PRIME
An Echo in the Stones

James Watson

Dedication

For Anita, Neil, Natalie, and Nicholas.

For being there.

Copyright © 2018 James Watson
www.jameswatsonauthor.com
The right of James Watson to be identified as the Author of works has been asserted by him in accordance with the copyright, designs, and Patents Act 1988. Apart from any use permitted under the UK copyright law, this publication may only be reproduced, stored, or transmitted, in any form, or by any means, with prior permission in writing of the publishers or, in the case of reprographic production, in accordance with the terms of the license issued by the Copyright License Agency.
First published as an e-book in 2018
All characters in this publication are fictitious and any resemblance to real persons, living or dead, is purely Coincidental.
Cataloging in Publication data is Available from the British Library.
ISBN: 9781838530624

Memories of an Avalonian Grandmaster.

Let me take you to a place, somewhere.
To show you the old ways man and time forgot.
Lives lost in scriptures of a bygone age
Destroyed by oppressors and victors alike.
Scriptures, where characters leaped off their page
And escaped their ink and paper cage.
So, listen before an old man's memory fades
I will take you to a place where all worlds meet.
Before my eyes grow dim, and my flesh grows cold
I will pass on my knowledge, these ways of old.
Then I can rest and find my peace, my solitude.
Memories passed down restored to script once more
Passed from father to son, mother to daughter the score.
I can at last find release from today's lies and deceit.
For in these pages is a place where all worlds meet
Where old ways and new may come alive.
Only then can I rest in peace with my mind
And can leave the real world far behind.
Here the echoes of my lives will
Teach and keep us connected still.
We will walk together; talk together.
Tread the unspoiled grass forever.
And when the time is right,
one day.
My memories and I will fly away.

James Watson

CONTENTS

1. NEW YORK 1974 AD 13
2. SOMERSET, ENGLAND 1599 AD 26
3. LONG ISLAND NEW YORK 1974 AD 55
4. THE WOLVES, 1604 AD 64
5. NEW YORK 1985 AD 77
6. SECOND REGRESSION 1985 AD 102
7. RED DREAMS 1985 AD 119
8. THE 'PRIMEVIL' INITIATION 1985 AD 150
9. THE SPONSOR'S 1985 AD 162
10. WHITE DREAMS 1985 AD 176
11. THE LAST REGRESSION 1985 AD 200
12. GLASTONBURY 1995 AD 212
13. THE PRIMEVIL GRANDMASTERS 1605 AD 222
14. EARLSWOOD MANOR 1996 AD 227
15. THE MASTER BEDROOM 1996 AD 241
16. MIDSUMMER DAY 1996 AD 257
17. GLASTONBURY HENGE 1996 AD 268
18. MORAG'S COTTAGE 1996 AD 282
19. THE HAND-FAST 1996 AD 300

Preface

There are people walking amongst us who live in the shadows. They look like us, talk like us, and interact with us. They may seem to come from all walks of life, but they are very different from the rest of humanity. They are not defined by skin, color or creed. The defining attribute that sets them apart from the rest of humanity is their ability to transmigrate their souls to their offspring after death. Therefore, they can recall memories of their ancestors going back to the beginning of conscious thought.

Their numbers are few, and they keep their abilities well hidden. Since the beginning of time, they have lived amongst humankind – protecting guiding us, and watching us evolve over the millennia. They have had many titles: Shamans, Watchers, Guardians, Angels, Fae, Fairies, various Gods and Goddesses, also Idols whose names have been lost in time. However, the title they give themselves is simply, 'Prime.'

Also, living amongst us is an equally secretive group. In the past, they too could remember their previous lives. This gave both groups infinite knowledge. But that's also where they diverged, with the latter exploiting this peerless wisdom – which gave rise to them being able to wield absolute power. And as we know, absolute power corrupts.

They are known as the 'Primevil' and can be found in the highest reaches of governments throughout the world. They are drawn to the dark side of humanity – wishing to subdue, conquer, control, or corrupt – and are responsible for countless wars and conflicts. Their bloodlines are diluted by centuries of rape and pillage, resulting in the loss of their ancestral memories. They are now as blind as the rest of humanity. Because they have lost their ability to love, they now only wish to destroy those who do.

Unknown to humanity, the 'Prime' and 'Primevil' have battled each other from the beginning of time. It is a battle that the 'Prime' is losing as evil looms around the world unchecked and unseen.

Amid this chaos, we follow the paths of six people, a love even death couldn't deny, as their souls transmigrate, and they are reborn in the twentieth century. Running in parallel is the unfolding of events related to the birth of twin girls in Somerset, England, in the year 1599 AD.

1. NEW YORK 1974 AD

Joan Masters groaned as her throat muscles squeezed back the scream raging in protest of the rude interruption to such a rare bliss that she had managed to finagle. Failing in vain efforts to cling tight onto those tendrils of a marvelous dream fading fast from her mind, she could only sigh heavily as she lay in bed. And waited. Hoping against hope that the echoing sound coming from down the hall would stop. Yet knowing that it wouldn't.

Peter felt an elbow in his ribs. As he began to wake, another elbow thrust brought him to his sense.

"Your turn," Joan said as she turned and pulled the blankets over her head. She wanted to go back to sleep, to recapture the wispy wonder of the unusual dream she was having – so real, so unusually vivid.

Peter lay there blinking, his head still fuzzy with sleep. "What do you mean, my turn? I slept in his room all last night. I must fly to Dallas at midday tomorrow, I need my sleep."

Joan fretted as she continued to lie in bed and listened to the sound of a child crying. It was Paul, her son. She lay there hoping he would go back to sleep, waiting for him to stop, but she knew he wouldn't. She eventually called out: "I'm coming, Paul. Don't cry."

Joan slipped on her dressing gown and made her way down the hall to Paul's room. "It's all right, Paul, shush, don't worry, mommy is here." She sat on the bed, and he wrapped his arms around her like a limpet clinging to a rock. "Shush now. Have you had another bad dream?" Paul did not answer but clung to his mother for all he was worth. "What was this dream about?"

Finally, his sobs subsided. "The men fell from the castle battlements. They were bleeding, Earl Llewellyn was bleeding."

She continued to stroke his hair, trying to soothe him. "It is only a dream, Paul," she whispered lovingly. "It's nothing to worry about, let me get in beside you." Paul calmed down with his mother close, his breathing slowed as he slipped back into slumber. These sleep terrors were getting to be nightly occurrences and Joan was at the end of her tether. Thinking back over Paul's young life of four years, Joan could not recall exactly when they first started, but the latest dreams seemed to be getting darker.

Badly needing sleep, she shook her head while lost in thought. *I cannot stand this much longer. I simply need rest.* She decided there and then that he was going to be an only child.

She sometimes wondered if those early fitful baby cries had been misinterpreted, if Paul had been troubled from the very beginning with bad dreams and sleepless nights. As he got older, he started to recount his dreams to his mother – and as she listened to them, she had an uneasy feeling of déjà vu. They were the same type of dreams that troubled her.

She shuddered, once again lost in thought. *I thought I was going crazy, and now Paul has them. Are we both possessed? Have I passed this curse on to him?*

This fear cemented a drastic change, for Peter and Joan Masters had always dreamed of having a large family. They were rich and had a lavish lifestyle. Peter's grandfather had immigrated from England to America in the early 1920s. His father was a keen golfer, and as the sport took off in America, he saw an opportunity to get in on the ground floor. He started a company designing and constructing golf courses. As the sport took off in a big way, so did their finances.

Some hours later, Joan discussed the latest dream with Peter as he read the newspaper over breakfast. He was compassionate and knew she had also been troubled by strange dreams for many years. She had been seeing a psychiatrist and had recently confided to that professional of not only having dreams she could not explain – but that she'd gone on to hear voices too. The mention of voices in her head had changed the attitude of the psychiatrist, and Joan stopped going. Now her son was showing the same symptoms.

"Do you think we should take him to a child psychiatrist, Peter?"

"Well, it didn't do you any good, dear. I don't think we need to pin the crazy label on him just yet."

Joan bristled as he said it, and Peter realized he had put his foot in it.

"Crazy like me, you mean." Joan pushed the chair backward angrily, and it fell over. She walked away.

Peter lowered his head and rested it on the table in exasperation. "I didn't mean that the way it came out." He listened for a reply, but there was only silence. He knew it was too late the moment those words left his lips. Again, he called her. "Joan, I didn't mean that. You know I didn't."

Joan returned to the table five minutes later with two cups of coffee. She wrapped her hands around her cup and, after sipping the hot liquid, wondered aloud. "Peter, have you ever used the word 'battlements' when telling Paul stories?"

Relieved that his wife had calmed down and was again speaking to him, he drew his attention away from the newspaper. "I don't recall telling him stories about castles full stop, let alone battlements. Why?"

She took another sip of her coffee. "Paul has just used the word describing them in his latest dream, and I can't remember using it either."

He flicked his broadsheet back up and continued to read, then added: "He has probably got it off the television. What was this dream about?"

"Oh, he said two men fell from the battlements of a castle with lots of blood."

Peter thought about what Joan had said before replying. "Another dark one then. I think he is getting all this from television, and he simply has a very vivid imagination. We need to keep an eye on what programs he is watching."

After another sip of coffee, Joan added: "You're probably right." Her thoughts, however, drifted once again. *Yes, Peter, you keep telling yourself that. What's the alternative? Our son is possessed, haunted, even? Yes, Peter, television is a safe answer. I need to find out what is happening to Paul and me.*

"Oh, by the way, he gave us another name, Earl Llewellyn. Have you ever spoken about an Earl Llewellyn?"

Once again, Peter looked over the top of his broadsheet and stared at his wife, deep in thought. He was momentarily distracted by her lucent green eyes, and his heart, as always, skipped a beat. "Llewellyn, you say. I know of several noble families in England's West Country by that name. And some in Wales, too probably lived in castles. No, I have never spoken to him about anyone called Llewellyn." He flicked his newspaper up once more and continued reading, then pondered aloud. "I wonder whom he gets his imagination from."

Joan continued to sip her drink, but she had picked up his sarcastic witticism. *Yes, Peter, I know you think it is all in my mind.*

*

Joan never took Paul to a psychiatrist, but he accompanied her to church every Sunday just to ease her mind in case he was possessed. However, several months later, she took him to see a spiritualist for a private reading without Peter's knowledge.

Joan Masters did not believe in ghosts or spirits, but her Son's well-being was of paramount importance to her. She had secretly attended several spiritualist meetings before and felt she could bring Paul along on the pretense of having his fortune read. She decided he would feel less threatened if she participated in a meeting at the end of the regular weekly session at the local spiritualist church.

From what she'd heard, the medium had a sound reputation and many pastoral members were excited to have her. At first sight, the medium looked to be in her fifties and had dark black hair down to her shoulders. On her fingers was a selection of gold rings. Her dress was black and contrasted with her pale complexion. However, her eyes were a striking green, piercing, hinting at her intelligence and unknown wisdom.

She could be a gypsy. Joan thought as her eyes narrowed, studying her. *Yes, she has gypsy blood, but she is not suntanned like a gypsy. I wonder when she last saw daylight, she has such ashen skin.*

The medium called Joan to her. They were alone as the last of the congregation had left, the woman smiled as she walked over to them. *Oh, and she has a gold tooth.* Joan mused, *definitely Gypsy.*

She took Joan's hand in hers and closed her eyes. "Let us see what we can see, dearie," she said and continued in well-rehearsed monotones. She announced that Joan was going on a long journey. It was a term used at most meetings and was well-worn.

Joan's heart sank as the medium continued. *Oh, here we go. I am going on a journey, am I? Doesn't everyone in America go on a journey every day? Have I wasted my money here?*

The spiritualist fell silent for a minute. She cocked her head to one side, giving Joan the impression that she was listening to some distant voice. Joan shook her head and was glad she hadn't told Peter she was coming here.

The medium turned to Joan with a perplexed look on her face. "You are a seer?"

"What!" The statement shook Joan and was unexpected. "What do you mean, I am a seer?"

"You have the gift. You have second sight. Did you not realize?"

Joan's forehead creased, and a shiver went down her spine. She did not answer and kept eye contact with the medium's piercing eyes.

"How could you not know? Can you not hear the spirits calling you?"

Joan felt the hair lift on the nape of her neck and thought. *Oh God, the voices are ghosts. Am I possessed? Oh no, could Paul be too?*

When she did not respond, the spiritualist continued. "Voices? Can you not hear them?"

Joan mumbled wordlessly in response, unsure what to say. Finally, the long-dreaded words left her lips. "Voices? Yes, I hear them."

The old woman shook her head in confusion. "In that case, why are you asking me for a reading?"

She studied the older woman's face. She was dumbstruck, and she dared not let her eyes fall away. "I did not know what they were, so I have been seeing a psychiatrist."

The medium was full of compassion. "You poor thing, you, poor, poor thing. You should have asked for a reading sooner."

The spiritualist continued to hold Joan's hands and meditated some more. Joan watched her eyes moving under her lids and studied every nuance on her face. After a couple of minutes, her eyes opened wide in alarm and startled Joan.

Unnerved, she started to back away, but the woman gripped her hands firmly so she couldn't leave.

"Mrs. Masters, your mother or father should have prepared you for this, for at least one of them must have had the sight?"

Joan turned away from the woman's piercing eyes. "My parents were killed in a car crash when I was very young."

The medium nodded. "Ah, I see, that explains it. I am sorry to hear that."

She turned to Paul and took his hand as well and held it for several minutes. Eventually, she released both their hands and repeated her first statement. "You are going on a journey, but not yet. The time is not right. You both need to go home to England, to your family's ancestral home, especially Saul. But not just yet."

Joan shook her head, disagreeing with her. "We are American. America is our home, and his name is Paul, not Saul."

The medium presented Joan with a tolerant smile, her eyes bright, piercing, and full of excitement. "You are new to this, Mrs. Masters. I can see that. If you listen to what I have to say, things may become a little clearer to you. You are very special, and this little one is so special you would not believe it. Does he hear the voices?"

Joan shook her head wordlessly. "No, I don't think so, but he is troubled by dreams."

The medium again nodded. "Ah, that's how it starts. Paul needs to return home to England, but the time is not right. His destiny is in England. Paul is very special, and she will call him when the time is right."

"Who? who will call him?"

"His lover will, he needs to find her to fulfill a prophecy. Like the rest of us, she has been waiting for him for almost four hundred years."

Joan could feel the breath leave her lungs. Her eyes, however, never left the face of the medium. "What do you mean special?"

The woman took her hand once more and placed her second hand on top. "Mrs. Masters, please breathe. You have gone pale."

Joan did as she said and took a deep breath.

"That's better. This has been a shock for you. I can see that. It has been a shock for me too. I have known about Saul, er Paul, for a long time, but I never expected to meet him. Mrs. Masters, you must listen to the voices. They know who you are. They know who Paul is. Do not ignore them. They are your kin, and they are trying to help. Oh, you poor thing. If only your parents were alive, they could have prepared you for this."

The medium's eyes then turned to Joan's son. Joan saw love and awe in them. She caressed the side of his face as if she was praying, worshiping him. "Nice to meet you at last. So, your name this time is Paul Masters. Right young Sir, let me take your hand and tell you your fortune."

Joan could not remember the journey back home. She had driven on autopilot, her mind elsewhere. There were so many questions running through her head. *Is this for real? Was she genuine? How does this affect my Christian beliefs? Am I comfortable with it? Why on earth did she rip up the cheque? And oh God, some woman will call Paul away from me. And these voices are my ancestors talking to me, advising me.*

She shuddered, parked the car in the garage, and closed the electric doors with the fob on her keyring. Again, she shuddered and sat in the dark, thinking. *Do I tell Peter?* She subconsciously shook her head. *No, he will flip, no, definitely not, he really will think I am nuts.*

A cry from the back seat disturbed her reverie. "Ok, Paul, mommy's coming."

Joan didn't tell her husband about taking Paul to the spiritualist meeting. She knew Peter – being a devout Catholic – would never have understood her reasoning if she had.

Sleep that night was fitful, but when she did, the dreams returned. Each time she slept, they were more vivid and realistic. It was the old lady of the woods once again, a dream that kept returning, time and again.

Once awake, she continued to hear the voices, but they were little more than echoes, faint, very faint, and for the most part, gibberish. However, the dreams grew stronger and appeared to be a continuous story. Each morning she lay in bed and recalled the dream.

Her mind was in turmoil. *Do I tell Peter about the spiritualist? Would he understand?* She shook her head wordlessly. *No, of course, he wouldn't, he really would think I am crazy.*

*

Later that year, however, Peter also started hearing voices and started talking in his sleep. He began calling out names of various places, so Joan wrote them down. She did the same for herself, and as soon as she woke each morning, she would make notes.

Peter did not see a psychiatrist himself. He did, however, copy names and places from his dreams into a small notebook. Some weeks later, he admitted doing so to Joan, and after they collated their notes, they realized that these were not just dreams.

"Peter, I think we have given it enough time, it's been a month now. Get your notepad out. We need to see if any of these dreams are the same. let's see if we are haunted. I have the notes that I have taken from Paul's book as well."

Peter did as she suggested, and they both sat up in bed.

"Ok, Joan, let's start with types of dreams. My most common one is dancing. I have several when I was dancing in a forest or the woods."

"Well, that's a start, Peter. Me too. I was often wearing a white robe, what about you?"

Peter counted the times on his pad. "Four, I have had four dreams wearing a white garment, and I have had six where I was wearing nothing, completely naked."

Joan looked pensive. "Naked. I have had three or four dreams in these last two months where I have been dancing around naked. However, two of them I can completely explain."

Peter looked across at his wife and arched an eyebrow questioningly. "Go on, this should be interesting."

"The first one was when we were in San Francisco at that all-night party, up in the woods where we met for the first time and got completely stoned."

Peter smiled as he reminisced, "God, that was a good party. I can still see you gyrating, dancing seductively around the campfire. That's when I realized I was falling in love with you for the first time."

Joan continued. "You then carried me over your shoulder like a fireman and off into the woods, and the rest, as they say, is history. The other naked dream was when we went to Woodstock in 69, and we were again stoned."

Peter again reminisced. "You were on my shoulders with your boobs out. How could we do that in front of all those people?"

Joan nodded her head in agreement. "Enough reminiscing, Peter, which leaves two, and these were two that I can't explain. I was dancing in a circle of clear ground in some woody area. I had a lamp in my hand, not an electric lamp, but a lamp with a naked flame. It was dark, I was spinning around with the lamp, and it created a magical effect on my eyes. There were lots of other people doing the same. I think it was some sort of festival."

Peter pursed his lips, and Joan noted the crease in his forehead. "That's interesting. Most of mine were in a forest and involved some sort of circle. They were always in the dark, and, yes, we held lamps in our hands. There was a big, flat stone slab in the middle and a couple was having it off on the slab. Everybody was watching and cheering them on. As soon as they finished, everyone, and I mean everyone, joined in making love to each other, a right old orgy it was."

Joan studied his face, and a feeling of déjà vu overcame her.

"Peter, I have had that dream several times. I spoke to the shrink about it. She said I was fantasizing, trying to recapture my youth, and that it was quite normal and nothing to worry about. I have had many dreams about dancing with the white robes on, again in the forest. I am not going mad if we both have the same dreams."

Peter leaned across and kissed her lovingly on the cheek. "I have never thought you were going mad, Joan."

She raised a brow, a cynical twitch, and added sarcastically. "Really, Peter, then why send me to all those shrinks? Okay, Peter. If these are not normal dreams, what are they?"

Their eyes met, and neither of them spoke for a while.

Peter eventually broke the silence. "An old film perhaps, perhaps we subconsciously remember a film from our past?"

"Oh, you mean like television influencing Paul." She said bitterly. "I don't think so. Anyway, I can't remember a film like that. Can you?"

Peter did not speak. He simply shook his head and changed tack. "Right, names of people in our dreams. I have loads, how about you?"

"I have plenty. I will read mine out, and you tell me if you have any that match."

Joan read out her list of names, followed by Paul's, while Peter cross-referenced them.

"We have plenty that match, but most are common garden names. I will read out the matched ones. Robert, Paul, Ben, Simon, Jed, Richard, Thomas, Stewart, Mia, Monkton, Llewellyn, Morag, Saul, James, Luna, Jake, Samuel, Eleanor and Christopher."

Joan chewed her lip deep in thought. "Ok, the real common names we need to cross off, I can understand the Roberts and Pauls, but there are some very unusual ones here. Monkton, Morag, Mia, Luna, Saul, Llewellyn. Peter, all three of us dreamed of someone called Morag, Mia, Saul, Luna, Monkton and Llewellyn. How can we explain that?"

Paul simply shook his head. "I can't Joan, maybe there is more to this than just having the same dreams, but I haven't got a clue what it is. What about places? Any names for places?"

Joan consulted her notepad. "Right, I have an Avalon, an Earlswood, a Glastonbury, a York, and a Bath."

Paul studied his notes. "I have a Glastonbury and an Earlswood, Joan. You're right, this is getting scary."

They were both lost in thought, trying to understand what was happening.

"Peter, do you think a ghost or something is haunting us, or maybe it's this place?"

Paul gave a derisory laugh. "I don't know, Joan. You know I don't believe in that sort of thing."

Joan decided it was time to let Peter into her secret and took a deep breath. "Peter, I took Paul for a private reading by a spiritualist."

He gave a contemptuous snort. "What!?" His voice was edged with scorn. "Why would you do a thing like that?"

Joan drew her eyes away from his. "I wanted answers. You thought I was going mad, and the shrink just leeched our money away and agreed with you."

Peter stared at his wife, his face getting redder by the second. She knew he would be upset, although he did not go to church as often as she did. He did consider himself a true Catholic and lived his life by Christian principles.

He raised his voice by a couple of decibels. "You should not have done that, Joan. That's mumbo jumbo stuff, and you know it is."

Joan studied her husband's reaction and thought he took it better than she expected. Feeling braver, she continued. "Anyway, I took Paul to see this spiritualist. I told him he was going to get his fortune told. He is only four, Peter, and did not understand what was happening. It was a rather interesting meeting. She said Paul was special and that I came from a long line of seers."

Peter studied his wife's face intensely, half expecting her to burst out laughing. "You believed that Joan, that you come from a long line of seers? You are beginning to freak me out. Do you know what, that sounds more like necromancy or even schizophrenia?"

Joan ignored his sarcasm. "She said the voices in my head were spirits trying to get in touch with me and that they would guide me."

Peter was angry, and his voice was getting louder with each syllable. "You really are worrying me, Joan. That's what necromancy means, spirits talking to you, guiding you." Paul ran his fingers through his hair and began to massage his temples. He then took a deep breath and let it out slowly. When he spoke, he had calmed down, and his voice was barely a whisper. "So, you believe in ghosts now?"

Joan could give as good as she got and argued. "Will you shut up and listen? I went to see her about Paul and his dreams. She said he is very special and needs to go back to the land of his ancestors, England, and fulfill his destiny."

Peter controlled his voice, repeated what she said, and looked her in the eyes. "His destiny?"

Joan remained unabated. "Some woman will call him when the time is right."

He couldn't hide the taunting in his voice. "Call him? Right, Joan, this may be hard for you to believe, but quite a few girls will give him a ring when Paul is growing up. It's what teenagers do. For God's sake Joan, how much did this cost?"

"Peter, she did not mean the telephone. Some woman will enchant him and call him back to join her in England."

"Enchant him?

"Yes, she said my parents should have prepared me for these voices and that we should prepare Paul so that he understands what is happening to him as well. Peter, the spiritualist charges one hundred dollars for a private meeting."

"I thought so, Joan, you have been had."

"Will you just shut up and listen?" she snapped. "When she realized who Paul was, she gave me my money back."

Peter fell silent, his face reflecting his confusion. "She gave you the money back. I don't understand, What's the point in getting a punter there and then giving them the money back?"

"My thoughts exactly. I went back the following week for a second reading, and they said she was only booked for one night and had left the area. So, she wasn't even after repeat business."

For a while, Peter looked blindly into space, deep in thought. He shook his head slowly. "It Doesn't make sense, Joan. Why would she do that?"

Joan placed her hand on his. "That's the point! It only makes sense if she is telling the truth. Peter, she said my parents should have prepared me. Obviously, they couldn't because they died so young. Now, this is happening to you, maybe you should talk to your dad and see what he has to say. We need to understand what is happening to us all.

"Anyway, I have always thought that I could tell the future. Now I understand why." Her voice had taken on a lighter tone.

His brow creased, reflecting his confusion. She was smiling. Why?

"All right, Joan Masters, prove it, tell me what the future holds."

Joan wrapped her arms around his head, pulled his face down onto her breasts, and laughed, " I predict you will lock the door within the next thirty seconds in case Paul wakes up."

Later, lying sated in the arms of the only man she ever truly loved, Joan drifted into a deep sleep and, as had become the norm for her, returned to the dream about the old lady of the forest.

2. SOMERSET, ENGLAND
1599 AD

The morning air lay cold and damp. The opal mist rising from the depths of the lake carpeted the landscape, hiding its secrets. Above the tree canopy, high streaks of orange pierced a clear gray dawning sky.

The old lady blinked. Using the heel of her hands, she cleaned sleep from her eyes as reality dawned and replaced the comfort of oblivion. The knot in her stomach tightened. The heat of the sun had not yet penetrated the tree canopy to dispel the mist. The fog crept silently as a specter from the lake, weaving its way through the forest, its insidious touch wrapping around the healer like a wet blanket.

The cold had gnawed at her body throughout the night and she shuddered as the feeling of despair engulfed her. Morag got to her feet and removed her sodden shawl, her old bones stiff and reluctant. She stood at the side of the bed waiting. Her life, she knew, was in the balance. Would she live to see nightfall? She doubted it.

Her eyes turned to the woman lying on the bed. Lady Llewellyn. Formerly Princess Mia from the land of Persia was dying. Lord Llewellyn, who was lying on the bed next to hers - had tasked the old lady to keep his wife alive.

It was only a matter of time, and Morag hung her head in despair. She checked the young woman's temperature and pulse, making a mental note of the pallor of her silky-smooth skin, then lay her hand upon the swollen belly and felt her heart weep for the life moving inside. The Princess was full-term pregnant and they were both going to die. With her likely to join this luckless duo.

Morag mopped the sweat from her brow as she turned nervously toward the person lying next to the Princess and prayed. *Earth Mother let him die first, I beg you.* Morag knew he would kill her if he didn't die before his wife. The plague had got them both, together with the baby so near, and yet so far.

It was a humiliating outlook for Morag, who was 'Prime.' – a title bestowed only on the most Elite of Druids – and a healer of the highest repute. She saw herself as someone who could draw on the arcane knowledge of the Avalonian Master Druids of old.

Like all women of that time living alone, she was aware of the whispers surrounding her. The healer was a welcome member of the forest community but she was also feared. In their minds, those who can cure can also kill – after all, she was not a Christian who feared God and despised everything unholy. Who knew what she got up to on her own in the forest? She kept herself to herself, and those that feared her kept their distance unless a community member was sick.

How then had this party found her in the middle of the forest, well off the beaten track? She rubbed her temples wearily as there was no way of knowing.

Why don't you save the child? The voice came unbidden from deep within her mind. It was not hers. It was one of the thousands of ancestors whose memories she carried within her. Prime memories – secrets that only the Elite Prime Druids could access at will.

Save the child how? She answered wearily.

Recall my memories, dearie, just think back. I did it when my Masters' favorite sow died just before she could give birth. Just cut her stomach across the middle and lift the baby out – you must be quick, mind.

Morag sat deep in thought and again she shook her head. *A pig is one thing – but a woman?*

We are all the same under the skin, my lovely. It was another voice, a different ancestor. * I knew of a woman that was run over by a cart – she was full-term and split in two. The baby lived for a few hours before dying.*

As she contemplated options, Morag recalled what she had been informed before the duo fell unconscious.

Lord and Lady Llewellyn had arrived by boat two weeks previously from France in perfect health, along with a troop of guards. Two days after landing on the English shore, the guards fell sick and died. When they arrived deep in the forest at the cottage of Morag the healer, their numbers were down to four. It had been too late for her to help the guards – and it was only a matter of time before these two would follow them. But the baby – could it be possible?

"Ten gold coins if you save her," the Lord had promised. More money than Morag had ever had in her lifetime. But no amount of money would save either the Lord or his wife.

Morag's silent reverie was broken when she felt the Lord grip her arm.

"Healer, my wife, how is my wife?" His hand, so weak, fell away moments later.

The healer edged away, eyeing him like a fly trapped in a spider's web. There would be no escape if the Princess died before him. Her eyes turned back to the woman lying on the bed, her voice barely a whisper.

"My Lord, I have told you, your wife will leave this world before sunset."

His eyes were blood-red, and he pleaded hoarsely: "No, you must save her! I have more gold in the wagon, name your price."

Morag cautiously shuffled further away. Every inch away from the Lord could make the difference to save her life. The extra inches between them gave her more confidence and she turned to face him once again. "I may be able to save your baby, but your wife is too weak."

"Damn the child she can have others, save my wife - she is special – you have no idea."

Morag thought he was evil. She had sensed it from the very beginning. She knew she should have run and saved herself, but the healer within her prevented it. "My Lord, no amount of gold will save your wife – but I may be able to save your baby if the Earth Mother wills it."

"Healer, I pray to God, you save them both for your sake."

Morag backed further away from the Lord but remained close to the Princess. "My Lord, I have heard that you've tried many healers on your journey here to me, so I know what to expect. I say again that your wife will not walk after today in this life. Her ancestors are calling her, they are waiting."

"Don't talk gibberish you old Witch, just heal her."

No more words were said as the Lord fell quiet. Hours passed and Morag watched bleakly as the chest of the ailing Princess rose and fell. As a healer, she had seen many people die, young and old. With yet more deaths looming, she looked around her. Surely no one could wish for a calmer, sweeter resting place, the peace almost Benedictine.

She heard the death rattle and stood over the Princess waiting for her chest to stall. There was nothing to alert her, even when the Princess exhaled one long last breath. Upon seeing that frail chest failing to rise in the seconds following, she took her sharpest knife and pulled aside the makeshift blanket to expose the pregnant belly. Then counted silently to confirm that life was truly gone.

Knowing she had little time left, Morag then drew the blade across the bloated belly. Liquid gushed out of the dead woman's womb as she lifted the baby out and placed it on a towel. She saw further movement in the womb. "Another one." She gasped as she lifted the second child out. "Another girl, two girls."

Time was slipping away while there was still more for her to do. She knew she must get them to breathe. She rubbed them both with the towel, trying to revive them – but there was no response. She checked their nostrils and throats for blockage, before lifting both girls by their ankles, and smacking their butts. First one, then the other began to cry.

"Mother, be praised," she cried jubilantly.

Hearing the excitement in her voice, the Lord awoke and somehow found the strength to raise himself slightly. "You have saved her?"

Morag took the knife in her hand and hid it behind her back, waiting. *'Earth Mother,'* she prayed. *I beg you to protect me from his wrath.* She turned to face the Lord but kept the knife hidden out of sight. "My Lord, I'm afraid your wife has left this world. But praise God we have a miracle, your daughters are safe. Yes, my Lord, you have two beautiful daughters."

A howling wail split the air as the Lord saw his wife's stomach sliced open. Anger lending him the strength to get off the bed, he staggered over to the body. Unable to comprehend the vision before him, he accused: "You have killed and butchered her, you hag! You have murdered her!"

Morag's blood ran cold. She felt an icicle envelop her heart and the knot in her stomach tightened further still, and her voice faltered. "M... my Lord, she was not cut until she died. Yes, she is dead, but look, my Lord, your wife lives on. You have two beautiful daughters."

The Lord's eyes never moved to his daughters; all he could see was his wife's butchered abdomen. "Murderer!" he shrieked hoarsely.

She looked at him pleadingly. "But I have saved your babies."

The Lord lunged and when she swung her arm to stop him, the weapon she had hidden came to light. He tried to grab the knife but failed. Backing away as far as she could, she held it high above her head in a defensive posture, ready to strike. He, however, still had her other hand in a vice-like grip.

Morag looked into his eyes. She could see no compassion, only hate and rage. He had not even looked at his daughters. Slamming the knife hilt onto his head, Morag broke his grip, and the Lord fell forward to the floor.

With his arms splayed on all fours, he growled: "I will have your head for this Witch!"

Acting instinctively in self-defense, Morag stepped over his back and simply sat upon him. This sudden weight immediately caused his arms to collapse.

"Get off me, witch!" He raged and tried to move but didn't have the strength.

Morag sat there, unknowing of what her next move should be. Her heart was racing and she clutched her chest in panic. She could hear the roar of the blood rushing through her ears.

He continued to try getting to his feet, but she bore all her weight upon him. Finally, he realized that he couldn't get free.

Morag came to the same conclusion and began to control her breathing, causing her heart rate to slow. She sat there as he struggled and weighed her options. Her priority was the survival of the babies. Morag also knew he would show her no mercy.

Her eyes drifted to the wagon, to a prize that could be hers. A wagon containing gold and finery from Persia. And then there were the horses – he called them "Arabian". They were the finest she had ever seen.

Not forgetting the babies. Morag was past childbearing age and was alone in the forest. Here were two girls to raise. Two companions for her old age. Girls to whom she could pass on her knowledge of ancient healing. She nodded her head thoughtfully and closed her eyes in anguish as she made her decision.

"My Lord, did your father ever teach you to play chess?"

The Lord responded weakly. "What are you talking about, witch? Get off me!"

She repeated the question slowly. "Did. Your. Father. Teach. You. To. Play. Chess?"

The Lord's voice was barely audible, exhausted by the effort. "Chess, no, never."

Morag's voice, however, had become strong and forceful. "I thought not, my Lord. Blame your father for your predicament. The first rule of chess is never to threaten if you can't back it up. It is the same in life. Never threaten anyone when you are in a position of weakness."

Morag grabbed a handful of hair, pulled his head backward, and drew the blade across his throat – slitting it from ear to ear. His legs thrashed violently and a gargled curdle left his lips as he grasped his throat in an attempt to slow the flow of blood.

Morag watched the pool of blood grow, a crimson halo fanning out to frame his head. She remained seated on his back as his body convulsed in spasms and paused for reflection as his life ebbed away. She had broken the vow all healers live by. She had taken a life. Tears ran down her cheeks as she sought support for her action from her ancestors, and found none. They were silent – not a whisper, not even an echo.

As he stilled, the years fell away from the hunchback that was Morag the healer. She stood upright – stretched her limbs and turned her attention to the babies. Quickly she cleaned their bodies and wrapped them in blankets. Both began to cry loudly, and when she started to rock one of them, it began to suckle her fingers.

Morag was surprised they needed to feed so quickly and was unprepared for this need. Her main objective throughout the night had been to outlive the Lord. She never dreamed the babies would live. But now they have – how could she feed them?

For a while, she sat on the Lord's bed in silent contemplation. *There's no one within a day's ride, and the babies need milk. Do I know anyone who has recently given birth and could be a wet nurse?* She searched her memories and the hopelessness of her predicament dawned upon her. *No one would come anyway – no one trusts me. How can I feed them? They need milk or they will die.*

An unexpected reprieve emerged right then when the Princesses' wolf came out of her den. It was her personal guardian and it had been attracted by the smell of blood. It approached the dead Princess cautiously, its ears flat against its head as it gave a blood-curdling howl that echoed through the forest. The response was instant, echoes returned from every direction.

Morag shuddered and looked at the two corpses stretched out before her. The retort from the other wolves sent a shiver up her spine. *So many, I did not realize there were so many wolves in the forest.*

Earlier, Morag had calmed the creature by enchantment, and the wolf now thought of Morag as the pack's new leader. She then remembered the wolf had given birth to four cubs just two days previously, and only two had survived.

You have milk wolf, yes milk, and spare milk at that? Morag's mind began to formulate a plan. *I can make an enchantment to make the wolf believe they are hers. It might work, it might just work. I must ask the old ones.*

Amid this rising hope, she saw that the sun had once more risen above the tree canopy and dispelled the gossamer-like mist. Ignoring the wailing babies, Morag sat cross-legged on the ground, closed her eyes, and began to meditate. She was calling upon her ancestors for guidance. Seeking the archaic wisdom passed down from the Stone Ages and beyond. Morag patiently listened to the hundreds of voices within her head.

A female Avalonian Grandmaster's suggestion caught her attention. *If you take the skin from the cubs that died at birth and fasten it around the babies, it will fool the foster parent into thinking that the babies are hers.*

At last! A smile emphasized the creases on her weathered face. She thanked her ancestor – then recited an enchantment to calm the wolf and collected the bodies of the two cubs that had died. She skinned both cubs, cutting off the legs where they reached the abdomen. After cleaning off the blood, she slipped the skins over the babies, putting their arms and legs through the holes in the skins, she then stitched the skins back together, covering the babies' bodies.

She admired her handiwork and nodded her head approvingly, further gladdened by the thought that the skins would help keep them warm as well. She lay the babies next to the wolf so they could latch onto the nipples. Immediately they clung on and began to suckle.

"It's going to work. Yes, it's going to work." She sang the words aloud and began to dance, hardly able to contain her excitement. Morag knew that by the time the wolf's milk passed through the babies' digestive systems, the smell would confirm to the female wolf that the babies were hers.

Immediate concerns taken care of; Morag focused her next efforts on longer-term gain. She took full advantage of being a shapeshifter, a rare talent that she'd kept hidden even from her fellow 'Prime.' Turning her attention to the dead Lord, she placed her hand across his forehead and bent his head backward. With the other hand on his chin, she opened his mouth and appeared to kiss him. When she breathed in deeply, nothing seemed to happen. It took a few moments for the skin of the Lord to tighten, wither, then shrink as the flesh underneath dissipated – until all that was left was only a skeleton covered in skin.

At the same time, her hair had started to change color, and the masculine features of the former Sir Robert Llewellyn replaced those of Morag. Moving quickly to the rear of the cottage, she collected an essence jar and removed the stopper. Placing her mouth over the vessel, she released her breath into it.

Morag labeled the jar with the name of the Lord and, after sealing it, put it on the shelf next to a row of similar jars. As her features returned to normal, she cackled: "Now, Sir Robert, you are mine to do with as I please."

She returned to the desiccated remains of the Lord and removed his rings and clothing. She tied a length of rope around both ankles and secured the other end of the rope to the harness of the horse used for pulling the wagon. She led the creature deep into the forest, dragging the Lord behind until she reached a clearing downwind of her dwelling.

After removing the rope from the body, she performed a simple ritual. "Creatures of the forest, I give this man back to you. For many years he has hunted you down. He has feasted on the bodies of your brothers and sisters. Now, his life cycle is complete, and it is your turn to feed on his bones."

With the ceremony completed, she walked back to her cottage to check on the babies and was pleased to see that they were sleeping.

Morag turned her attention to the Princess and took time to examine the dead woman. The deceased's hair was long, jet-black, and straight without the hint of a curl. Her eyes were emerald-green, in sharp contrast to her silky smooth olive skin. The most unusual feature of this woman, however, was her height. Being almost six feet tall, she was eighteen inches taller than most forest women and the tallest woman she had ever seen.

The healer, like most people of the forest, was a Celt. Most were little more than four feet six inches tall, some slightly taller. Her own hair, although now gray, used to be a dark yellow. Most people of the forest had complexions similarly fair as hers, alternatively a very light brown or the color of sunbaked barley.

She looked back at the girls, fast asleep, and wondered what the girls will look like if they survived into adulthood. *Sir Robert was also tall. They too will be tall then, tall, and magnificent girls.*

Morag removed all her clothing, revealing the body of a middle-aged woman. She moved across to the Princess and kissed her in the same manner as the Lord. Again, she breathed in deeply – taking in the essence of the dead woman. As with her husband, the Princess's skin contracted with the essence extracted and Morag took the form of the Princess.

Excitedly she ran to the mirror in the cottage and examined her new form. She twisted and turned, taking in every aspect of her new body. She reached for the hairbrush - and began to comb her hair. Hair that fell to her waist. Then, lifting her ample breasts, she felt the heavy milk inside. Her eyes drifted to the babies still sleeping alongside the female wolf and wished the milk was natural. She then ran her hands down her unmarked stomach and legs and liked what she saw.

Morag fell silent, sensing something strange within her. *What's this? This is unexpected. I feel different.* She paused for a time as strange sensations began coursing through her body. *What is it? Power, I feel her power, so much power. Avalonian power, I'm sure of it. So, you were a sister!*

Her eyes drifted back to the corpse of the Princess and reappraised her. '*So, my Princess, you had powerful talents and skills that are different from mine, but skills I can use. So, it was you calling me these last few nights. You who warned me of the Lord. Thank you, Princess. By doing so, you have saved my life and I Morag of the North Wood will repay the debt. Your daughters will have love and devotion from me for the rest of my days.*'

Once again, her form slowly returned to that of the healer. *Yes, my dear, I will have so much fun being you as well. This has been a wonderful day, a glorious day.*

She took stock of what she had acquired. Wagons containing unknown finery. The gold, the horses, and two girls. Girls that could hopefully inherit their mother's gifts and possibly her looks. She mused as she recalled the Princess's image in the mirror. *They will charm any prince or noble in the land if they do. Yes, this has been a wonderful day.*

*

Against all odds, the girls survived, and the wolf cared for the girls as if they were her own. They grew stronger every day, as did the wolf cubs which grew rapidly.

Three months later, Morag was busying herself doing the everyday household chores when she sensed something was wrong. There were no bird noises and the forest creatures were utterly silent. She searched the heavens and could see a flock of rooks circling in the sky in the distance. A rook's parliament was held daily in the tall ash tree, but that was always at the first light of dawn. It was now midday, so something or someone had disturbed them.

"Someone's coming," she said for her own benefit, and after collecting the babies from the wolf's den, hid them in the cottage. "Wolf, you go back to your den and stay there," Morag commanded as she went back into the cottage.

A group of soldiers on horses approached and as they came to a halt outside, a man's voice called out. "We come in the name of the Earl. Is there anyone at home?"

She quickly hurried to the rear of the cottage where she stored the essence jars. Opening the one labeled Lord Robert Llewellyn, she took a deep breath.

Wolf now moved to the entrance of her den and a guttural growl resonated from deep within her throat. All at once the horses began to panic, and their riders struggled to bring them under control.

One soldier cried out, "Captain, a wolf, a giant wolf."

Another cried, "Kill it."

A powerful male voice called out from inside the cottage. "There will be no need for that!" As the soldier's eyes turned to the cottage, Lord Robert Llewellyn stepped out.

The captain called out triumphantly, "Lord Llewellyn, you're alive,"

The Lord waved his hands dismissively. "Yes, as you see, captain, I am very much alive."

"Sire, we have been searching for you for months."

"Well, now you have found me, captain. What can I do for you?"

"Lord, your father sent several patrols out looking for you when you failed to arrive at the castle a month after your ship docked." As he addressed the Lord, the captain started to dismount.

Robert put both hands, palms out, facing the men and commanded, "Stay back, do not get off your horses."

The captain froze with one leg in the air. "What is it, my Lord?"

"My men and I caught the plague on our way home. Every one of my companions has died."

The soldiers immediately backed their mounts several feet from Sir Robert. Seeing his Lordship's unkempt condition and lack of dress, the captain inquired, "Are you well now, my Lord?"

His Lordship began to cough and again waved his hands dismissively. "No, I still have the plague but I am recovering."

"The Princess, Lord?"

"The Princess also has the plague, but she too is recovering. She is very weak."

"Your child, Sir Robert, has it survived?"

"Yes, I have two daughters and both are well. The healer Morag is attending to them as we speak."

"Praise God Lord, two daughters. Will you be able to travel back with us today?"

The Lord shook his head. "I fear it will be a long time before we can travel." He then rested his weight on a table outside the cottage, feigning weakness.

"But Lord, your father instructed us to return with you."

"Don't be stupid! My father would not want me to return with the plague you fool!"

The effort of his outburst appeared to weaken him significantly and he sat down. After almost a minute's silence, he continued in a more moderate tone. "We were treated on our journey by many healers, but my men died one by one, we were down to just the four of us when we arrived here. Sadly, the other two did not make it. But this healer is the finest in the land. She has treated my wife and me for many weeks, and we are getting stronger."

The captain moved on his saddle uncomfortably. "We too have fine healers, Sire. You can be treated at the castle in comfort."

"No, Captain, don't be ridiculous we cannot leave this place."

"Sire, your father's orders."

"I said no, Captain!" The Lord let his head hang with fatigue, then continued. "The healer says the herbs she needs only grow in this forest, and she says only fresh herbs picked daily will heal us. I cannot risk traveling until we are both cured."

"But Sire."

"I said no you fool, and I won't repeat it! According to the healer, it will be at least a year before we will be free of the plague. I will return to the cottage and write my father a letter. Give it to him, and he will understand. I will put my seal on it to prove you have found us. Do not get off your horses and stay exactly where you are. There is no way we are traveling back to the castle while we still have the plague."

Sir Robert walked back to the cottage, clinging to any object that would aid his support. Wolf, in the meantime, was watching the men and stood between them and her den growling.

The captain called out to the Lord. "The wolf, my Lord, is it safe? I have not seen a white one before, or one so large."

"She will not harm you if you stay where you are. The wolf belongs to my wife, it is her protector and never leaves her side. She has two cubs in her den, so you will be safe if you stay on your horses."

Fifteen minutes later, the Princess walked out of the cottage and the men fell silent. She was taller than most of them and her skin was olive-brown. She wore a long green dress with a gold-colored belt, and unusually for women of that time, her hair was loose and fell to her waist. She was stunningly beautiful, a woman the likes of which they had never seen before.

Morag could sense the men's admiration and was enjoying the sensation. It had been long since any man had admired her, and she noted her beauty transfixed them. "My husband asks me to give you this." She said and held out a sealed letter.

The officer was staring open-mouthed and did not comment.

Morag had deliberately emphasized the Princesses' foreign accent. "Well gentlemen, how you say in this country, has cat got tongue?"

The officer eventually pulled himself together. "B-beg your pardon, my Lady."

"It is all right, captain. May I have name?"

"Roberts, my lady."

"Captain, the title you give is wrong, I am Princess, not Lady. You must use title, Princess, when you address me, understand?"

The captain nodded. "Sorry, my Lady - I mean Princess."

"Captain Roberts, would you kindly take letter to father-in-law?"

The captain took the letter and the Princess gave him her warmest smile. It was a smile the Princess had practiced throughout her lifetime and one that made most men weak at the knees. It was a tool she regularly used to good effect.

"You must forgive husband for being abrupt. He very weak. He say - you search for many months?"

"Aye, aye," the men chimed in unison.

"As you can see, we are not well, but safe. We sought this healer because she lives deep in forest, so we have less chance of passing on the disease. So, you brave men must leave this place. I could not bear it if even one of you were to catch it." Her eyes moved to each soldier in turn, and her smile never wavered and she noted the effect on them was profound.

"Of course, Princess, we will do as you say. But I am concerned for your safety as you are alone here."

"We not alone. We have 'Wolf'." Hearing her name, the wolf moved alongside the Princess, and her growl became louder. She reached across to comfort her and to keep her close.

"It's all right, Wolf. It's just father-in-law's soldiers." Wolf could smell the primeval fear emanating from both the men and horses. The Princess placed her hand on its head and the creature sat by her side and the growls began to subside.

"Truly a magnificent beast, You're Highness, a giant, but it is still just one creature."

"Yes, but what a creature." The Princess continued to stroke the wolf. "This is a royal wolf, bred from the largest and finest wolves in my country. She do everything I ask of her. She can kill a bear, snap a man's neck, or rip throat out in a second."

The captain winced but was unconvinced. "But it is still just one creature, and an arrow could bring it down. Your Highness,

I will leave several men, and they can camp at the side of the road to keep an eye on you from a distance."

"No!" The Princess replied sharply, and the smile left her face. "Husband say we no draw attention. Leaving men nearby, it do that!"

Softening her features, she added: "Husband, say you go back to next village and spread word we have plague in forest. This will deter anyone from venturing nearby. Morag tells me no one lives around here for miles. We be safe as long as we careful."

"Whatever you wish, your Highness."

The Princess lifted her arm to her forehead, feigning fatigue. "I feel weak and must rest, so go now and report to father-in-law. Tell him as soon as we healed, we send word for you to return and escort us back." She again turned and smiled at each of them in turn. "Now please, captain, take your men and go." She shuffled back to the cottage, and after closing the door rested her ear on it and listened as the captain barked his orders.

The men turned their horses and retreated. Wolf watched them leave and, when they were out of sight, the creature turned and went back into her den.

A feeling of relief and euphoria overcame Morag. *See the look on their faces, they adored me. With just a simple smile, they were wrapped around my little finger. They didn't suspect a thing. With this body and my gifts, anything is possible.*

*

The wagon did indeed contain gold and other treasures. Morag kept the horses and began to breed them. After six months, she decided it was time to tell Earl Llewellyn that both his sick son and wife had survived but were still not strong enough to withstand such a long journey.

In the guise of his son, she sent a message to the Earl seeking to have a grand house built in the forest. Being on the southwest tip of the Earl's, estate, the land would serve as a long-term residence for his growing family. The costs would be met and paid for with the dowry from the Princess.

A request for forty craftsmen to be sent south to construct the property was granted, and the construction began almost at once. She still used the subterfuge of the plague to keep the workers and forest dwellers away from the cottage. However, Morag never once stepped outside without using one of the many guises she had stored in her essence jars.

*

Communicating with the spirit world came as naturally to Morag as breathing. She found comfort in her solitude and was at peace with the forest and the creatures that shared it. From the very beginning, she taught the girls the ways of the Ancients and shared how they became the first people to control fire. Then onto the hunter-gatherers, a new people that moved north from the plains of Africa and confronted the Ancients, and how, over time, they interbred with them. This group with mixed blood set themselves apart from the rest of humanity. They alone could recall their past lives, they alone were fully aware.

She told them of the Wood and Stone Henges and how humankind could predict the seasons by building them. And the vision these early peoples had to create a place of learning - where all men were equal and free to study the heavens and live in harmony with nature. A place they called Avalon, and later how the invaders from Rome destroyed it.

She taught them about the flora and fauna of the forest and how to observe them and learn their ways. To study the seasons as they unfolded, to enjoy simple pleasures like feeling the wind in their faces, and be in touch with the elements. To gain comfort from basic pleasures like walking in streams and feeling the water on their feet as it journeyed through the forest to the great sea. She taught them about the destructive force of fire and how to control it. And how to touch the stones and listen to their echoes.

Throughout their early years, Morag's life was dedicated solely to the instruction of the girls, passing on to them the 'Prime' wisdom and archaic memories passed down through the ages since time began. She was at pains to point out how special they were, what they could achieve in their lives, and that one day if they learned their lessons well, they may be accepted into the Prime Sisterhood of healers.

She told them of the Shamans and Arch Druids, men and women, practitioners of the healing art and early magic, whose memories they would soon recover, and the ancestors that will reside within them for the rest of life's journey. Ancestors that will advise and comfort them, passing on knowledge from the clear springs of ancient wisdom.

She taught them how to converse with animal and plant spirits, skills gathered through countless lifetimes. Skills the rest of humankind sought from them, healing arts they wanted and feared.

She cautioned the girls that humankind would always fear someone who can heal and that it caused discomfort to those whose souls are dead and whose spiritual eyes are blind. When this happened, the healer would become feared and proclaimed, a 'Witch.' Someone to be judged, punished, and even killed.

She told them the beauty of carrying the memories of their parents, brothers, and sisters, the joy of healing others, and the love of life itself. And to be aware of the dangers of the dark forces that corrupt and destroy and how they are fed by jealousy, anger, greed, suspicion, envy, hate, corruption and other dark thoughts. Thoughts and deeds that worm their way into the soul, blackening it forever. Forces that sucked out life's beauty, causing sickness and despair.

Morag was also aware these girls were different from most other children. They had the genes of their parents. Their father, she knew, had been a cruel man. However, their mother was a healer, a sister, and a seer with powerful new wisdom. Wisdom passed down a path unknown to anyone in these lands. What secrets? What healing practices may they have when eventually their memories are awakened?

These girls were the daughters she could never have, and they now filled her life day and night and gave it purpose. The skills she hoped to pass on to them would make them extremely powerful women, with talents that could corrupt or blossom.

The girls were becoming more aware, and distant memories came to the fore daily. Both girls now seemed to be in contact with their mothers' spirit, and they seemed perfectly comfortable with this. Due to Morag's teachings, they not only expected to receive the 'Prime' memories of their ancestors, but they looked forward to them with anticipation.

She knew these girls were unique. Every day, weather permitting, they ventured into the forest, where they settled down and continued with their instruction. Their favorite places to study were near the lake or stream so they could be in close contact with the lake spirits and, of course, their mother.

Morag found the lessons were simply reawakening distant memories. Once these memories had come to the fore, they were there forever. This made teaching them extremely easy, and soon the girls were retaining knowledge that an average person would take a lifetime to accumulate.

*

It soon came time to introduce them to the Sisterhood and inform the Earth Mother's representative at Avebury. This was a return journey of almost a hundred miles and it presented many dangers. Taking two five-year-old girls and three wolves would undoubtedly draw unwanted attention. Leaving the girls on their own for an extended period of time, even with their protectors guarding them was not an option. She would need to get there and back within a few hours.

She was reluctant to leave them unattended but she had no choice. She called the girls and told them she was going on a journey and they were to stay in the cottage with their wolves - who would watch over them while she was gone.

Ursula bit her lip, a trait she always did when she was worried, and turned to Morag, "Nana, will you be gone long?"

"Only one night, little one."

She tugged at Morag's skirt, and her watery green eyes looked up eagerly. "Can we go with you?"

Morag smiled down at her daughter. "It's a very long journey, Ursula - too long for you or your sister to travel in one night."

"If it's a long journey, how can you go there and back before sunrise?"

"Easy child, I will fly."

Both girls burst out laughing until they realized she was serious. Sarah posed a question, her green eyes as big as saucers. "I didn't know you could fly, Nana!"

"I can't," she said smiling down at them. "But I know a bird that can."

Once again, both girls began to laugh. "Nana, You're too heavy. It would have to be a huge bird."

"The bird will carry my spirit. My body will be here with you, sleeping in my bed."

"So, you will be with us, but asleep in your room?"

"Yes, but I will be in a very deep sleep, so you won't be able to wake me until I return. I will go into my room and lock the door from the inside so that no one can disturb me. Then I will call a bird to carry my spirit and I will be back by dawn."

Both girls fell silent as they absorbed this new information, then Ursula quipped. "Will you call your Raven totem, Nana?"

"Not this time child. What bird would you take for this journey?"

"A hawk because they are the fastest birds - so you will be back before dawn."

"That's very true. What bird would you choose, Sarah?"

Sarah bit her lip, copying her sister, and thought for a while. "I would call an owl."

"Yes, Sarah. I will be calling an owl. I could have called a goose - or a nightjar - as they both fly at night – but not a hawk. Hawks cannot see in the dark."

"So why did you choose the owl over the other birds?"

"Good question, Ursula. As Sarah realized, the owl can see in the dark. It also has very few predators, and it flies on silent wings. If you listen when an owl is on the wing you will hear no sound. If I chose a goose, it would make too much noise. A goose can't fly far without making a honking noise, and this would draw too much attention to me. Although swift and graceful, the nightjar is a small bird, a bird small enough to be attacked by other birds of prey."

Both girls looked up at Morag, their eyes still as big as saucers and steeped in wonder. "Is it dangerous when your spirit is carried by another creature Nana?"

"Yes, Sarah, it is a most dangerous time. Anyone whose spirit dwells in another body is very vulnerable. If that creature is killed, the spirit may not find its way back and be lost forever."

Both girls looked horrified and clung to her skirts as their eyes looked up pleadingly. "Then you mustn't go, Nana."

Ursula echoed her sister. "No, Nana, you mustn't go - we need you, please, stay."

Morag bent down and hugged her wards, her eyes moist with emotion, and tried to comfort them. "I must make the journey - but you girls can help. Did you know your mother was a seer?"

The girls replied in unison. "What does that mean, Nana?"

"A seer is someone who can look into the future and tell if something bad is going to happen. When you go to sleep, I would like you to ask your mother if it is safe for Nana to make this journey. Would you do that for me?"

"Yes, Nana, but what if she doesn't come?"

"I'm sure she will come. She has been expecting me to make this journey for quite a while."

"You are going to see the Earth Mother, aren't you?"

Morag felt the hair lift on the nape of her neck. She had not mentioned the creator of all things to her. *So, Ursula is in contact with the spirit world as well. I was beginning to think it was just Sarah.*

"I'm going to see the representative of the Earth Mother. How did you know Ursula?"

"Mother told me, of course."

"I see, when did she tell you this?"

"Yesterday." They said again in unison.

Morag hugged the girls. "It looks like I'm always the last to know. Did she say when?"

Ursula replied, "She said tomorrow night just after sundown, but she did not say you would be calling a bird."

"Then I know my journey will be safe because she's already spoken to you."

The following evening, Morag prepared herself for the journey. It was a journey she did not want to make. She was aware that when the spirit left its host, the body itself was very vulnerable and one step away from death - and it was something she dreaded doing.

She prepared a concoction of exotic mind-expanding elements from the forest's flora. Archaic knowledge obtained by communicating with plant spirits across the ages. Potions to slow her heart down to the very minimum.

After calling the three wolves to her, she instructed them to guard both girls and to stay by their sides until she returned. Ghost would watch over Sarah and Shadow would stay with

Ursula. Wolf herself would remain in Morag's room to watch over her as she slept.

Morag locked all the doors to the cottage, and after putting the wolves in the girls' room, she returned to her bedroom and bolted the door. The window was left open enough for the owl to enter. And after retiring to her bed, she began to call the owls of the forest.

Within minutes, a pure white barn owl answered her calling and flew into the room, a phantasm. It settled at the foot of the bed and waited as Morag's breathing began to slow until she was barely alive. A glow began to emanate from Morag and encompassed both the owl and the bed. Eventually, the owl turned, flew out of the window as silently as it came, and was gone.

The owl flew swiftly south, skimming the treetops of oak, juniper and birch, and it made the 42-mile journey in just over two hours. Finally, she could see the giant stone circles of Avebury below her.

*

A stray memory came of how the Stone Megaliths near the village of Avebury were first erected during the Neolithic period. The sanctuary comprised three separate stone circles. Its outer circle is the largest stone circle in the world. These stone circles and the earlier wooden ones were ceremonial centers. Places where people from the Early Neolithic onwards would meet up to worship their 'Earth Mother' in her various guises.

The two main meetings were the summer and winter solstice, the longest and shortest days of the year. At these meetings, multiple marriages would take place. Tribe and family members who had passed away would be honored. News was exchanged and future ceremonies were organized. There were animal sacrifices to thank the Earth Mother for her bountiful supply, and hopefully, encourage her to grant them good hunting in the coming season. And when humankind turned to the plow, a successful harvest.

The Henge was steeped in folk law and ritual practices. They began as meeting places for the early hunter-gatherers. Being nomadic it was challenging to meet up with other groups. They needed a focal point to meet, somewhere distinct from the surrounding area.

At first, they used wood to construct the henges. Wood was plentiful at this time because most of Britain was covered in forest. After selecting a meeting place, they formed a large circle and inverted a ring of trees around the circumference. They left the roots in place so they acted like branches. This prevented the trees from regrowing and it made the circle as conspicuous as possible. It was a meeting place, a focal point for the tribes to meet twice a year. In later centuries when the population and manpower increased, they built them out of stone.

The only time references they had was the longest and shortest days of the year. At these points in time, they would meet. It was the beginning of humankind's 'organized society.'

The population of the British Isles was in the thousands. It was a place to meet when someone was of age and needed a partner, whether for one night or a whole lifetime. The ceremonies would be alcohol - and narcotic-fueled and resulted in copulation on a grand scale. This encouraged diversity in the gene pool and the offspring of these encounters were both more robust and healthier. It also helped link the various tribes together, which the tribe elders noted and encouraged.

Later came the Shamans and Priests – grasping the potential to use these practices as tools to control society - as religion has done throughout history. Later they increased the annual ceremonies to four, using the spring and autumn equinox.

At one of these forthcoming meetings, Morag wanted to present her daughters. The person she needed permission and guidance from was the 'Earth Mothers Representative' in this area. The name people used for her was simply 'Mother' or for ceremonial purposes, 'Earth Mother'.

Mother was the embodiment of images and sculptures found in graves and temples discovered in later centuries and was obese to the point that she could hardly walk. As the Earth Mother's Representative, it was her duty to replicate this image, and with the excess food presented to her, it wasn't difficult.

She could be quick to anger and very stubborn. Her moods could be dark, her temper quick. However, she was not chosen to be the 'Mother's Representative' for nothing. Her mind was sharp, and the memories passed along her ancestral line gave her immense knowledge.

*

The owl was circling above her dwelling in the early hours and Morag was hoping she was a morning person. It landed on the windowsill and hooted several times.

Her sleep disturbed, the Earth Mother' sat upright and came face to face with the owl. She blinked several times in disbelief and the tone of her voice reflected her annoyance. "Who in the name of the 'Mother of all' is this? Do you not know what time it is?"

Please forgive the intrusion, Mother, I need your advice.

The Earth Mothers' representative snapped. "Could it not have waited until tomorrow?"

No, Mother, it would have been complicated. I have children who are now alone and I must return before sunrise.

"Very well, give me a moment."

'Mother' raised herself with difficulty and sat cross-legged on the floor and meditated before once again addressing the bird. "Who is this that wishes to consult with the Earth Mother?"

My name is Morag.

"Morag, from the north forest?"

Yes, Mother.

"Morag, the Earth Mother welcomes you."

Mother, I have two daughters, born not to me, who have the gift and I believe they are special.

The Earth Mother sighed heavily. "Special, are they? All mothers think their daughters are, special. Why do you think they are special?"

Their summers are now five in number, and...

"Five!" she snapped, cutting her short. "You can't tell if a child is special or has any gifts at five. You woke me up to tell me this?"

Mother, if you listen to what I have to say, you will understand. I need guidance and I can speak to only you.

"Morag, this had better be good... speak."

Five summers ago, a Lord came to my dwelling, the son of Earl Llewellyn. He was returning home from a great journey overseas. He had with him his wife, who was regarded as a Princess in her country. They and their companions had caught a plague while on this journey. They came to me for healing.

"Wait, is this the Lord that killed two of our sisters?"

It is, Mother.

The Earth Mother gasped in disbelief. "And you helped him?"

I tried Mother, but I did not have much choice. His wife was with child and ready to give birth. We have a duty.

"I see, but what happened to them?"

Lord Llewellyn and his wife died. I am here because his wife was a seer and she had the gift.

"Ah, I see. Were you able to recover her memories?"

Yes, Mother, and they are new memories.

"New memories?"

Completely new.

"Are you sure about this? We have not had new memories for hundreds of years?"

I am sure Mother. This Princess came from a distant land. Her skin was olive-brown and her hair jet black without the hint of a curl. She was almost six feet tall, nearly as big as Lord Llewellyn. I had not seen her kind before.

"So, you obviously managed to save the baby?"

Yes, both babies survived.

"Babies?"

Yes, Mother, she had two daughters.

"You are rearing these children as your own, I take it. Does the Earl not want them?"

I recovered the essences from both Lord Llewellyn and the Princess. When I took her form and recovered her memories, I realized her marriage was a business arrangement between the families. She hated him. He was a cruel man and she did not want his family to rear her children.

"I see, so you're raising them as your own."

Yes, Mother. When the Earl's men came looking for them, however, I took the form of Robert Llewellyn and the Earl's family thinks he is still alive, and the Princess too.

"Morag, if they lived with the Earl, they would live in comfort."

They will live in comfort with me and are also very loved. The Earl is building a great house by the lake in the woods near where I live and we will live there.

"Do the girls know you're not their mother?"

Yes, they know. They call me 'Nana' and they know their parents are dead. What they don't know is I killed their father.

"You killed him?"

Yes, he was trying to kill me when his wife died. I knew he had killed our sisters and I was expecting it because the Princess had warned me in a dream. She had foreseen her death and that I would save her daughters and lead them to the light. I hoped that when he saw I had saved his daughters, he would bond with them. But no, he saw his wife's body and went into a rage. If he had had the strength, he would have killed me there and then. The plague was too advanced, so it was only a matter of time. Anyway, it was a mercy.

"So, you think these girls are special."

They are unique and have recovered lots of memories already. I think they will significantly benefit the Sisterhood with the correct guidance.

"Excellent, Morag, we will present them at the next meeting. But I will not tell anyone about what we have said tonight. The fewer people who know we have children with possibly new memories, the better. Also, there will be less chance that people who, shall we say have taken a darker path, could be drawn to them. I will see you at the summer solstice."

One more request, Mother. I will probably need help guiding them, especially when we move into the large house – people we can trust. Can you recommend anyone?

"I will think on this. I would like to judge for myself how special these girls are. I will give you my decision at the solstice."

Then I will take my leave.

The owl turned and fled.

The Earth Mother sat for a while, deep in thought. *Children are usually born with memories. Some newborn babies are distressed and cry when remembering their earlier death. Some, who are contented, either don't remember or had a gentle passage from their previous life. Then the memories fade. Being 'Prime', all children recover them but not until puberty. For girls to remember at such a young age is unheard of. Then again, if they are from a new line, who knows what is normal for these people? This is exciting news. Yes, we must keep them close. We must also keep them away from the dark brothers and sisters who may want to corrupt them.*

*

The journey back was swift. The owl flew straight through the bedroom window, perched on the bed, and waited. After ten minutes, the owl was again bathed by a glowing light. It grew larger until it encompassed both the bird and the bed.

Morag began to stir and verbally said "thank you" to the bird, which then turned and flew back into the forest.

The exhausted healer slept through to midday, waking suddenly when Wolf roused her by licking her hand.

"Thank you, Wolf, I'm getting up now."

She stretched her stiff muscles and went through to the scullery.

"Nana, you're back," cried both girls as they rushed over to her and wrapped their arms around her legs. As Morag looked down upon her daughters, her heart melted and she could see the joy on their faces.

"Goodness, girls, what a welcome. Were you worried?"

"Yes, Nana, you said it was dangerous."

Both girls' eyes were once again as large as saucers. She knelt beside them, lifted them both, and rested them on her hips.

"Yes, but I chose wisely Sarah, and thanks to your mother I knew the owl was a perfect host. Remember, girls, it's important to make the correct decisions throughout life. If you are not sure about something, consult with your mother, me, or your ancestors. Then you will be safe because we are here to guide you."

As soon as Morag put them down, Ursula tugged at her skirt. "What did the Earth Mother say, Nana?"

"Yes, Nana, what did she say?" echoed Sarah, who was jumping up and down with excitement.

"She said we are to go and see her at the summer festival."

"Does that mean we are going to fly too?"

"No, girls, we will have to make the journey on foot."

As the words left her mouth, she fell silent and was lost in thought. *How are we going to get there? We can't take the horse and cart the roads are simply unsuitable. It would take a week on foot with a couple of five-year-old children – I could ride on a horse, but there is no way the girls could.* Sarah asked. How long will it take on foot Nanna?

"Almost a week I think, but don't worry we will take our time, Sarah – unless I can think of something else."

Sarah then proposed excitedly. "We could ride on our wolves as you do on your horse, Nana."

Morag waved her arms dismissively. "I don't think your wolves would let you ride on their backs, Sarah. You're being silly."

"But Nana, Ghost lets me sit on her back."

"So does Shadow," quipped Ursula.

"They do? Your wolves let you sit on their backs? When did this happen?"

"About two moon cycles ago, when our mother first started talking to us."

"You must show me. I have never heard of children being carried by wolves."

The children ran outside and called their wolves. They were never out of earshot and arrived almost at once. Each wolf went up to its companion. The wolves remained motionless and simply stared at the girls.

Morag watched them and was expecting some sort of verbal communication. The girls, however, said nothing. They merely looked into their creature's eyes and after a couple of moments, both wolves lay down in front of them. The girls stepped across their backs, and the wolves stood up.

"How did you do that? What did you say? How did you speak to them?" The questions left Morag's lips in a rush, she had never seen anything like it and was dumbstruck.

"Easy Nana, you just ask."

"How did you ask Sarah? I didn't see your lips move."

"They looked into our minds and asked us what we wanted them to do."

"I see." Morag shook her head, trying to clear her thoughts, then added, "Is that the same for you, Ursula?"

"Yes, Sarah could do it first. She talks to most of the animals and she showed me how to do it. I can't do it with all the animals, just Shadow."

This was further news Morag was unaware of. "You can talk to other animals, Sarah."

"Not talk, Nana. But I know what they're thinking, and they seem to know what I think."

"How long has this been going on? No, let me guess. Since you started speaking to your mother two moon cycles ago?"

"Yes, Nana."

Morag again felt the hair on the back of her neck rise and her stomach twisted with excitement. *They can talk to animals without speaking. No one does that these days, I have heard that the Avalonian Grand Masters used to do it, but it is a skill lost in time - and their control over the wolves is unbelievable.*

"Will they walk with you on their back?"

"Of course, Nana. Watch."

Both wolves then began to walk around in a circle.

Morag shook her head in amazement. *Unbelievable, totally unbelievable.!*

"They will run too. Watch."

"No! Ursula, be careful."

Instantly both wolves began to trot.

"Nana, they can go really fast."

"No, stop!" Morag yelled, but it was too late – the wolves had gone.

Unperturbed by the danger, both girls began laughing hysterically.

"Stop, stop, come back. Come back this instant!"

Morag felt her heart race as the wolves picked up speed and she rested on her staff for support. Finally, the wolves slowed to a trot, then walked back. Morag outwardly held her excitement in check – and managed to keep calm and not let the girls see how frightened she had become.

"That was very interesting, girls. Walking will be acceptable, but no trotting or running unless you are in danger. Now, I'm starving, so let's get something to eat."

Morag chuckled inwardly, again deep in thought. *That will solve the problem of transport. Mother will not believe her eyes.*

3. LONG ISLAND NEW YORK 1974 AD

Peter's father was a widower, his wife had died just after their golden wedding anniversary. He lived in a gated house on Long Island, New York, with just one housekeeper and a dog. He liked his privacy but was always happy to see his family.

Over the evening meal, Joan skillfully guided the conversation to the dreams that they were all having. His father did not comment at first, but as he listened to their comments his mind drifted back to his youth and to a conversation he had had with his wife.

He eventually placed his knife and fork down on his plate and cleared his throat to indicate that he was about to speak. "You say Paul has these dreams as well?"

Peter nodded to confirm it.

"I see. This takes me back a bit. Your mother used to say that dreams like the ones you have just described are windows to the past. She came to terms with them - God rest her soul - and swore they were simply the memories of her ancestors."

Joan looked at Peter and she could see the relief on his face. "That makes sense, Peter, and it certainly makes more sense than ghosts talking to us all the time."

Peter's father cocked his head studying his son. "You hear voices as well?"

Again, Peter and Joan exchanged awkward glances before nodding in unison.

"Joan has been troubled by them for years dad, but I have only just started hearing them."

"Do you mean lots of people talking simultaneously?"

"Yes, dad, that's exactly what I mean. Why, have you had the same problem?"

Peter's father inhaled deeply before continuing. "Yes, when I was very young - that is. However, your mother was troubled by them all her life, but we kept it quiet. We did not want people to think she was going nuts. She said she could have full-blown conversations with them - like they were different people. I stopped hearing the voices when I was very young."

"Ok, dad, that would explain Paul and me having these dreams, but what about Joan? And mom for that matter. Were the dreams you and mom had the same? or were they different?"

"It's hard to remember now son, as I said the voices got less and less as I got older, but I can't remember the dreams. Your mom found comfort in them. I remember getting very worried about her at one point. She used to ignore them when I was around, but I often heard her chatting away like there was someone in the room, especially when she thought she was alone."

Peter again glanced over at Joan, who appeared to be lost in thought. "It looks like it is just some hereditary trait on my side of the family at least, so we are getting somewhere."

"Dad, can you remember any names or places from those dreams - or what the voices said, anything that springs to mind?"

He shook his head. "Tell me the names you have - and let's see if any of them jog my memory." Peter reeled off a list of names, and nothing jumped out at him, so Peter again changed tack.

"What about places? Have you heard of Glastonbury, Avalon, or Earlswood?"

His father laughed wholeheartedly. "Of course I have, I was born at Earlswood Manor, Glastonbury in the Vale of Avalon."

Joan interrupted. "You were born there? Then it is a real place - it really exists. Peter, the spiritualist, said Paul would be drawn back to England, to the place of his ancestors. She said a woman would be calling him to come home when the time was right. Maybe she is already calling him. Maybe she is calling all of us."

Peter's father couldn't hide the surprise on his face. "You have been told a woman would be calling him back to England. That is an unusual thing to say."

His eyes turned to Paul and he addressed him in person. "It reminds me of something your mother said to me when we were very young. She said she had been calling me and that is why I was drawn to her. She said her mother had taught her how to do it before she died. As you know she was only ten when it happened - and I have never heard of anyone else using the term 'calling' other than by telephone. How strange."

*

The meeting with Peter's father was informative, but it raised even more questions. Joan could understand Peter, and even Paul inheriting memories about Earlswood manor, but how could she be having the same dreams? Her family as far as she knew had never lived there. Joan wanted answers; It may have comforted Peter knowing his mom and dad both heard voices, but it still troubled her.

The following day Joan was chasing her breakfast cereal around her plate absentmindedly with her spoon and was deep in thought. *So, I am not mad. I might be possessed, but not mad. How do I feel about that? Well, surprisingly not as bad as I think I would have done last week, so much has happened in such a short space of time. Peter took the spiritualist thing well. I think he realizes he has wasted a lot of money on shrinks, which serves him right. Thank God, at last, I have proof I am not mad.*

"Maybe we should go to this Earlswood Manor and spend some time in Glastonbury? We could do with a break - we never seem to stop working these days."

Peter raised his eyes above the newspaper which he insisted on reading over breakfast and shook his head. "I don't think we can get away just yet. We have the golf course in Dallas halfway through construction - and I must finalize the plans for the one in Florida. Maybe next year. Why don't you just give them a ring?"

Joan continued to chase the cereal around her plate and snorted. "Give them a ring and say what exactly. Can you help me, please? Why am I dreaming about your house and town? Get real."

Peter continued speaking, but he now did it through the newspaper. "Ask them to send some brochures. Dad said it was a hotel now, so I am sure they would do that."

Joan Masters cupped her cup of coffee in her hands and looked thoughtfully into the swirling liquid. *I might just do that.*

*

Jed Stevens was manning the reception desk at Earlswood manor. When the phone rang and a lady with a strong American accent engaged him in dialog about the manor. She seemed very pleasant. She commented on his strong Welsh accent and he did the same saying they did not get many Americans ringing them.

The conversation was cordial and Jed gave her a quick rundown of the manor's history with plenty of facts, and even legends about the place. Thinking she was enquiring to visit the manor, he offered to send some brochures and the booking forms.

"May I have your name and address please?"

"Joan, Joan Masters... May I just ask. "Does Saul, Mia, or Morag still live there - or any of their relatives Jed?"

Jed fell silent, and the pregnant pause was deafening.

When he did not answer immediately, she raised her voice. "Are you still there!?"

"Er, I was just thinking..." He said nervously. "Do you know their surnames by any chance? *What on earth is going on here?*

"No, sorry."

"Why did you ask?"

"Oh, it's just something that came up in conversation at my father in laws house over our Sunday meal. He was born there - his family owned the house in the early 1900s."

Why, why would they talk about someone that had been dead for four hundred years? And think they might still be alive? "I can ask around Mrs. Masters." *How do I answer this without compromising myself?* "I was thinking does the word Prime mean anything to you Mrs. Masters?

"Yes, I think my father-in-law mentioned someone with the surname 'Prime.'

So, she thinks Prime is a surname, I think I am safe here. "I can ask around, there are a couple of staff members that have worked here for years - they will know if anyone will. So, your father-in-law was born here. If you don't mind me asking? What prompted the conversation about the Prime family?

"You will laugh, I keep dreaming about them, and my father-in-law said it was someone from the manor. He is going a bit senile now, but he is sure he remembered them from his youth."

Now it is beginning to make sense. Could it be, could it really be?"

"I see Mrs. Masters. Well, I will ask around, and if there are any relatives still living - I will put the contact details in the brochure. May I have your address?"

When Jed put the phone down, he sat pensively as he considered his next move. He needed to meet with her quickly before it was too late.

He picked up the phone, and his hands were visibly shaking. He dialed a number from memory. "Earth Mother, I think I have found a sleeper - I must go to New York at once."

*

The very next day Jed was given a two-week holiday and flew out to New York. He made his way to Joan's house and casually rang the doorbell.

As he waited for someone to answer - he took in the surroundings. He was unused to city life and danger seemed to be around every corner. His heart was filled with mixed emotions and he prayed that he was not walking into a Primevil trap.

Joan opened the door - and Jed was pleasantly surprised when he saw her eyes were bright green, and she smiled openly.

"Can I help you?" she said as she bent down to pick a newspaper off the floor.

Jed laughed nervously. "We spoke on the phone a couple of days ago. You asked for some brochures on Earlswood Manor, and I thought – being as I was passing - I would drop them off in person." Joan stood there, open-mouthed, unable to speak.

Jed prompted. "You asked about certain people, you remember, Morag, Saul and Mia. I have information about them. It is a little sensitive, and I felt I should not talk to you over the phone."

Joan's mouth was still open. Finally, she realized and closed it. "Jed, is it?"

"Yes, Joan, do you think we could go somewhere where we could talk?"

Joan stepped to one side to let him pass. "Yes, of course. Please come in - my husband will be home soon." Jed followed her into her kitchen, where she began to fill the kettle. "Well, Jed, this is a surprise. Would you like a coffee?"

He shook his head. "Any chance of a cup of tea?"

"Sorry, Jed."

He waved his hands dismissively. "Maybe a glass of water then." She smiled openly again, and it lit up her whole face, and his heart skipped a beat. *She's 'Prime,' I am sure she is.*

"Well, Jed, this is a surprise," she turned and rested her back on the sink studying his features. He was six feet tall, strong looking with deep blue eyes. She found him pleasantly attractive, even though he was a few years older than her.

"What an amazing coincidence - you coming to New York and can drop off the brochures just days after we spoke?"

He smiled, to ease the situation. "No, it wasn't a coincidence Joan, the brochures were just a front to come and see you. Once I spoke to you on the phone, I realized that we needed to meet up."

Joan's hand reached into the sink behind her and grabbed a knife, she held it out of sight behind her back; the solid feel reassured her and the smile left her face. "My husband will be back shortly. I think you should leave."

Jed continued. "Oh, I think he should hear what I am about to say before I go."

Joan continued to study him, she was wary but he didn't seem to be threatening in the slightest, and she wondered if she was missing something.

"Jed." She said nervously. "People do not travel halfway around the world without a very good reason. What is this all about?"

Jed looked around. "Do you mind if we sit down? This is going to take a while." Joan did not speak, but she indicated which chair he should sit on by nodding her head.

Jed sat down and quipped. "You can bring the kitchen knife if it makes you feel more comfortable until your husband gets back."

Joan watched him suspiciously and sat opposite him, and Jed noticed that she had taken the knife with her."

Jed sighed. "Sorry if I have frightened you, Mrs. Masters. It was not my intention. Do you want to talk now, or shall we wait for your husband to return?"

"Jed, would you please tell me what this is all about?"

Jed clapped his hands and rubbed them together. "Right, ok. Could we start with you telling me what you know about Morag, Saul and Mia, and please don't say they were your father-in-law's friends?"

She was about to say just that and found her mouth wide open once again.

When she did not speak, Jed continued. "You had a dream about them. Is that correct?" Joan nodded. "Joan, if you don't mind me using your first name. You have had many dreams you cannot understand - am I correct?" Again, she nodded.

"What about voices? Do you hear voices?"

Again, she gave an affirmative nod and put the knife down on the table.

Finally, she found her voice.

"Yes, I hear voices. Are you a spiritualist?"

Jed pursed his lips and shook his head. "No, Joan, but I know why you hear voices and why you are having these dreams. That is why I have come all this way. You need help, and, I'm sorry to say you are in grave danger." His eye's bored into hers, measuring her. "Have you told anyone about Morag, Mia and Saul? It's very important."

Joan took a deep breath and looked suspiciously into his eyes. "Only my husband and my father-in-law."

"Thank God for that, just family. If I say the word Primevil does that mean anything to you?"

A frown crossed Joan's face. "Is that a real word? I have heard of Primeval, not 'Primevil,'"

Jed continued to study her face intensely. "Do any of your dreams contain images of people in red robes mutilating or abusing people?

The color drained from Joan's face.

"Yes, and they are always nightmares. I have felt troubled by them for years, and when I have one of them I can't sleep - I haven't even told my husband about them."

Jed chewed his lip thoughtfully. "Ok, first the bad news, the people in the red robes are real people - no, not people, less than people, less than animals. They are called the 'Primevil,' The images you see in your dreams were real events - and believe me it is just the tip of the iceberg, they have happened in the past. One of your ancestors witnessed the event, and you have inherited the memory from your ancestor. It's a memory - not a dream."

Joan's eyes were fixed on Jed's, taking in his every word, and she found herself holding her breath impatiently. "Then why am I in danger if they are simply inherited memories?"

She watched as Jed took time to continue.

"Right Joan, if, as you said you have kept it in the family and told no one, then you are safe. These 'Primevil' are very powerful, they control several governments and even some countries. They have eyes and ears everywhere, and they are our mortal enemies. If they know who you are and what you are, you would be just one more victim in one of your red dreams. So, tell no one - you must keep this to yourself."

She glanced cagily at him. "Then I think it's time you told me what I am."

Jed clapped his hands hard excitedly and rubbed them together, and Joan nearly jumped out of her skin.

"Now for the good news. I am one of the good guys, and you, Joan Masters, are a 'Prime' stray."

*

Jed stayed at Joan's house for the next seven days. He explained who and what she was, and he taught her how to meditate and reach her inner self. He advised her on how to communicate with the ancestors embedded within her. He explained the different dreams she had had - and what they meant. He discussed the red dreams and explained why it was necessary to remember them. He implored her to fixate on the white dreams and be guided by what they represented.

The emphasis was always on secrecy, if the 'Primevil' did not know Joan and her family existed, they were safe.

She promised to bring Paul to Earlswood as the spiritualist had foretold, but not until he had finished his studies when he would be twenty-five. She drove him to the airport, thanked him, and said Jokingly she would see him in twenty years.

When Joan began to dream that night, she felt relieved that it was a white dream and snuggled into the bedclothes with renewed interest.

4. THE WOLVES, 1604 AD

Morag rose early the following day. She had found sleep hard to come by. The events of the previous day had troubled her greatly. The girls' power over their wolves was disturbing, and it was simply unheard of to communicate with land animals without speaking. During the night, she searched through memories that went back to the Stone Age and beyond and found that only a select few Avalonian Grandmasters ever had this ability.

The sun was rising over the tree canopy surrounding the cottage and the mist from the lake was ascending to the heavens once again. The sky was filled with rooks and other corvidae flying in great flocks celebrating the joys of life. The air was filled with birdsong, it was going to be a beautiful day.

She addressed Wolf verbally. "Today, I am going to take the girls out deep into the forest. We need to broaden their horizons and I want to witness their interaction with other animals, especially Sarah. I am sure Ursula is exaggerating, but I need to be sure. I also want to see if it will be possible for them to travel on the backs of your daughters."

She cupped Wolf's head in her hands and stared into its eyes as the girls had done - and tried to communicate telepathically with her.

How much do you understand, Wolf? Can you read my mind as well? Just sit down if you can. She waited, but nothing happened.

She called the girls to her. "Girls, we are going on a trip today. We will take my horse Jasper and the baskets and trowels. I want to show you some important plants. Plants we need for food, plants we need for healing, and plants we need to avoid. I want you to get your wolves ready and let us see if they will carry you on a journey. Oh, and for a special treat today, I will be traveling as your mother."

"Yes, yes," cried Ursula excitedly. We haven't seen mother for ages."

"Now remember, always call me Mother when I take her form. You must get used to it and if we meet people on our journey there must be no slip-ups, ordinary people wouldn't understand."

"We know Nana," the girls replied.

"Very good, now call your wolves." The girls called out to them, and they came at once. Morag took the form of the Princess and dressed simply so anyone seeing her would think she was just a commoner foraging from the village.

"Mother, you look scruffy?"

"Today, Sarah, we will be getting our hands dirty. Dressed like this, people will not give me a second glance. Now get on your wolves."

The girls cupped the wolves' heads, looked into their eyes, and both animals lay down. The girls stepped over the backs of their respective wolves, and both creatures stood and waited. Morag watched her daughters studying their technique and shook her head wordlessly. *Amazing.*

"Sarah, you lead, and Ursula you follow your sister. If you get frightened, call out."

The animals moved off without the girls saying anything verbally, and the Princess followed with her wolf guarding the rear.

It was a strange sight, two young girls at ease on the back of giant wolves who appeared to be as gentle as horses strolling through the forest.

An hour had passed when Ghost, the lead wolf, stopped and, turning her head looked at Shadow. Suddenly, both wolves began to growl. The Princess called out to the girls.

"Why have you stopped?"

Sarah answered her mother nervously, "There are people up ahead. Ghost thinks they are some of the builders who are working on the big house."

Ursula added, "Shadow says they already know we're here."

"Does she indeed?" *Very interesting.* "If they know we're here, be prepared for some unusual reactions. I will lead, you girls follow when I give you a signal."

As the Princess moved into the clearing the men stopped working and removed their headgear. "Your highness, we didn't recognize you - this is an unexpected honor."

Princess stood aloof on her horse with her back straight and looked down menacingly at them. "What are you men doing here?"

"We have been tasked with marking trees suitable for timber. It's for your new house, my lady." The man looked around and seeing she was alone, said. "Is it safe for you to be so deep in the forest without an escort, my Lady?"

She continued to look down on them as if they were insignificant insects and the men withered in her glare. She snapped her fingers, and both girls moved into view sitting astride their wolves. The startled men gasped. It was a sight that no one had seen in this country before.

"As you can see, the Princesses and I have personal protectors - the wolves will keep us safe. Lord Llewellyn has approved, but thank you for your concern."

She paused and looked at each man in turn. "I was under the impression that my husband had informed you I am to be addressed as Princess."

"B - beg your pardon, Princess - er, sorry." The man fumbled with his hat nervously.

"Don't let it happen again," she snapped and left, closely followed by her daughters.

Morag made a mental note. *That was interesting! Both girls seem to communicate with their wolves, and they make formidable guards. Their keen eyes, sense of smell, and instinct for danger will be beneficial. It's no wonder the Princesses' families used them for protection, though it's a pity those workmen saw them riding on the wolves.*

Morag called the Princess from deep within her head.

Well done, Mia, I resurrect you for one morning - just one morning, and you do this, you were supposed to be keeping a low profile.

The group continued for a couple of miles until the Princess called the girls to a halt. "We will make our way to the stream where it joins the lake down at the bottom of the valley." Upon arrival, the Princess dismounted and spoke words of comfort in his ear. "Girls, if you can dismount from your wolves, we will start your lessons." First, Ghost then Shadow simply sat down and the girls slid down their backs into a standing position.

Mia smiled. "Well, girls, you made that look easy."

"It was easy, Nana. Our Mother said that was the way she used to do it."

"Sarah, you say your mother used to ride on wolves?"

"Yes, Nana, when she was very young like us. She used to go on Wolf's grandmother's back - she was her guardian until she got too old.

Ursula added. "They always carry the royal children and mother says they always will."

"Well, that's interesting, but remember girls now I am in the form of the Princess - you must call me mother - not Nana. Right girls, let us get to work. Collect your basket and trowels and follow me to the stream's edge. There are plants growing here, important plants - plants we use for food - and plants we use for medicine. This one is called Yarrow."

One by one, Morag pointed out the merits of various plants and how to recognize them by the shape of their leaves. She informed them what time of the year the plant flowered and how much of the plant they could remove without killing it. Where in the forest to find them and what time of year to harvest them - what their uses were - which were poisonous - and which plants they should avoid.

The Princess noticed Sarah had a confused look on her face. "Is there something troubling you, Sarah?"

"Yes mother, I have no memory of any of the plants that you are showing us."

This surprised Morag as the girls had always taken new information in their stride. "What about you, Ursula?"

"I don't know them either. The land mother came from was nothing like this. We did not have big forests with streams running through them. The land was mainly sand, and the plants were all... different."

Morag's spirit interrupted the Princess. "No trees, just sand?"

"There were some trees, Ursula said defensively, but they were all... different. Sometimes it was just sand as far as you could see and not a tree in sight. There were no streams or lakes, just small, isolated pools surrounded by trees."

Sarah added. "Mother called them oases."

Morag commented thoughtfully. "That must be an extraordinary land?"

"Just different and hot, so hot the sand burned your feet, and you always had to wear sandals."

"So, girls, these plants are all new to you both. In that case, I will concentrate on instructing you and your mother on the different flora and their uses. You may find this harder because You're not simply reviving old memories."

Sarah turned to her mother. "The wolves are hungry. Is it all right if they go and find some food?"

Mia's gaze moved over to the wolves lying in a group on the ground. "Is that what they are asking, to go hunting?"

"Yes, Mother."

"In that case, Sarah, tell Ghost and Shadow they can go together. Tell Wolf she is to stay with us to keep us safe. Your wolves must bring food back for their mother. Can you do that?"

"Yes, Nana."

The young wolves trotted off into the undergrowth without a word being spoken; Wolf settled down by the girls, and Morag made a mental note that Sarah had complete control of the creatures.

"Girls, I think it's time for us to eat as well." She unpacked the food and spread the blanket on the ground by the stream. As she sat with her wards listening to them laugh and giggle. Morag, even in the guise of the Princess, thought she was as happy as she had ever been in this lifetime. She let her mind wander, wondering what the future held for the girls and what the Sisterhood would do with them.

A couple of hours later, a rustling noise from the undergrowth heralded the return of the wolves. The faintest of smiles creased Mia's lips as Morag noted that they had indeed brought a large rabbit which they presented to their mother.

Later they walked along the edge of the stream, and the Princess continued to instruct the girls about the different flora using Morag's memories, patiently explaining their various uses. They were having difficulty remembering, so Morag persisted with this instruction time and again.

*

The seasons moved forward, and it was time to introduce the girls to the Avebury Sisterhood and, hopefully, participate in their midsummer festivals. Morag was particularly excited this year. The influence of Princess Mia was getting stronger daily - and she began to fantasize that she should participate in the form of the Princess. Her mind drifted back to the first time she took her form - and the reaction of the soldiers that came looking for Lord Llewellyn. She absentmindedly nodded her head. *Yes, they adored me.*

Mia agreed. **Of course, they adored you - all men will - believe me - I know - even some women if it takes your fancy. Come on Morag - we can have fun. When did you last have fun? One last dance for old times' sake.**

Mia, you know what the Earth Mother said. We are to keep a low profile.

Boring, boring.

Morag's will was weakening. She felt butterflies in her stomach - and squeezed her crotch tight in anticipation. It had been several years since she last participated. She remembered the embarrassment of failing to be selected as a 'dance Partner' as her looks faded. But if she took the Princesses' form, she would be treated as an exotic guest. The thought appealed to her but was it her thought – or was the will of the Princess taking over?

*

The day of the journey finally came. The Princess decided she would be traveling on her favorite horse, 'Wind.' She had packed her traveling bags which Jasper the packhorse would carry. She also brought several small pottery jars that held the essence of different people, among them the Princess and Lord Llewellyn. Mia took a supply of dried meat, fruit, bread, and various medical supplies. She also packed several of the Princesses' dresses, exotic costumes suitable for ceremonies, and a couple of traveling tents. The girls couldn't contain their excitement as this was their first big journey.

Morag had informed the villagers that she would be traveling with Lord Llewellyn and surgery would be closed for a while. The construction workers at the nearly completed Earlswood Manor had a visit from Lord Llewellyn, and he told them he would be traveling south for an important meeting and not expect them back for at least one month.

At the crack of dawn, the party set off. They managed to travel between fifteen and twenty miles a day, and Mia kept the pace leisurely with frequent stops for the horses to rest and the wolves to hunt. As they traveled, the Princess continued to instruct them on the different flora, and at times they stopped to collect fresh vegetable root crops, early cherries and wild strawberries.

On the fourth day, they came to a large river. Morag had made this journey many times. She knew the river had a bridge crossing nearby but was unsure if it was up or downstream. She called the girls to her and informed them that she needed to call one of the birds to carry her spirit - because she would be able to find the bridge quickly from the sky.

The Princess started to meditate to call the bird to her, but Sarah interrupted. "Nana."

"Can you not see I'm meditating," she said irritably, "and don't call me Nana, I'm mother, remember? What do you want?"

"Why don't you just ask the bird which way to go?"

"You know I can't talk to creatures like you can, Sarah. "How would you ask a bird which way the crossing is?"

"Is it a ford or a bridge?"

"A bridge."

Sarah skipped away towards the river and called back, "There are wading birds down by the water. I will see what they think."

After ten minutes, Sarah returned. "We need to carry on downstream. They all thought the same, Mother."

"Well done, Sarah. Let's see if they are correct." *This could be interesting. Let's see if she is right.* Morag turned to Ursula. "Are you managing to communicate with any other creature besides Shadow yet, Ursula?"

She let her eyes fall to the ground. "Only Shadow, sorry, Mother."

The Princess hugged her close. "Don't be sorry, Ursula. You will have many gifts you are not aware of yet."

The party followed the river downstream and saw the bridge in the distance. Morag called the Princess from the deep recesses of her mind. *Remember, do not draw attention to the girls.*

The girls dismounted from their wolves as they saw the bridge in the distance and crossed the bridge on foot. Even so, an exotic-looking lady on such a tall slim horse, followed by three giant wolves and two children, caused them all to stare.

The countryside began to flatten out and traveling became a lot easier. The Princess, however, had decided that they should travel well back from the road but parallel to it, she was still concerned that people might see them traveling down from the north.

The wolves had alerted them to people traveling along the road on several occasions. On one occasion, they made a detour to avoid a site where people were sleeping. It turned out that the wolves' sense of smell was a significant advantage. Wood fires they could smell many miles away, and Morag was thankful they traveled with the wolves on many occasions.

Morag called Mia once again. *Mia, there is a smell that is troubling both the wolves and me. Be very careful. Hide the girls and investigate.*

She led the girls off the main path and deep into the undergrowth, where she prepared food for the girls and left them with their guardians.

Wolf led the way toward the smell. She traveled on foot, leaving 'Wind' tethered by the girls. She knew what she would find well before she reached the fire. The scene that she beheld both sickened and appalled her. The burnt houses were still smoldering, and corpses were scattered on the ground. They had all been slaughtered, men, women, children and even animals. Not only slaughtered but mutilated beyond belief.

Morag knelt and held the hand of a dead child. Her mind exploded with images. Men were riding horses circling the village, their faces hidden by grotesque masks. The intruders corralled men, women and children.

Morag gasped at the atrocities she had seen. She could feel the terror and confusion of her last moments and prayed to the creator of all to guide her spirit back to her - and began to weep openly. Finally, she got to her feet and spoke verbally to her wolf. "They are back wolf, God help us." She sighed despairingly, then headed back to the girls.

There was nothing she could do except bear witness. She committed the scene to memory, a memory she would pass on when she died.

Realizing they were only a day's ride from Avebury, she took them down a route to the west, well past the site. When they had done this, they veered to the east until they were south of the meeting place. After finding the road to Avebury, they traveled along it in a northerly direction. They greeted as many people as possible, always stopping to talk and asking for directions. The excitement was now palpable within the group.

"Your mother thinks you should ride on the wolves." Although she was in the form of the Princess, it was Morag's voice that emanated from her. "She wishes you to make a grand entrance. I feel your mother's influence growing in me. The longer I'm in her form, the stronger the influence becomes. She was a very important person in her own country, and now that I have taken her form for so long, I seem to be influenced by her more and more. I feel she wants you to be the same in this country. 'Mother' won't like it, but it seems I have no choice. Climb on to your wolves. Now remember what I taught you, we do not communicate with animals by thought, do we? How do we do it?"

The girls replied, "We must say the commands out loud."

"What did we say about the memories?"

"We haven't recovered them yet."

"Good. The only person who knows anything about your gifts is the Earth Mother's representative. And don't forget you must call me mother from now on.

A mile further down the road, Ursula's wolf slowed down. "Ursula, What's the problem, why are you hanging back?"

"It's Shadow, she is very nervous, and she senses lots of people and animals."

Sarah added, "Mother, Ghost is as well. She thinks we should not go any further."

Morag sat lost in thought for a while. *I should have foreseen this. The young wolves have only ever been in contact with a handful of people at one time.*

The party halted in the middle of the road. "Girls, I want you to reassure your wolves. Try telling them that this is an extension of their pack. Tell them that this pack offers no threat and that they are not to harm anyone unless you are physically attacked."

Ursula responded, "Yes, we have done that but I think their mother should lead. She has met many people and is comfortable around them."

"Good idea, Ursula. Wolf, you lead, and I'll follow. You girls follow behind me so your wolves can see how their mother reacts. We must expect quite a reaction from people at the gathering. To arrive on the backs of your wolves is your mother's idea. I think we should walk without drawing attention to ourselves. But no, she wants a grand entrance, quite a woman your mother."

As the Princess was speaking, several horses approached from behind at speed. They were going in the direction of the gathering. Thinking the children were on ponies, they drew close to them. Ghost, the rear wolf, turned her head to see who was approaching, and the horses realizing they were wolves, panicked and ran off the road. The startled riders got their horses under control and positioned themselves about forty feet away.

The Princess could feel the rider's edgy fear. She could feel their reluctance to greet them and decided to ease the tension. "Greetings gentlemen," she called out at the top of her voice. "I greet you in the name of the Earth Mother." - Her voice once again emphasized her foreign accent. - "Tell me, is this road to summer gathering at Avebury?"

She could still feel the sense of agitation and alarm emanating from the travelers, who just stared in amazement. Wolf moved between the travelers and the Princess, her body in contact with her leg and the horse, a low guttural growl rumbling deep within her throat. The travelers backed their horses further away.

"I am Princess Mia. We have traveled far and crossed the sea to be with you. The Earth Mother expects us, and we are honored guests."

One of the travelers shouted, "Are you taking the wolves to the festival?"

"The wolves are perfectly safe and under control, and yes, we are taking them to the festival. Are we on the correct road?"

"Yes, your highness."

"Would you be so kind as to warn people about our mode of transport? We do seem to be alarming everyone we meet."

"I can understand that my Lady. I've never seen wolves that big, and I've never seen wolves that let children ride on their backs."

"In my country, all royal children have a guardian assigned to them from birth. They are their transport and their protectors. They will not harm anyone as long as no one harms my daughters. As you see, my protector is so gentle." The Princess lowered her hand to touch Her wolf's head, gently stroking her until the threatening growl subsided.

"So, gentlemen, warn travelers we pose no threat."

"Yes, your highness." With that, they continued their journey at speed. The Princess and her daughters watched the men disappear into the distance. Overhead a buzzard circled, and its mewing cry pierced the air. The Princess watched it as it spiraled higher and higher. Was her cry a warning? She meditated momentarily, searching for their immediate future. Her ancestors were quiet, and the signs were good.

"Well, girls, I know I shouldn't be allowing this, we should have traveled on foot, your mother will now get the reception she wants. I have tried to change back to my form many times on this journey, but the Princess is fighting me." *Yes, Princess, you are very willful, we should not be drawing so much attention to our daughters, please, please, please give me back control of my body.*

The Princess ignored the comments of Morag, who realized she was beginning to lose control as Mia urged the horse forward.

"Girls do not be afraid - these people are our kin. They will welcome us, but they will also be wary. I am speaking as your birth mother now. Complete the journey and hold head high - with back straight, be proud you are royalty, the daughters of Kings and Princesses' and remember never to show fear. Our ancestors will show you how to behave and what responses to give, consult them now."

The party continued along the road. As they got closer, they could see many people looking from the tops of trees and high ridges. More and more people gathered as the news spread quickly.

They approached Avebury in what today is called 'West Kennet Avenue.' The avenue comprises one hundred pairs of standing stones that run parallel to one another for one and a half miles, forming a ceremonial entrance leading directly to the Sanctuary of the large outer circle.

"Mother, What's that noise?"

Mia stopped the horse, turned to Sarah, and listened. The faintest of smiles creased her lips. "You can hear them?"

"I can hear something…What is it?"

Mia turned to Ursula. "Can you hear anything?"

"Yes, mother."

"What can you hear?"

"Whispering. I think people are hiding behind the stones."

Mia nodded her head thoughtfully. "What sound do you hear, Sarah?"

"Singing, Ursula's right, it's coming from behind the stones."

Mia turned the horse and led her daughters around the stones in a complete circle. There was no one there.

"I don't understand, Mother. Where is the noise coming from?"

"Touch the stones, both of you." The girls did as she instructed and placed their hands flat on the cold monoliths, they both began to smile.

Ursula was the first to realize where the sound came from. "It's the stones themselves."

Mia's smile filled her face. "Well done, both of you. Very few people can hear the 'echoes in the stones.' Morag taught you about communicating with them when you were very young. These are ancient stones and their power is very strong here. This avenue has seen many things, they know we are 'Prime' and are drawing us to the sanctuary of the circles. Now let us continue."

Following their mother's lead, the wolves began to calm down. There was a sharp turn in the road ahead, and as the lead wolf turned the corner into the avenue, there were gasps of alarm from the crowd, followed by murmurs of admiration at the sight of the tall Princess on her exotic horse. The girls turned the corner next, and the crowd's gasps of astonishment escalated. People close to the roadside were fearful of the wolves and fought their way back through the crowd and hid behind the standing stones. The Princess and the girls simply looked straight ahead, holding their heads high, ignoring the onlookers.

They continued along the avenue. The crowd parted in front of them, then closed behind. As they journeyed onward, the crowd, who numbered in the hundreds, followed close behind. Up ahead, she could see the reception committee. At the center was a large man resting on a wooden staff. He had a white beard and long white hair. On each side of him were two younger men, and at their sides, two older women also dressed in white robes. At earlier festivals, Morag had met the older man many times. The younger men she knew as Simon and Stephen. Since her last visit, they had grown into men, however, she did not recognize the two women.

5. NEW YORK 1985 AD

Joan Masters stared at the letter in front of her, and her vivid green eyes glanced across at Paul sitting sheepishly at the other end of the table. She ran her hands through her graying hair. "What does your tutor want to see me about?"

"Paul's eye's drifted from his mother's,' he sighed nonchalantly and took a bite of his apple.

"I don't know, who knows what teachers think."

Joan's eyes were still locked on her son, measuring him. He got up to leave the table. "Sit," she said in a raised voice.

Paul sighed once again and slumped back down in his chair.

"I don't know, I said." His eyes turned back to his mother, challenging her. "I don't know – honestly."

"No idea, you have absolutely no idea at all?"

Paul shrugged his shoulders and mumbled. "There was a lot of interest in some of my paintings."

Joan raised a brow cynically. "Not a painting of Jenny, whatshername?"

"Walker – no, I haven't painted her mom, I haven't got a clue why they want to see you. Why do you always assume I am in trouble?"

Joan looked away from her son, re-read the letter, and placed it on the table. "Paul, you are always in trouble, that's why." She rubbed her temples wearily. Tell her I will call in after your last lesson tomorrow."

A man's voice called down from one of the rooms above.

Joan sighed. "Go and see what your grandfather wants."

*

It had been five years since she had sold her house and moved in with Peter's father on Long Island. His health had been failing for some time, and his Son's disappearance had shaken him badly. It had been ten years, and they still had no clue where he was. Paul's grandfather had taken his father's place as a role model, but it was not the same, he lacked discipline. Joan had taken over the running of the family business, first temporarily until Peter returned. As the years rolled by, she was now well and truly embedded at the helm.

The following day she found Paul seated outside his tutors' office. "Sorry I'm late, any idea what this is about?

Paul pursed his lips and shook his head. "I am not sure, but all my paintings have been removed from the storeroom."

Joan whispered conspiratorially. "Please tell me you haven't got any more girls to pose naked for you?"

The door opened before Paul could answer, and a small woman with a round face smiled nervously at her. She wore large round owl-like glasses that were in fashion at the time. Her hair looked like Michael Jackson's did in his youth with a perm that had been way overdone. She shook Joan's hand weakly and presented her with a nervous smile.

"Thank you for coming at such short notice, please come in."

Joan positioned herself opposite the tutor and steeled herself for what was about to transpire. The look on her face gave nothing away, The tutor opened a large folder, took out several paintings, and spread them across the table.

Joan took a deep breath. "Look, if it's a nude painting of Jenny whatshername, it was her idea - she threw herself at him – you should have her here as well - she has no morals whatsoever."

The teacher looked puzzled, "Jenny, who?"

Paul interrupted angrily. "There are not any paintings of her – I told you."

The tutor continued when neither Paul nor his mother was forthcoming with the name.

"Paul is becoming an outstanding artist; I like his work."

She spread the paintings across her desk upside down so Joan could study them. Joan had to agree that the paintings were good. She had seen sketches he had done in his room, so she knew he had talent, especially the drawing of Jenny whatshername.

The tutor, however, never looked once at the paintings, her eyes were fixed on Joan's – measuring her reaction. Joan could feel her neck turning red as she studied each painting in turn, and nodded thoughtfully; she had seen images like these many times in her dreams.

"Yes, I agree, Paul has talent. Is that what this is about?"

The tutor appeared to be open and friendly.

"We sometimes call parents in to give them good news Mrs. Masters."

She laid out a different choice of paintings. Again, Joan studied them one at a time and began to feel uncomfortable.

"As you see, some are very explicit." Her eyes never wavered from Joan's face. Joan's eyes, however, were fixed on the paintings.

Joan cleared her throat awkwardly. "Yes, he has a very vivid imagination."

The tutor laid out a different selection. This time, the people were all dressed in red robes, and the nightmarish scene was a lot darker. People were being tortured, and maimed. The hellish pallet was in dissimilar shades of red.

Joan's blood ran cold, she had seen these same images repeatedly in her nightmares throughout restless nights when sleep would not come. She had discussed them with a man called Jed ten years before and knew what they represented and, for a moment, was lost in thought.

So, Paul is tormented by the same 'Primevil' images as me. Maybe it's time to explain to him what they are.

The tutor's eyes never wavered. "Have you any thoughts on this latest batch of pictures?"

Joan pursed her lips thoughtfully. "There are pretty dark – aren't they." She continued to study them one by one, then placed them on one side. "Your point being?"

The tutor didn't answer the question, she simply replaced the paintings with several others.

"These are my favorites," she said, spreading out an assortment of sketches of various parts of a woman's face. One showed just the eyes – green eyes. Another was a view of her head from the rear with her black hair hanging down her back. Next, a side view centered on her ear, and lastly, a full-frontal of the whole face emphasizing her high cheekbones and full mouth. You were drawn to the woman's eyes, drawing you closer, vivid green and an imitation of Joan's.

Joan gasped and looked at her son. "She is so beautiful, Paul, is this her?"

The tutor's eyes followed Joan's and rested on Paul, who shrugged his shoulders.

Joan turned her eyes back to the painting. "I did not realize you were so talented, son."

"Which brings me to the point, Mrs. Masters. Paul would have little trouble gaining entry to any art college in the country with paintings like these."

Joan turned to Paul. "Is this what you want – to go to art college?"

Paul shook his head. "No way."

The statement took the tutor by surprise. "Oh, you seem to enjoy your painting so much, I just thought…."

"No." Paul said sharply, "I will be going to business school to help mom run the family business."

The tutor turned her attention to her notes. "I see there is not a Mr. Masters on the scene.

Before Joan could answer, Paul, quipped. "That's because he is dead."

Joan countered. "He's not, he's missing." For several moments the room fell into an awkward silence before Joan continued. "My husband is missing - it's a long story." She waved her arms dismissively and turned her attention to her son.

"Paul, if you want to study art, it's ok with me."

Again, Paul simply shook his head. The tutor leaned back on her chair and turned her attention to the Paintings. "Paul, do you mind if we discuss the content of the paintings?"

His face presented a wan expression. "Sure, fire away."

"They seem to follow a particular Pattern, we seem to have four themes, we have several with a joyous scene of dancing outdoors in the woods around a fire at night – are they supposed to be Druids or something?" Paul did not answer and stared the tutor out. "Two, we have several much darker scenes, these seem to be people wearing red clothes and mutilating people." Again, Paul said nothing. "Three, we have rather explicit sex scenes, and four, these exquisite sketches of this beautiful woman. Who is she?"

Paul's eyes turned to his mother, who nodded her head slightly. He turned his attention back to the tutor. "I dream a lot, and I always have, these are some of my most vivid dreams." The tutor lifted her cup of coffee in her hands and investigated the swirling liquid thoughtfully. "And the woman?"

"He gave a rueful shrug of his shoulders. "Her too."

The tutor turned to Joan. "You asked Paul if it was a particular woman – do you think you know her?"

Joan began to feel awkward sensing a trap. "Ok, where is this going? We have just gone from praising Paul for his good work to giving him the third degree."

Again, the room fell silent, and the tutor turned her attention to the red paintings. "Mrs. Masters, you have to agree these particular paintings are disturbing."

Joan bristled and threw her arms into the air and was almost spitting with anger. "Now we are getting to the nitty-gritty. This is why you have called me in, not some rubbish about being good enough for art school."

The tutor turned defensive. "No, no, no, well... partly."

Joan shook her head in dismay and began to get to her feet. "We're off."

"Please, Mrs. Masters, we need to talk about this now - we have to report…."

Joan's shoulders sagged. She turned and slumped back on the chair, her body language reflecting that of her son when he was about to be admonished. "Go on then."

The tutor looked uncomfortable and drew her eyes away from Joan before continuing. "The school counselor looked at the red paintings and he would like to discuss them with Paul in person."

Joan controlled her breathing and her composure. "I see, and if I do not approve?"

"It's for his own good we need to get to the bottom of these things before..."

Joan got to her feet, walked across to the window, and looked down into the street. She started speaking with her back to the tutor and lit a cigarette.

The tutor snapped. "I don't allow smoking in my office."

Joan inhaled deeply and created a ring with the smoke, and Paul hid the laughter in his eyes. Joan ignored the tutor and pressed. "Have you ever heard of the term inherited memory?"

Indignantly the tutor pressed her glasses to the bridge of her nose. "Well, yes - when applied to animals."

Joan continued to stare out of the window, but her eyes were seeing images lost in time, and after a pause, she continued. "There are several ongoing studies to evaluate the theory that humans also have this ability. These dreams that Paul is painting are like the ones I have several nights a week. So, you see, he is not some latent hell-bent hatchet man about to run amok amongst your students." Joan turned and sat down; her eyes still red with anger.

The tutor stroked her chin thoughtfully. "So, you are both experiencing the same dreams?"

"More or less, his grandmother did too. The dancing, the ceremonies, the light, and the dark ones – not the woman, she has tormented Paul since childhood." She turned her gaze to Paul.

"I take it that's who you were painting?"

Paul again turned his eyes to the floor and nodded.

The tutor continued to stare into her coffee. "So, let me get this straight, you both have the same dreams, as did his grandmother – and that is what Paul is painting?"

Joan quipped. "In a nutshell."

"Are they Druids or something?"

Joan waved her arms in the air dismissively. "I wish I knew, some past lives or something - who knows."

The tutor put the coffee down. "Have you considered reincarnation? It has all the hallmarks, and it certainly could be a possibility?"

Joan, who now had full control of her emotions, spoke clearly and calmly. "Who knows reincarnation - Inherited memory? What's the difference, the point being Paul is not about to chop your students up." Joan got to her feet, made her way to the door, and placed her hand on the handle.

Before she could leave, the tutor called out. "Did you know professor Gaskill is calling for volunteers to be regressed to see if there is any proof in the theory of reincarnation?"

Joan released the handle and sat down. "Here at the college?"

"Yes, he is taking on one hundred students, I am sure he would be interested in adding you and Paul to the study. It might give you some answers."

"You mean he will hypnotize us?"

"Yes, it's all very safe, they follow the strictest guidelines."

Joan rubbed her temples thoughtfully. Her mind drifted back to her conversation with Jed all those years ago. *You are only safe if no one knows about you, you are dead if it becomes common knowledge of what you and Paul are.* Her gaze drifted across to Paul. *He must know some time, no, not yet.* "I don't think so." Again, she got up to go, but Paul interrupted.

"I'll do it."

Joan turned on him. "Over my dead body, come, we are leaving." She opened the door and pushed Paul out. When he left the room, she again turned to the tutor. "I mean it, I do not want a hypnotist anywhere near my son. Do you understand?" Before the tutor could reply, Joan leaned across, snatched the painting of the mysterious woman, and slammed the door in her face.

•

Several days later Paul Masters chatted with several other students outside professor Gaskill's office in the waiting room. They were hoping to be accepted for the regression trial. He had been given a bullet list that he had read and had ticked all the boxes that applied to him.

A girl's voice called from the crowd. He waved to Jenny, who walked over to him and joined him in the queue. She was an attractive girl with long brown hair that reached down to her shoulders, she had a full mouth and a friendly smile. Paul thought her crowning feature was her vivid green eyes. Eventually, they both handed in their forms and the authorization from their next of kin, in Paul's case, his mother.

"I didn't know you were going to apply for this Jenny, it seems exciting, doesn't it?"

She nodded to the door opposite. "Several students have gone in there, and they assess you to see if you are susceptible to hypnosis." Just as she spoke, a student came out looking glum.

Jenny called out to her. "How goes it, Kay?"

The girl shook her head. Jenny whispered in Paul's ear. "Four have gone in, and only one has been added to the list."

Paul looked crestfallen. "I thought it was a done deal – just turn up."

Jenny pursed her lips and whispered in his ear. "Apparently not." After a pause, she added, "I think I have a good chance." Her green eyes sparkled mischievously. "After all, I am very open to suggestions."

Paul suppressed a smile. "Mom found the sketch I drew of you in my room."

The color drained from her face. "What!"

"It's ok, I told her I was using my imagination."

She stared him out. "And she believed you?"

Paul shook his head thoughtfully from side to side. "She has her doubts but just feign ignorance if she brings it up – it always works for me."

Jenny leaned across and whispered in his ear. "It's a good job she can't see my butt, I still can't get those dam symbols off. What did you call them?

"Runes."

"Yeah, runes. What sort of ink did you use? It's like a tattoo, my butts raw with all the scrubbing."

Paul turned sharply to face her. "Don't rub them off – they are Pagan, we are only drawn together while they are visible."

Jenny squeezed his hand affectionately. "How do you know this stuff?"

Paul sighed heavily, "I just do, I don't know how." He waved his arms at the crowd gathered before them. "That's what this is all about – I need to find answers."

Paul was called in next, and he kissed Jenny on the cheek.

"Here goes."

Professor Gaskill was reading his form, checking the various tick boxes. He did not look in Paul's direction. "Paul Masters, I believe?

"Yes, professor," he said nervously.

He glanced at Paul and studied him over his spectacles. "I was rather hoping you would turn up. Your tutor mentioned you the other day. If I remember correctly, she said your mother was against letting you participate in the trial?" He studied the consent form, and the signature looked genuine.

Paul held the professor's gaze. "She changed her mind, she's like that, blows hot and cold as it were."

The professor placed his form on the pile and smiled. "I am so glad, your tutor said you have been troubled by strange dreams for some time."

Paul did not answer; he simply nodded his head in acquiescence.

"Good. If you could rest on the couch and make yourself comfortable, we will see if you are susceptible to hypnosis."

Paul stretched out on the couch. The hypnotist was a man in his sixties, and the assistant was a woman in her forties. They both smiled openly to put him at ease.

The professor slipped a cassette into the tape deck. "As you can see the sessions are being recorded – we have to be transparent at all times, no one will be allowed to listen to the tapes without your guardian's consent. Are you happy with that?" Again, Paul nodded.

Paul looked around the room, taking in the décor - or lack of it, a typical professor's room, not somewhere that was conducive to relaxation.

The hypnotist spoke softly. So softly, Paul could barely hear his voice and had to listen intensely, taking in every syllable. It was both melodic and rhythmic, and he felt relaxed in no time. He could feel his mind separating from his body. Eventually, he found himself in a tranquil state.

"When I count to ten, you will be fast asleep." By the time he got to five, he was under the influence of the hypnotist.

The hypnotist turned to the professor. "He's the best yet, he was under in no time."

The professor looked shocked. "Are you sure...? Already?"

The hypnotist looked in the direction of the medical assistant and nodded. No words were spoken, and the nurse took a sharp needle and pricked the back of Paul's hand. There was no response. She turned to the professor. "He's well and truly under."

The hypnotist turned his attention back to Paul.

"Paul, you are coming out of deep sleep. If you can hear my voice, just nod your head."

Paul responded by doing just that. The hypnotist's voice continued in its smooth, melodic tone.

"Do you know where you are?"

Paul looked around the room and closed his eyes once more. "I am in the professor's study."

The hypnotist turned his eyes to the nurse again. "Would you double-check?"

The nurse pricked the back of his hand, and again he didn't flinch. "Definitely under."

The hypnotist smiled approvingly. "Professor, you can put him at the top of your list. Shall I wake him up?"

The professor picked up his file and double-checked all the tick boxes.

"This is the one I am most interested in. His tutor said both he, his mother, and his grandmother continually have rather unusual dreams, all similar in content. Do you think we could ask him a few questions?" He looked at his watch, "five minutes, maybe."

The hypnotist turned his attention back to Paul.

"Paul, listen to my voice. We are going on a journey, and don't worry you will be perfectly safe. I want you to remember your earliest thoughts. Can you describe them for me?"

Paul's eyes moved under his lids, he breathed in contentedly and smiled. "Joy, warmth."

"Where are you? What can you see?"

Again, his eyes moved behind his lids. "In the water by the shore, there is light, warmth."

The three observers exchanged puzzled glances, and the hypnotist pressed. "You are in the water. Where are your parents?"

Paul shook his head, "No, parents, I am alone, but now I am more."

The hypnotist blinked, confused by his response. "Paul, how old are you?"

"I have no age, but at last I can renew."

The professor tapped the hypnotist on the shoulder. "Ask him to relive his happiest event?

"Paul, describe the happiest event you can remember?"

His face filled with joy, and he laughed openly. "My hand-fast."

The professor grabbed the hypnotist's shoulder. "Did he just say his hand-fast?"

The hypnotist nodded. He looked at the assistant. Check again. I am sure he is trying to trick us." The assistant stuck the needle in the back of his neck and left it sticking out.

"I tell you he is definitely under, not a flinch."

The professor's face blanched. He was visibly shaking and he began to take notes. "This is unbelievable. Ask him how old he is."

"Paul, how old are you?"

Paul looked puzzled. "Who is Paul?"

"Sorry, what is your name, and how old are you?"

Paul's voice had lost its American accent. "Saul, my name be Saul, and I can count fifteen summers." The group again exchanged surprised glances. "Saul, in what year were you born?"

"In the year of our Lord fifteen ninety-eight."

"You say your happiest time was your hand-fast. Where was your hand-fast held?"

"It be at the stone circles at Avebury Henge, o course."

"You were hand-fast at a henge, what country is that in?"

"What a daft question, why England where else."

The nurse turned to the others. "There is a henge at Avebury in Wiltshire England, it's very famous."

The hypnotist looked at his watch. "Your five minutes are up, do you want me to wake him up?"

The professor shook his head. "Not really, I would rather send the others home and listen to him all evening. This is what we have been searching for." The professor sighed heavily. "I suppose you should, but act normal, don't say anything to alarm him.

"Paul, when I count to ten, you will wake up and forget all the things you have remembered. Do you understand?" He nodded his head in agreement. On reaching ten, his eyes fluttered open.

"Well, was I under? I was under, wasn't I?"

The professor smiled. "Welcome to the trial, Paul, you have been accepted."

Paul's face lit up. "Yes! And you managed to hypnotize me?"

"Yes, Paul. Is any evening best for your first session?"

"Cool, Tuesdays, Wednesdays and Fridays are good."

The professor jotted the days on Paul's sheet. "Ok, then shall we say Tuesday at six?"

Paul left the room, and when he closed the door, they all began to speak at once. The professor held up his hands to quieten them. "Right, is he genuine? All their eyes turned to the hypnotist.

"You saw his lack of reaction when we stuck a needle in him, he did not flinch in the slightest. You can't shut your mind off to pain like that."

The nurse added. "The needle in his neck was quite deep, there would have been some reaction."

The professor stroked his gray beard thoughtfully. "Oh God, I hope this is genuine. He seemed to go under straight away. I couldn't understand his response to our first question, but this hand-fast story is intriguing, and he has already given us a year and a place, this is unbelievable." He walked to the door and leaned out, "next."

*

The following Tuesday, Paul rested his sports bag on the chair next to him and smiled to himself. His mother could not believe his latest fad as he had never shown any interest in sports of any kind. The gym club was run after school three days a week, and Joan did not think twice when he asked if he could attend. He glanced at the ticking clock, irritated by the sound, and wondered why clocks were so noisy when you were in a quiet room.

He checked his watch for the third time in as many minutes, confirming that they were running late. He could hear voices on the other side of the door. Finally, it opened, and a girl walked out. As the girl turned into the corridor, the professor called to her. "See you at the same time next week."

He turned to Paul and smiled. "Please come in."

Paul entered, made his way to the couch, and settled down, making himself comfortable without being asked. The professor sat on a chair and took out his notepad. "First, tell me why you want to be regressed."

Paul looked at his two companions, they were the same people from the first session. He stuttered nervously, "I – I hope it will explain my dreams."

The professor eyed him warily. "Ah, yes, these are the dreams you have been painting in the art class. Am I correct?" Paul nodded. He opened a large folder and took out several paintings. "I took the liberty of asking the art teacher for a few samples." His eyes drifted over them, one at a time. "You're an outstanding artist. Can I ask you what this one represents?"

The painting he placed on the desk in front of him was of several female dancers dressed in sheer white dresses. The scene was set in a forest or wood, and several large stones were standing on end, they were twice as tall as the people dancing around them.

Paul shrugged his shoulders. "It's one of my happy paintings. I seem to be at peace with the world when I have these dreams."

The professor lay a second painting on top of the first. "And this one? It was one of the red paintings."

Paul shook his head and frowned. "I don't like these paintings, they scare me - they are my nightmares. I don't know what they represent, and I thought if I painted them and studied them, I would understand what they mean."

The professor lay a further painting down on top of the others. "And this one?

Paul laughed, and he felt his neck redden. "Well, it's an orgy of some kind - maybe a celebration. They always seem to be enjoying themselves in my dreams, I'm not sure what it represents."

The professor placed the last painting on the top of the pile. "And who is this?"

Paul picked it up and looked lovingly at the sketch, his eyes taking in every aspect. It was the study picture, showing just the eyes of the green-eyed woman.

Paul sighed. "I wish I knew; I am hoping you will be able to answer that question for me, I have dreamt about her for as long as I can remember."

The professor placed all the pictures on one side. "Apparently, your mother has had similar dreams?"

"Paul's eyes turned away from the professors. "Yes, and my grandmother on my father's side, but she died a long time ago."

"And your mother did not want to join the trial?"

Paul shook his head, his eyes still fixed firmly on the floor. "No, she is dead against it, hypnotism that is."

The professor sighed heavily. "That's a pity. Right Paul, I will run through things so you know how it will pan out. Firstly, there will always be three people in the room with you: Mr. Jones, the hypnotist, Ms. Evans, who is a trained nurse, and myself. The sessions are being recorded, and the trial will last six weeks. You will have access to all copies of the tapes, but not until the trial has finished, do you understand?"

Paul nodded his head in agreement once more. "Good lad." The professor walked away. "Then we will begin, it is over to you, Mr. Jones."

The hypnotist went through the usual procedure, and within minutes, Paul was in a deep hypnotic trance, and the professor spoke into the microphone on the tape deck.

"Subject. Paul Masters, Tape one, parental consent is given…." The professor studied Paul nervously. There was a standard set of questions, names, addresses, ages, etc. The hypnotist reeled them off. Without warning, the nurse pricked the back of Paul's hand with the needle. She smiled at the professor and felt confident he was under the hypnotist's control.

Then he began.

Paul, I want you to return to your earliest memory." The professor placed a hand on the hypnotist's shoulder. "No, take him back to the hand-fast."

"Paul, I want you to go back to your hand-fast at Avebury. You were happy that day, I believe."

A smile spread across his face. "Aye, it were fine day."

The assistant whispered to the professor. "That's an English Westcountry accent, I have heard it on the television." The professor made a note on his pad and the hypnotist continued.

"Why are you so happy?"

Paul laughed. "Well, she be a lush maid, I'm luckiest man alive."

The hypnotist's voice continued in its melodic tone. "Saul, what is the name of the woman you are to be hand-fast to?"

"Why it be Sarah, o course."

Again, the professor wrote the name down, and a smile spread across his face. He liked names, names could be traced.

"Saul, where do you live?"

His forehead creased with a frown. "Wot you wanna know that for?"

The hypnotist faltered for a second as the tables had been turned and the question was now aimed at him. "I am new here, Saul, I was just wondering."

He shook his head disdainfully. "Lunney, o course, I thought everybody knew thaaat."

"Is Lunney a village or a house?"

"Lunney castle, you oaf, where you be from?"

"I am from the east, a long way away."

Paul snorted. "Where's that too?" The hypnotist turned to the others. "What is he asking?"

The nurse proffered. "I think he is asking where in the east."

"Saul, I live in London."

Paul replied tartly. "Thought you be from there. Folk round here says nofin comes from London sept trouble.."

"London is not that bad, Saul have you ever been there?"

He shook his head once more. "Ark at e, no, too far away, takes yonks' to get to London. My brother has, though, his regiment be there."

The professor nudged the hypnotist. "Name. Regiment."

"Saul, What's your brother's surname and regiment?"

A frown creased his forehead once again. "You be nosy buggers. Why all the questions?"

"Just being friendly, I thought I might say hello next time I am in London."

Paul pursed his lips and nodded. "He be Lord Peter Monkton."

The professor gasped. "Yes, a Lord, we can trace him easily. Ask him the regiment."

"Saul, what is his regiment called." Silence filled the room, and Paul's head moved from side to side like he was thinking.

"Guard of honor or somfin like that. Can't remember which one, though, cus he's just changed regiments. You wouldna catch him in barracks anyhow, he be stayin with his uncle in Mayfair. 201, Mayfair Mews, if you want to meet him, he be there when he stays in London."

"Yes, yes, yes." The professor scribbled the address down, and his hands were visibly shaking. "Ask him his uncle's surname."

"Saul, what is your uncle's surname?"

Paul laughed. "Monkton, o course, me dad's cousin." The professor continued to make notes, then changed tack.

"Ask him about this, 'Sarah.'"

"Saul, what is Sarah's surname, and where does she live?"

"She be a Llewellyn, from Earlswood."

"This Earlswood, is it a town or a village?"

Paul started to laugh. "Ark at e, Londoners, everyone knows Earlswood, it's a big estate, you can see it from Glastonbury Abbey."

The professor continued to make notes. "Ask him when he first met this "Sarah."

"Saul, you, and Sarah seem very much in love. Tell me how the two of you met. The professor quickly put a new tape in the cassette and sat back.

"O, aye, we be in love alright, loved her from the first time I set eyes on her, she was in her fifth summer. It was the midsummer festival at Avebury in 1604.

There was a commotion at festival, some riders cum and told everyone three Princesses were a comin. They said the two girls were riding on the backs of giant wolves." He chuckled. "No one believed um, but we joined the crowd anyway, there were hundreds of people a waitin. We don't normally get Princesses, see, so everyone wanted to get best view. Then this woman entered the avenue on the biggest horse I ever saw, white it was.

Suddenly the crowd started running away from her." He laughed openly then continued. "Then I saw why; me Sarah was sitting on the back of a giant wolf. It were as white as horse - never seen a white wolf afore. She just sat there like she were ridin horse, and wolf just let her sit on its back like it were normal. There were two of them, sisters they were, twins. That's the first time I saw me, Sarah."

The three of them looked at each other in amazement, and the professor drew his finger across his throat. The hypnotist turned again to Paul.

"Saul, you are feeling tired. Go to sleep for a while and rest, and I will wake you shortly."

The professor waited until Paul's breathing became even. "Can he hear us?

The hypnotist shook his head. The professor did the same before adding. "This does not make sense, girls riding on wolves. Did they still have wolves in the early fifteenth century in the UK?" Have you ever heard of anyone riding on the back of wolves?"

The nurse quipped. "Only in films."

The nurse took the needle and stuck it in Paul's hand, he showed no reaction whatsoever.

The hypnotist held his arms in the air in exasperation. "I tell you he is well and truly under. Ok, I have never heard of anyone riding on wolves either, but this guy certainly believes this, Sarah did. Look, we have lots of names, dates, places, and loads of facts to get our teeth into. Shall I wake him up and you check the facts?"

The professor looked at his watch. "We still have forty-five minutes left - it seems a waste. Ask him what happened next.

"Saul, you can wake up now. You feel refreshed, tell us what happened after you first saw Sarah."

Paul's face once again filled with joy at the memory. "Well, the Princess and her daughters cum down the stone avenue, all the women were hidin behind standing stones, all scared like. Their party came to a halt afore the Shaman, and there was problem as he refused um entry. Princess Mia was in middle, with the two daughters on either side, and her giant wolf stood in front o Princess, guardin her like. The crowd see-in the wolves meant em no harm, felt braver, and fanned out, surrounding um in a semi-circle. The Princess waited, her head held high, and Sarah did the same until the crowd's noise died down. All three just sat there till thee could hear pin drop. Then Princess Mia placed her hands together as if she was a prayin. The other girl and me, Sarah, did the same."

*

"Greetings, Shaman, I am Princess Mia, high priestess of the Shashanti, daughter of Princess Hattie, granddaughter of Princess Ria of Persia. We have traveled a great distance to meet you, and we have crossed many countries and seas. We come to honor the Earth Mother and wish to participate in your ceremony and join the festivities. Your Earth Mother knows we are coming."

The acolyte to the right of the Shaman opened a book and quickly looked through the pages, he turned and whispered in the Shaman's ear, and Mia noticed the subtle shake of his head.

The Shaman responded. "It seems, Princess, that we have no record of you wishing to attend this meeting. Of course, you are welcome, but you must leave your wolves tied up somewhere as we have children playing freely around in the sanctuary, and they could be harmed."

The Princess towered above the welcoming committee, sitting astride "Wind," She was used to intimidating people. In her mind, the best way was to present an air of superiority, and it was a tool her line used regularly. She could feel the eyes of the crowd bearing down upon her, and they were hanging on her every word. It was time to impress the onlookers, and as was her way, she deliberately looked down upon the welcoming community as if they were insignificant insects.

"Be assured no one will be harmed unless someone harms the Princesses."

The Shaman stood his ground. "You must leave them, or You're not welcome here."

The Princess looked straight ahead, ignoring him. "I am welcome here. As I said, I have already spoken with the Earth Mother."

His voice began to lose its authority. "You must leave now!"

Princess Mia stared down at the Shaman, she was not used to being disobeyed. She could see the effect she was having upon him by the bead of sweat coalescing on his forehead, and the slightest smile creased her lips. "Does the Earth Mother herself confide in you, Shaman?" She paused for effect.

When there was no response from the Shaman, the crowd waited hanging on to her every word. "No, Shaman Bramel, son of Wilmer, from the house of Gent, no, she does not."

The acolyte to the left started to snicker.

"This is not a laughing matter, Acolyte Simon, son of Wilmot, you too, Acolyte Stephen, son of Griff. Does she confide in you? No, she does not."

. "It seems you have us at a disadvantage Princess."

Again, she turned away from him and looked straight ahead. "I have you at a disadvantage Shaman - because she confides in me. Now go, speak to the Earth Mothers' representative. Tell her the visitor that called to see her in the form of a bird has arrived with her daughters and that her party has been refused entry."

The Shaman's voice faltered. "W - we have not refused you entry, just your wolves."

The Princess took a deep breath. "The wolves are tied to the Princesses by enchantment, and they cannot be separated – it is impossible even if you command it. They are guardians, Persian royal wolves. They have served as our guardians for centuries. We have many enemies, so if they are not allowed in, we cannot enter." After a minute's pause, the silence became overbearing, and she shouted at the top of her voice.

Go!"

One of the acolytes turned and fled. The Princess was in her element, she was the center of attention. While she waited, she started accessing deeper into Morag's memories, and she chuckled inwardly.

"Tell me, Shaman, how is your wife?"

"She is well, Princess."

"Does she still have her migraine headaches?"

"She does. How do ...?"

"How are your children? Have the boys found partners yet?"

"They have."

After digging deeper into Morags memories the barest of grins creased Princess Mia's lips. "What of your daughter by the priestess? Is she well?"

The Shaman's eyes darted from side to side. When he replied, his voice was barely a whisper. "I have no daughter by any priestess."

"Goodness, did you not know? ... Oh, I see. Do you mean you haven't told your wife yet? You can't hide anything from me, Shaman, as I can see spirits even you can't."

The crowd gathered closer as the conversation got more interesting. The Shaman studied the Princess and wondered how she could know these facts. As far as he knew no one knew about his daughter.

The Princess was also studying the Shaman and answered his question as if reading his mind. "You do not get to be high Priestess by accident, Shaman."

The acolyte ran back and again whispered in the Shaman's ear. The Shaman collected himself and stood to one side, allowing them to pass. "It seems you are expected after all."

The Shaman bowed slightly and now gave them the customary greeting to honor guests.

"I, Shaman Bramel, son of Wilmer, welcome you in the name of the Earth Mother." The three travelers put their hands together as in prayer, and the Princess replied.

"I, Princess Mia, daughter of Princess Hattie, granddaughter of Princess Ria, and High Priestess of the Shashanti in the land of Persia, greet you Shaman Bramel, son of Wilmer."

It was customary to greet people you had not met before by giving your ancestors' names and positions in society and family ties. The more important you felt you were, the more names you would give. This greeting had enough family ties to impress most onlookers, and the Shaman had only given one. With access to the mother's memory, both girls understood what was happening.

First Sarah, and then Ursula spoke next, taking the Shaman by surprise. "I, Princess Sarah, daughter of Princess Mia, High priestess of the Shashanti, granddaughter of Princess Hattie, great-granddaughter of Princess Ria, greet you Shaman Bramel, son of Wilmer."

Ursula followed. "I, Princess Ursula, daughter of Princess Mia, high priestess of the Shashanti, granddaughter of Princess Hattie, great-granddaughter of Princess Ria, greet you Shaman Bramel, son of Wilmer, the carpenter."

With that, the Shaman stepped to one side to let them pass. He had picked up this sleight on his father's occupation. The statement astonished him. He could understand a High Priestess communicating with spirits, but the daughter, a mere child. How could she have known my father was a carpenter without communicating with the spirit world?

As they entered the great outer circle, the girls stared in wonderment. Neither the girls nor the young wolves had seen so many people. They gathered around them in their hundreds. Acolyte Stephen led them to what was a large reception tent.

The Princess dismounted. "Girls, stay here. Keep your wolves comforted. I will take Wolf; I want to see where they put us." The Acolyte opened the tent to let the Princess in. What are your requirements, your Highness?

"We would like to be away from the center of activities. We need a grassy area for the horses, the edge of the wood would be good so that the wolves can hunt for food."

"I think I can help you there. We have two or three tents for you to inspect if you follow me."

The acolyte took them around all three tents, and the Princess chose the one most suitable. She turned to the acolyte. "Would you inform Mother that I would like to visit her when it is convenient?"

"Of course, You're Highness." With that, he bowed and left.

She called Wolf, who had positioned herself outside the tent. "Get the girls." The Wolf turned and trotted through the crowd, who dispersed sideways as she advanced. She came to a halt in front of the girls who were still sitting on her daughters. The girls were in mental communication with her, but they remembered Morag's instructions.

Ursula called out to Sarah verbally. "I think she wants us to follow." Sarah turned and looked at the wolf before giving her a verbal command.

"Lead the way, Wolf." The wolf turned and trotted off with the girls following behind. There were murmurs of approval emanating from the crowd, who were now beginning to be less fearful of the wolves. Arriving at the tent and being followed by a group of onlookers, Sarah told her wolf to sit, then she slid down its back, straight into a walking position.

Ursula then did the same. Both girls again told their wolves to stay verbally, which they did. Again, murmurs of approval emanated from the crowd. On entering the tent, Ursula said excitedly, "Do you see how many people are here?"

Sarah added, "I didn't think there were this many people in England."

The Princess smiled at her daughter's reaction. "Well, girls, this is the main meeting of the year. Everyone who is anyone wants to be here."

Sarah asked, "Why mother? What is so special about this place?"

"It's a holy place where we 'Prime' celebrate and honor the Earth Mother - and this is the summer festival, the day when the sun is in the sky the longest. But there are many other reasons to be here. People have come to be married or handfasted. Some 'Prime' and Druid have come to find new mates, try out new partners, and see if they can find someone special to spend the rest of their lives with. Some just come to have a good time or check out what happened to their friends and relatives who have moved away. Most unattached people come for the fertility rituals on midsummer's day."

"Ursula creased her brow and asked. "What are fertility rituals?"

The Princess meditated for a few seconds and replied, "You're not old enough to know, but you will remember when the time is right."

The Acolyte Simon returned to the tent. "The Earth Mother will see you now if you follow me."

"Girls, stay here, you stay too, Wolf." She followed the Acolyte through the crowd and could feel their eyes on her from every direction. She had forgotten how strange her looks were. Her height was the main factor. Her hair was another feature, although, unlike the rest of the population of the UK, the Pagan women still wore their hair loose for meetings - its color and length were other factors. Added to that - her skin color was a lot darker. She relished being the center of attention again, it was where the Princess thought she belonged.

Morag, however, was not comfortable. She had not been considered attractive even in her youth, and for Morag, it was a pleasant surprise, but Morag now had a feeling of unease building up inside her. She had been in the Princess's form now for four days. The decision to ride the wolves into the meeting was precisely the opposite of what she had planned to do.

Was the Princess's influence growing inside her? Was her will stronger than hers? Was she taking control? Would she become just a puppet at the mercy of Mia?

*

Paul Masters had been released from his hypnotic state. The hypnotist had removed any lingering memories of Saul and the happenings in 1605 AD. He glanced at his watch as he came around and fifty-five minutes had passed. His eyes drifted across to the professor. "I take it you managed to hypnotize me and I have not just been asleep?"

The old professor smiled at him. "We are not allowed to divulge what took place or what you may or may not have said at this point, but I can tell you that you have been hypnotized."

A broad grin stretched across Paul's face. "Cool, man. Were you able to regress me?"

The professor pursed his lips and shook his head. "That I can't say - but I will say you're an interesting case.

Paul nodded his head thoughtfully. "What happens now?"

The professor collected his notes into a tidy pile and tucked them under his arm. "I don't know about you, but we are all going home. Is the same day and time ok for you next week?"

Paul nodded his head in approval and left the room.

The professor waited until he heard the outer doors shut, and Paul's footfalls fade into the distance, and put his notes back on the table. He turned to his colleagues', his eyes searching theirs, and sat back down. "Well, what did we make of that?"

The room was silent, and then two of them tried to speak simultaneously. The nurse submitted. "You first."

The professor continued. "Ok, so what do we have here? Is this a past life experience, or is he somehow reliving some sort of fantasy? We have girls riding on the backs of giant wolves that appear to be as big as donkeys. We have hundreds of Pagans or Druids who are somehow practicing their ceremonies unbeknown to the puritan regime controlling England at that time. And what is this Morag character all about? It sounded like she was some kind of spiritualist with another spirit taking possession of her body."

He flapped his arms in the air in exasperation and turned to the others. "It must be some sort of con or trick to discredit the trial, it must be?"

The nurse added thoughtfully. "We have lots of data we can check before next week. This Lord Monkton should be easy – I mean, the nobility is easy to trace, and then there's this Sarah Llewellyn living on a large estate on the edge of Glastonbury. His description of her is confusing. In the beginning, he said she was a Princess, later a maid, either way, there should be some sort of record. That's where they hold the pop festivals these days.

The nurse's voice trailed away under the derisory stare of the professor.

"What has pop festivals got to do with anything?"

The nurse retorted indignantly. "I am saying that Glastonbury Abbey is a ruin, but the village that grew around it has become a famous town – so we again have a place."

The professor turned once again to his notes. "Oh, and there is the fact that this girl Sarah can talk to animals." Again, he flapped his arms in the air, "I mean, really." He sighed. "I was pinning my hopes on this one, he had by far the best profile - it has to be a con."

"I think this was real."

The professor turned to the hypnotist; half expecting him to laugh.

"You do?"

"I know for a fact he was under my control. Some of the things he said did not make sense to us, but he had a primitive mind. This was an age of superstition, Witches, Druids, and Pagans. He saw what they wanted him to see. His mind was probably manipulated somehow, so don't put it down to just a trick. Do the checks, see if these people existed, and check the names and the dates. After all, he is by far the most interesting case I have ever come across."

The nurse piped up, "I agree – he seemed genuine to me."

The professor wearily got to his feet. "Very well then, but I have an awful feeling about this. See you all tomorrow evening."

*

6. SECOND REGRESSION 1985 AD

A week later, Professor Gaskill read the fax several times, and his hands were visibly shaking. He slid It into the file belonging to Paul Masters, lit a cigarette, and sat thoughtfully contemplating the first week's regression trial.

He had interviewed over one hundred students checking to see if they were susceptible to hypnosis. Fifty percent were not and had been rejected. After the first week, only ten students were asked to return for a second session. Of those ten, only five appeared to show signs of an earlier life experience.

His eyes once again drifted to the folder of Paul Masters', and he was lost in thought. He inhaled the smoke from his cigarette, savoring the moment, and let it out slowly. He turned; stubbed it out, and his anticipation was palpable.

Paul Masters made his way to the couch, feeling excited, soon, he would have answers. He knew only ten students had been recalled for the second week's regression. He also felt confident that they would not waste another hour of their time if he had not interested them somehow. He had not told his mother he was taking part in the trial. Of late, he found her very controlling, everything had to be done her way. He didn't like deceiving her, but he had no choice - this was important to him.

He put his sports bag on the side of the couch and lay back at ease with the situation. The fact that the dreams had returned with a vengeance made him confident that the answers he had been looking for were just around the corner. Five more sessions, that's all - and then he would know.

Professor Gaskill had kept the study notes to himself and had butterflies in his stomach. He turned to the hypnotist.

"You may begin."

The hypnotist turned the tape recorder on. "Paul Masters second session."

His voice now took on its familiar melodic tone, and Paul soon slipped under his control.

"Paul, can you hear me?"

Paul responded with an affirmative nod, and he continued.

"Paul, I would like you to go back before the darkness, back to your previous life. Will you do that for me?

Again, he nodded in the affirmative.

"Paul, can you tell me your name?

"Jamie, Jamie McFadden."

The hypnotist blinked and turned to the others, who looked just as surprised at his reply. The professor signaled him to continue.

"Jamie, what year is it?"

His eye's opened, and he dived onto the floor and screamed, "get down."

The nurse rushed over to him, but the professor grabbed her arm. "Wait."

They watched as he crawled along the floor, his face pressed to the ground. The hypnotist continued. Jamie, what year is it?"

He screamed, "Do you not ken the year man, for god's sake, get down."

"No, what year is it?"

"Jesus, nineteen forty-four, get down, or you will be blown to pieces."

The hypnotist continued, his voice smooth and melodic.

"The danger has passed, Jamie, you are safe. What day is it?"

Paul shook his head. "Do you not ken tha day either?" You banged your heid or somat, it's the sixth of June."

"Jamie, where are we?"

"Normandy."

The hypnotist turned his eyes to the professor, who signaled him to stop by running his finger across his throat.

"Jamie, you are safe now. Go to sleep for a while, and I will wake you shortly."

Paul fell silent, and the hypnotist quipped. "That was unexpected."

The professor smiled and nodded his head approvingly. "Totally unexpected. I take it we are talking about the Normandy landings?"

The hypnotist nodded his head. "Makes sense to me, sixth June nineteen forty-four, we all remember that from our history lessons."

The nurse looked perplexed. "I don't understand. I thought he would go back to being Saul, and now he is someone called Jamie and speaking with a Scottish accent?"

The professor again smiled, and the nurse could not remember him smiling so much. "Multiple lives, we have multiple lives. When Mr. Jones took him back, he said to return to his previous life, not his happiest memory. So, we have someone who can recall his earlier life and others. He rubbed his chin thoughtfully. "I wonder how many lives he can remember. We can ask him shortly, bring him back, and get his name, rank, regiment, and commanding officer, if this is some kind of trick, there is no way he would know that, and we can check with the army records."

"Paul, it is time to wake up, you are safe, the danger has passed.

Can I ask your name, rank, regiment, and commanding officer?

Jamie stood to attention without being asked and reeled them off without hesitation. "Private McFadden, 22nd Armored Brigade, my commanding officer is Brigadier Hinde, Sir." He followed it with a salute,

The hypnotist imitated an army officer. "At ease, Private." His melodic voice continued.

"Lay back down on the couch, Private, and rest."

Paul did as he commanded, and the hypnotist waited for him to settle before continuing.

"Jamie, I want you to go forward one day. What can you see?"

Jamie's eyes moved under his lids, but his face had drained of color.

"Nofin."

"He's gone white." The nurse said anxiously. "Do something quickly."

"Jamie, what is the next thing you remember?"

His face began to smile, and the color returned to his face. "Preschool."

The hypnotist blinked. "What year is it?"

"Nineteen-seventy-three."

The nurse gasped. "Oh God, he died on the beach at Normandy." And promptly her eyes began to fill with tears.

The hypnotist continued. "What is your name?"

"Paul Masters."

The professor drew his finger across his throat, and the hypnotist again put him to sleep. All three looked at one another without speaking, and the hypnotist noticed the professor was visibly shaking. The hypnotist eyed him warily.

"I take it you believe him. What changed? You thought he was trying to trick us last time?" The professor took the fax from Paul's file.

"I have been keeping something from you both. I engaged a genealogist in the UK to check out the info we got from Paul Last week. It seems Lord Peter Monkton did exist and was stationed in London at that time. He had a younger brother, Saul, and he lived at Lunny Castle, which also still exists. The other thing." He went on watching them closely. "Sarah Llewellyn was not a maid, apparently, the term "maid" is an old Westcountry name for a young woman. She was also of noble birth, and she did live at Earlswood Manor near Glastonbury at that time."

The nurse looked wondrously at the recumbent Paul, oblivious to the conversation. "So, this is all real, we don't just die and rot away, we are reborn, or some of us are."

The professor took a deep breath. "This is what I have been searching for all my life, proof, substantial documented proof. He turned to the hypnotist. "Ask him how many lives he can remember.

"Paul, you have had a good rest. Do you know what year it is?"

"Nineteen-eighty-four."

"And where are you?"

He opened his eyes and looked around. "In professor Gaskill's office." He closed his eyes once more and rested his head back down.

"Very good, Paul, how many previous lives can you recall."

A perplexed expression crept across his face. "Well, all of them, of course." All three exchanged glances.

"Can you not give me a number?"

He shook his head. "Impossible."

"Paul, when I asked you your first memory, it was by the water's edge somewhere. What year was that?

"It was not a recorded year, we only started to record time recently, it was way back at the beginning, before anything - the beginning of life."

Again, the professor signaled to stop.

The nurse proffered, "Is he saying he is remembering the beginning of life on Earth?"

Mr. Jones pursed his lips. "Well, there you have me, it certainly sounded like that."

The professor stroked his chin thoughtfully. "This is unbelievable. I have read hundreds of studies of previous lives, never and I mean never, have I heard of anyone recalling more than three lives." He turned and stared at Paul. "Imagine what we can learn from him if this is genuine."

"If all this is true." The nurse said wondrously. "Out of the hundreds and thousands of lives, he must have had, the happiest time in his whole existence was meeting this, Sarah Llewellyn." She wiped a tear from her cheek. "It's so romantic."

Even the professor himself was choked. "Ok, Mr. Jones, take him back to his Sarah, let's see what transpires next

*

Arriving at the grandest tent on the site, the Acolyte rang a bell above the entrance, and a voice from inside simply said, "Enter." The Acolyte informed the Earth Mother that the Princess had arrived.

"Tell the Princess she may enter."

The Princess found the "Earth Mother" sitting cross-legged on the floor and draped in a red shawl. The Princess placed her hands together in greeting and spoke first.

"Greetings, Earth Mother. I, Princess Mia, High Priestess of the Shashanti, daughter of Princess Hattie, granddaughter of Princess Ria, representing the kingdom of Persia, greet you."

The Earth Mother replied formally, "Greetings, Princess Mia, the Earth Mother welcomes you." She turned to the acolyte and dismissed him with the wave of her hand - and glared at the woman standing in front of her.

"Who is standing in front of me? And don't say, Princess Mia." The Earth Mother's voice was sharp, and she didn't try to hide her anger.

"It is both the Princess and I, Morag." She said nervously.

"If I remember our last conversation, we decided to keep a low profile. And you come here with your charges riding on wolves and start tearing strips off my Shaman."

Morag's voice faltered. "I - it wasn't my intention Earth Mother. The longer I'm in this form, the more influence the Princess has over me. It was her idea to do this to impress people. She is a very powerful woman who is used to getting her own way – and I am having difficulty controlling her."

The Earth Mother looked at her in amazement and raised both arms in exasperation. "Well, why come as the Princess at all!?" She was almost shouting.

Morag looked to the ground feeling uncomfortable, her eyes avoiding the Earth Mother, searching for the courage to answer her. "It's silly, really."

The Earth Mother stared the Princess full in the face trying to intimidate her, "I'm all ears." She said coldly.

Again, Morag's voice faltered. "A - as you know, I haven't had a mate for many years. When I'm in this form, I can feel her power over men, the admiration, and the unbelievable sexual attraction she exerts over everyone. I just thought..."

The Earth Mother tilted her head, teasing her, enjoying her discomfort. "Yes?"

"I just thought..."

"Go on?"

"I thought I might go to the ceremony in her form."

The Earth Mother slapped her thighs as she rocked back and forth and roared with laughter. Standing in front of this gross woman laughing at her seemed to diminish Morag. But stand there she did, her face and neck turning redder by the second.

"Forgive me, Mother, for I have made a fool of myself. I will leave you now."

"No, no, no, stay. I'm not laughing at you, Morag, I'm laughing with you."

Morag continued, her eyes still fixed firmly on the floor, "It may be hard for you to understand, but I have been lonely for many years, so I thought maybe one last time, being someone everyone deSires, would be... fun."

The Earth Mother's face softened. "As Earth Mother, I get many men wanting to honor me. I remember a time before I was appointed, and I too was lonely, so I understand, but if you go to the ceremony as the Princess, you probably won't be able to sit down for a month. But what fun you'll have."

Relief flooded Morag's face, and she found the courage to raise her eyes from the floor. "So, you approve."

The Earth Mother placed her hand on hers and felt guilty for causing Morag discomfort. "I approve. Now tell me about your charges. What news do you have for me?"

"First, Mother, I must report a massacre that we came across on the way here. It was on the north side of the river, a day's ride from here. There were houses on fire and the corpses of men, women, and children scattered on the ground. Mother, they had been mutilated beyond belief."

The Earth Mother's face darkened. "The work of the "Primevil?"

"Yes, Mother, it has all their hallmarks. They had certainly been tortured."

Morag could see the color drain from the Earth Mother's face, and her eyes clouded over.

"Morag, could you collect any memories?"

Morag gave a rueful shrug of her shoulders. "I was too late. I consoled a little girl's spirit – she was bewildered, and I prayed to the creator to guide them all to her – but there was nothing else I could do.

The Earth Mother closed her eyes in anguish and sighed heavily. "Do not mention this to anyone at the meeting. I will have a word in private with his Lordship. It's his land, and I don't want to put a damper on the celebrations.

Suddenly the cloud that had covered the Earth Mother's face had gone and was replaced with a forced smile. "Tell me about your girls."

"Mother, you will not believe what I am about to tell you," Morag said excitedly. "They have recovered some of their memories already."

Immediately the Mother's face became stern. "Have you induced them?"

Morag snapped indignantly. "No, of course not, they are far too young. Mother, I am now learning things from them. New treatments, poultices, medicines, and remedies not known to us.

"They can also control their wolves by mental communication. Sarah can look into the minds of most forest creatures. She even asked some birds which direction was that crossed the river on the way here, and they told her. We came across a stag a few weeks ago. It was trapped by its antlers in a thorn bush. The creature was terrified because we were accompanied, as always, by the wolves. We already had enough food to last for days, and we did not want to displease the Earth Mother by taking its life unnecessarily. So Sarah spoke to the stag without using words and told him he was safe. She said she told the wolves not to harm him - then got the stag to lower its head - so I could free its antlers and go backward out of the bush. The wolves then stepped to one side to let the stag leave. The stag simply walked past the wolves and left without a single word being spoken."

The Earth Mother looked stunned. "Morag, I've never heard of a power such as this."

"Mother, I have searched all the memories I possess, and no one has, not since the Romans killed the last of the Avalonian Grandmasters."

The Earth Mother fell silent for a while, deep in thought. "If what you say is true, these girls are extraordinary."

"That's not all, Mother, they can hear the stones."

"That's ridiculous." She said indignantly. "Morag, even I cannot do that."

"It's true. I have always been able to do it, and so has Mia. We all heard them as soon as we entered the Avenue."

The Earth Mother shook her head in disbelief. "Morag, the Princess comes from this land… Persia?"

"Yes, the titles I gave you are her true titles. I think this country is far to the south. The girls were having trouble recognizing the forest's flora as they were new to their memories. Their land is very hot and covered in sand."

"I have heard of it. Yes, it is to the south and very far away."

The Earth Mother's face looked troubled. "I think the Princess was wrong to draw so much attention to the girls. The dark brothers and sisters would love to control this power."

Morag nodded her head in agreement but added.

"She's not a complete fool. The Princess journeyed to the east and then south of Avebury in secret so that we could approach from the south. She then spoke to everyone she could find to make people think we were traveling from the south - and told everyone she had traveled from across the sea to be at the meeting. So, in the future, if people try to find them, they will be looking in the wrong country and in the wrong direction."

The Earth Mother pursed her lips and nodded her head thoughtfully. "Clever lady."

"Yes, and very powerful, as I said, I am having trouble controlling her."

"There is one other thing that is worrying me. I sense we may have a problem with Ursula."

"What sort of problem?"

"It might be nothing. As I have said, Sarah can communicate with the animals, but Ursula can only communicate with her wolf. I feel she's getting very envious of Sarah. Also, the forest creatures are wary of her and run and hide whenever she is near. As we both know their father was a cruel man. I worry that some of that wickedness may run in the family. When I approached your Shaman, I gave him a list of several family ties - as I have done with you. The Shaman only gave one, his father. The girls realized Mia was putting him in his place. Sarah copied her word for word, but Ursula added his father's profession. Being a carpenter, it was obviously a further put-down. The Shaman noticed. But I sensed a wicked feeling of pleasure from Ursula."

Mother replied, "Creatures of the forest run from everyone. I also get pleasure from putting the Shaman in his place. Morag, I would not worry about this too much. Jealousy and envy, however, can be the worm that attracts evil. You must praise

Ursula when she achieves something, and it would help if you made her think she, too, is exceptional. Maybe you should play down Sarah's achievements a little. The Earth Mother fell silent and then turned to Morag. "How did she know about the carpenter?"

The Princess shook her head from side to side. "Mother, I have no idea."

"Very interesting. I will look forward to meeting the girls. Do they know they must hide their gifts?"

"Yes, Mother."

"As you are no doubt aware, the reception meal is tonight. I will position you and your daughters on my table. It is the high table, the one for visiting dignitaries. Princess Mia from Persia with the young Princesses will be expected to be on my table."

"This is a great honor, Mother. In all the years I have attended the festival, I have not got past the third table."

Mother added. "There are several visiting dignitaries, one from the East, two from the far west of Wales, two from Ireland, and Lord Monkton and his sons."

Mia's voice came to the fore. "Is that the Lord Monkton that owns the surrounding land?"

"Yes, he holds the title deeds for Avebury. His guards passed you on horseback, the ones that reported your daughters were traveling on wolves."

The Princess looked puzzled. "I was not aware that they were soldiers - they were not dressed as such."

The Earth Mother shook her head and sighed heavily. "I want to speak to Morag, Princess please keep quiet. Now, where were we? Ah yes, Morag, it's been many years since you attended the festival. Things have changed. The Protestant church has decreed that all Pagan worship is banned, and they are feeding falsehoods to the masses. Apparently, we are in league with the Devil. We perform human sacrifices and we eat babies, and they are telling everyone that sex is to be outlawed outside of wedlock! We are fortunate that Lord Monkton has given his men strict instructions to turn all outsiders away."

"I met him in my youth, he was very handsome. Is he one of us?"

"He is 'Prime,' but he tells everyone he is just a Druid. If it were not for him, we would not be able to hold the festival. He comes from a long line of sorcerers and has many gifts, including retaining the memories."

Mia interrupted. "Do his children retain them as well?"

The Earth mother sighed. "They are too young. The eldest, Peter, is nine, and the youngest, Saul, is just six summers. He has no daughters, but his sons might be good company for your girls. Now Princess, will you be quiet."

The Princess ignored the Earth Mother and pressed. "Is there a Lady Monkton?"

The Earth Mother addressed Morag. "I see what you mean, she is very willful. No, she died in childbirth with the youngest son Saul, and he never remarried. He has never been the same since - they were very much in love. These boys could make good marriage prospects for one or both of your girls. Right, you two, when we meet during the festival, I will address you as Princess Mia. So, Princess Mia, I will see you tonight, and Princess - please be good." She waved her arms dismissively, signaling they should go.

When Mia arrived back at her tent, she was confronted by a group of onlookers, mainly children. The girls were allowing them to take rides on the wolves, and the wolves themselves seemed to be reveling in the attention.

Sarah ran up to the Princess. "Mother, these are our friends."

"Are they indeed?" Turning to the children, she could see a sea of upturned faces looking at her.

"I, Princess Mia, welcome you children of Avebury."

"Mother, this is my new best friend, Saul."

Mia eyed the boy warily, she studied his attire and noticed how fine he was dressed. "I, Princess Mia, welcome you, Saul Monkton"

Saul looked surprised and asked, "How did you know my name?"

"I am a High Priestess. I know many things, Saul. Please would you take hold of my hand?" Saul lifted his hand and gave it to the Princess. "Saul, I see you have a pure heart, and your mother spirit watches over you. She says she will always be by your side, yours, and your brothers."

A male voice called out from the rear of the crowd.

"That was very impressive, your Highness."

Seeing how the young boy looked at this man, the Princess made a calculated guess. "Lord Monkton, I am honored to meet you."

The Lord took in the beauty of this woman, the likes of which he had never seen before. He studied her features, but it was her green eyes that took his breath away. "Yes, very impressive. Have we met before?"

The smile she presented to him had been practiced by her and her ancestors over the centuries and was a tool she exploited to gain an advantage.

"No, my Lord, I have just arrived in this country."

His Lordship turned to the young boy standing next to him. "May I introduce my eldest son...."

The Princess cut in. "Ah, Peter Monkton, I am pleased to meet you?" Peter bowed to the Princess, who then took the child's hand.

Mia held the boy's hand and looked deep into his eyes. "You too have a pure heart, and I see you will be a warrior one day." The boy beamed a smile and looked up at his father. This, too, was a calculated guess. Most noble families had one son in the army. She caught a glimpse of Ursula, hanging back, and taking a deep interest in the eldest son.

The Princess held out her hand for Ursula to join her. "This is my daughter, Ursula. She and Sarah are twins." Ursula lifted her eyes, looked directly at Peter, and put her hands together in greeting.

"My name is Ursula, daughter of Princess Mia, the High Priestess of the Shashanti, granddaughter of Princess Hattie, great-granddaughter of Princess Ria from the land of Persia. I greet you, Peter, son of Lord Monkton."

They bowed to one another and stood next to their parents with the introduction over. Mia and his Lordship studied one another for a while, and it was Lord Monkton that spoke first.

"Do you not have any prophecies for me, Princess?"

"May I take your hand, my Lord?" The Princess placed his hand between hers, closed her eyes, and again smiled pleasantly. Your wife's spirit is with you also. She watches over all three of you." The Princess then paused for effect, tilting her head - as if listening to someone speaking in her ear. "I see!" She said and turned her head to one side as if listening to other voices. "I see." She repeated and turned to his Lordship. "Your wife tells me you have not remarried and were deeply in love."

His lordship took a deep breath and sighed. "Yes, that is true."

"She said you have her permission to take a wife if you wish, but she knows you will not. She also says you must stop mourning her and start having fun." Again, she tilted her head. "I see." Then said. "Are you sure?" Another pause. "As you wish."

She turned to face the Lord. "She said you should join in the fertility festival, even if it's just for fun." The Princess raised an eyebrow. "How very understanding of her, my Lord?"

Lord Monkton looked shocked. "She said that?"

"She did."

His lordship pursed his lips, and the Princess noted the frown creasing his forehead. "I will think about it."

"Will we see you at the reception meal tonight, my Lord?"

"You will."

"Until tonight then."

Mia turned and went back into her tent, closely followed by Ursula. Mia removed her cloak and eyed her daughter with curiosity. "That was a very formal greeting, Ursula."

"Of course it was. You only meet your husband once for the first time, so you should do it properly."

Mia could not hide the astonished look on her face. "Your husband? Why on earth would you think that?"

"You forget, I come from a very long line of seers. Peter and I get married along with Sarah and Saul ten years from now."

Mia studied her daughter with curiosity. "Your mother told you?"

Ursula angrily stamped her feet. "No, I can see for myself. I have told you before that I have the sight, but you never believe me."

The Princess tilted her head, measuring her daughter once more. "Can your sister see the future also?"

Ursula pursed her lips and shook her head. "I don't believe so."

"So, you think you have the gift of foresight? Will you be happy?

Ursula placed both hands on her hips and snapped. "Mother, you know a seer cannot see their own future."

It took all of Mia's willpower to hide her smile.

"Of course, how silly of me, but you did see your future with this boy."

"I did, mother."

Mia hugged her daughter and kissed her forehead. Something Ursula could not remember her doing in the past. "Go and mix with the other children and enjoy your day."

Morag once again paused for thought. *So, Ursula is already getting the gift of sight, and that is how she knew the Shaman's father was a carpenter. *What of you, Princess? How clever of you to trick and impress the Lord - using snippets of information gained from the conversation with the Earth Mother. You are a trickster, Princess Mia – nothing more.*

A voice replied from deep inside her head.

You must use every trick at your disposal, Morag, but it's not just tricks. These boys may marry our daughters in the future as Ursula prophesied. The Lord is impressed with you. It would help if you discussed with him the hand-fasting ritual, we have plenty of gold for the girls" dowries, and the betrothal ceremony could take place this week. I see he also deSires you. Like all men, his mind is centered a foot below his navel and is easy to read. The seed is now set for the fertility ceremony, and remember you are his prize - do not be too eager.

The girls continued to play with the other children. Ursula followed Peter around all afternoon like a puppy following its master. There was four years difference in their ages, but they didn't look out of place as the girl was tall. Saul and Sarah were as thick as thieves. They disappeared for hours and ventured deep into the forest, playing by the stream and getting covered in mud.

Like Sarah, Morag noticed that the forest animals did not shy away from Saul. *That's comforting, Princess,* Morag said from deep within her mind.

*

The reception meal was just before sunset. The high table was the most prestigious and the one everyone wanted to be invited to. The Princess had dressed the girls in green dresses to match her own. Of all the dresses the Princess owned, this was her favorite. It was long, almost to the floor, and shimmered in the firelight. It had two side splits and a panel in the middle. The splits went up to her thighs, which showed her long elegant legs. She knew this had a profound effect on her male companions. Another tool she used often.

The Princess was used to making grand entrances and had deliberately waited until everyone was seated. In her mind's eye, she had to be the last to arrive. As they made their entrance, the Earth Mother smiled inwardly as she observed the reaction of everyone at the table. The Princess and her daughters approached the Earth Mother and placed their hands together and greeted her formally.

"Greetings, Earth Mother."

The Earth Mother greeted them. "Welcome to our table - please be seated."

She sat next to the Lord - and the girls were positioned opposite the boys.

The feast was fit for royalty. There was all manner of meats from the forest - Swan, duck, wild boar, deer, vegetables and fruits in abundance. Wine and mead and a selection of forest mushrooms were plentiful. Servants and Acolytes topped up their drinks as soon as the glasses were empty, and cleared the plates when they finished.

As the evening wore on, the laughter increased with the amount of wine and mushrooms consumed. Lord Monkton engaged the Princess in all manner of conversation. Where she was from, the various countries she had crossed to get here, and what her country was like? The subject finally got around to the whereabouts of her husband.

"My husband and I no longer share the same beliefs." She said sheepishly. "He has become a Papist. As you know, Rome is committed to destroying our way of life. The bastard has destroyed all the images of our Earth Mother, and I must keep them hidden. He forbids us to go to rituals and meetings."

She then leaned across and whispered in his ear. "He even insists we only make love when he wants another child." The Princess lifted an eyebrow invitingly and studied his reaction before taking another sip of wine.

The Lord did the same, and studied every facet of her face, measuring her. "But he has let you come here?"

Her eyes moved to the goblet in her hand, and her voice faltered. She swirled the red liquid around, studying it as she searched for the correct words, implying English was still a new language. "He has allowed us to travel to the Northern Countries, but he does not know about my little… diversion. He wants me to find future husbands for the girls and arrange for them to be hand-fast until they reach fifteen. In our country, marriages are arranged by the parents of both parties. They consider how rich each family is, how much land they own, what contacts the family has, and if there are any strategic advantages in such a union. Love has nothing to do with it."

The Lord nodded his head pensively. "It is similar in England - marriage is used to bind families and even enemies together. I was lucky. I found a woman with the same beliefs as myself, and because I was the second son and would not inherit the estate, I was allowed to marry for love. I got the best of both worlds as my brother died before he could have a male heir, so the estate passed to me."

The Princess gazed deep into the flickering flames of the fire, and her mind seemed distant for a time. "Yes, I know, your wife told me." She sighed heavily. "I was not so lucky. I did what my family ordered. He is twenty years older than me and so fat he can hardly walk. Before my wedding, I had never even met him. On my wedding night, I cried myself to sleep." She emptied her goblet and immediately an acolyte refilled it, she took another sip and sighed once more and added. "And still do most nights. I long to experience the dance of love, even if it's just for one night. Her green eyes looked temptingly over the goblet at his lordship. "That's another reason I am here, to find true love."

The Lord looked quite surprised. "Do you mean you will be participating in one of the dances?" The Princess laughed openly, and his Lordship realized she was getting quite intoxicated.

She lifted both eyebrows and made her eyes as large as possible, enticing him. "I thought you would have guessed by now, only one, my Lord." She leaned closer and whispered in his ear. "I believe you call it "The Dance of the Free Spirits." The statement took his lordship entirely by surprise. He choked and spat his wine back into his goblet. When he composed himself, he took her hand and laughed openly, and he patted it affectionately.

"I am sure you will find many partners at the dance - but whether it will lead to true love." He shrugged his shoulders. "Who knows."

She returned his smile. "My Lord, I will know."

The Princesses voice inside Morag was getting stronger by the day, and once again, it came, unbidden. *He wants you, Morag, but don't appear too keen. Keep him longing for you.*

Morag became aware of a new sensation and realized she was beginning to see into the mind of the Knight. It was another of the Princesses' gifts. She, too, could see his deSire, his lust even, and Morag called the Princess. *So, it was not all conjuring tricks – you really can see their thoughts.*

Laughter once again came unbidden from deep within her. *Morag, keep that to yourself, tell no one. It will get stronger, at this moment you can only see a fraction of what I can. Looking at the minds of the men gathered here, we will have one hell of a festival.*

7. RED DREAMS 1985 AD

Paul found himself once again on the couch. He looked at his watch, and they had run over by ten minutes. He turned to the professor. "I take it I have been regressed once again?"

The professor shook his head. "Nice try son, you know the rules."

Paul looked at each of them in turn, and all three returned a wan expression. "Do you want me to come again next week?" He said hesitantly.

The professor continued to write something in his file and said nonchalantly. "If it's ok with you, yes."

Paul agreed and chewed his lip thoughtfully. He thought he would have gained some snippet of information, and left the room disappointed. Once again, when they heard the outer doors close, all three sat down. Ms. Evans spoke first.

"If he is tricking us, he has an amazing imagination, I mean, inventing this Earth Mother character and describing how they introduced each other, the meal, the types of food, and the preparations for this festival they are going to."

The hypnotist added excitedly. "I can't wait to hear about that. I have been reading up on these Pagan ceremonies since last week. Did you know the Romans and the Catholic church destroyed all records of festivals and ceremonies? We know so little about the Pagan and Druid lifestyle, and what we do know was sourced by the victors, and we know how biased that can be."

The professor's smile was once again missing. "Yes, very realistic, but we must offset this against this ridiculous statement that this spiritualist, or whatever she is, seems to have the ability to change her form, and not just carry someone else's spirit. Oh, and this Morag's spirit can be transported by a bird and can communicate with someone miles away. This must be a fantasy of some kind, it would never stand up to any sort of scrutiny. And. - He paused for effect. - "We did not have any facts that we could check this time."

The hypnotist, however, was once again more positive.

"I still think this is a man with a primitive mind. The bird taking this Morag's spirit must be hearsay. Did he actually see this Morag woman change shape.... No. This is how they controlled the minds of primitive men, tricks, deception, and hearsay. I think this whole thing is mind-blowing. Ok, we can't check this hand-fast story, but we can check this Jamie character's records. We have name rank and number, and if he is tricking us, I bet you one hundred bucks he gets the commanding officer's name wrong."

The professor smiled wickedly. "Yes, yes, we can. I will contact the British army records office, and all being well, we should have an answer by next week."

*

Jenny Walker was waiting for Paul as he left the building. "Hi." She said and walked over to him. Paul pressed his lips into a line and shook his head. "You look glum?" she proffered - and when he didn't respond - slipped her arm into the crook of his, as they walked side by side. "What's wrong?"

He gave a heavy sigh. "They are keeping me in the dark, I am not even sure that I have been regressed at all, and now I have to wait another week."

She studied his face intently. "Did you know there are only four of you left on the trial?"

Paul looked surprised. "No."

She tugged his arm playfully. "There you go, they wouldn't have asked you to come back if they could not regress you."

Paul's face brightened. "Yes, your right." He took a deep breath and nodded his head to himself thoughtfully. "Yes, you are right, I just have to be patient."

Jenny leaned across and kissed his cheek. "Do you feel like hanging out for a bit?"

Paul's eyes grew darker. "For a bit of what?"

She squeezed his hand and opened her eyes wide, invitingly. "Well, Paul Masters, as you know, I am always open to suggestions." To emphasize the fact, she fluttered her lashes at him.

He smiled. "It depends. Do you still have the runes I painted on your butt?"

She pursed her lips. "You know I have, I can't get the dam things off. I had to cancel swimming this week, the teacher would have thought it was a tattoo and told mom." She glanced warily at him. "You still got yours?"

Paul nodded and added. "I am not trying to get mine off, we are tied to each other while wearing them." His eyes locked on hers and she could see his carnal deSire. "Do you not feel it, their power pulling us together? I can't stop thinking about you. We are tied you and me - there is no escape for either of us."

Jenny leaned over and kissed him once more. "I like it when you talk dirty, your place or mine?"

Paul laughed. "You think mom will let you in my bedroom again?"

Jenny began to walk quicker, pulling him along behind her. "My place it is then, mom finishes work at eight, so we have only got forty-five minutes."

*

That night Paul had a dream. A red dream. He tried to wake himself but couldn't. Since the regressions started, he seemed to dream constantly. He found the white dreams comforting, and he found the ceremonies sexually arousing. He found love in the face of the green-eyed woman. The red dreams, he hated.

He was an observer, a child hiding in the bushes. His mother had hidden him there. Men and women on horses were raiding their village. The thatched roof of his home was ablaze, and people were running everywhere, shouting, and screaming, while horses galloped around the perimeter, preventing anyone from escaping. He was like a rabbit frozen in the headlights of a car. One by one, the people were slaughtered, some left maimed, barely alive. The women were rounded up and tied hand and foot. Inevitably the men succumbed, and those still living were tied to stakes in the ground.

Paul could feel their terror and helplessness as they were resigned to whatever fate awaited them. It was always like this in the 'red dreams.'

He tried to wake up time and again but couldn't. For some unfathomable reason, he was compelled to witness these events. What were they? Why was he dreaming these horrors?

He had no deSire to do these things and could understand why the teacher was worried about his mental health.

His head thrashed around in his sleep, and he called out a warning. The children were lynched one by one, their legs thrashing, trying for purchase on the air around them, their families, tethered, watching. He gasped and tried to lift one, preventing the rope from taking its deadly toll, but his body was paralyzed and it could not respond.

His role, as always, was simply to see the event. The screams of the parents echoed in his mind, he clasped his hands to his ears, trying to shut the sound out. The women and men were raped, abused repeatedly then slaughtered. Finally, the men that were staked to the ground and forced to witness the event were disemboweled and left to die. "Why, Why," he screamed out loud. No answer came.

Joan Masters was watching her son, tears in her eyes. She knew he had to bear witness. She had been troubled all her life by these same dreams. After seeing Paul's paintings at the school, she realized he was becoming aware. The red, white, and ceremonial dreams were hers. She had passed them down to Paul as they had been passed down to her by the child observing the event many lifetimes before. He needed to remember." It was painful, but He was 'Prime.' He needed to witness these events to pass them on to his children and grandchildren, they all needed to witness the 'Primevil' and their atrocities.

He would get over it.

She stroked his forehead, feeling the sweat on his brow, and watched as he became aware of his surroundings as his eyes blinked rapidly. She saw the relief on his face when he realized it had been, once again, just a dream.

"You Ok, son?"

Paul looked up, he could see the compassion in her eyes and shook his head warily.

"Describe it to me."

Paul lifted himself on his elbows and rested his head on the headboard, his body drenched in sweat. "Another red one. What was it about?"

"I was a child hiding in the bushes. They circled my family's home with horses, burnt the house down, and killed everyone – my brothers and sisters, my mom and dad, everyone."

"Joan nodded. I remember that one, not very pleasant."

He sighed heavily. "Why do I keep dreaming these awful things? It's not like I have any urge to kill someone."

"You will work it out soon. All I can say is that you needed to see that image, it is important. To you, it was only a dream, but it was that child's memory, and he does not want anyone to forget his pain."

Paul shook his head in disgust. "You and your dam memories."

She placed her hand on his to comfort him. "Family memories; our family's." Joan changed tack.

"How are you doing at the gym club?"

Paul's eyes fell away from Joan's. "Err, Ok."

She tried to lighten the mood with a smile. "Do you have any events I could go to?"

He shook his head anxiously. "Mom, I am not that good yet, in about a month maybe."

She gave him a peck on the cheek. "Can't wait." As she got up to go, she looked back. "You ok now?"

He nodded. "Yeh, but leave the light on."

*

The hypnotist read the fax the professor had received from the British army records office. He scanned it, the name, rank, and regiment were all correct. He read on and gasped. "He got the commander right as well – bloody hell."

Mrs. Evans gave a wry smile, she took the fax and read it herself. Her eyes turned to the others, searching, looking for their reaction. "This is it, we have done it. It is definite proof. We asked him a question he could not possibly have anticipated, and he answered at once."

Professor Gaskill stroked his beard thoughtfully and looked at Mr. Jones. "Is this the proof we have been looking for to support the transmigration of the soul? I think she's right - It certainly looks that way to me. What do you think?"

He shrugged his shoulders. "I have thought he was genuine from the beginning. What do you want me to do today? Do you want to try another life, get some facts, and double-check the findings?" He was about to answer, but Mrs. Evans cut in.

"We should continue with Saul's story. Anything we learn about these Druids and their ceremonies will be a first. I have done a lot of research this week. According to the only records we have, which were written by the Romans two thousand years ago, they sacrificed people, ate babies, summoned spirits, and communicated with the dead. They controlled the weather by invoking fog and mist at will and were able to communicate with the creatures of the forest, as Saul said this Morag woman could do. They, like the Buddhists, believed in this transmigration of the soul. Look, we have found someone whose ancestor was an actual Druid, no wonder he is the top candidate for our trial. We know absolutely nothing about these people, and you can bet your bottom dollar the Romans invented half these stories to justify wiping them out."

Mr. Jones agreed. "I think she is right. We should run this through before moving on to a new life."

When Paul entered the professor's study for the third regression session he went straight to the couch. Since the last meeting, he had had three red, one white, and one ceremonial dream, and with the physical demands of Jenny Walker was exhausted by the lack of sleep. He rested his head on the cushion and longed for rest before the hypnotist started to regress him. Professor Gaskill eyed him warily.

"Are you all right, Paul"

"I am feeling very tired, Sir. Professor, do you mind if I ask you something?"

The professor rocked his head. "Depends, as long as I can stick within the guidelines of the trial."

"This all started with me having these dreams, and since we started the trial, I dream even more, why is that, and what do they mean?"

"Well, there, now you have me, son." The professor pursed his lips and shook his head, and Paul watched as he chewed his lip thoughtfully. "Sorry, Paul, I can't see a connection there."

Paul smiled inwardly, and his heart lifted. *He took a long time to think that one through. That must mean they are managing to regress me, so I will have answers soon.* It was not with trepidation but with anticipation when he closed his eyes.

"Can you hear me, Saul?" As was the norm, he simply nodded.

"Saul, you have told us how you first met Sarah at the midsummer meeting at Avebury. Could you describe what you see around you? We are especially interested in the ceremonies and the people taking part in them. I have never been to a ceremony, but I would like to. Would you do that for me, so I know what to do when I go?"

Paul nodded, and his voice took on the West Country lilt once again. Arr, I be glad to tell ye. The following day be classed as a "day of greetings." People would meet up with kin and anyone who had lost touch. We would exchange news and gossip. Like who has had bairns or grandchildren? Who passed on to spirit world? Who be hand-fast or lost a partner through illness or marriage breakup since they last met? Today be day they seek out new partners, new mates. We talk a lot and drink a lot. It be a grand day.

It be same each year since we built henge. Bin repeated at midsummer and midwinter for thousands o years until Romans destroyed Avalon. We must meet in secret now, see. First, it was Romans, and now these Puritan bastards persecute us. Praise be to Lord Monkton and his men for turning any non-believers away. It be only place us 'Prime, 'and Druid" can meet up as our numbers are so few now. Folk rarely journeys far these days, even for festivals, unlike old days when we followed bison and mammoth. Folk rarely travels more than ten miles from where born now. So, at festival we can meet new folk, make new mates, and maybe if we're lucky take dance we um.

There be workshops where new magic and potions be taught, even for kids. That's when trouble started for me, Sarah. It was in children's circle, Druids were watchin for special kids - kids with gifts. Druids were always lookin for special kids.

Ursula and Sarah were singled out, see. Having their 'Prime' memories already gave, um, unfair advantage. During first day, several tutors felt it necessary to seek urgent meetin with Earth Mother to pass on news.

*

The Princess's daughters were summoned to visit the Earth Mother in the late afternoon. Accompanied by their mother, the girls waited anxiously outside her tent. Eventually, they were told to enter. The Earth Mother was flanked on one side by Shaman Bramel and the other by Acolyte Simon. She greeted the trio.

"Greetings, Princess Mia, Princess Ursula, and Princess Sarah."

They responded in unison. "Greetings, Earth Mother."

"My Shaman and Acolyte Simon bring me news that your daughters are showing potential." She then turned her attention to the girls.

"Are you enjoying your time here?" Both girls nodded their heads enthusiastically. Then the Earth Mother turned her attention to the two men.

"Would you be so kind as to leave us? I wish to talk to the Princess and her daughters in private." The Shaman was not expecting this but reluctantly left the tent. Again, the Earth Mother waited for their footfalls to fade. Eventually, she turned her attention to the girls.

"Your mother tells me you have recovered some of your ancestors" memories?" Both girls were unsure how to respond and looked to their mother for guidance.

"It's alright. I've explained everything to Mother. You can talk to her openly.

Ursula spoke first. "Yes, Earth Mother."

"Child, you can just call me "Mother."

"Yes, Mother."

"The Princess has not induced you. She hasn't given you any potions to aid recovery?"

"No, Mother."

The Earth Mother looked sheepishly at the Princess. "Sorry about that, Morag. I had to be sure. Have you any gifts you can tell me about?"

Sarah replied first. "We can talk to the wolves with our minds."

"Yes, tell me about that. How can you do that without word commands."

"We just look into their minds. It's quite easy."

"So, you do not have to use words?"

"That's correct, Mother. At the festival, we are using verbal commands. Morag told us to do this to hide our gift; she said it would draw too much attention if we Didn't."

"That's very wise of Morag. I am sure she wouldn't want to draw too much attention to you." Her eyes looked across at Morag, who picked up the witticism.

"Tell me, Sarah, you say you can communicate with most creatures. How did you ask the birds which way to go for the bridge on the river?"

"It's difficult to explain."

"Try."

She looked hesitantly at her mother, who nodded her approval. "I do not use words. I use pictures. I can look into their mind, and we are one, they seem to understand pictures."

"Ursula, Morag tells me you have another gift that you discovered just this week?"

Ursula also looked at the Princess for guidance, and she gave her a nod.

"I think I have the gift of foresight." It was Sarah's turn to look surprised.

The Earth Mother raised an eyebrow. "Do you now? This is an extraordinary gift. It would be best to keep this a secret because those in power always wish to control people with foresight. They see your gift as a powerful tool that could give them the upper hand in matters of state and war. Morag tells me you foresee that you will marry Peter Monkton."

"Yes, Mother."

"If you do, I think it will be a good match. They too carry 'Prime' memories. You to Sarah when you marry Saul because both family's gifts would combine perfectly."

Sarah glared at her mother, waiting for a response. The Princess shrugged her shoulders apologetically and turned to her daughter. "Sarah, I don't know if this will come to pass, it is what Ursula has informed me."

Sarah instantly flew into a temper. "Well, I'll marry whomever I like, not like my mother."

Princess Mia tried to appease her. "Just because Ursula said it would be so doesn't mean it will happen. Do you not like Saul?"

"I've only just met him, and yes he is nice, but I will decide, not Ursula." The Earth Mother raised her hands to quiet them and shooed them away. "It seems you have lots of things to talk about, so I bid you all farewell." The trio bowed, backed out of the tent, and left.

As the girls walked away, Sarah could no longer control her temper and kicked Ursula on the leg. "Did you see that coming, Ursula, or this?" The Princess just managed to grab Sarah's hand before she could slap her.

Ursula responded, "You're just jealous because I have a better gift than you. You can't stand being second best. You always must be the special one, and all you can do is talk to animals."

Princess Mia grabbed them both by the arms and held them apart. It took all her strength to control them. "What on earth has gotten into both of you? Stop this at once?"

Lord Monkton, who was following behind, commented.

"Looks like you've got a couple of wild cats there, Princess."

Sarah, her anger growing stronger by the second, turned on his Lordship. "And, if you think I'm going to marry your son, you've got another thing coming."

"What on earth is the child talking about, Princess?"

"Sorry, your Lordship, Sarah misunderstood something the Earth Mother said."

"What was that?"

"She simply said that your children's gifts and my girl's gifts complement each other and that they would be suitable mates."

His Lordship pursed his lips and raised his brow in surprise. "Would they indeed?"

"Sarah said in response that she would not be forced into an arranged marriage after seeing how badly my husband treated me. She thought we were about to hand-fast them together."

Sarah was still squirming and trying to get at Ursula, and his Lordship tried to calm her down.

"Sarah, Sarah, keep still. Look, no one is going to make you marry my son. When either of my sons get married, it will be for love, and no one will be arranging it without both parties wanting it."

"It's just that Ursula said…."

At this point, the Princess felt the need to chastise her. "Sarah, that's enough. Ursula is just a child like you."

Lord Monkton, who was now getting quite inquisitive, asked. "What did Ursula say, Sarah?"

"She said she has the gift of foresight and that we would both marry your sons."

"Sarah, your sister's much too young to have a gift like that. You're being silly."

Seeing the situation going from bad to worse, the Princess tried to rescue it. "Yes, Sarah, you are both too young to have any gifts. Now say sorry and be quiet."

Ursula, not to be outdone, joined in. "Well, you tell him, mother. You know I'm right. You're a seer, so you tell him."

"For the sake of Earth Mother, Ursula, be quiet."

His Lordship commented. "Is this true, Princess?" Silently Morag delved inwardly. Ok, Princess, how do I rescue this?

"Don't be ridiculous, she is much too young."

"I mean, is it true you are a seer?"

Princess Mia lowered her voice to a whisper, "All the females in my line are, yes. That's why the Kings and Princes marry us. Not for love like you, now if you excuse me." She grabbed the girls, who were still fighting, and walked away. The Lord, who was deep in thought, watched her leave.

Shaman Bramel, who had also heard their conversation, commented to his Lordship. "She has her work cut out with those two. Remarkable girls, I believe."

His Lordship, who was still taking in the enormity of what the Princess had said to him, agreed. "Yes, Shaman Bramel, quite remarkable."

The Princess didn't try to hide her feelings back in the tent.

"What on earth possessed you both? What did we say when we came? Do not tell anyone about your gifts. So, what was the first thing you do? You shout out that your sister already has the gift of foresight and that I am a Seer. Do you not realize what danger you have put us in? It will be all around the festival. A gossip like this travels fast. I am frightened, and I know Morag is frightened too. How could you have been so stupid? You are too young. I should not have brought you here."

After a sustained length of silence, everyone calmed down.

"Listen, Sarah, just because Ursula thinks she has foresight, it doesn't mean she has. Even if someone has the gift of foresight, it is one of many paths that can be taken, and it is not set in stone. We must play this incident down as a trick that went wrong. Ursula, you must tell everyone who asks that you were trying to trick Sarah. Do we all understand how silly we have been?

"Yes, mother."

"Girls, go out and play. If we have another incident like this, we must leave. Do you understand?"

"Yes, mother."

"Now go. Keep your wolves on alert." Little did she know it was already too late.

*

That evening the Princess was summoned to see the Earth Mother. When she arrived, she found Lord Monkton standing outside her tent. He approached the Princess. "Have you been summoned also?"

The Princesses' voice deep inside Morag could be heard worming its way to the surface. *He's a handsome man, Morag. You would need a tall man. The gentry is always taller. He would make a fine father for our girls.*

"Yes, my Lord. Do you know why?"

"I've no idea unless it was something to do with your daughter's outburst." They rang the bell that hung above the entrance and waited, and a voice from inside invited them in.

"Greetings, your Lordship. Greetings, Princess."

They replied in unison. "Greetings, Earth Mother."

"I've summoned you here to inform you that it is common knowledge throughout the festival that you, Princess, are a seer, as is your eldest daughter, and your youngest daughter can "bewitch the forest animals to do as she bids. Do you have any comments to make on the subject Princess?"

The Princess was unsure how to reply to this question with his Lordship standing next to her. Her eyes glanced over to his Lordship.

The Earth Mother snapped. "His Lordship might as well know the truth, everyone else at the festival does."

"The girls got a little carried away. Sarah thought Ursula and you were arranging a marriage for her. They are good girls, Mother, but they fight like cats and dogs. It is unusual for Sarah to start an argument as she is normally the passive one."

The Earth Mother raised her arms in exasperation. "So, it's my fault?"

Mia lowered her eyes and looked at the ground submissively. "She's only a child, she simply misunderstood."

"Be that as it may, the whole festival is talking about it. Whether it's true or not, you and your daughters are in danger. There are always 'Primevil' spies at these meetings. We never know who they are, but they will surely have heard already."

The Princess argued her point. "We have our protectors, the wolves. I've already told the girls to alert them. After the row, I thought it best."

The Earth Mother turned her attention to the Lord. "My Lord, thank you for coming. I thought you should know in case there is any trouble."

"Thank you for keeping me informed, Mother. If I can supply some sort of protection, I certainly will."

The Earth Mother turned her attention once again to the Princess. "What do you intend to do, your Highness?"

"I do not want to put anyone in danger. I had told the girls to spread it around the festival that it was just a trick Ursula was playing on Sarah, but it seems it was too little too late. You are right, Earth Mother – the girls are in danger - we must leave. I was so looking forward to treating them to a festival – there is no way my husband would allow it in my own country."

Seeing his chance to get to know the Princess better slipping away, Lord Monkton stepped in.

"I could have some of my men keep an eye on the girls, discreetly, of course."

The Princess looked for approval from the Earth Mother, who replied, "With your men and the guardians, they should be safe, but it must be your decision, Princess."

Mia turned to his lordship and smiled openly. "In that case, I accept your protection."

Lord Monkton turned to the Princess. "Good, I am looking forward to seeing more of you. I will go and see to my men."

The Princess placed her hand on his arm to prevent him from leaving with a mischievous glint in her eye. "Before you post your men on guard duty, we must get the girls to introduce them to the wolves, just in case they get confused and eat the wrong ones."

His Lordship was taken aback for a second, and then realise she was joking and departed. As she always did, The Earth Mother waited for the footfalls to fade before speaking. When they did, they both burst out laughing.

The Earth Mother clapped her hand elatedly. "Well, Princess, tomorrow night at the festival, I know who will be first in line to honor you.".

The Princess let her eyes fall to the floor in embarrassment. "Yes, you do not have to be a mind reader to see his thoughts. She subconsciously rubbed her thumb across her fingers deep in thought. "Yes, but how will he be paired with me?

"Princess, everyone dancing will know who you are."

Mia's brow creased. "Really, how?"

The Earth Mother raised her eyes to the heavens. "Think about it. You're a foot taller than any other woman dancing, and your skin is olive-colored while everyone else is pale white. You will stand out like a sore thumb."

"Yes, of course, how silly of me, but how will I recognize him?"

"That is going to be the hard part. When his wife was alive, he always used the same mask year after year. It was a face mask made of feathers, the turquoise of the kingfisher, the whites of the swan, and the robin's red. He did not expect to be dancing, so he probably has not had time to prepare a new one. So hopefully, the mask should be the one we are used to."

The Princess looked troubled. "What if he didn't bring his old mask with him - I'll be stuck?"

The Earth Mother's mind moved quickly. After all, you didn't get to be 'Mother' by being slow-witted. "Ok, Princess, this is what we will do. I will have a word with Acolyte Simon, and he will assist his Lordship with his costume. When You're dancing, look to the Acolyte, who will give you a signal. He will move his staff from his left hand to his right, then turn his back to you when you have chosen correctly. You realize that I am only doing this because I think joining your two families is essential. The signs are good. They match perfectly, and I do not want our 'Primevil' brethren to get their hands on either girl.

"Thank you, Mother. You are as efficient as ever." The Princess bowed and left the tent. As her footfalls faded away, a second set followed her.

*

Midsummer's day finally arrived, the most celebrated day in the Pagan calendar. The daylight hours are the longest and usually the hottest days of the year. After the building of the Henge, this day could be predicted with accuracy.

The first Henge was made of wood and built while humankind was still hunter-gatherers. After studying the heavens for centuries, they began to understand the pattern of the seasons.

The Shamans could now predict when the seasons changed by positioning the trees and later upright stones in a particular position in conjunction with the sun and moon. For the hunter-gatherers, this gave them a significant advantage. It gave them time to stock up on food for the winter. The tribes would know when to cease following the herds and make camp for the winter months. They could now calculate what time of year would be best to have a child. The wise Shamans worked out that exactly nine months from midsummer's day took you to the twenty-fourth of March

In March, food was plentiful, and the women, not having to follow the herds of migrating animals, had rested for six of the most challenging months of the year. It was a win, win situation. To achieve this, you had to have rules. You could break them, but you would be at a disadvantage, and the survival of you and your offspring could depend on it.

The first rule was abstinence from sex as much as possible until the summer festival. If there were sex out of season and pregnancy, the healers or the medicine women would supply potions, enchantments and even physical intervention to stop it from going full term. For this reason, the midsummer festival was the highlight of the year. So much so that, three thousand years after humanity turned to the plow, it is still celebrated by those that still carry the memories, although in the utmost secrecy.

The Princess had been on edge all night, reliving the previous day's events. The girls had introduced the wolves to Lord Monkton's guards, who were instructed to observe them discreetly.

Hearing a voice behind her, the Princess turned to find Lord Monkton approaching.

"Good morning, Princess. Did you sleep well?"

"A little unsettled, I'm afraid, what the Earth Mother said to the two of us put me on edge. But it's a beautiful morning, a fine day for the ceremony. You're taking part, I see: your wife is pleased.

"Well, Princess, I haven't participated since my wife died, so I'm not sure."

The Princess waved her hands dismissively. "Lord Monkton, it wasn't a question."

"Oh! Is this something you have foreseen?" Her smile captivated him, but she did not answer his question in case he didn't participate.

From what I saw, all I can say is the lady will be well and truly honored!" The Princess laughed, her face full of life.

Lord Monkton took her hands in his and returned her smile, "Hopefully, we will meet at some point?"

The Princess raised her eyebrow. "You can count on it, my Lord."

*

The nurse tapped the hypnotist on the shoulder.

"Ask him to describe the scene. Ask him what happened to the children. Find out if they are involved in the ceremonies."

The hypnotist turned to the professor, who responded with a gentle nod of the head.

"Saul, I have always wanted to go to the midsummer festival, but we are not allowed them in London because of the puritan regime that runs the country. Could you describe what you see? Were you and Sarah involved?"

Oh, arr it were big day, always was. It were hustle and bustle from morning to dusk. People were preparing food, and cattle, pigs, and poultry in their hundreds were led off to be slaughtered. Stalls were set up to supply trinkets, you could get feathers of all colors, and sea shells, woad, and all sorts of body paints and cloth for the costumes. All people were busy like. There were barrels of mead, wine, and bowls of mushrooms were scattered everywhere.

This night was to be a celebration not to be forgotten - but it was not for us children. In the early afternoon, the children were taken to tents deep in forest where we played games. Just before dusk, all us children were led to the oldest oak groves in forest - where we would form a large circle and sit on the ground.

In the center of the circle, an elder would keep us entertained by telling stories. This was how we passed on knowledge down the ages. We used to start with a poem; poems are easier to remember, see - and us children would be encouraged to recite poems together. I remember first poem I ever heard. I was sitting with, Sarah. We watched wide-eyed as the old Druid settled on the roots of the oak tree. I had never seen anyone that old, his hair was long and white. And his voice echoed around the grove.

"Let me take you to a place, somewhere.
To show you the old ways man and time forgot.
Lives lost in scriptures of a bygone age.
Destroyed by oppressors and victors alike.
Scriptures, where characters leaped off their page
And escaped their ink and paper cage.
So, listen before an old man's memory fades,
I will take you to a place where all worlds meet,
Before my eyes grow dim, and my flesh grows cold.
I will pass on my knowledge, these ways of old.
Then I can rest and find my peace, my solitude.

Memories passed down will be restored once more,
From father to son, mother, and daughter the score.
I can at last find release from today's lies and deceit.
For in these tales is a place where all worlds meet,
Where old ways and new may come alive.
Only then can I rest in peace with my mind.
And I can leave the real world far behind.
Here the echoes of my lives will,
Teach and keep us connected still.
We will walk together and talk together.
Tread the unspoiled grass forever.
And when the time is right,
one day.
My memories and I will fly away."

"We would sleep in the tents all night, and for Sarah, and Ursula this was a new experience. The wolves were in earshot outside our tents. The soldiers, to their dismay, were guarding the girls, they weren't happy, they were hoping to join in with the dancing.

Dusk approached to find people still shuttling back and forth, making last-minute changes to their costumes and makeup. The costumes were scant and designed to attract, and the use of feathers was abundant. The white of the swan, the raven's black, the gray of the heron, and even the turquoise of the kingfisher were prized.

The grownups kept scuttling back and forth to stalls bartering for ornaments for their costumes. There were beads of wood in different colors, and strings of land and seashells arranged as frills or necklaces. Body paints of blue woad, reddish-yellow ocher, and white chalk were used to paint elaborate designs on their bodies. On their heads, they wore elaborate headdresses with feathers hanging from their hair and around their waist - the more daring the costume, the better. A simple mask hid the faces of all participants, and their costumes were hidden under a white Druid robe and hood which always covered the headdress. At the setting of the sun, the grownups would gather around one of the two inner circles of the Henge.

We always waited until the sun dipped below the horizon for ceremony to begin. A lone drum always started the festival. At the far side of the Altar Stone, a large luxurious red cushion was placed on the floor. Dozens of other sleeping mats were always placed around the Altar in a complete circle. All were positioned so that the narrow side faced the Altar Stone in the center. Then another row and another, so there were fifty sleeping mats emanating outwards from the Altar Stone in a circle. Looking from above, the Stone would stand for the sun. The cushions radiating outwards imitated beams of sunlight, the light of life.

With the mats in place, a single pathway was left from the circle of Standing Stones to the Altar Stone. Since time began, it was known as the decree aisle. The drumbeats faded into silence, and the anticipation of the crowd was always palpable.

The Earth Mother arrived at the sound of piped music and took her place on the large cushion sitting cross-legged and removed her shawl. She, as always, was naked and painted head to toe in red ocher to represent the blood the mother had shed to give birth.

This was the image passed down through our memories and it had to be recreated exactly to appease the creator of all things and mother to us all. Once the music stopped, the crowd stood in complete silence, waiting for her to address the congregation.

*

"Greetings my children, and welcome to the midsummer fertility festival at Avebury."

The crowd roared with excitement.

She paused, waiting for the congregation to fall silent.

"I will call on Shaman Bramel to conduct our sacrifice to the Earth Mother, creator of all things." Standing behind the Altar, the Shaman was handed a lamb. Two Acolytes held the creature down while the Shaman cut its throat. For an instant, it squealed and then fell silent.

Then, the Shaman ceremoniously held the knife above his head and waited until the crowd fell silent. When they did, he lowered the blade and dissected the lamb.

At this point in the ceremony, there was complete silence. The Shaman would consult with the creature's spirit, and he would examine every part of the lamb for omens. If they were favorable, and after consulting its spirit, the festival would take place, or they would all have to return home.

The Shaman stood back; he had finished. He signaled his two Acolytes to collect the parts of the creature and placed the remains on two plates. Turning to the Earth Mother's Representative, he made a signal to her.

The crowd waited.

The Earth Mother milked the occasion, stretching out the tension, and then nodded to the two Acolytes. This was a signal for the animal's remains to be returned to the forest. This gesture would appease the forest spirits and honor the sacrificial lamb, and its parts were to be left as food and not wasted.

The crowd roared. People who had attended before knew that this was the signal, and the omens had been good. Before the Acolytes left, the white blanket that covered the Altar was soaked in the lamb's blood, coloring it red, the holy color of life and the Earth Mother.

The first ceremony was the hand fast. This ceremony is for families or couples who wish to be joined together in marriage at a future date. They wore elaborate costumes to impress and enchant their partner.

All participants had the ground ivy vine tied to their wrists but not, as yet, joined. Both the women and men wore feather necklaces around their necks, and their bodies were scantily clad and decorated with runes and enchantments. They carried gifts to be presented to the Earth Mother, ready to place at her feet.

The waiting couples lined up in the decree aisle leading to the Altar. The crowd continued humming, a background noise that would continue throughout the whole ceremony.

The Shaman called the first couple, who approached the Earth Mother and stood before her. She blessed them in the creator's name, and the couple presented their offering to her and bowed. She then tied the man's left hand and the woman's right with the vine. They stayed bowed while she anointed them by painting a red line on the forehead of each. Then, still bowing, the couple backed away until the Shaman called the next couple.

The ceremony was repeated until all the couples were blessed and hand-fast. This part of the ceremony can take a long time, depending on the number of betrothals. During this period, the crowd continued to consume wine and anything else they wished, and the beverages were all designed to lower inhibitions.

The wedding ceremony was next. The drumbeat returned, a single beat slowly picking up speed; horn and flute followed. The first selected participants stood waiting. These couples wished to fulfill their hand-fast and be joined in marriage, and they lined up with their partners in the decree aisle. They, too, were scantily dressed, with the women wearing a simple veil covering them from their heads to their knees. The men wore elaborate headdresses and necklaces of feathers from the forest. Around their waist was a short skirt made of beads or frills, as with the hand-fast, the couples" bodies were painted with elaborate designs, spells, runes, and enchantments. Each of them had a vine around their wrist. Symbolically, it represented the same vine that joined them at the hand-fast ceremony.

The Shaman called the first couple forward. The couple approached the Earth Mother's representative, and they stood before her as she blessed them in the name of the Earth Mother. A gentle hum emanating from the crowd backed up by pipe and flute was always in the background.

The scene was one of love and harmony, and the crowd recognized it as the most sacred ceremony in both the 'Prime' and Druid calendars.

Once blessed, acolyte Simon and Priestess Sophia led the first couple to the Altar, where the man climbed up and lay on his back on the red covering. Priestess Sophia helped the bride to sit astride him. There was always an assumption that the bride would be a virgin, so to prevent embarrassment, the covering was already stained with the sacrificial blood of the lamb.

Between the Acolyte and the Priest, they gently guided the couple together. When her hymen had broken and witnessed, they once again knelt before the Earth Mother, who re-tied the symbolic vine that had bound them together at their hand fast.

In the eyes of the Prime Druid community, the couple were now joined in wedlock, and the applause from the onlooker intensified as the union was sealed with a kiss. By completing this simple act of penetration, they had honored the Earth Mother and consecrated their marriage.

The ceremony was repeated until all the couples had married.

When the last couple had been blessed, they all walked deep into the forest, where they honored each other in private for the first time.

With the weddings completed, the crowds, now in high spirits due to a combination of alcohol and narcotic mushrooms, started to stand, the excitement rising in anticipation of the last ceremony.

This was the ceremony most single people had traveled to participate in, 'The Dance of the Free Spirits.' It was a dance anyone could join in, but at this time, it was usually for people who, for some reason had lost or separated from their partner. The dance had its roots in antiquity from a time when people needed to replenish the tribes with children to keep it workable.

In those days, humankind was little more than animals. The tribes of hunter-gathers rarely met other groups because the population of Britain was so small.

These were loose groups of people. Usually comprising of an Alpha male that leads, a Shaman to converse with the spirits, and a Medicine woman.

The women of the tribes were high-ranking and usually owned a hearth of their own. This gave them status, and most men deSired a woman with children and a hearth. Here was a woman that the Mother of all had already blessed. To share her hearth would mean that, with her will, this woman would one day carry his child also.

The men would be gone on hunts for weeks, and life was fragile. It was customary for women to have many sexual partners within the group. At the midsummer meetings, there was a chance to meet new people and hopefully, new partners to possibly join their tribe, and it was this dance of love that is now called, 'The Dance of the Free Spirits.' It was also where people with a pure 'Prime' bloodline could seek out their own kind.

The dance was left until the end of the proceedings and generally continued throughout the night. The early Shamans introduced it to diversify the gene pool by mixing blood, and it was also the ceremony that Morag would be attending in the form of the Princess.

The gong sounded again, and the crowd roared, men were always on the right, women on the left. In loose pairs, they walked down the aisle towards the Altar Stone. On reaching the Altar they knelt before the Earth Mother, who blessed them individually by simply brushing them with an elder branch across each shoulder. The men turned to the right, the women to the left, and they formed a large circle.

The Earth Mother whispered to Mia when it came to the Princesses' blessing, but there was a sharp edge to her tongue. "Princess, we were overheard at the tent. I am sure the 'Primevil' know. Lord Monkton's mask has disappeared. It's up to you to find him." The Earth Mother brushed her with the elder branch on both shoulders, and then the Princess backed away to the left.

The circle of dancers was now complete. They removed their robes and let them fall to the floor. Again, the onlookers roared, edging them on. Both women and men wore very little. His Lordship wore a short skirt made of beads, just long enough to prevent embarrassment. Around his neck, a necklace of feathers spread out evenly around his chest, and everyone wore masks to hide their identity.

The Princess wore a turquoise face mask, and around her neck were several necklaces, her breasts were bare and stood out firm with gold tassels hanging from her pierced nipples. She had a gemstone in her navel, and around her waist, a green belt hung down with a gold buckle fastening just above her pelvis. The rest of the belt supported a short frilly skirt hiding very little. On her wrists, she wore several bands of gold. Her body was decorated with runes, magical symbols, and scrolls emphasizing her ample breasts and written in red ocher and blue woad.

Lord Monkton was dumbstruck. Her beauty filled his senses. Never had he seen a woman the likes of her. He felt the reaction between his legs and nervously looked down at the scant garment covering his privates.

The drumbeat sped up, and the participants began to dance. Many dance styles were being performed, but everyone was unique. The purpose was not to be part of the crowd. It was to shout out, this is me - I am the best. Some men encircled the women, captivating them within his own private circle. Some danced wildly erratic dances, showing off their athleticism. Some were slower and more fluid. The women tended to be more provocative, with gyrating bodies, and their arms moving in suggestive patterns.

The Princess chose a dance like a modern-day belly dancer, with bells on her fingers. Her hips gyrated seductively, enticing all who were nearby. Her suitors were many, and she danced with each, then turned away to try another.

For Morag, it was the dance of a lifetime. It was apparent that every dancer knew who the Princess was, this attention was a new and joyous experience. With the newfound ability of mind reading gained from the Princess, she could see the deSires of the others, and they were carnal and centered on her. Morag could also see who was 'Prime 'and who was Druid. But, unlike her ancestors, she was not here to procreate.

Morag felt the awakening of urges and deSire surface that had been lost for a decade or more - and squeezed her crotch tight with anticipation. *They all want me. This will be the best festival ever.*

The Princess, however, had other ideas. *Do not get carried away, Morag. There is more at stake than seeing how many times you can honor the 'Mother' in one evening. We must arrange the hand-fast for our daughters, and there is only one family suitable here tonight.*

The dancing became more intense, and the male dancers more forceful, several touching her seductively. One dancer wrapped his arms around her from behind, his hands cupping her breasts and pulling on the tassels that hung down from her nipples. She felt him rubbing his manhood against her buttocks, taunting her, teasing her, she gasped in anticipation, thinking it was his Lordship. When she turned around he was a foot smaller than her.

Again and again, she rejected them by turning away. It seemed like every man there wanted to couple with her and her alone. Morag was enjoying every minute. Never had she felt so elated.

However, there was only one man the Princess wanted. The second she had set eyes on his Lordship, she had decided she wanted to hand-fast her girls to his family. On the other hand, Morag wanted them all, never had she experienced such an urge to copulate on a grand scale. *The Earth Mother was right, I can have them all.*

The Princess's mind was working overtime. *Where are you, your Lordship? It's so hard to tell when none of the faces are visible. How am I going to find you? Ok, You're tall, as tall as me so that rules at least thirty out. He's heavily built, so that leaves another five out. He's in his forties, so those two are much too agile. This one has a blonde hairy chest, so that rules him out. That leaves just the one with the black hairy chest. Yes, it has got to be him. He's as big as I am. If you get this wrong, Princess, you've blown your cover as a seer.*

Concentrating now on this individual, she danced the most exotic dance her memories held. A dance several of her ancestors had used with success over many lifetimes. He, in turn, seemed captivated by her and danced with her alone. Other dancers tried to join in but they were simply rejected by turning their backs on them. More and more revelers were leaving the circle with their selected partners. The Princess took the hand of her partners, who bowed eloquently and the two of them joined the others and waited.

Eventually, the crowd fell silent as the last of the dancers' found partners, and everyone's eyes turned to the Earth Mother and waited for the signal. After a nod of her head, the Shaman struck the gong, and the couples ran to get to the cushions as close to the Altar as possible.

Seeing the most prestigious ones already taken by the young and agile, the Princess called to her partner. "The Altar, get to the Altar - quick."

Her partner hesitated. "You don't usually use the Altar in this country... It's sacred - for weddings."

She pulled him closer to the Altar and joked, "I'm from a different country, so how would I know? Be bold and go for it." He looked hesitantly towards the Earth Mother who had been watching and she nodded her approval.

Walking over to the Altar, he lifted her with ease and sat her down. All around them, the dancers proceeded to honor the creator, but the eyes of the crowd were on the Princess and her partner. She could sense their intrigue – she could feel their deSire. Once again, she was the center of attention – somewhere she always expected to be, and she reveled in it.

He went to join her on the Altar, but she placed both her hands on his chest to restrain him. For a moment, his Lordship faltered. Unsure, he looked into her green eyes, enhanced by the red from the fires, and gasped as he saw them darken. Her tongue circled her lips seductively, teasing him, tempting him.

The Princess leaned back on her elbows, lifted her bare feet to the edge of the Altar, and spread her legs wide-encouraging him. There were roars of encouragement from the watching crowd. Like all of them at the dance, she was naked under her short skirt, and his eyes were drawn to her source of pleasure as she continued to open and close her legs, tempting him like a moth to a candle.

He found himself transfixed, as his eyes took in every detail, every fold. He felt like a fly trapped in a spider's web. One false step and his soul would be lost. She presented the hint of a smile, and her eyes opened wide enchanting him, and drawing him closer to his doom.

The Princess was aware of his deepest deSires by delving deep into his mind. It was a tool her line had used since the beginning of time, a tool that set them apart and gave them complete control over men.

The crowd had fallen silent, and the audience waited.

Eventually, the Princess pulled his head to her groin and lay back in anticipation. His Lordship needed no further encouragement and searched for her special place, her place of pleasure. The crowd again roared their encouragement.

She gasped loudly so all could hear. "Yes, that's nice. Oh yes. Your wife said you were good, she was so lucky. A little higher, please, yes, oh yes, Holy Mother, yes. You are so strong – so much better than my husband."

Unbeknown to his lordship, the Princess's voice had taken on the subtle tones of autosuggestion. She moaned and arched her back. She could feel her nipples harden, and her respiration quickened in anticipation. There were continuing roars of encouragement from the onlookers. This was the reaction she wanted, and it was for their benefit, too, she could feed off their deSire.

When the Princess felt she was ready, she released his head from between her thighs and gasped. "I am ready, my Lord. Join me. You want me more than any woman you have ever seen, I can see it in your eyes. Never have you wanted a woman so badly. You have been looking for me all your life, waiting for me, take me now, and I will be yours forever."

Groaning in anticipation, he pushed her backward and cupped her breasts, one in each hand, took each nipple between his thumb and forefinger, and twisted gently. She moaned and screamed for the benefit of the audience. Her enchantment was working on them all, both men and women. She pulled him towards her and submitted like a virgin as he thrust forcefully time and again into her willing, expectant body.

The crowd continued to roar encouragement as they had done at this ceremony since the beginning of time, their 'Prime' memories as fresh today as it was at this ceremony for the early hunter-gatherers-whose sole aim was to mix their blood. As she began to climax, she howled like a wolf, and the crowd fell silent as the wolves of the forest replied.

As they lay on the Altar sated, the crowd's attention turned to the others. Still wrapped in each other's arms, his lordship gasped at the emerald green of her eyes and the unbelievable love he felt for her. He knew then his soul was hers forever. She ran her tongue around her lips, kissed him, and smiled contentedly. "We are now as one and I have finally found my one true love. You, my Lord, are mine."

The enchantment was embedded into his soul.

*

Couples that had honored the Earth Mother left the circle and made their way to the Standing Stones, where they watched and encouraged the young and more virile participants. Lord Monkton lifted the Princess off the Altar and joined them. Some would go back to the circle and dance again, seeking fresh partners and lovers. Others drifted away into the woods for privacy. The ceremony continued through the night as the participants' minds clouded in a narcotics haze

The Princesses' partner finally removed his mask and bowed.

Taking her hand, he kissed it. "Princess, I thank you for the honor. How did you know it was me?"

Her eyes locked with his and Lord Monkton gasped at their beauty, depth, and intensity and, for a moment, forgot to breathe, and as she smiled, his heart once again missed a beat.

"My Lord, I knew it would be you before I set foot in this land." The smile on her face was replaced by laughter, and she kissed him gently. "Don't look so surprised, my Lord. I am, after all, a seer, these things do not happen by accident, the Earth Mother guided me to you, and you, alone."

He held his breath as he measured her. "Why me, Princess?"

"She said you were my one chance of happiness and that our children needed to meet, she also said they could be the last hope for the true 'Prime.'

The Lord shook his head in disbelief studying every nuance on her face. "The last hope you say, what is it they are supposed to do?"

"Lead mankind back to the light, apparently, the 'Primevil' are getting too powerful." Mia took both his hands in hers and stared him directly in the eye, her melodic voice like smooth water at the top of a waterfall hiding the enchantment in the torrent hidden below.

"My love, the Earth Mother has decreed that both couples must begin a new 'Prime Dynasty.' We must guard them and guide them."

Lord Monkton shook his head in disbelief. "This is a lot to take in, Princess." For a while, he gazed into the distance with unseeing eyes. "I will think about it. In the meantime, I will understand it if you wish to return to the dance, every man here wants to honor you."

The Princess took his hands in hers, lifted them to her lips, and kissed them gently. She once again looked deep into his eyes. "There was only ever going to be one dance for me, my Lord. It was only ever going to be you."

She laughed openly.

"What is it? Why are you laughing?"

"It is I that am honored, my Lord, I told you yesterday your dance partner would be well and truly honored, well I am, and I need no other lover but you. Perhaps we can go somewhere quieter."

Morag screamed from deep within the mind of the Princess. *What! I never agreed to this. They all want a dance with me, so give me back control of my body.*

His Lordship kissed her hand. "Would you like to join me in my tent, Princess?" Again, Morag screamed. *No, not yet, we must go back, I've waited all my life for a dance like this.*

The Princess replied. *It is for the greater good, Morag. I foresee this man will comfort us both for many years to come.*

The Princess shook her head. "No, my Lord, but I would like to walk in the forest so we can be completely on our own." Her smile captivated his heart as it did for all men, and hand in hand, the couple wandered deep into the forest and finally found a grassy hollow. They lay together and made love at a gentler pace, honoring themselves and the "Mother."

Something moved in the undergrowth nearby. His Lordship was instantly alert. "Who's there?"

"I think it's Wolf, your Lordship. She's just keeping an eye on me. Sorry." She called out to the creature. "Wolf, go back to the girls." Immediately, the wolf could be heard moving through the undergrowth, back in the direction of the girls' tents.

"It's incredible, those giant creatures understand every word you say." Mia was savoring the moment in her lover's arms deep in thought. *I wonder what you would say if I told you I didn't need words.*

Suddenly the air was split with the loudest wolf howl imaginable. Mia sat bolt upright and screamed, "The girls!"

Within seconds, she was on her feet and running downhill towards the children's tents, His Lordship followed, hard on her heels.

After arriving at the tents, they found a scene of devastation. Everywhere people were lying on the ground, dead or unresponsive.

Mia burst into the girl's tent and found the occupants in their beds, fast asleep. She shook them hard, trying to wake them to no avail.

His Lordship, who had finally caught up, called out to her. "The girls, are they all right, Princess?"

Mia turned to Lord Monkton, her face ashen white with shock. "They are not here, my Lord. They have been taken. How could this happen? Where are the protectors?"

His Lordship turned on his heels, ran out of the tent and called back to Mia. "They are here - laying on the ground."

Still, in a dazed state, she walked over to them numb with shock. They were motionless on the ground. "Are they still alive, my Lord?"

"I don't know, Princess. You check."

She bent down and put her ear to their chests and listened. She then smelt their breath. "They have been poisoned, she said inconsolably, but they are still alive. What about your soldiers, my Lord?"

He turned and froze when he saw his men motionless on the floor. He checked on them, one after another. Then slowly, his eyes lifted to Mia's and he simply shook his head.

Pulling herself together, Mia looked in all the tents. "There are only two empty beds, my Lord, so I think it's just my daughters that have been taken."

His Lordship was overcome with shock, and his face was pale and drawn. He closed his eyes in dispute and turned to Mia. "Princess, if this is the work of the 'Primevil,' they must think they are exceptional in some way."

Mia said, "They are. I told you all our children are special. Mother was right - what have I done - I should have gone back to my country, and now your men are dead; they must have heard the gossip around the festival."

The love dance of the free spirits was now in its final throes. The Earth Mother rose, put on her shawl, and left the circle. The remaining participants were oblivious to her and were in no fit state to help anyway. With the aid of Shaman Bramel, she made her way to the girls' tent and went over to his Lordship.

"Your Lordship, what is the position? I have been told your men are dead?"

"All four, yes, and the Princesses have been taken. The other children are unconscious, but we are unsure if it is poison or just a sleeping potion. The wolves also look like they have been poisoned, but they are alive at present."

The Earth Mother moved over to the Princess, her anger rising at what she perceived was the cause of this outrage. She controlled her emotions but there was a sharp edge to her tongue. "Well, Princess, is this enough attention for you? I told you to be discreet, to blend in, and this is what happens when you draw attention to yourselves and let your girls ride in on the backs of giant wolves. You promised you would be discrete - you have caused this."

His Lordship was taken aback at the Earth Mother's outburst. "If anyone is to blame it is me." He said apologetically. "I promised her protection, but I underestimated the lengths the 'Primevil' would go to get the girls. I will go and arrange a search party to track them down."

The Princess interrupted. "Your Lordship, Mother is right. I have been stupid, but I do not think any of your remaining men are in a fit state to search for anyone tonight. Our priority is to treat these children before it's too late. I also need to attempt to save the protectors; we will need them to rescue the girls. Mother, if I could make a request, would you arrange for your best healers to assist me in helping the children and wolves, the ones that are still coherent?"

His Lordship looked shocked. He placed two hands on the Princesses' shoulders and shook her gently. "But your girls, Princess, my men and I must rescue them at once?"

As she examined one of the children, the Princess replied, "They will not harm the girls because they are too important. We will know where they are soon enough. They think my daughters are special, but they do not know how special."

8. THE 'PRIMEVIL' INITIATION 1985 AD

Professor Gaskill stopped the tape, and the room fell into silence. He cleared his throat awkwardly. "Well, that was interesting."

Mrs. Evan's neck had turned red, and she was fanning her face with several sheets of A4 paper. "Interesting! God, that was so hot, so descriptive." She walked over to the sink. "Wow, I need a glass of water." She sat back down and turned to the others. "Well, that seemed very realistic and informative."

Mr. Jones said thoughtfully. "Mankind has used the term 'Earth Mother' in the past, along with many others to portray a large voluptuous woman." He rubbed his chin thoughtfully. "I think these days the Druids have an Arch-Druid to oversee the ceremonies, and I am as sure as I can be they don't have mass orgies at midsummer."

"Your right, they could not keep something like that out of the press." Mrs. Evans picked up the pile of A4 sheets of paper, and once again began fanning herself.

Mr. Jones's gaze took in the recumbent form of Paul with renewed interest and had difficulty hiding his excitement. He cleared his throat awkwardly. "So, the Earth Mother represented these 'Prime' Druids, and her role is now lost in antiquity. Of course," He added, hoping that he had controlled the emotion from his voice. "We have found small figurines of fat, large-breasted women made from mammoth ivory and later clay all over Europe for over thirty-six thousand years. They have been called many things, 'Earth Mother,' 'Venus figurines' and 'Great Mother,' to name a few. So, it fits with this image Saul is describing."

"So," Mrs. Evans said thoughtfully. "When Saul said these Druids came for a dance for just one night like the hunter-gatherers - it was to spread the gene pool, nothing more. A right old orgy by the sound of it, at least the Romans got that right. No human sacrifice though, just the one lamb and his description was so vivid. I mean the Earth Mother, naked but colored red from head to toe. And the mats placed around the Altar, radiating outwards, imitating the sun and light."

The professor, forever the pessimist, again pointed out the negatives. "Again, we have nothing we can verify. This Morag woman is intriguing, she can disguise herself as another woman, and no one can see the difference. She can talk to animals and can read people's minds. Oh, and she is a seer and, like her daughter, can see the future, all very fantasy-like."

Mrs. Evans managed a faint interrogative, "Ah ...? Here we go again. We are doing Saul's life because we have no information about the Druids. Already we have a description of the ceremony, the standing stones, the dancing, the hand-fasting, and the marriages. And the Romans did say they could communicate with animals and birds, which in theory we can confirm. Professor, you are always so negative."

Mr. Jones hid the smile that had crept across his face. Mrs. Evans's outburst was totally out of character.

"No, Mrs. Evans, I'm just being professional. This is all just hearsay, nothing we can cross-reference. This word 'Prime' is interesting though. It seems to set them apart from the other druids, and he keeps going on about these memories being passed on."

Mr. Jones looked at the boy with renewed interest as he now knew that Paul was a stray, but he would keep that close to his chest. "When he introduced us to the festival." He added. and was pleased the excitement he felt was not reflected in his voice. "Saul said he could remember building the henge and hunting both the bison and mammoth."

"Another thing," Mrs. Jones added. "The description of the wedding and the hand-fast, very precise. Men walking one-way, women the other, and the type of clothing and how they decorated their bodies. And only having to penetrate the hymen to cement the relationship in the eyes of this, 'Earth Mother.' All fascinating stuff.'

The professor sighed and slumped down in his chair, defeated. "I was hoping to give my sponsors some exciting news, but I am not ready yet, most of this is hearsay. Mrs. Evans looked surprised and turned to face him.

"Sponsors?"

For a moment, the professor looked uncomfortable. "Err, yes, didn't I mention them?"

Mr. Jones turned abruptly to face the professor, and a feeling of dread began creeping up his spine. He glared at him. "No, you Didn't, who are they?"

The professor looked sheepishly away from them both. "A company called 'Lost Genealogy,' they are sponsoring hundreds of these trials. We are free to publish and take any credit for our findings." His voice had dropped to an awkward whisper, and he added. "After we let them see any data first."

Mr. Jones added dryly. "You should have told us, professor, we are a team." The feeling of dread had now centered on his heart.

The professor dismissively waved his arms. "It's all above board, and it just slipped my mind. Anyway, it is time to wake him."

As Paul Masters left the building, Jenny smiled and walked up to him. He did not return the smile and seemed lost in thought. She gave him a moment. Still, Paul said nothing. Slipping her arm through the crook of his, she walked in step.

"You, ok?"

"Just knackered." Still, he hadn't smiled.

She studied his eyes and tugged his arm playfully. "It's not me wearing you out, is it?"

Paul laughed. "No... Now you mention it, your athleticism isn't helping, but it's these blasted red dreams, I think I am going crazy."

"The ones you keep painting – the scary ones you said your mother and grandmother had?"

Paul sighed. "Yes, but it is wearing me down now, I can't sleep, and those lot in there are not telling me anything."

Jenny leaned across and kissed him on the cheek. "So, we will give it a miss tonight then. I just thought, being my mom is on a late shift, we could – you know?"

Paul glanced sideways at her. "What time does she finish.?"

She licked her lips seductively. "Ten."

He continued to study her face. "You still got the runes?"

She raised his brow. "I have stopped trying to remove them, and anyhow, I am enjoying the sex more than swimming. Anyway, don't worry if you're tired."

Paul squeezed her hand and finally smiled. "I can't fight off the power of the runes either. Your place it is then."

Later, Paul dropped into a deep sleep. They had only made love once this time but had managed to climax together. She didn't disturb him because it would be a good hour before her mother returned from work.

She studied his face and took in his features, his straight nose, his wavy hair, his lips, and his facial hair that seemed to get thicker every time she saw him. She turned her attention to his body, lean but quite muscular. She smiled as she realized the runes were still on his butt and wondered if he had retouched his up too. She was sure he had. Was she in love? She was not sure. Undoubtedly there was a strong physical attraction between them. The sex was great, but was that down to these magical runes he had drawn on each of them, pulling them together? Or was it lust? She hoped it was love. She had to agree he was troubled though, tormented even. Silently she hoped the regression trials would give him the answers he was looking for.

Paul called out in his sleep. "No, don't, please don't!" It startled her, and she went to wake him. She then stopped with her hand raised in mid-air, unsure what to do.

"Let me go!" He screamed again. She watched and waited.

Paul had broken free and was running through the forest. Branches and brambles scratched and tore at his skin, he didn't care, he had to escape. People were chasing him, but he was nimble, and he knew the forest like the back of his hand. They wore red robes. Red robes always terrified him, even though he was unsure why. He dived into a thicket of brambles, crawled beneath them, and frantically covered himself with dried leaves. He could hear them getting nearer and felt sure they could hear his blood as it roared through his veins. He held his breath and closed his eyes.

Hours passed, and he lay there, too terrified to move. It was dark before he heard people chanting in the distance. He cleared the leaves that were covering him and looked around. Lights danced through the bare-branched trees, below each light, a robed figure weaved its way to the Henge.

Leaving the safety of the brambles, he followed discreetly at a distance. Like a monkey, he climbed the old fir tree that he knew overlooked the Henge and waited.

The Henge was lit with flaming torches staked around the perimeter. The red-robed figures stood upright in a circle as a line of men and women were paraded before them like cattle. Each had a rope around their neck and fastened to the person in front. On reaching the circle, they knelt, head bowed, resigned to their fate.

Paul again called out, but it was a whisper, barely audible. "No, in the name of the Earth Mother, no." Paul's forehead was covered with sweat as his head thrashed from one side to the other. Jenny picked up her slip and mopped his forehead, unsure what to do. Then remembering Paul had said his mother told him he had to witness these dreams, she pursed her lips and reluctantly let him dream.

A woman was lifted to her feet by the rope around her neck, she did not resist as they removed her clothing. Meanwhile, her companions stared at the floor motionless. Four men lifted her into the air and paraded her horizontally around the circle. Each robed figure laid a hand on her head reverently as they took her to the Altar, where they lay her on her back with her arms and legs spread-eagled, which they lashed to posts fixed in the ground.

Still, she did not resist.

A giant of a man lay his hand on her head, and suddenly she appeared to be aware of her surroundings and began thrashing at her restraints - until she realized it was futile. Eventually, she lay still resigned to her fate. Paul watched, horrified, as the robed figures removed their clothing and took it in turn, to rape her. The crowd cheered and egged each rapist on. She did not cry out and did not scream. The onlookers fell silent when the giant ceremonially raised a dagger above his head. He lowered the knife in a sharp downward movement, then stopped just above her breast, and cut the restraints. The onlookers cheered and greeted the woman like a long-lost friend with open arms.

Once the greetings were completed, the giant led the woman who was still naked to the other participants. She walked up and down the line and chose another victim. After cutting the rope, she lifted her by the neck and handed her to the giant.

The procedure was repeated time and again, men and women. All appeared to be in a trance until they were lashed to the Altar.

One woman resisted more than the rest and screamed throughout the whole ordeal. When the giant raised the ceremonial knife at the end of her torment the crowd knew what to expect and began to chant. The giant brought the knife down hard into the middle of her chest several times, then after pulling out her pumping heart, held it aloft so all could see."

Paul screamed out. "No!" At the top of his voice and sat upright, his body covered in sweat. Jenny watched as he became aware of where he was. He had tears in his eyes and was almost crying.

She pulled him close to her and hugged him. "Another red one, I take it?"

He did not answer.

*

Since the disappearance of Paul's father ten years before, Joan Masters had gradually taken over complete control of the company. They had gone from strength to strength. Apart from the occasional meal, she had shunned other men. One day she knew Peter Masters would once again walk through the door after being released from some godforsaken prison where he had been held against his will – she was sure of it.

She played the tape on the answering machine once again. It was a man's voice and he was well-spoken, the accent, possibly English, maybe Australian. She did not recognize the voice. He wanted to meet up, his voice was anxious, even alarmed. She played the tape a third time and shook her head. "No, I don't recognize his voice, he is definitely not an old dinner date." She had spoken the words aloud for her own benefit as she was alone. She chewed her pen thoughtfully and dialed his number. After two rings, he answered.

"Thank God you called. Can we speak?"

"Who am I speaking to?" She said questionably.

"You do not know me, but I am Paul's hypnotist."

The color drained from her face, and a chill crept up her spine. She closed her eyes in anguish and shook her head. "What hypnotist?"

"I am assisting Professor Gaskill at the regression trial at the school."

Joan snapped angrily. "I have not given my permission for him to be hypnotized. How dare you hypnotize him!"

Mr. Jones fell silent. For a second and was lost for words. "What! I read the signed authorization form myself, we would never hypnotize any child without parental consent. Anyway, we need to talk."

Joan could feel her temper rising. "Dam right, we do."

"Mrs. Masters, I need to speak to you today, it is life or death."

It was at times like this that Joan felt alone. Peter's father was upstairs but now mentally incapable. Oh, how she missed the strength she gained from her husband's presence. She sighed heavily. "Come around now. Oh, do you have our address?"

"Yes, it is on the authorization form you didn't sign, give me twenty minutes - and don't speak to anyone."

Joan replaced the phone on the receiver and rubbed her temples anxiously. *Oh God, Paul, what have you done now?*

Peter's father's house was gated, and surrounded by CTV cameras. She watched the car as it pulled up and studied the man as he pressed the intercom button. "My name is Jones; we spoke a short while ago."

There was no answer, but the motor on the gates started to hum, and the gates began to open. He turned and jumped in the car. Joan noted how nervous he was as he scanned the area before driving in. She went to her gun locker, pulled out a revolver, checked to see if it was loaded, and placed it behind a cushion on the sofa.

The CTV showed the car pull up outside the front door and the man as he got out. A further CTV camera took his face as he pressed the doorbell. She was sure they had never met. With a feeling of apprehension, she opened the door. He was smartly dressed and appeared very nervous. She addressed him with a wan smile.

"Mr. Jones, I take it?"

He smiled weakly. "Thank you for seeing me so promptly. May I come in?"

She waved him in and locked the door behind her. He followed her into what appeared to be a reception room and gestured for him to be seated.

"So, you are my son's hypnotist, are you? You do realize he did not have my permission to be hypnotized?"

Mr. Jones placed the authorization form on the table.

Joan scanned it and shook her head in despair. "I'll wring his neck when he gets in - you realize it's a forgery."

"I gather that now Mrs. Masters, but he was very convincing. May I ask why you were so against him being regressed?"

Joan studied his features, trying to measure the man. "First, you tell me why you are here?"

Mr. Jones got to his feet and began to pace up and down and appeared to be deep in thought. Joan waited.

"Your son, to say the least, is a fascinating case." He turned and faced Joan and locked eye contact with her."

Her face gave nothing away, she was an outstanding businesswoman and knew how to debate. "Mr. Jones, would you get to the point? Her voice belied a certain amount of irritation."

"I believe you also experience your son's dreams, as did your mother-in-law?"

Joan did not answer and kept eye contact with him. He waited for the response and when none was forthcoming, he sighed heavily. "Mrs. Masters, I am your friend?"

Joan lifted her brow cynically. "Really, Mr. Jones, I have only just met you. How can I possibly know if you are a friend or not? Will you please get to the point?"

He again sat opposite her. "I have regressed Paul back to three previous lives." She did not react, so he again continued reluctantly. Two of his earlier incarnations I have been able to verify.

"And?" She said impatiently, "you said I am in danger. What is this all about?"

His eyes darted from side to side, and his voice fell to a whisper.

"If I were to say Paul is 'Prime,' would you know what I mean by that statement?" The room fell silent as each waited for the other to speak.

Eventually, Joan pressed. "'Prime' what?" She continued to study every nuance on his face.

He got up and once again began to pace around the room, then began to rub his hands through his hair, mentally searching for his next statement. "Oh God, you don't know what I am talking about – do you?" He rubbed his temples deep in thought, then sat down opposite to her once again, and turned to her. "You did not seem surprised that I had managed to regress your son. Why is that?

"I know Paul has had previous lives, we all have, I believe in reincarnation. He did not need to be regressed, that's why I didn't want him being hypnotized, you shouldn't be hindered by the actions of your previous lives - and he knows that too."

"And you have never heard the term 'Prime' before?" He watched as Joan blinked several times, unsure how to answer.

Mr. Jones's face lit up. "You have, haven't you?" The wan smile did not fall from her face, but she did not answer. "It's just that Paul has used the term several times in one of his previous lives - and I know what it means."

Joan presented her poker face giving nothing away. "So, Mr. Jones, why don't you tell me what it means?"

"It means Paul has descended from a tiny group of Druids that can remember their previous existences and recall their events and memories."

Joan looked at her watch and did not hide the irritation in her voice. "I will ask you one last time, why am I in danger?"

"It's not just you, but Paul as well. Mrs. Masters, if he lets it slip that either of you are 'Prime' your lives will be worth nothing."

Joan got to her feet, signaling to him that it was time for him to go. "I want this regression stopped. I do not know what you are talking about, but I will tell him not to mention it to anyone."

Mr. Jones remained seated. "The thing is," he continued. "And the reason for this impromptu visit is that I have been informed that the regression trial has been sponsored by a company called Lost Genealogy." He locked eyes with Joan once more. "It is a company I have never heard of. I have done some checking, and I can find no record of them. It's just that there are people that set traps for us, the 'Prime' that is, and this could be one of them."

Joan sat back down. "What sort of people?"

"They call themselves the 'Primevil. Have you ever heard of them?"

Joan shook her head and once again got to her feet. "Sorry, Mr. Jones, I do not know what you are talking about. When is Paul's next regression?"

"Tuesday at six."

Joan shook her head in dismay. "Gym club, I thought that was too good to be true. She rang the bell, and a servant came through. "Thank you for taking the trouble to warn me, but I really do not know what you are talking about."

As he turned to leave, he handed Joan a business card. "Ring me anytime, Mrs. Masters. If you see any strangers or have unusual phone calls, ring me."

The second the car left the drive, Joan turned to the filing cabinet, searching for her old address book. Finding the moth-eaten book that she hadn't seen for years, she thumbed through the pages, settled on a number, picked up the phone, and dialed it.

The Earlswood Manor reception desk phone rang three times before someone answered. She recognized the Welsh accent. "Jed?"

"Yes, who is speaking?"

"It's me, Joan Masters. You came to see me in America ten years ago."

The phone went silent for a time, then Joan heard the surprise in his voice. "Well. Well, Joan, how are you and your son, Paul is it?"

"Paul is a teenager now and a handful. That's what I am ringing about. Can we talk? I need some advice, 'Prime' advice?"

"Of course, you can, Joan. How old is he now? Thirteen, fourteen?"

Joan sighed. "Fifteen." Before she could continue, he interrupted.

"He should have recovered his memories by now, has he?"

"No, no, but he is troubled by those awful dreams I used to have. Anyway, unbeknown to me, Paul has been enrolled in a regression trial. The hypnotist has just called around to see me in a right state. He said that he is 'Prime' and thinks Paul is as well. Since you told me we should keep a low profile, I have told no one. He tells me that Paul keeps mentioning that he was 'Prime' in an earlier life, and it is all on tape. He is concerned because he has just found out the regression trial has a sponsor, a company called Lost Genealogy, and they have the right to examine the tapes before they publish the trial results. He said he could find no record of them, and he thinks it might be a 'Primevil trap.'" Joan waited, and the line fell silent. "You still there, Jed?"

"Yes, Joan." His voice was reflective, and she waited. "Do you have this guy's name and phone number?"

"Yes, I have his card in front of me, his name is Bryn Jones, and he is a professional hypnotist. He looked about fifty-five, maybe sixty-five."

"Is he Welsh?"

"No, I don't think so, not going by his accent anyway. Oh, and this company "Lost Genealogy – have you ever heard of it?"

"No, Joan, but I will make some inquiries and ring you back. It is the sort of trap they keep setting for us – you were right to call me. Joan, you must realize this is war, and they are winning hands down. Thousands and I mean thousands, of us are trapped each year, and it is never a pleasant death. Changing the subject, you say Paul has still not recovered his memories – he should have done by now?"

"No, but he is tormented because he does not understand what's happening to him. That's why he disobeyed me and signed up for this trial. I wish my husband were here to help."

"Peter is no longer with you?

Again, the line went silent before Joan responded. "He's traveling, and I don't know when he will be back."

"Look, Joan, when Peter gets back, the three of you fly out and stay at the hotel, and I can arrange to get his memories induced here at the henge."

Joan bristled. "What! No, no drugs, no way. After my problems with drugs in my flower power days, he is going nowhere near them. They must come naturally or not at all. Paul will be going to university in two years, if he has not remembered by the time he is twenty-five, we will talk then."

Jed sighed frustratingly down the line. "Joan, it's quite safe, and it's for his own good. When he realizes what he is capable of later in life, he will not thank you." When there was no response, he replied testily. "Very well, think about it. I will make some inquiries and ring you back." And Joan," his voice softened. "It is lovely to hear your voice again."

"You too, Jed, talk to you soon." Joan sat and stared at the phone, unsure of what to do next. Pouring herself a bourbon, she sat back and closed her eyes, weighing up her options. So many questions ran through her mind.

Should she have taken up his offer of inducing Paul's memories? Is this a trap? Is this Mr. Jones really 'Prime.' or could he be one of the 'Primevil' trying to trap her and Paul? Lost in thought, she drank the bourbon too quickly and choked. With tears in her eyes, she continued with her train of thought. *Both Jed and this Mr. Jones think we are in great danger if these 'Primevil' work out who and what we are. Oh, Peter, how I wish you were here.* Joan was disturbed from her reverie by a banging noise from the ceiling above. She downed the last of her bourbon and called out, "I'm coming, grandfather, no peace for the wicked."

9. THE SPONSOR'S 1985 AD

Joan Masters stared at the CTV screen. The image was distorted by rainwater on the lens. A car pulled up at the electric gates and before the driver could get out, she pressed the button to activate them. She stared at the sheets of rain sweeping across the yard, dark and gray reflecting her mood.

She met Mr. Jones at the front door herself as he dashed in to avoid the downpour. She gave him a weak smile and at once pinched her lips straight. "Do come in, Mr. Jones." He followed her to a different room this time, furnished lavishly, a sitting room. She gestured for him to be seated on one of the sofas, and he sank into the soft leather as he did so. "Drink?"

He eyed her warily. "Err, coke, please-I'm driving."

"Ice?

"Yes, please." He studied her as she poured him a coke and added bourbon to hers. She was attractive, even, charismatic, and was beginning to age gracefully, her hair, showing the first signs of gray was hanging loose. She had strikingly green eyes, and he wondered if they were colored contacts. Her clothes were casual but expensive. She was used to money.

She handed him his drink and sat on the chair opposite, crossed her legs, and locked eyes with him.

"I owe you an apology, Mr. Jones." She presented him with another weak smile, but it left her face moments later. "I have made some inquiries since we last met. You are known to be 'Prime,' by my acquaintance, I had to be sure you see." She took a sip of her bourbon. "You can't be too careful. So, Paul has compromised us both."

His forehead creased with a frown. "I hope not, and I understand your reaction to my first visit. May I ask who your friend is?"

Joan looked warily at him. "No, you don't need to know that, but he has confirmed to me that you are a true colleague. So, Mr. Jones, how do we rectify this?"

He shrugged his shoulders and sighed. "Did your friend have any information about this company, 'Lost Genealogy?'"

She took another sip of her drink, swirled the remainder around her glass, and stared into the liquid, searching for the correct words. "He agrees with you, it's probably a trap. They have used this scam in dozens of countries, and it is a well-known ploy. They set up these trials looking for sleepers, or as we now call them 'strays,' who have, for whatever reason not recalled their ancestral memories and are unaware of who and what they are. He does not know the numbers, but he reckons it is in the thousands each year worldwide."

Mr. Jones looked stunned. "Your friend is very well informed, and I had no idea it was so widespread. Is your friend local? There are so few of us left these days, and I could do with meeting…."

"As I said, Mr. Jones, the less you know about him, the better. There is a reason, you see. Are you sure you would not like a stronger drink?

He eyed her suspiciously. "No, why?"

"There is something you don't know about these trials."

His eyes remained locked on hers. "Go on."

"Paul and I are not the only ones in danger." She took another sip of her drink and again stared into the glass. "It seems when one of these trials unearths a stray, they become prone to accidents, fatal accidents. I am afraid they leave no witnesses." She paused to let him absorb the information and saw the color drain from his face. He ran his hands through his hair and bowed his head in submission.

"Oh shit."

Joan finished her bourbon, got up, and poured herself another. "Yes, aptly put …. bourbon?" He shook his head silently in denial. Joan sat down, tucked both legs under her, and lay back casually. He studied her and wondered just how many drinks she had had. "Mr. Jones, do we know if this company has been kept informed regarding Paul's regression?"

He gave a rueful smile and said thoughtfully. "I will have to ask the professor, until our last session, I was unaware there was a sponsor. At the last meeting, he said that he was hoping to give them some good news but was unsure whether Paul was making the whole thing up or not."

Joan's mind, as always, was razor-sharp. "So, the way I see it, we have two options. We discredit Paul's trial as a prank, or I get all the proof back myself - tapes everything." For a moment, the room fell silent.

"That is only going to work if he has not already kept them informed, I will have a word with the professor."

"If I remember correctly, you said Paul's next regression is Tuesday at six." She watched as he nodded in the affirmative. "In that case, I will call around during the regression, so Paul is unaware I'm there and debunks his recollections. It would help if you told me everything he has said so far,

For once, his face lightened. "I can do better than that, I have copied all the tapes." He placed them on the table in front of her. "I'm sure you will find them most enlightening."

*

The following Tuesday Joan watched her son walking hand in hand with Jenny whatshername openly across the schoolyard, and she shook her head silently. His hair reached down to his shoulders, and she mentally decided it was time for a haircut. They did not seem to have a care in the world. Paul hitched his sports bag onto his other shoulder, turned, and gave her a light kiss. It was pleasant seeing his loving side, she sighed, momentarily lost in thought. *Young love. They would not be as carefree if they knew what I know.* Paul walked past the gym into a building on the far side of the yard. *So that's where the professor's office is.* She sat back and waited.

Joan opened the folder in front of her and rapidly scanned the A4 pages. Pages she had virtually copied word for word from the tapes. She memorized as much as possible and chewed her lip thoughtfully as the storyline progressed. Jed had helped Joan ten years before, teaching her how to meditate and control the voices from within. She could recall specific snippets of information from earlier lives, but she knew deep down she was only remembering the tip of the iceberg.

After reading the transcript of Paul's regression, she was stunned at the detail and wondered if she should have her memories induced as Jed had advised one day. She shuddered; did she want to remember? Jed had said she would gain immense knowledge and possibly even recall the answer to what they call, 'the first question,' the meaning of life. Joan wasn't sure if she wanted to know that either. She looked at her watch, the session was thirty minutes in.

She tucked the folder under her arm and made her way to the professor's study. She pressed her ear to the door and could hear Paul talking. Silently she slipped inside, and all eyes turned to her in unison. The professor put his finger to his lips, signaling her to be silent. She realized Paul was in a deep hypnotic state and sat down without being invited and began to listen to her son.

*

The Earth Mother herself checked the children and breathed a sigh of relief. "The children will be ok their breath has a distinct smell. It's just a sleeping potion."

The Princess, however, thought the wolves had been poisoned. "In that case, if you can look after the children - may I have your permission to treat the wolves because I might lose my daughters without them?"

"Go ahead." She said impatiently. "The children are not in any immediate danger." The Princess asked one of the healers to fetch certain herbs and spices to prepare a broth for the creatures. The healer scurried away.

Mia turned to the Earth Mother. "I also need charcoal."

The Mother shook her head and her face reflected her bewilderment. "The best I can offer is the burnt wood surrounding the fire's hearths."

"That will do nicely. However, I need some way of administering the broth." She turned to his lordship. "My Lord, would you have a hunting horn I could use? I will have to destroy it."

"I have one in my saddlebag, I will get it." He turned and ran.

The Princess called out to stop him. "Can you cut the end off so I can use it as a funnel?"

"Of course."

The healer returned with the ingredients for the concoction, followed by a second person carrying charcoal.

The Princess placed all the ingredients into a bowl, and with a pestle, she ground the ingredients together and finally added hot water. The smell was obnoxious. She then added as much charcoal as she could, and the result was a black, unpleasant-looking liquid.

His Lordship returned with the horn moments later and handed it to the Princess.

"Will that do?"

"Yes, that's excellent and it will do nicely. If you could lift the wolf into a sitting position, so her head is above her stomach please."

The wolf was heavy, so he called over a couple of men who between them sat it upright. The Princess held the horn to the creature's mouth and poured the liquid into it. After emptying the bowl, she did the same to the second animal. She then stood back and studied both creatures. When she was satisfied she turned to the onlookers. "Thank you everyone all we can do now is wait."

Mother had been watching the proceedings and called the Princess over to her. The herbs you used, I can understand, but the charcoal, why charcoal?"

"It is a remedy from one of the Princesses' memories. She believes it will soak up the toxins or poisons. I only hope it's not too late - the quicker you can administer it, the more effective it becomes. How are the children coming along?"

Mother gave Mia a comforting smile. "They will sleep tonight the sleep of the dead - but at least they will wake tomorrow."

"In that case, I can do little here, so I will go and rest in my bed."

The Earth Mother looked aghast. "Princess, how can you sleep at a time like this?"

Princess Mia waved her arms dismissively, "who said anything about sleep? I am going to call a bird. Will you let his Lordship know what I am doing, and maybe he could put a guard outside my tent?"

The Earth Mother nodded her approval. "Of course, Princess, but wait for the guard before meditating. Will you use the owl again?"

"Yes, it's by far the best bird for the night flying."

The Princess returned to her tent, lay on the bed and immediately began to call an owl. She didn't want any owl as there were unknown dangers ahead, she wanted the biggest in the forest, the European eagle owl.

Minutes passed. Gut it seemed like hours, then as silent as the night an owl arrived by her bedside. Mia was lying on the bed in a deep meditative state. A glow spread out from her head and encompassed the bird. Then as silently as she arrived, the bird flew back into the forest, taking the spirit of the Princess with it.

Flying high, the bird began a spiral search pattern of ever-increasing circles. It flew ten miles from the henge before spotting the kidnappers. They had camped, and all were asleep except for one guard.

The owl flew down to the girls, a phantasm to the slumbering guard.

The owl started to pull the blanket away. Both girls were startled for a second but soon realized what was happening.

"Nana?" They said in unison.

Yes, girls, it is your mother and me. Are you all right? Have you been harmed?

Sarah replied, "We have not been harmed, we have only just woken. What is happening mother, why have we been brought here?"

They are not the ones who were watching over you last night. The four men that were guarding you are all dead. Girls, the people responsible for this are the 'Primevil.' They are devious wicked people who will stop at nothing to get their way. Do not antagonize them. Do everything they say. They want your gifts and your powers, so they will not harm you. Pretend you're listening to their falsehoods, find out as much as you can about their plans, and look for any weaknesses. If you move on before we get to you, try to leave a trail, but do not do anything stupid. If you make a plan, discuss it together so that Ursula can foresee any possible outcome. If that path fails, make another until Ursula finds a safe one.

Sarah whispered to the owl, "I will speak to the forest's creatures, and they will tell you where we are."

Mia said. *You forget, Sarah, that we can't talk to them like you, so we would not understand.*

"Then I will get them to talk to Saul. Yesterday, I taught him the basic technique of doing it, and he seemed to pick it up straight away."

The owl turned its head in surprise. *Saul can talk to the creatures too?*

"Yes, as I said, he found it quite easy."

That's good news girls. I must return now as they have poisoned your wolves, so I must treat them. I just wanted to let you know that we will come and get you.

Sarah's eyes began to fill with tears after hearing about their protectors. "Nana, please, you must make Ghost and Shadow better."

We will do all we can. Get some sleep as tomorrow is going to be a busy day.

The owl turned and as silently as he came, was gone.

Arriving back at the tent, the owl landed on the floor. His Lordship, who was sitting by the Princess, was quite startled. The owl ignored the Lord who could only stare in awe as a glow emanated from the owl and encompassed the head of the Princess.

A minute later the owl turned and, in an instant, was gone.

His Lordship took the Princess's hand as she began to wake.

"Are you alright, Princess? Did you find your girls?"

Gradually she became more and more aware of the world around her. "Your Lordship, you watched over me. Thank you."

His Lordship repeated himself. "Your girls, did you find your girls?"

The Princess sat upright and was, by now completely awake. "Yes, they are about ten miles away. Four men have them, and they are unharmed. I told them to get some sleep and not to worry. Your Lordship, according to Sarah, Saul can converse with the creatures of the forest - did you know this?"

His lordship looked puzzled. "This is news to me - are you sure you're quite awake?"

"Sarah said that she taught Saul how to do it yesterday – apparently - he found it quite easy."

His lordship was astounded. "Do you mean the rumors that your youngest girl can bewitch animals is true?"

"Yes, they are true, and it's one of the reasons the 'Primevil' want them."

"Does that mean your eldest daughter really is a seer at five years of age?"

Mia cupped his Lordship's head and kissed him gently on the lips. "Yes, and at six, your youngest son can already talk to animals. It seems the Earth Mother was right, our children are exceptional."

"Princess, I must ask, did you induce their memories."

Mia glared indignantly at the Lord. "No, of course not. In my line girls start to recall their memories from the age of three upward. The older they get the more they recover. By the time they reach puberty, they are fully conscious. At present, my girls only know a fraction of their gifts, but they seem to be able to control their emotions from their earlier existences and take them in their stride.

How about you, my Lord? Were you induced, or did you simply recover them yourself?"

He shook his head. "I was induced at fourteen, but Maria's came naturally to her by the time she reached puberty. Anyway, your girls are safe, and that's good news."

The Princess turned to face the Lord, her voice was restricted by the need to know and her eyes took in every nuance of his face. "The wolves, my Lord. How are the wolves?"

His Lordship's face darkened, turning his eyes away from hers.

"I am not sure, Princess, so maybe we should check on them." They made their way to the Earth Mother.

The Earth Mother looked surprised to see that the Princess had returned already. "Do you have any news? Did you find them?"

"Yes, Mother. They are about ten miles south of us and are unharmed. I told them to get some rest, and I informed them that we will rescue them as soon as possible. How are the wolves doing?"

"They are responding well. It seems your charcoal is working its magic. They have both vomited, so that should be a good sign."

"Good, good. That's what the broth was for."

Mia turned her attention to the wolves. They were laying on their sides, she fussed them and smelt their breath. The Princess looked up to the Earth Mother and smiled weakly. "Thank you, Mother. I think they will be fine, so there is nothing more we can do tonight, it's been a busy day and I need to rest. The Princess directed her gaze to his Lordship and she held out her hand.

"I could do with some protection tonight. May I join you in your tent?"

"Of course, my Princess. It will be an honor."

Although she was tired, the Princess found sleep hard to come by. She realized what the Earth Mother had said was true. She had been foolish and should have been more discreet. Now four men had died and she could have lost two of the protectors. Her mind was alert to the fact she nearly broke the line of the protectors. It was something she hadn't foreseen and resolved to breed them again if they survived.

After dawn, she went down to check on the wolves, and all three came to greet her. She sighed with relief and silently thanked the Earth Mother for returning them to her. After checking first Ghost, and then Shadow, she could see they would survive. However, she did sense distress, extreme distress because they were separated from the girls.

"Don't worry. We will go and find them shortly. Now you must go and hunt, for you will need your strength today."

The wolves trotted off into the forest. Turning, she saw his Lordship walking towards her. He had a smile on his face.

"Morning, Princess. Your wolves seem to have recovered."

"Yes, they will be fine and have just gone to get some food, they will need to build their strength up today.

She shielded the sun from her eyes with her hand and looked up at him. "Did I wake you this morning, my Lord? I couldn't sleep."

"It is understandable. I, too, had had a restless night. We need to consult with the Earth Mother."

"We will consult with Mother, but first, we must eat, as we will also need our strength today."

Lord Monkton was taken aback by how casually she seemed to take it all. "Princess, I'm surprised how calmly you are taking this. Let's go now, we must find them quickly."

The Princess shook her head, disagreeing with him. They will have moved on by now, so we will have to wait until they get in touch. First, get your men fed, armed, and ready. You need to get Saul. I can communicate with my wolf, but not the forest creatures."

His lordship shook his head in disbelief. "Princess, as far as I'm aware, Saul has never communicated with any of the forest creatures, even if Sarah says he can."

"Your Lordship, I had watched the two of them together when they were alone in the forest on the second day. The forest creatures trust Saul, just like they do Sarah. They feel comfortable around him, that's a sign they can sense he means them no harm. We should take him with us just in case he can."

After eating, they met up with the Earth Mother, who was accompanied by Shaman Bramel. The four sat cross-legged on the floor in her tent, discussing what they should do to rescue the girls.

The Earth Mother spoke first to the Princess. "So, you believe the girls will get in touch with us through the forest's creatures?"

"I do not doubt it, Mother. They will get in touch shortly. If they do not, I will call a bird again. Do we know of anyone leaving the ceremony early? If we do, it may give us a clue as to who the kidnappers were?"

The Shaman replied quickly to this question. "Many have left already your highness. It is quite normal after the dance of the free spirits, and people who have traveled great distances always tend to go early."

Mother interrupted him. "Thank you, Shaman, but get the Acolytes to list who has departed anyway. This may give us an advantage in future dealings with them. Quickly do it, this is very important before any more depart." The Shaman left the tent and hurried away. The Earth Mother turned to the Princess and addressed her.

"If we have not heard from them in the next two hours, the search party should head south to where you saw them camped last night. We can then at least follow the trail, and you, Princess, can call one of your birds to start a new search. She turned her attention to the Lord. May I have your thoughts, please?"

"I agree, Mother. I would add that I think we should go now as the trail will be fresher. I have instructed my men to take provisions for several days. If we get a message, we can leave in an instant if that is all right with you, Princess."

"Yes, your Lordship. Please continue to make your preparations. I too, will get my horse and traveling tent ready."

His Lordship left, and the Princess bowed her head. These words were for the Earth Mother alone.

"Mother, please forgive me for I have been foolish and have cost good men their lives, and before long, more will die. I never dreamt they would take them with the Lord's men and the protectors guarding them."

The Earth Mother waved her arms dismissively. "I too underestimated them, Princess. Somehow, they deduced how powerful they were from what possibly was a childish prank between your girls. They were so sure of this power that they were even prepared to kill. They must have sensed something we have missed. It is possible that one of them, or even both, has a dark side they have sensed before we could."

Both women fell silent for a while, lost in their thoughts. Finally, the Princess commented. "I have watched them grow and I believe both girls have good hearts. Ursula is quick to temper, and she does not like Sarah to better her at anything, but this is quite normal for girls so young. When we arrived on the first day, I sensed an unusual pleasure in her for putting the Shaman down by implying he was just the son of a carpenter."

The Mother gazed into the distance with unseeing eyes, deep in thought. "That is interesting but not necessarily a sign of evil. Yes, but thinking about that. Anyone listening would have found it very interesting that she knew the Shaman's father's" occupation without hearing it from you."

"Yes, Mother. It could have been anyone in that crowd, and half the congregation was there.."

"So, Mia, we are no better off, but a misplaced word like that is all it needed to alert them." The Acolytes Simon and Steven then rang the bell on the tent, and the Earth Mother's voice from inside the tent bid them to enter.

Acolyte Simon spoke first, addressing the Princess. "I am happy to report all three wolves have returned from the forest, and all the drugged children have now woken from their slumber. All seem perfectly fine."

The Princess greeted the news with a smile. "Excellent, Acolyte Simon, but what of the list you were requested to make."

"List your highness?"

"The list of people who have left the festival early."

"I know of no list, your highness?"

The Earth Mother now interrupted the conversation. "Acolyte Steven, do you have the list?"

"Mother, no one has asked me to make a list either."

"So, you say that Shaman Bramel did not ask you to do this task within the last hour?"

"That is correct, Mother, but we will see to it at once."

Mother once again waved her arms dismissively. "It is too late for that. Would you find the Shaman and bring him to me now?" The Acolytes turned swiftly and left the tent.

"Mother, what is it? What are you thinking?"

"Princess, the Shaman knew how important it was to find out who left early and who could have been responsible for taking the girls, yet he did not pass on my instruction."

The Princess, her mind drawing the same conclusion, added. "He also could have been alerted by Ursula's knowledge of his father's occupation." Acolyte Simon then ran back to the tent, stopping to ring the bell.

"Acolyte, what news do you bring me?"

"The Shaman is not well. He is in his tent, and we cannot wake him." The Earth Mother and the Princess looked at each other, a frown forming on the Earth Mother's face.

"Thank you, Acolyte Simon. Would you get a healer to quickly check him for drugs or poison?" He again turned and fled.

"So, Princess, we have two possibilities. Either the Shaman has been poisoned, or he is trying to contact them and is in a deep meditative state."

The color left the Princesses' face, and it became that of a corpse as the feeling of dread crept up her spine.

If the Earth Mother's face were not still colored red from the ceremony, hers, too, would have blanched and she bit her lip thoughtfully.

The Princess expressed her concerns verbally.

"If he is meditating, his spirit could have left his body and is now on its way to pass the information to his brethren, and the kidnappers will be aware Sarah can contact us through the forest creatures - and that we are waiting for a message."

"Then the girls are in considerable danger, Princess. We must act fast. Go and check on the Shaman yourself and send the Acolytes to me. Go quickly."

Arriving at the Shaman's tent, the Princess found an elderly healer checking him over.

"Healer, I am Princess Mia. May I enquire as to the Shaman's health please?"

"Yes, Princess. I am aware of who you are. The Shaman, in my opinion, is simply meditating. I have only made a preliminary diagnosis, and I can find no signs of poison. His breath does not smell, and his pupils react to light. I do not think we should worry too much. He will be fine, but I think we should let him wake up in his own time."

"If I could check him as the Earth Mother is quite worried about him."

"Of course, Princess, please do."

The Princess double-checked the healer's findings. "Thank you, healer. I agree with your diagnosis, and I will tell Mother that she has nothing to worry about."

Turning quickly, and with her heart filled with dread - she made her way back to the Earth Mother. Arriving at the tent, she found she was in conversation with his Lordship."

"Well, Princess, what is the news of the Shaman?"

"It is as we feared, Mother. The Shaman is in a deep Shamanic trance."

The Earth Mother staggered, and both Mia and his lordship grabbed her arms to support her. They lowered her to her bed and placed a cushion under her head.

She gasped "Then we must assume he is trying to contact the kidnappers, and the girls are now in great peril. They have taken two of our most promising sisters from under our noses, this is a violation, an outrage. The most promising we have had for thousands of years, theirs to manipulate and control and turn to the dark."

Mia shook her head in despair. "This could be the end of all 'Prime.' And my poor children could be lost forever.

An agonizing scream left Mia's mouth and it was the cry of a wolf.

*

Joan Masters cleared her throat, and the hypnotist eyed her warily.

Her voice was barely audible. "You need to stop."

The expression on the professor's face was as dark as thunder. He turned to the hypnotist and drew a finger across his throat, indicating that he should do as she requested. "I take it you are from the sponsors?"

Her voice was set with anger. "No, professor, I am Paul's mother."

10. WHITE DREAMS 1985 AD

Mr. Jones instructed Paul to go to sleep, and all eyes turned to Joan Masters.

"Firstly, professor, you are regressing a minor without parental consent."

The color drained from his face. He lost his composure and eyed her suspiciously. "What? Why?" No, that is not possible, I have his consent form here."

He got to his feet, then opened Paul's file, took out the consent form, and slapped it on the table in front of her.

Joan scanned it and shook her head.

"It's a forgery, professor. I told his tutor in no uncertain terms that he was not to be hypnotized, yet no one thought to check with me. I can have your job for this, God knows what damage you have done?"

Shock stole his breath, and he collapsed back into his chair. She watched as he massaged his temples nervously. When he spoke, it was barely audible.

"He was very convincing, Mrs. Masters, and is the most amazing subject I have ever come across. So far, he has recalled multiple lives."

Joan sneered, her voice cold and calculated. "Lives like the one we just heard. A woman's conscience being carried by a bird, and people talking to animals, really, professor? God, where do they find people like you? What other lives has he recalled?"

The professors' voice and confidence were broken. "A - a soldier who died on the beaches of Normandy in the D-Day Landings."

She pursed her cheeks together, turned, and fired him with a stern look. "Did you get a name, rank, and regiment?"

The professor's face brightened momentarily. "Yes, Private Jamie McFadden 22nd Armored Brigade, he even gave his commanding officer's name when prompted. We checked them all, and he was correct in every detail."

Joan laughed sarcastically. "I take it You're talking about Brigadier Hinde, Professor?" The professor closed his eyes in anguish but said nothing. "He is family on my husband's side, Paul is fooling you."

Mr. Jones interrupted. "I can assure you, Mrs. Masters, Paul was, and is, in a deep hypnotic state."

Joan waved her arms dismissively. "That may be, but Paul knows everything about the Normandy landings, he wrote an essay on it last year using his great uncles' diaries. And this charade, I am afraid professor, is a reenactment of the novel I have been writing for several years, almost word for word. She again waved her arms in the air. "For God's sake Professor, I mean, talking to animals!"

She opened her bag and placed the manuscript in front of him.

"If you don't believe me read it. I was on my way to my proofreader but I thought I would pop in and see Paul at his gym club, only to find he hadn't joined, and they told me to come here."

The professor quickly scanned the manuscript and fell silent. After several minutes he threw it back down on the table. "Dam and blast." He looked at his colleagues. "It's almost word for word."

Ms. Evans shook her head sadly. "Well, he had me fooled, there was so much detail. Has he done this deliberately?"

Mr. Jones commented. "He was always in a hypnotic trance, so it is not deliberate. He is probably bored with his life and fantasizes about the characters in Mrs. Masters' book, the same with the battles of the 22nd Armored Brigade." He turned his eyes to the professor, measuring every nuance on his face. "Thank God we did not inform the sponsors."

The professor's eye's blinked rapidly, and his gaze fell to the floor.

Joan got to her feet and glared at the professor menacingly, her voice cold and threatening. "I will take every tape you have of my son's regressions, and I mean every single one!"

She turned to the hypnotist angrily. "And you will remove any lingering memories of this event! He must be removed from the trial at once, or my lawyers will be camped out on the dean's doorstep tomorrow morning! Do I make myself clear?"

The room was silent, the atmosphere oppressive. The professor wearily got to his feet and handed the box of tape and Paul's file to her. He was visibly shaken, and his voice, broken. "I – I do apologize, Mrs. Masters."

She glared at him. "And the one in the tape deck."

He seemed to shrink and diminish. "Err, sorry, of course."

"You." Again, she turned to the hypnotist. "Will inform my son that he has been excluded from the trial - do I make myself clear?" He nodded in the affirmative, and Joan left, slamming the door behind her.

When he heard the outer door shut, Mr. Jones turned angrily to the professor. "What have you told the sponsors?"

The professor sighed heavily. "Not much, really.

Mr. Jones glared at him. "You are messing with my reputation. What have you told them?"

"It was just a bullet sheet I had to fill in after every session. There are certain names they are interested in, and if we came across them, we were to inform them straight away."

Mr. Jones could feel the chill creeping up his spine. "What names?"

"Oh, in our case, just the one, 'Prime.'"

The chill reached the hypnotist's heart as his worst fears were laid bare before him. They were obviously the 'Primevil' and were searching for strays or the 'special one,' as Joan's informant had predicted, and they had been caught hook, line, and sinker. He had slept little the night before, and his next move had been prepared for in advance.

"I will make us all a coffee, who wants one?"

Mrs. Evans smiled wearily. "Make mine a strong one." The professor simply nodded, and the atmosphere in the room was one of gloom and dismay.

"So, we are down to three subjects, and their answers are simply monosyllables. No detail, nothing that can help us prove that transmigration of the soul is a possibility. Mrs. Evans walked over to the professor to comfort him, and when she did, Mr. Jones slipped a sedative into both their drinks.

As soon as Paul was brought out of his regression, he could sense the oppressive atmosphere in the room. He looked at his watch and saw the session had finished twenty minutes early.

He scanned the professor's face. "Why have we finished so early?"

The professor pensively regarded the rest of his coffee in his cup, finished it, and stood up. "I am sorry, son, this is as far as we go with your regression trial. We feel that we have found no proof of any earlier life experiences. You have been dropped from the trial."

Paul was dumbfounded. He was sure they would find something. He shook his head in disbelief and replied angrily. "Four weeks, it took you four weeks to decide that!" He looked at each of them in turn, and they turned their eyes from his one by one. "Four bloody weeks, and that's it?"

The professor shrugged his shoulders. "Sorry, son."

With a face like thunder, Paul stormed out of the room and slammed the door behind him, and once again, the room fell to silence.

"He took that well." Ms. Evans said, trying to break the mood. She finished the rest of her coffee and sank back down into the sofa. "God, I'm tired.

The professor opened his file. "The girl, Judy Marshall, is next."

Judy Marshall lay back on the sofa and closed her eyes in readiness. She was a pretty girl with short blonde hair that appeared natural. Judy was slightly overweight but carried it well. Mr. Jones calmed her and relaxed her skillfully. However, she was not the only person falling into a hypnotic state in the room.

Later that evening, Joan Masters answered the phone. She recognized the accent at once. "Mr. Jones, how did it go?"

"Hook, line, and sinker, the professor believed his job was on the line. How did Paul Take it?"

"We have not discussed it, but he is in a foul mood, poor boy. He is looking for answers to questions that can't be answered easily. I know nothing about the trial as far he is concerned, and I will keep it that way."

"Ok, Joan, just to keep you in the picture, the professor did contact the sponsors regarding Paul, he did not mention his name, but he did inform them that one of the trial subjects mentioned the word 'Prime,' it was a keyword they were searching for."

"Oh, God." She gasped, and she felt a chill envelop her.

Mr. Jones kept his voice calm, trying not to alarm her. "However, I think I have sorted it." He added casually. "I have hypnotized both the professor and Mrs. Evans, and they will remember the word in context with Prime-Time television. They also no longer have any recollection of Paul even attending the trial. So, Joan, be vigilant and let me know if anything happens out of the ordinary. I will not be calling on you in person again just in case I compromise you or Paul. One more thing, and I am saying this as a friend, Paul will continue with his dreams until you get his memories induced, and he will not thank you if you leave it much longer before telling him." Please give it some thought. Bye for now."

Joan stared at the phone, unsure of what to do next. How she wished Peter would walk through the door. *Would he agree to Paul being induced?* She doubted it. *Could the 'Primevil' have already trapped him like they were trying to trap them all?* So many questions, so few answers.

That evening Joan's sleep was disturbed by loud noises in the house. After the conversation with Mr. Jones, she decided to keep her revolver under her pillow. She grabbed the gun and removed the safety catch; her heart was racing. She positioned herself behind the bedroom door expecting someone to burst into the room, but no one came.

Again, there was shouting, and this time she recognized the voice. "Paul," she screamed and ran down the corridor to his room and kicked the door open. Joan held the revolver in front of her with both hands sweeping from left to right as she had seen them do on television. Her hands trembled, and the blood coursing through her ears deafened her. The room was silent. She waited half expecting someone to pounce, and then Paul cried "Sarah."

Joan collapsed onto the side of her Son's bed and sat there as her heart returned to its normal rhythm. She watched as his eyes moved rapidly behind their lids and wondered where his mind was this time. Her heart ached as her name again left his lips. This time, it was as gentle as a prayer. "Sarah." He whispered.

She settled down. Oh God, he is searching for her once again. Hopefully, it is a white dream, it usually was when he was with Sarah. Until the end.

"No," Paul screamed again and sat up in bed. Joan looked into his eyes, and they were unseeing, and she realized he was not in this time.

She lay him back down and comforted him. "Find her, Paul, find her and keep her safe. You know you must remember." Eventually, he drifted back to sleep.

*

The wolf's howl echoed the Princess's cry and the hair lifted on his Lordship's neck. "I have lost them to the evil ones, and they will blacken them forever. I must warn them somehow! Mother, I will call a bird."

"Princess, I do not think we have time. The Shaman could be there already. I took the liberty of instructing the Acolytes to summon a meeting of the 'Sisters of Avebury,' to see if we could contact the girls telepathically. We must join them in the North Circle." She turned her attention to the Lord.

"You're Lordship, take your men south, to the point the Princess said they camped last night."

"Yes, Mother."

He turned to go, but the Princess stopped him.

"Your Lordship, take the wolves and your boys, especially Saul. If we can contact the girls, I will instruct them to contact your group."

"Very good Princess."

He turned on his heals and fled.

The Princess gave a piercing whistle, and the three wolves arrived moments later. Taking Wolf's head in her hands, she verbally instructed her.

"Go with the men, find the girls, protect them and take your daughters, let the creatures of the forest guide you. I will catch up in some way. Go now with his Lordship."

All three wolves turned and followed the Lord.

The Princess made her way to the Altar Stone, where she found a circle of twenty women sitting on the floor cross-legged in a circle. A pentagon had been drawn in the soil surrounding the circle. The Earth Mother assumed her position in the center, and the Princess joined the sisters on the ground. Immediately Mother addressed them all.

"Thank you all for coming at such short notice. As you are all aware the two Princesses have been taken, we think, by the 'Primevil.'"

There were murmurs from the sisters. After a pause, she continued. "You may or may not be aware that four of his Lordship's men were killed last night. Our dark brethren have no regard for life, and we fear for the girls' safety. We also have reason to believe the Shaman was one of them."

The sisters began to whisper amongst themselves, and again Mother waited.

"The Shaman was at a meeting with Lord Monkton, Princess Mia, and me when the Princess informed us that Sarah could communicate with the forest's creatures. When he discovered this, he at once retired to his tent. He is now in a deep trance, so we must assume he is trying to contact his fellow kidnappers to warn them."

The sisters, all tried to talk simultaneously, and they were brought to order by Mother when she snapped. "Sisters, all join hands. We do not have time to debate this."

Sitting within the pentagon surrounding the Altar, the sisters linked hands, and 'Mother' acted as the mouthpiece of them all.

"Great Earth Mother, guide our thoughts, and may our calling reach our sisters in peril. We call the Princesses' daughters Sarah and Ursula. They are deep in the forest, and we think the evil ones have taken them. Carry our thoughts to them. They are young but are aware. Hear, our prayer."

The sisters sat in silence and waited. Moments later, a small voice responded deep in the heads of all the sisters.

Who is this? Am I dreaming, or is someone calling me?

It is the "Earth Mother" calling, Ursula and Sarah.

I am Ursula. Is that really you, Earth Mother?

It is the Earth Mother's representative from Avebury. Are you both safe?

Yes, we are safe. How are we talking to you?

The Avebury sisters are meditating; our combined conscience is allowing me to use telepathy. Your mother is here; you may talk to her now if you wish.

Mother, are you there?

Yes, Ursula. Have they harmed you or your sister?

No mother. They say they are trying to protect us and take us somewhere where no one can harm us. We were up at dawn, and we are now heading straight toward the sun.

So, Ursula, they are taking you Southeast, back towards the mother country. Is Sarah safe as well?

I can hear you now, mother, and, yes, I am safe. They are telling us that you were manipulating our minds and that our skills would be stunted if we continued to be misled by you.

Girls, listen to me. They are not aware of how much of your 'Prime' memory you have recovered. Consult your ancestors, listen to what they say, and be guided by them.

You told us this yesterday, mother, and we are playing along with them.

Good girls. Listen. We think Shaman Bramel is in league with them, and he knows Sarah can talk to the creatures of the forest, and we think he is on his way to warn your guards.

The girls answered in unison. He is not here, mother.

No, the Shaman is in his tent. He is in a deep Shamanic trance, so his spirit has left his body. He will have taken the form of another, but who or what we do not know. I fear he may harm you or drug you to prevent you from communicating. Has anyone joined your party this morning?

No, we have the same four men that were guarding us yesterday.

Ursula interrupted. I can foresee that he has taken the form of a Raven. He will be here soon.

Well done, Ursula. We need to kill that bird. Look at the different paths that we can take to destroy it. Look at which creatures Sarah must summon to help.

Quick as a flash, Ursula said. *There are several paths, but most of them will fail. It will take more than one bird to kill it. If you call the eagle owl you used yesterday and a Sparrow hawk, success is far more likely, two sparrow hawks and the owl should bring almost certain success.*

Good girl. You're using your powers wisely already.
Did you hear what Ursula said, Sarah?
Yes, mother. I will summon them now, and I have already called a male wolf. He is making his way back to Avebury to guide the search party, and ghost and Shadow are expecting him.
Good girls. I am so proud of you both. Remember, go along with what the guards are saying, and do not give them any reason to harm you. We will soon be back together. Be brave, my daughters.

The circle of sisters sat in silence, waiting for Mother to speak.

"Well, that went well, my sisters. We will soon see what our younger sisters are made of."

*

Lord Monkton and the rescue party finally arrived at the campsite the girls had used the previous night. They continued to follow the trail, which appeared to be going Southeast. Then, in the distance, he heard the howl of a wolf.

The three wolves stood still, their senses on high alert with their ears pricked as their eyes scanned the forest. Then, a lone wolf came running toward them. Ghost and Shadow ran towards him, and all three greeted each other. The male wolf then turned, and all four wolves headed south. Lord Monkton, who realized what was happening, told his men to follow.

Sarah had contacted the sparrow hawks, and two were circling high above. The owl, awakened from its slumber, was making its way south.

Ursula sensed something and grabbed Sarah's arm. "He's coming. I can feel him. He is getting close." Sarah looked up and alerted the sparrow hawks, who began to dive.

The Raven, who was gliding in just above the treetops, did not know what hit him. First one, then the other, hit the bird in mid-air. The raven fell to the ground, and both hawks followed him. All three birds began fighting on the ground, feathers, and blood flying everywhere, and then from nowhere came the eagle owl who began to rip the Raven to pieces.

The guards, who saw what was happening, ran towards the birds to separate them but were unsure which bird was their compatriot and stood back. As the raven fell silent, the two sparrow hawks fled to the bushes, followed by the owl.

The men bent down to examine the Raven, whose wings twitched in the throes of death. Ursula stepped down off the horse and turned to the men.

"Why were the birds fighting?"

"I am not sure, Princess, I think it may be a messenger."

Ursula responded. "In that case, it's a matter of life or death." The man closest to the bird turned his back to her, and Ursula stood on the bird, breaking its neck.

She then climbed back on her horse, looked down at the men, and said, "My life, his death."

Sarah, meanwhile, had dismounted and retrieved one of the hawks that had been injured and held it against her chest, comforting it. One of the men ran to the bird and raised his sword.

Sarah screamed. "Don't kill it, it's the messenger, can't you see that they were all trying to stop it from getting to us? Ursula killed one, and the other two got away." The man hesitantly sheaved his sword.

"Sorry, your highness. I thought she had killed the messenger."

"Can you not tell?"

The man shook his head in denial. "I hear nothing from this bird, Princess."

"Well, I do. This bird is saying it is carrying the spirit of Shaman Bramel." Is the Shaman one of your brethren?"

"He is your highness."

"Well then, there is no way I would know that. The bird is injured, that's why it can't talk to you, but it should be able to fly. It's telling me that we are walking into a trap, and men are waiting up ahead. He said we should double back quickly and follow it."

Throwing the bird into the air, it circled and headed north as instructed by Sarah. The party followed and now headed back towards the rescue party.

The girls looked at each other, a nearly visible smile creasing their lips. The owl was still circling high overhead, and Sarah contacted it telepathically.

Tell the rescue party to wait. We are coming back towards them and to get ready to ambush them.

The owl flew north towards Lord Monkton, his men, and the wolves. It then swooped down in front of the lead wolf and landed on the ground. The wolves came to a halt, followed by his Lordship and his men.

One of the men called out, "Why have we stopped, my Lord?"

His Lordship ignored him and called Saul to his side. "This is obviously a messenger. If you can communicate with these creatures as Sarah said you can, now is your chance to prove it."

Saul got off his horse and knelt before the owl, his head only inches from the bird. Nothing was said and Saul turned to his father.

"We must set a trap. The girls have tricked the kidnappers, who have doubled back and are heading straight for us, and they have killed the Shaman."

"Killed the Shaman." Lord Monkton said in an astonished voice. "The owl told you this."

"Yes, father, but we must hurry."

His Lordship took control of the situation and had his men spread out undercover. "Saul, can you tell the wolves to do the same?"

"I have told them already, father."

His Lordship shook his head in disbelief. "Oh, well done, already? Right, Saul, and you too Peter, take your bows but hang back in the undergrowth. Let my men and the wolves do the fighting."

The owl flew to the top of the tree and watched. Suddenly, a hoot from the owl high above alerted his Lordship, and he told his men to get ready. The lead horse came into the clearing, a second hard on its tail. Ghost leaped into the air, followed by Shadow. Both horses reared up, with their hooves pawing the air, and the startled riders fell to the floor. In an instant, the wolves locked their jaws around the men's throats as the men screamed and thrashed until they eventually stilled. The two remaining men, leading the girls by a tethered rope tied to each horse, were lagging and halted after hearing the screams.

The lead man turned to his compatriot. "Did you hear that? Was it a scream?"

"I didn't hear anyth...."

Mia's wolf leaped at the lead man, knocking him off his horse, and got him around the throat as soon as he hit the ground with another death bite. The remaining man, whose horse was tethered to Ursula's, turned to flee, and the smaller male wolf gave chase and leaped at the man - but was knocked to the ground. The man then slashed at the creature with his sword, injuring it badly.

Still holding the tether, he again tried to flee, but this time an arrow brought him to a halt as it hit him straight in the chest, then a second, then a third. The man fell to the floor, dead.

Princess Ursula sat terrified on the horse and began screaming uncontrollably. A rustling sound came from the bush up ahead, and then a familiar voice called out.

"Are you harmed, my Princess?"

"You... you saved me, Peter, you saved me." Ursula jumped to the ground, ran to him, and hugged him for all her worth.

"There, there, Ursula, you are safe now. They are all dead."

Ursula, whose face was full of dread, turned to Peter. "Sarah, what about Sarah? Where is she? Where is my sister?"

"She is safe, and she's with Saul. Your wolves killed the others."

His Lordship galloped into the clearing wielding his sword and brought his horse to a halt.

"Peter, you have the Princess – well done. Did the kidnapper escape?" He followed Peter's eyes and spotted the man with three arrows sticking out of his chest."

"Well done son. They are your arrows I take it? Peter nodded, and his Lordship turned his attention to the Princess. "Are you hurt, Princess?"

"I'm unhurt, my Lord, thanks to your son. Where is my sister? Is she harmed?"

Sarah ran to Ursula, and the girls hugged one another for all they were worth. When the trio returned to the others, they found Shadow fussing over the male wolf. He had been injured in his battle with the fourth kidnapper and had several slash marks across his back.

Saul watched over him, showing his concern, and asked Sarah if he would live.

"He will need treatment, and I fear he will not survive without my mother's help,"

Sarah instructed the owl to report to the Earth Mother. It turned and headed north towards Avebury and was gone in an instant.

The bodies of the men were stripped of all clothing and possessions and left to feed the creatures of the forest. His Lordship's men collected the remaining horses, and the group headed back to Avebury.

The Avebury sisters were still sitting in an unbroken circle when the owl flew down to Mother on the Altar. Moments later, she nodded, and the owl was gone.

The Earth Mother addressed them all. "Thank you, everyone. It seems our young sisters are safe, so we can rest now."

The Princess turned to the Mother. "I must go to them."

"There is no need. They are hurrying back to us, and no one has been harmed. You are to prepare for one injured wolf with deep slash wounds to his back. Saul is bringing him on his horse."

Mia immediately got to her feet. "Thank you, mother. I will start making a poultice and get a needle and thread." With that, she was gone.

The Earth Mother dismissed the circle of sisters and made her way back to the Shaman's tent. There was no one there, so she walked inside. The Shaman was on his bed as if he were asleep. After checking his pulse, she lifted the blanket, pulled it over his head, and spat on the ground.

Three hours later, the rescue party returned. Crowds had gathered to welcome them back. Princess Mia stood waiting as both girls trotted into the camp on the backs of their wolves. They dismounted and ran over to her, and she welcomed them with open arms.

"Girls, you are both safe. Did they harm you?"

Ursula was the first to respond. "We are safe thanks to Peter, he saved me, and he shot my kidnapper with three arrows."

Sarah added excitedly. "And the wolves killed the other three."

The Princess looked concerned. "One of the protectors is hurt. Which one?"

"It was not one of ours. Sarah called a male wolf, the one she sent to the search party to lead them to us."

Sarah pulled at Princess Mia's robe sleeve to get her attention. "We must treat the wolf quickly. It is badly hurt, and Saul has it on his horse."

Sarah led the Princess to Saul, who had lowered the wolf to the floor with the aid of two men.

"I have prepared a poultice for this already." She said then added. "The owl said you were bringing an injured wolf, I am so relieved I thought it was one of ours. There is hot water on the fire. Sarah, clean the wound, and I will get the poultice."

Saul watched over Sarah as she treated the creature and whispered. "We must save him, Sarah, he almost gave his life for you."

Ursula stared into the distance, her eyes searching their future. "He will live. I have foreseen it. He fathers" cubs to both Shadow and Ghost in the future."

Sarah bent her head forward and whispered in Ursula's ear. "Ursula, be quiet, you must not tell everyone you are a seer."

Ursula gave Sarah an incredulous stare. "Sarah, it's no longer a secret, that's something else I've just seen."

Princess Mia arrived with the poultice, needle, and thread. She sedated him with a sleeping draft and then removed the hair around the wounds using a sharp knife.

She kept checking his life signs until he was fast asleep, then she stitched one wound and left Sarah and Ursula to do the others. Then she applied the poultice and covered the wounds with bandages.

"Well done, girls, that stitching is perfect. I think this wolf will survive."

Mia turned her attention to Ursula. "Well done, you used your skill of foresight to take the correct path in our dealings with the kidnappers and managed to get your birds to kill the bird."

"Thank you, mother, but I did have to give it a helping hand, the soldiers were going to release the raven, so I trod on it."

"You... killed the Raven?" The Princess felt a feeling of dread creeping up her spine, but outwardly she was calm personified. "Well, it all worked out fine in the end. I am so glad you are both safe." However, silently she made a mental note. *I must talk to Mother.*

*

The Earth Mother was sitting cross-legged in the center of the Altar. It was a pleasant evening, and the sun's heat had given way to the mist creeping up from the lake, working its way through the trees, along the stream, and collecting in the hollow of the Henge.

She addressed the Avebury Sisterhood.

"As the Earth Mother's representative, I have called this meeting to explain what has happened over the last couple of days. Some of you are fully aware of the facts, but many rumors and stories are circulating, becoming more fanciful. We have once again been deceived and violated by the 'Primevil'. You may or may not know the Shaman is dead."

There were murmurings throughout the circle of sisters, so Mother waited for them all to stop before continuing.

"He held a position of trust for several years, so we can assume the 'Primevil' are aware of our innermost secrets. He was complicit in the kidnapping. He knew our young sisters were special, although the Princess and I went to great lengths to hide the fact."

The Earth Mother did not hide the sarcasm in her voice, and the Princess avoided her stare.

"Upon arrival, Princess Ursula let slip she knew the father of the Shaman was a carpenter, even though she had never met him or encountered anyone here. That was all it took to alert him. He contacted his masters, and now our young sisters are forever in great peril. He recognized their power, but he underestimated them greatly. One of the gifts is that they can communicate with the forest creatures."

Again, the Earth Mother waited for the mutterings to die down, and then she continued.

"When he realized the girls could contact us through them, it forced his hand because he had to inform the kidnappers. He chose to do this by calling a bird to transfer his spirit to warn them. By doing so, he left himself vulnerable, which the girls exploited.

Thanks to you, my sisters, we were able to contact our younger siblings. Sarah, in turn, called two sparrow hawks and an eagle owl, and they attacked the Shamans Raven before it could pass on the message."

All the sisters started talking simultaneously, so the Earth Mother again waited for them to stop.

One of the sisters raised a question. "Why so many birds to kill one raven?"

Mother was pensive for a time, unsure how much information she should pass on to them, considering that all here helped destroy the Shaman. She made her decision.

"Many paths were searched before choosing the number of birds required to kill the raven, as you all know, they are huge birds with few predators, and the path chosen was the one known to succeed."

The sister replied. "To decide that we would need the powers of a very powerful seer. We have no one here powerful enough to do that?"

Mother's eyes again slid across to the Princess, who remained silent with her eyes fixed firmly on the ground.

Once again, the sisters talked loudly amongst themselves. The Earth Mother waited patiently for silence. Then the same sister spoke again.

"Mother, I know you are saying they have foresight at just five years of age., But surely the number of birds was down to Princess Mia?"

The Earth Mother's eyes turned to each sister in turn. She was going to have to tell them.

"You were all witness to our communication with the girls through our meditation, so I am surprised you need to ask." The Earth Mother sighed. "Not both girls, only one of them. Ursula."

The entire group of sisters erupted in conversation. Knowing the enormity of this statement, Mother let them take time to absorb it. Meanwhile, the Princess continued to say nothing.

Another sister raised a question. "These girls, have they been forced to regain their 'Prime' memories? Have they been violated?"

The Princess raised her eyes from the ground and spoke forcibly. "My daughters have never been mistreated. Unlike the people of this land, we do not need to force the memories on them. From the age of three, they start to surface naturally. That is why Kings and Princes choose my line for their wives or concubines."

Her eyes took in each of the sisters one at a time, daring them to argue.

After a long pause, she continued.

"Think, my sisters. If you have a kingdom and your wife is a seer. What power you have over your adversaries? She can advise on matters of state and war. No, my sisters, my line does not need to force our daughters. That is why we are the most prized seers in my land. That is one of the reasons the 'Primevil,' want them."

For several moments an awkward silence fell upon the circle. When no one spoke, the Earth Mother, again, took control.

"So, my sisters, the Shaman is dead along with the four kidnappers, and we have our sisters back safely in the fold. Princess Mia will address you further shortly, but as the Earth Mothers representative for Avebury, I wish to thank you all because, without the circles' help, the girls would have been lost to us forever."

"Tomorrow, the Princess and her daughters are heading back to their own country. She brought them here hoping they could find suitable life partners and be hand-fasted, but now that the 'Primevil' are aware of them - she feels they will now be safer back in Persia. His Lordship will provide an escort to keep them safe on their journey until they board ship in Plymouth."

The Princess once again addressed the meeting. "I wish to thank you, my sisters. Without your help, my daughters would be lost to me. My time with you has been very special to me. Your festival was very touching. I particularly enjoyed your love dance, the 'celebration of free spirits.'" The sisters en masse roared with laughter.

She waited for the laughter to die down. "I am sorry to say we will not meet again in this life, but in the future - who knows? I will remember you always, in this life, and forever. Having helped me rescue my daughters, you have bestowed the greatest of gifts on me."

Mia turned to the Earth Mother and addressed her. "In return, my sisters, I, Princess Mia, High Priestess of the Sisterhood in Persia, will share the 'Prime' memories of the sisterhood in my land."

Excitement erupted throughout the group. The Earth Mother quickly stepped in to quieten the meeting. "Sisters, please sisters, quiet, please. We are all very excited to receive this honor. It is always a joy when a sister shares her memories. I was hoping the Princess would do us this honor, but I dared not ask. My sisters, this gift to us is special because they are new memories, for the first time in over two hundred years, we are receiving completely new memories from a distant and strange land."

The meeting again erupted in conversation as this was unprecedented in their lifetime, and they were brought down to earth when Mother asked them to join hands.

Mother started the proceedings.

"I will now pass you over to the Princess, but everyone must calm themselves as we need to go into a deep meditative state to receive this gift."

The Princess changed places with the Earth Mother and sat in the center of the pentagon. Time passed, and when the Princess felt the order was ready to receive the memories, she started.

"Holy Earth Mother, I, Princess Mia, High Priestess of the Land of Persia, thank you for guiding me to this land and the sisters of Avebury. I thank them for helping me in my hour of need and will now pass on my 'Prime' memories in appreciation for rescuing my daughters from the evil ones."

"So, sisters, as you know, this may take a little time, probably more than you think. Get yourselves comfortable." She waited until she could sense calm and tranquility throughout the group and then addressed them

"I can feel the circle is now strong and complete. I will say no more; we are as one."

The circle was as quiet as the grave, and the sisters - were statuesque and in a deep trance. Hours passed, and the moon rose in the evening sky and its light flickering through the tree branches danced eerily across the faces of the sisters.

The Acolytes Simon and Steven stood watching over them and became worried. More people gathered and began to stare, but the Acolytes kept them at bay. One of the Acolytes felt the need to call for his Lordship. He arrived almost at once, and the first Acolyte greeted him.

"Your Lordship, thank you for joining us. I have never seen the sisters in such a deep trance for such a long time. The ways of the Sisterhood are strange, so I am unsure if we need to take any sort of action."

His Lordship observed them for a short while. "How long have they been meditating?"

"They commenced the meeting just after the evening meal. The moon has passed its zenith now." His Lordship continued to observe the sisters. There was no movement, but they did not seem in distress.

"If I were you, Acolyte, I would leave them to continue. Just keep the crowds away. I must prepare for the Princess's journey to Plymouth." He turned quickly and went back to his men.

Eventually, the sisters came out of the trance and began to discuss the memories they had received.

The Earth Mother closed the meeting, and each of the sisters took it in turn, to thank the Princess personally and wish her a safe voyage back to Persia.

*

Early the following day, the Princess called to see the Earth Mother in her tent. After ringing the bell, she was bid to enter.

"Good morning, Princess."

"Good morning, Mother. May we talk?"

"Yes, I can see you are worried about something. How can I help you?"

The Princess paused, unsure of how to proceed. "It's something that happened to the raven that carried the Shaman's spirit."

"Go on, Princess. It is obviously troubling you."

"The birds did not kill it, they only injured it, and Ursula had to finish it off by crushing it under her foot."

After absorbing this information, the Earth Mother took a while to speak. "Did she come into contact with its skin?"

"Not that I am aware, Mother."

Mother shook her head dismissively. "Then there should be no danger. Surely, she was wearing foot coverings of some kind, shoes, boots?"

"Boots, I believe, Mother."

"Then the risk is minimal. I do not think the Shaman was full,' Primevil,' just a puppet useful for his basic skills. Any essence he would pass on to infect her would be minuscule, so I can't see how they could have contaminated her. However, it is another thing to keep a lookout for, and You're going to have your hands full looking out for them."

"Thank you, Earth Mother. You've put my mind at rest. This brings me to another request, the new manor House will be completed very shortly, and we will be expected to live in it. I will need people I can trust to assist me in guiding the girls, people who will need to know who I am. I can't go around being the Princess for the rest of my life, as it's too draining. She is very willful, as you have noticed."

The Earth Mother thought for a while, then asked a question. "What sort of jobs will they be required to do?"

"Everything. I have no idea how to run a household. The girls will need a scholar who can guide them with reading and social behavior, even how to dance, and all the skills they will need to move into society. We will need workers for the fields, a blacksmith, and a cook. We are comfortably well off, so I will be able to pay them."

"I am sure I can arrange that, but you will need to inform the brothers and sisters that I send to you who you are."

"Yes, Mother, when the time comes, of course."

"What of his Lordship? He will be your neighbor. When he finds out you live in the next estate to his, I'm sure he will want to see a lot more of you, in more ways than one."

"That's a pity. He will no longer want me when he sees what I look like, and I feel a great fondness for him."

The Earth Mother's eyes creased, and she started to laugh. "He may surprise you. What makes you think you know what he looks like?"

"What?" Morag said, hardly able to believe her ears.

"Yes, Princess, he can change faces too. I am sure He's about ten years older than he looks, making him the same age as you. The pair of you made this ceremony memorable in more ways than one, watching both of you flirting with each other and both felt they needed to be someone else to attract the other."

The Earth Mother rocked back and forth, laughing. Then, seeing the expression on the face of the Princess, she slapped her thighs and laughed uncontrollably.

"Another matter, Mother. The deception of me traveling to Plymouth. Can we discuss this? I can't see how it will work without informing his Lordship. We said it should be our secret, but it would mean the girls and I were sailing to France, going ashore, and returning later. Who's to say they are not already waiting for us at the port? If they could arrange a kidnapping as quickly as they did, I'm sure they would have people at the ports, the ships, and the docks."

"What do you suggest, Morag?"

"We need to let his Lordship in on the plan. Even with the Princesses' diminished skills of a seer and that of Ursula's, we both know they will be married in ten years - so he must be 'Prime.'

The Earth Mother sat quietly thinking while Princess Mia waited. "After our last misjudgment, Princess, I'm loathed to let more people in on the plan, but you are right. I think we can trust him. I have already sent for him on a different matter. He should be here shortly."

The bell above the doorway of the tent rang. The Earth Mother bid the person enter, and Lord Monkton stepped inside. Both women burst out laughing, unable to contain themselves. His Lordship, unsure why, waited until they finished before speaking. "It seems I have arrived at an amusing moment."

The Princess regained her composure first.

"I do beg your pardon, your Lordship. It was a private joke, a female joke, sorry."

"It's good to see you in such high spirits, Princess, after your ordeal."

"Yes, and it's thanks to you and your sons that it is possible."

His Lordship now looked at the Earth Mother and addressed her. "You sent for me?"

"Yes, your Lordship, but something else has come up since I sent that request, and it needs to be dealt with first. Before we speak, would you go outside and casually walk around my tent? What I have to say next is for the three of us only, and I want no one in earshot."

His Lordship looked puzzled but did as she bid. Returning to the tent, he sat down beside the Princess and waited.

The Earth Mother spoke first. "There has been a deception, and only two people are aware of it."

His Lordship replied, "What sort of deception, Mother?"

"First, I must tell you a short story. Several months ago, an owl arrived at my bedside in the middle of the night. The messenger spoke of a Princess that came to one of our healers for help five years ago. This Princess was a powerful seer and she sensed she was the only one that could help her daughters. At the time, the healer did not realize she was a sister and treated her and her husband."

His Lordship interrupted. "This healer could not sense she was a sister?"

"That is correct, it will soon become clear if you listen to the story. This Princess and the Lord were dying of a plague they contracted while traveling overseas. The Princess was unable to communicate because she was near death. At the time, the Princess was pregnant, full-term. The healer knew she could not save either parent, but she thought it might be possible to save the unborn babies."

Again, he interrupted. "How on earth could anyone save the babies of a dying woman?"

The Earth Mother rebuked him firmly. "Stop interrupting, and you will find out."

She then continued. "On the point of death, the healer cut them out of her stomach and revived them." Again, he interrupted.

"The Princess died?" He looked sideways at the woman sitting next to him hardly able to comprehend what she was saying.

Mia pursed her lips. "Yes, I'm sorry to say I died that day."

Lord Monkton, who was overcome with emotion, said nothing. He simply stared at the ground as his eyes began to fill with tears, and when one fell to the floor, the Princess held his hand to console him, and then she too, began to cry.

The tent went very quiet for a time, with no one speaking.

When the Earth Mother thought they had had enough time to control themselves, she continued.

"So, this healer saved the twin girls. When the healer harvested the Princess's essence, she realized she was one of us, and looking back on her memories, she saw the husband was a cruel man. The Princess requested the healer keep the girls away from their father-in-law, Earl Llewellyn."

After controlling his emotions long enough to speak, his lordship raises a question.

"Lord Llewellyn, Earl Llewellyn's son on the estate to the north of mine?"

"Yes, the same one."

"So, the young Lord is dead. And these are his daughters?"

"That is correct." His Lordship's eyes looked across to the Princess and raised another question. "This healer is now raising the children on her own?"

"Yes, my Lord, but that's not the end of the story. Earl Llewellyn thinks his son and daughter-in-law are alive and well, and is having a grand house built for them, about forty miles away from you."

He turned again to face the Princess and saw her tears reflected his own. "How on earth did you manage that, Princess?"

"By deception. When anyone calls, I am either the Princess or his Lordship. It has been difficult, but so far, I have succeeded."

"So, you are now going to take them back to Persia because of their danger?"

Before the Princess could respond, the Earth Mother again took control of the conversation.

"This is the real deception. The Princess went to great lengths to appear her party arrived from the south. We must do the same, but this time she must journey south to disguise the fact that she needs to go north to get back home."

Lord Monkton studied the Princesses face intensely. "So, you are not taking them back to Persia, you are going to live in England."

"Yes, we are to be neighbors, and hopefully, we can renew our acquaintance from time to time."

The Princess still held his hand, and he returned the compliment by placing his other hand on top.

"Yes, Princess, I would like that very much, very, very much. They sat holding hands for a while without talking, and the Earth Mother did not interrupt their thoughts. His Lordship then jumped to his feet, and his mind moved to the next problem. He began walking back and forth, deep in thought.

"In that case, we need to make different plans.

11. THE LAST REGRESSION 1985 AD

On the morning of the last regression trial, professor Gaskill received a fax from the trial sponsors. Two representatives were going to observe the last session. He crumpled the fax and tossed it in the bin. "Dam," he said out loud for his own benefit as the room was empty.

The trial had been a total disaster, instead of proving the soul could transmigrate after death, it did precisely the opposite. None of the three students left in the trial provided him with any tangible evidence he could check or verify, and he had nothing.

He checked the time. There were still eight hours left before the first of the three students would arrive. He replied by fax immediately, informing them their trip would be fruitless, briefly he relayed the findings of the trial, and silently prayed they would not turn up.

Halfway through the first session, a black stretched limo pulled into the school parking lot. Several students gathered around hoping to see someone famous - but soon dispersed when they failed to recognize them. The woman was five feet six inches tall with a slim build, she wore a tight black mini skirt, a white blouse, and a black jacket and was balanced precariously on three-inch black stiletto heels. The man was six foot ten and about two hundred and forty pounds and had to turn sideways to get through the door. He wore a black suit and tie, and both looked immaculate. If you saw them in the street, you would say she was a celebrity, and he was her bodyguard.

They made their way to professor Gaskill's office without asking for directions.

The woman opened the door silently and crept in. The professor turned and put his fingers to his lips, indicating they should be quiet. She took a seat, and the giant sat on a chair by the door. They both watched as the hypnotist's voice echoed softly throughout the room.

Mr. Jones felt a chill run up his spine, but he kept his voice steady and controlled. His eyes turned to the professor seeking an explanation, but he turned away." The chill moved to his heart. He noticed they kept their sunglasses on even though the room was dimly lit. Their faces were impassive and statuesque, and every nerve cell in his body screamed the same thing. 'Primevil,'

He could feel his neck turning red and the sweat coalescing on his temples, and he silently prayed they had not noticed.

The trialist, Sandra Bennet, answered his questions without supplying any evidence that he or the professor could verify. After forty minutes of monolog and single-syllable answers, she was revived.

The professor turned nervously to the observers. He addressed the woman. "I take it you are from our sponsors. Did you not get my fax?"

She turned her face toward him but didn't remove her sunglasses. "Fax. No. When did you send it?"

He began to stutter. "E- e-eight or n-n nine hours ago."

"Ah, no, professor, we were in the air and have come straight from the airport." Her face did not smile or show any sort of emotion.

The professor collected a folder of papers and began to sort through them as he spoke. "I am afraid you have had a wasted journey-we have no data to confirm the transmigration of the soul whatsoever."

The trialist gasped. "What nothing after six weeks. Nothing?"

The professor turned apologetically to her. "Sorry Sandra, nothing we can verify. You can have copies of the tapes before you leave tonight."

The woman cut in. "We will decide who has copies and whether the data collaborates with our theories." Her face was still impassive.

The trialist got up to leave and slung her bag angrily over her shoulder. She turned and aimed a tirade at the professor.

"You promised we could have copies. If I had known this, I would not have wasted six weeks of my time." As she put her hand on the door handle, the woman in black stopped her.

"Where are you going?"

The trialist turned her anger upon her. "Home, where do you think?"

The Lady in black looked perplexed. "Do you not want to get paid?"

The girl faltered. "Paid?"

All eyes turned to the professor, but the lady in black answered.

"Yes, paid. You have completed the trial, and it has taken up a lot of your time. We are very grateful even if the professor could not confirm our theories."

The lady in black turned her attention to the professor with a puzzled look on her face. "You did not tell them they were getting paid?"

The professor stuttered. "Err, n-n-no, I was w-waiting until the end of the session." His voice trailed away as he finished the sentence.

"I bet you were." Ms. Evans snapped. "How much?"

The lady in black once again answered the question for him. "One thousand dollars for each trialist that completes the trial."

Sandra let out a squeal of excitement. "A thousand dollars. You are going to pay me one thousand dollars?"

The lady in black's face still lacked any sign of emotion. "Yes, when the last trialist has finished, which should be in the next two hours. We always hand over the cheque personally, so I should hang around if I were you." Again, the girl screamed with excitement.

The professor, who appeared annoyed, told her to wait in the adjoining room and keep quiet.

"How come they are getting paid, and we're not?" The comment was directed at the professor, and once again, the lady in black answered for him.

"Why, Mrs. Evans, both you and Mr. Jones are."

All eyes turned again to the professor who began to turn red. Mrs. Evans snapped. "How much?"

"Five thousand each." The lady in black replied and turned to the Professor. "My, my, professor, have you not told your colleagues either, what a naughty boy you are."

The professor snapped back angrily. "Don't be absurd, I was keeping it as a surprise until the end of the trial."

"You bastard." Mr. Jones got to his feet and faced up to the professor. His face was red with rage. "No wonder you didn't tell us about the sponsors."

The lady in black stepped between them to keep them apart and placed a hand on his chest to push Mr. Jones away. As she did so, she stopped abruptly and could not hide the surprise on her face. A wicked smile creased her mouth.

"You need to calm down, Mr. Jones. You can sort out your differences after we have gone." As she spoke, the door opened, and the second trialist entered the room. He was a red-haired young man with pale freckly skin. He immediately sensed the atmosphere in the room.

"Is everything ok, professor?"

The professor gestured for him to take his position on the couch. "Yes, come in, Simon, and please make yourself comfortable."

Simon assumed his position, and the professor gestured to the man and woman dressed in black. "We have two observers for your final regression, they represent the sponsors for the trial. Are you ok with that?"

The boy nodded his head in their direction.

"Sure."

"Very good, then if you could begin, Mr. Jones."

Once again, the melodic tones of Mr. Jones echoed around the room. The session lasted just under an hour, and both the observers' faces remained impassive. Several times Mr. Jones let his eyes drift in their direction and he felt sure this was a trap. Their eyes, hidden by the sunglasses, gave nothing away.

He had noticed the wicked smile that creased the woman's face when she touched him and wondered if his fear had prevented him from controlling his mind. Or was he worrying for nothing? His eyes flickered towards the giant, who seemed impassive, and whose face constantly looked directly at him, and his heart filled with dread.

He knows I am 'Prime,' I am sure he does, I must keep my mind closed – oh God, what can I do? His eyes drifted to the professor and then to Mrs. Evan's. Both appeared unaware of the imminent danger. *Are they keeping us all here, or am I just imagining all this? Am I safe? - are any of us?* As his thoughts came to the fore, his voice faltered and broke. He cleared his throat, and again the beads of sweat began to run down the sides of his face.

As the last trialist was revived, the room filled with conversation, and the two trialists in the adjoining room joined them in the professor's study. However, the giant remained seated, with his eyes fixed firmly upon Mr. Jones. The lady in black turned her attention to the professor. "Do you have any coffee?"

The professor turned to Mrs. Evans. "Could you do the honors, please?

She glared at him. Two hours had passed since the revelation about the money, and her anger had not receded.

"I am not paid to make coffee, do it yourself." The professor reluctantly got to his feet, but the lady in black stopped him.

"I'll do it. Who wants coffee?" As she filled the kettle, she counted the people who wanted coffee. Her eyes drifted around the room; everyone had said yes except for Mr. Jones. She turned her attention to him. "Would you prefer something else... tea perhaps?"

He shook his head. "Not for me, thanks."

She spotted several cola cans as she opened the fridge to get the milk. "The professor has three cans of cola in here. Would you like one of those? After all, you look very hot – it's so warm here, don't you think? You certainly look like you could do with a drink." Her voice had taken on a melodic tone, it was very subtle, but Mr. Jones had spotted it.

An iron fist gripped his heart, and his eyes darted from side to side like a rabbit caught in a car's headlights - unsure which way to run. The giant was seated by the door. There would be no escape that way. He stuttered. "C-cola would be great, thanks."

She opened a can and was about to pour it into a glass when he stopped her. "I will have it in the can thanks." She hesitated, turned her back on him, put the glass down, and then handed him the can.

"Would anyone else prefer cola?" She looked around the room, and everyone dismissively shook their heads. The room eventually filled with conversation, and the atmosphere became more relaxed. However, the giant's eyes remained fixed in the direction of Mr. Jones.

Mrs. Evans made a beeline toward the lady in black. "Five thousand pounds, I had no idea, but that will come in very handy."

The lady in black turned her wan face towards her, her eyes still covered by sunglasses.

"You are most welcome, Mrs. Evans, it took up a lot of your time."

Mrs. Evans's eyes drifted towards the giant seated in the corner. "He Doesn't say much?"

The lady in black's eyes followed her line of vision. "Mr. Damien, he is only my driver, your right," she said disdainfully, "he does not say much." She wrapped her hands around the coffee cup, warming them. "Nice coffee Mrs. Evans."

She took a sip, and Mrs. Evans followed suit.

"Yes, the professor likes his coffee – although this tastes a little bitter to me."

The lady in black took the time to talk to each of them. She seemed pleasant and even managed the occasional smile. Gradually the room began to quieten as the sedative in the coffee started to take effect. She nodded approvingly and turned her attention to Mr. Jones, who had begun to feel drowsy.

For once, the lady in black smiled openly. "Well, well, well, what do we have here?"

Mr. Jones began to lose his balance, and she saw him close his eyes as he suddenly realized why. *She opened the can, I thought I was safe with a can, I must close my mind.*

She removed her sunglasses to reveal eyes that were as black as night. She again smiled wickedly and stroked the side of his face in a parody of affection.

"Yes, Mr. Jones, you must keep your mind shut - who knows what I might find there." She placed her hands on his chest and gently pushed him backward. Mr. Jones lost his balance and sat down on the chair, and the room fell silent.

She turned her attention to the professor, who appeared to be sleeping. She slapped the side of his face to wake him up. "Come on, professor, wake up, you want your money, don't you."

His eyes flickered open. "Oh, Goodness, I must have dozed off."

Her voice again took on the melodic tone of autosuggestion. "You are exhausted? Professor, I understand, but before we can give you your money we need to know which student used the word 'Prime?'

The professor closed his eyes, and she noted his eyes were moving under his lids. He shook his head before answering. "One of them used the term 'Prime television,' but I cannot remember which one. I will have to go through the tapes – is it important?"

Her eyes drifted to the giant, and he shook his head disdainfully.

"Professor, when you faxed through the bullet sheet, you said one of the trialists used the word 'Prime' singularly?"

Although he kept his eyes closed, he again shook his head. "Sorry, I did not realize the difference – my mistake, I was only trying to stick to our arrangement."

The lady in black turned to the giant. "What do you think?"

He got to his feet, walked over to the professor, stooped down, and removed his sunglasses. His eyes were bright yellow, and his pupils were cat-like. After a few moments, he shook his head and growled. "He knows nothing?" He turned his attention to Mrs. Evans and held his head close to hers.

The lady in black slapped her face as she had done to the professor, her voice once again was gentle and melodic. "Mrs. Evans, it's been a long day, and I know you are tired, but you need to wake up." She watched as her eyes fluttered and opened.

"Goodness, whatever has come over me - I am so sorry."

"It's ok, Mrs. Evans. We were just wondering which of the trialists used the word "Prime?".

She shook her head to clear the fog in her mind. "'Prime'? She fell silent for several seconds before trying to answer. "One of them recalled the first Primetime television programs, that's the only time I remember them using the word."

The giant got to his feet. "She thinks the same, her mind is an open book. Shit, we have come all this way for nothing."

The lady in black laughed.

"You think? She turned to the hypnotist, who was now fast asleep. "He is 'Prime' through and through. He closed his mind, but it was too late, and I managed to read his thoughts. He knows he is trapped."

The smile stretched across the giant's face. "Is he now? so, we are not wasting our time after all."

The lady in black paced back and forth as she contemplated their next move. "If the hypnotist did not know about our sponsorship, he would not have known about the bullet point sheet either." She pursed her lips thoughtfully. "In which case he may have wiped their minds, so one of these three could still be a stray."

She turned and looked at each of them. "Which one is the question? I am hungry let's have some fun. Tie the hypnotist to the chair."

Mr. Jones, who was unconscious, did not resist as he was bound by hand and foot.

The lady in black slapped his face. "Time to wake up, Mr. Jones."

His eyes flickered open, and once again his heart was filled with dread. Her dead eyes met his, and he could feel the malevolence evil creeping across his skin. He knew the blackness of her eyes reflected her soul. Her voice once again took on the melodic tones of mind control.

"Mr. Jones, how nice to meet a fellow 'Prime.' Tell me which of the trialists is a comrade, I only want to help. We can't let them fall into the wrong hands-can we?"

Mr. Jones looked straight ahead. His statuesque face remained impassive as she kissed him on the mouth. She took his bottom lip between her teeth and bit it seductively. His face remained unresponsive.

"Come on, Mr. Jones, you know you want me. Am I not the most beautiful woman you have ever seen? You have dreamt and fantasized about me many times, and at last, here I am."

She began to unbutton his shirt and kissed him on the neck and chest. "I will do anything you ask of me, just point out our comrade, and you can take me in your arms."

Mr. Jones did not move a muscle, his face white as flour.

The giant got to his feet and looked directly at his face trying to penetrate his mind. He shook his head. "You're wasting your time he has closed his mind off completely. I have seen them do it many times, he knows it is hopeless and he is about to die."

She indicated to the giant to get the professor by nodding her head in his direction. The giant lifted him to his feet by his collar. She slapped Mr. Jones's face hard and glared at him. "You have made your choice Mr. Jones. Your silence will kill them all, we only want the 'Prime', the others can live just point the trialist out, and the others can walk free."

Mr. Jones's face remained statuesque, his unseeing eyes staring straight ahead. The strength of the demon was so immense that he lifted the professor off the floor by his throat with one hand. He dangled him in Mr. Jones's line of vision so he could witness his demise. His legs thrashed, seeking purchase in midair as he clutched the giant's hand - trying to break his grip as his life slipped away.

One minute later he was dead. The lady in black slapped his face once again. "That was your fault, you caused his death. Now you don't want the same thing to happen to the rest of them, do you? Do you think one 'Prime's worth four humans? Give the trialist up now, and when they wake, the others can walk free."

She nodded her head towards Mrs. Evan's. The giant grabbed her by the throat and lifted her off the ground as he had done with the professor. Again, he dangled her in his line of vision as she let out a gargled scream as she clutched his hands trying to break his grip.

The remaining trialists began to wake as her life ebbed away. The lady in black's voice took on its melodic tone once again. "Your dreaming, rest your heads for a while. Go into a deep sleep, and I will tell you when it is time to wake up."

Mrs. Evans's eyes bulged, and her arms fell limp. The lady in black slapped him once again. "Two down, Mr. Jones, three to go. Look at them, Mr. Jones, they have their whole lives before them."

The demon grabbed her arm. "Stop you are still wasting time, we have to kill them anyway; they have seen our faces."

She sighed. "You are right, I just wanted to be sure one of them wasn't the one our Queen is after. His mind was shut so tight I was not getting the slightest energy off him. Ah well, if I can't get it that way, I will do it the old-fashioned way."

She sat down on his lap facing him, and kissed him hard on the mouth, then breathed in deeply drawing out his life's essence. His arms and legs thrashed against their restraints, as he tried to break free. But there was no escape. The lady in black began to glow with light emanating from her eyes and ears. Her hair stood on end as the static charge of positive and negative energy collided. Eventually, the resulting glow engulfed her body as she shuddered and climaxed in ecstasy for several minutes as she absorbed his life force.

Sated, she collapsed on the husk that had been Mr. Jones minutes before. She lay there for several minutes before the giant lifted her off his corpse. He held her in his arms, cradling her like a baby and whispered. "You, ok?"

Slowly she became conscious once again, he watched as she moistened her lips, and her eyes flutter open. When she realized where she was she turned on the giant and snapped "Put me down." He lowered her gently into the standing position and held her steady as she found her balance.

He repeated. "Are you ok?"

She staggered away, looked in the mirror, and straightened her hair. "Holy shit, that was better than all the lovers I've ever had in one hit. It's been years since I had one all to myself." Quickly she regained her composure, straightened the creases out of her dress, double-checked her image in the mirror, and returned to business.

She barked an order to the demon. "Remove his restraints." She then walked purposefully over to a gas stove and turned it on. After taking a candle out of her handbag she lit it at the other end of the room.

The demon turned to the three remaining trialists. "What about them?"

She snorted. "They couldn't close their minds at all, so Saul isn't one of them. They will sleep for hours, and it's time to go."

The giant closed the blinds to the professor's office, switched off the lights, and closed the door. The schoolyard was deserted as they left the building and they calmly walked to the limo.

Jenny walker watched from the shadows. Paul had not been to school or answered her calls all week. When his mother intercepted them, all she would say was he wanted to be left alone. After making her way to the professor's room, Jenny spotted the limo and waited. She watched as the other students went in and found it unusual when no one came out. She needed to speak to Paul in person, she was sure his mother was not passing on her messages.

When the lights went out and the limo drove off, curiosity got the better of her. After waiting fifteen minutes she tried the door. It was open, so she called out but there was no response. Her mind was full of questions. Where were they all? Where was Paul? Why have they turned the lights off? When there was no reply, she switched on the light. It was the last action of her life.

*

That evening Joan Masters stared at the television in disbelief. The local news program was showing pictures of four fire trucks tackling a fire at Paul's school. The police were putting the explosion down to a gas leak. There were seven casualties. The three remaining participants in the trial, along with Mr. Jones, Mrs. Evans, and the professor. They had all been killed outright, along with a woman that had not been identified.

Joan watched the television and was horror-struck. The color left her face, and she staggered to a chair for support. She knew it was no accident. *Why did they kill them all? Why? Only Paul mentioned the word 'Prime'? God, it is true, they are pure evil. Will I be next? Will Paul?*

She shook her head silently, unable to comprehend the horrors she saw on the television screen. Her mind, which was usually razor-sharp - was numb with terror. *Will the fact that he had been excluded from the trial divert suspicion?* Tears began to fill her eyes as she searched desperately for answers. *The only reason to kill all three is if they did not know who had said the word 'Prime'. In that case, does that make us safe?*

She sobbed openly. *Oh, that poor Mr. Jones, they killed all seven and managed to get a member of the 'Prime' by default. God Peter, where are you, I cannot do this on my own and I can only hope and pray that Mr. Jones did not reveal Paul's name.*

That night Joan did not sleep. From that day forth, she slept with the revolver under her pillow. When she went out, there was always one in her bag. The days turned to weeks and the weeks into years. She prayed for the souls wickedly cut short every night and always thanked Mr. Jones for his silence and sacrifice.

12. GLASTONBURY 1995 AD

The wolf cross scratched the front door of Morag's old cottage. After nearly four hundred years the building had been improved and extended many times. The cottage was no longer situated in the center of the forest and lay to grass on three sides and ran as a meadow to the lake. The third side was still forested, affording the cottage protection from the north winds and privacy from the guests of Earlswood manor.

Again, she scratched the door, but there was no reply. The creature turned, wandered around the back, and this time scratched at the rear door. Still, no one answered. Lifting herself on her hind legs, she rested a paw on the latch and pulled down. It was locked.

The dog's name was Bella, and it was one of three names the descendants of Sarah Monkton had used alternatively over the centuries for their guardians. She was the mother of Ghost and the protector of Alice's mother.

The dog sat on the porch and began licking her wound and waited. The fur down one side of her body was burnt and missing. She licked the flesh, trying to clean the wound and stem the blood oozing from it. It had been twenty-four hours since the accident, and the creature was getting weaker.

The car she was traveling in had been involved in a crash, and both her masters had been killed outright. The dog had been trapped in the burning vehicle, which began to fill with a colored swirling gas which was the essence of her charges, 'Prime' essence.

The creature knew instinctively what her next task was. Like the 'Prime,' her memories were immense and older than time. As her fur began to burn, she continued with her duty and licked the faces of her charges, and their essence passed through her saliva to her. Finally, she couldn't stand the pain of the flames any longer and had hidden down low between the rear seats.

The firefighters had the fire out in minutes. It was evident to the fire officer that the occupants were dead, but he instructed the leading firefighter to continue to spray the two corpses through the window as he offered up a silent prayer.

The smell of burnt chicken filled his nostrils. He knew, from experience however that it was not chicken. "Poor sods," he muttered to anyone in earshot - then added. "What an awful way to go," His voice was barely audible.

A firefighter turned and called out. "There's a dog in here, down between the seats. A second fireman opened the rear door, doused the animal with a fine spray, and laid it on the ground.

The officer barked. "Continue to spray the creature. Cool its skin down." After checking it over more closely, he issued a further order. "Will someone call a vet?"

He lifted his eyes to his colleague and shook his head. "This animal is done for - it's burnt to a crisp all down one side."

Bella knew she was mortally wounded, but she had one task left to fulfill. A task her line had conducted hundreds of times in the past. She had slipped past the firefighter and made her way back home. The officer futilely attempted to catch the dog but it was too late as Bella limped across the field, out of reach.

Bella continued to sit on the porch and was in both physical and mental distress as she attempted to clean the wound. She had to perform her last task and was rapidly running out of time. Her ancestors were now a mixture of wolf and dog, and her instinct was to bark, but the wolf's howl carried much further.

Alice Llewellyn was slim, green-eyed, and almost six feet tall, her hair was jet black without the hint of a curl - and it reached down to her waist, and when she walked, it was cat-like and graceful, unusual for a woman so tall.

Ghost heard it first. She raised her head and tilted it to one side as a bird would listening for a worm. Turning to her owner, she let out a bark.

Alice Llewellyn looked up from her task of collecting kindling deep within the wood. "What is it, Ghost? What have you heard?" Again, the dog barked, and she, too, tilted her head and listened. She could hear nothing.

Turning to Ghost, she communicated telepathically. Like all the women of her line, Alice Llewellyn could communicate with the forest's creatures. A gift passed down from Sarah Monkton almost four hundred years ago.

A puzzled expression creased her forehead. *What is it, Ghost? You think you have heard the howl of a wolf? Are you sure?*

Suddenly, she heard it as well, and a shiver went down her spine. She dropped the kindling and ran back to her cottage and her mind was filled with dread. *Something terrible has happened. I know it has. I have not heard Bella howl in years. Oh God, please, Earth Mother, do not let it be bad. Do not let it be bad.*

Arriving at the cottage, she could see Ghost fussing over her mother, licking her side where the fur had burnt off. Alice stopped dead at the sight of her mother's guardian. The hair lifted on the nape of her neck, and her heart froze. Kneeling at the creature's side, she stroked her head to comfort her, as you would an injured child. Immediately, the dog began to lick her hand frantically. "What has happened, Bella? Where are my parents?"

Alice lifted her hand to her face and stared at it horrified as tingling sensations emanated from her fingers. It was a sensation she had felt in many lifetimes, and her eyes began to fill with tears as she realized what it meant - and stared at her hand in disbelief. *Both Bella? Both of them...Gone? How? When?*

With her mind now linked to the guardian, she could sense that she was mortally wounded. *Oh, you too, Bella, and you have traveled so far to get here.*

Alice Llewellyn fell silent and began to meditate. Finally, she remembered to breathe, took a lungful of air, hugged her mother's guardian, and continued with the mental communication. *I have them now within me, Bella. Thank you your task is done.*

Alice Llewellyn sat on the porch with Ghost beside her and cradled Bella's head on her lap. She held her in her arms all night, as the essence of both parents passed over to her. Finally, sleep overcame her, and she felt solace in her oblivion.

The mist from the lake had crept silently through the forest like a spirit and surrounded her. Something touched the side of her face, and she woke with a start – was it a spirit? or was it only mist? She felt the side of her face, and her fingers were wet with dew.

A feeling of despair overcame her, her parents were dead, and Bella was stone cold on her lap. She let out a deep sigh and wished she were still asleep. Alice shook Bella and found she was stiff with rigor mortis and closed her eyes in despair. She called the spirits of Bella's ancestors to guide her back to the creator and thanked her for protecting her mother faithfully throughout her life.

Alice turned to Ghost, who continued to fuss over her mother and communicated with her again. *She is gone Ghost. It looks like it is just you and me now, so we are on our own.... again.*

Around her, the grays of early morning had given way to orange clouds of spun gauze in the pristine blue sky. Wearily Alice rolled Bella off her lap and got to her feet, her muscles reluctant and stiff.

She buried Bella in an area of woodland where she had buried dozens of her ancestors over the centuries and prayed to the creator of all things to watch over her.

When she returned to the cottage, she found two policemen waiting in a parked car. *Oh dear, Ghost, it looks like we have visitors. Dam blast.* She hesitated but held herself together, pursed her lips, and greeted them.

As she approached the driver wound down the window. He was in his forties and overweight. He was accompanied by a female officer in her late twenties, and Alice noticed neither of them smiled. The officer looked up. "Am I addressing Miss Llewellyn? Miss Alice Llewellyn?"

Alice presented the officer with a wan smile. "Yes, officer. Would you like tea or coffee?" Without waiting for a reply, she turned and entered the cottage. "I'll put the kettle on." The officers looked at one another, took a deep breath, and followed her.

As they entered the cottage, she began to fill the kettle with her back turned to them. "Please take a seat, and before you say anything, I know my parents are dead. How did it happen - was it in the fire?"

"Yes, Miss Llewellyn." The officer felt relieved that he didn't have to break the sad news, and it reflected on his face. "I was unaware you knew," Alice said nothing and stared through the window. "Tea or coffee?" She asked without looking back and then added, "Sugar? Milk?" The officers exchanged glances as they were surprised by her lack of reaction.

"How did the fire start, officer?

"Sorry, Miss Llewellyn, I didn't realize you were not aware of the facts. It was a car accident, a drunk driver, I am afraid.

Alice continued to look out the window with unseen eyes and repeated the officer's comments.

"A car fire" She nodded her head thoughtfully. "How awful! Did they suffer?"

The officer cleared his throat and again exchanged awkward glances with his constable. "No, Miss. Llewellyn, They would have died instantly. We want someone to identify the bodies. Could you accompany us to the station?" The kettle began to boil, and it bought Alice back out of her reverie.

"Sorry, officer, I have seen many people who have died in fires, and I wish to remember them as they were, not burnt to a crisp. You may take a DNA sample if you wish, but you are wasting your time. I know my parents are dead."

Again, the officers exchanged glances before the female constable took the kettle off Alice and began to make the drinks, her voice gentle and filled with compassion. I will stay with you for a while. "You're in shock, but we do need you to come down to the morgue and identify the bodies."

Alice pursed her lips and turned to face the officers. She smiled weakly, and when she addressed them further, her words were like water slipping over the ridge of a waterfall, smooth and melodic that hid the torrent hidden below the surface.

"This is not up for discussion. You do not need me to identify the bodies. I have things to do, and preparations to make for the funeral. I have already told you that I know my parents are dead. There is nothing more you can do here, so finish your drinks, and please leave." The officers sat with her for a while and chatted until they finished their drinks. They then turned and went away, unaware of the hidden enchantment.

As they made their way back to the car, the female constable commented. "She is weird, she didn't bat an eye, not a tear, nothing."

The officer agreed. "Takes all sorts, but I would not want to look at my family burnt to a crisp either, she was right, we can send someone around for a DNA sample.

Alice sat on the porch and rocked back and forth in her favorite chair. She turned to Ghost and spoke verbally. "I don't know about you, Ghost, but I am going to get pissed." She went back into the kitchen and returned with three bottles of beer. "I always hate recovering the memories. Oh Ghost, this can be so upsetting."

She assumed her favorite meditating position and sat with her legs crossed, and her ankles pulled towards her with her wrists resting on her knees and the palms of her hands facing upwards. She began to slow her heart rate and could feel the tension leaving her. She needed to be at peace with the world, but the circumstances made it difficult.

She began to concentrate on the different scents drifting in the wind. There was honeysuckle mixed with the various roses that climbed the cottage walls and the gentler scents of the trees, maple, juniper, and beech, deep in the wood. She listened to the birdsong, a skylark so high it was invisible to the naked eye, and then to the wind in the branches of the trees, and the secret whispering of grasses as they, in turn, danced a melody with the wind. Her attention turned to the bulrushes swaying seductively. She felt as near to peace as possible in the circumstances and took a deep breath and let it out slowly.

The memories of both parents began to get clearer. She concentrated until they filled her mind, body, and soul until they were one.

Alice laughed at the good times and felt sad about others. She saw the moment of her birth and felt the joy of her parents as they held her for the first time. Tears trickled down her cheeks as their memories were shared with her. *Oh, mother, father, I miss you so much already, I cannot bear this.*

She wiped her nose with the back of her hand, took a deep breath, and continued to follow the paths their lives had taken through their memories. She relived the achievements of both and realized how much good they had done in their lives. She saw the joy on the faces of the people they had helped. Time passed as she absorbed their memories and noted the lessons learned throughout their lives.

Deeper into the memories, she found their innermost secrets, and her heart skipped a beat. She relived the memory again, hardly believing what she was recalling. It was a secret that they would reveal to her on her twenty-fifth birthday. She said the words aloud, trying to understand what she was remembering. "Saul is alive. He walks the earth." She repeated it, remembering more. "Saul walks the earth, and Jed knows! Jed knows! Why have they been keeping this from me? Why?"

Again, she dug deeper. "Jed has known for twenty years. Why has he kept it from me? What's this? He is only one year older than me?" She took a deep breath, hardly comprehending what she had recalled, and her heart began to race.

We are the same age at last, after four hundred years, we walk the earth simultaneously. Why Mother? Why Father? How could you have kept this from me?

Alice ran to the stables and leaped on to her horse. She didn't bother with the saddle as she always rode bareback as her ancestors did centuries before. When Alice arrived at the manor, she let the horse run free and sprinted to the reception desk. Before she could confront Jed, he wrapped his arms around her and hugged her close. "Oh God, Alice, I've just heard. Are you ok?"

The guest of the manor stopped and stared. Alice saw his concern, and for a second, her anger subsided. "Jed, it is ok, and we are all together."

Relief flooded Jed's face. "Thank God, Alice. I thought for a moment your parents' memories had been lost."

Moments later, her anger returned with vigor. She broke free from his embrace and pushed him away. "Jed, why did you not tell me about Saul?"

Jed froze, studying his young friend. He was surprised at the change of tack and the anger in her voice. "What do you mean, tell you about Saul?

Alice shook her head in disbelief, studying the older man whom she had trusted all her life. "Jed, I have my parents' memories." She tapped her head, indicating the union with them. "Let me refresh your memory, Joan Masters, America Twenty years ago. You have known where my love is for twenty years, and you and my parents have kept it from me. Why?

Jed rubbed his hand through his thinning hair and looked uncomfortable, and his eyes turned away from hers. He grabbed her by the elbow, pulled her into his office and closed the door. He took a deep breath and studied her. "Alice, it might not be Saul."

Alice was studying every nuance of his face. "My mother and father think it's Saul. Why don't you?" Her eyes were filled with rage, and they burned into his.

Again, he ran his hand through his hair. "Alice, Joan Masters' son is… blind."

Her heart faltered. "Blind? When you say blind, do you mean he has lost his sight?"

Jed shook his head. "No, blind, as in, he has no memories. He does not know who he is or what he is." Jed watched as her forehead creased, and she bit her lip, a trait she did when confused.

She shook her head from side to side, disbelieving what he was saying. "How can he not know who he is? and what on earth is he doing in America? Jed, I cannot believe you have kept this from me, blind or not. Why?"

Jed looked at the floor sheepishly. "Sorry Alice, but your parents, and to be more precise, Joan, wanted Paul to finish his education. "It was discussed, and they all agreed to wait until you were twenty-five before they told you."

Alice stepped back. "Jed, you don't need to be educated if you are 'Prime.' You are a font of eternal knowledge - all you must do is recall your memories and listen to your ancestors."

Jed waved his arms in the air dismissively. "As I said, Alice, Paul is blind to the memories, and the same went for his mother and father. That's why I went to America twenty years ago - to help Joan recover hers."

The crease in Alice's forehead spread in confusion. "And does she remember now?"

"Yes, well, a little, but Alice, I am not even sure it is Saul. What I can say it is someone who knew you, your mother, Ursula, and Morag. It might not be Saul."

"Jed, it was wrong for you not to tell me. I must go to him straight away, and I must help him." She turned to go, but he grabbed her arm to stop her.

"You can't, Alice, you know you can't, not now. Remember, now your mother is dead, you are the new keeper of the henge, it is passed to you by rite, and then there is Sarah, you can't leave."

Alice threw her arms in the air and screamed at him. "I will never forgive you for this, Jed." Jed's face paled. He had not wanted to keep it a secret from Alice but was overruled by Joan Masters.

"Alice, have you been drinking? I have never seen you act like this?"

Alice burst into tears and, through the sobs, screamed. "Yes, Jed, I have just lost both parents, and I'm pissed, but not as pissed as I am with you." She called back as she began to leave. "If I can't go to America, I will bring him here."

Jed rushed over to her and grabbed her elbow to restrain her.

"You can't, he's blind - it is too late for him."

She studied his face intensely. "What do you mean it is too late?

He could not stand the pain in her eyes and looked away. His voice was barely audible. "You can't take the chance. You know as well as the rest of us how dangerous it is to be forced to regain memories at such a late age. He could turn towards the dark and, with his latent powers, be the biggest tyrant the world has seen for thousands of years."

She snatched her arm away angrily and screamed once again. "Not my Saul. If anything, he will become the savior of humanity, and together, we can fulfill Mia's prophecy." She stormed to the door, stopped, then turned back and shook her head in dismay, her voice as cold as ice and full of venom. "Jed, I will never forgive you for this." After slamming the door, she staggered out of the foyer, oblivious to the condolences of the staff.

Later that night, Alice Llewellyn assumed her meditating position and contemplated what she was about to do. *What if Jed says is true, and it is not Saul?* She shook her head. *I could not bear it. What if it is him, and he does not want me? What if he has already found someone else? Has he got a wife? Will he come back to me if he cannot remember us? Would he be content here? America is so big, and Somerset so small. What if I call him and he does not come?* She shook her head, dismissing the thought. *That would mean Jed is correct, and it is not him. He will have no choice but to come if it is him. Yes, I must call him. It is the only way to be sure. What if he wants me to go to America? I cannot leave Sarah, not now.*

Alice pulled her legs up to her chest, rocking back and forth, her heart racing. *Worst scenario, what if he gets drawn toward the dark? The 'Primevil' would welcome him with open arms. No, Saul would never do that. Then again, if he did, we would have to kill him. Could I kill him?*

The mist rose from the lake, its icy fingers creeping across her skin. Her mind changed tack. *Was that the Witches' malevolence probing, working its way into my mind?* "Begone Witch, he rejected you once and will do it again." She spoke the words verbally to give her courage and pressed her lips into a straight line. *Was that simply the mist or her - probing?*

She shook her head, hoping to clear the negative thoughts, and began to meditate. When she found peace, she began the enchantment to call Saul back to her as she had done throughout every lifetime in the last four hundred years.

Caged in her prison, the Witch cackled to herself. *We will see dearie, we will see who he really desires.*

13. THE PRIMEVIL GRANDMASTERS 1605 AD

The 'Primevil' Council for Somerset and the Southwest of England was summoned to an emergency meeting at the Wood Henge in the shadow of mount Avalon in Somerset. The ten most powerful Grandmasters in the area were present. The hooded figures wore red robes and sat cross-legged on the bare earth. The early evening mist drifted across the ground, settling in the hollow centered on the Henge. Fog, like loose linen, draped across the landscape. The air was damp and musky, and a smell of rotting vegetation hung about like a cloying veil.

The ten hooded figures sat silently, waiting, heads bowed. The meeting was due to start at sunset. In front of each of them was a pole six feet in length, rising vertically out of the mist, and at the top, a cross perch.

One by one, the birds flew in. They positioned themselves, one on each perch. Every bird that arrived was a hawk of some kind, and nine birds in all flew in. They waited for the tenth, but no one expected it to come. One hour passed before a hooded figure spoke.

"It seems we are all here, so we will begin. This meeting has been called to debate the happenings of the last two weeks. Your choice of bird tells me you have heard the rumor that one of the Grandmasters has left us. First, I will outline the events leading to his demise, and it will then be open to discussion.

The Grandmaster in question contacted our 'Primevil' colleagues six days ago. A Princess from Persia had arrived at their festival with two five-year-old daughters. He was extremely excited because even at the age of five, one of the girls displayed all the attributes of a seer."

The birds began to chatter amongst themselves, and the Grandmaster waited for them to quieten down before continuing.

"When addressing him for the first time, she knew his birth line and his father's occupation. This girl had arrived in this country just a few days before and had no contact with anyone at the festival before meeting him. He was ordered to observe this child and report back to us.

During the festivals, a row broke out between the two girls about an arranged marriage for one of them, and he heard the one say that, like her mother, she was also a seer. These girls also had an uncanny ability to control animals, having arrived at the festival on the backs of two giant wolves."

Again, the birds chattered.

"A decision was taken to remove the girls from their mother to be educated correctly. Our brother, who was also a seer, foresaw the different paths that could be taken, and he chose the one that he thought guaranteed success. He decided the greatest chance of success coincided with the dance of the free spirits. By this time, most of the revelers were incoherent or otherwise engaged. Four of our men killed their guards and took the girls making their escape in the dead of night.

The following day he was attending a meeting between the girl's mother and the Local Earth Mother and was very surprised that the mother was untroubled by the fact that the girls had been taken. They had readied a rescue party, but no one seemed to be in any hurry to rescue the girls. In the meeting with the Earth Mother and the girl's mother, they let it slip that one of the girls could communicate with animals - as we do birds and was waiting for a message to give them their location.

The Grandmaster felt he needed to inform our brothers that the girls could be in contact, and as the Shaman could not physically leave the meeting, he decided to call a bird to carry his spirit and warn them. However, it was intercepted by three birds of prey, and the girls" wolves killed all four men. We lost five brothers, and the girls were reunited with their mother."

Another speaker lifted his head, indicating he was about to speak. He was acting as the bird's voice that sat perched above him.

"If our brother was a seer, how could the path that guaranteed success fail?"

Again, the birds all began to chatter.

Another man sat upright and addressed the meeting. "If one so young could out-see a seer, she would have great potential."

Another man joined in. "You're suggesting a five-year-old girl could out-see a Grandmaster. You're talking nonsense."

All the men in the circle, except the one with the empty perch, joined in the discussion.

Another man asked, "Where are the girls now?"

The Supreme Grandmaster replied, "We are not sure at present. We did try to retake the girls on several occasions on their journey back to Persia, but our comrades failed repeatedly. We were informed they were heading for the fishing port of Plymouth and had forty men waiting at the port, but suddenly they diverted to the port of Portsmouth. At one point, we had laid an ambush, but at the last second, they again changed route.

Once more, a man lifted his head and commented, "The girl or her mother obviously foresaw the ambush, very impressive."

The Supreme Grandmaster continued, "Next time, they were spotted on the outskirts of the town of Portsmouth. So, the decision was taken to wait until they arrived at the boat before the next attempt to remove them. Their guards were to escort them to the ship, then leave when the ship sailed. We waited until they arrived in France, and one of our brothers managed to separate the mother from her daughters by directing her to a coach depot well away from the boat. Our men then overpowered the guards, and when we went into the cabin, all three had already fled."

Another man spoke, "So the child, or the Princess, also foresaw that trap, very clever. Where was the boat going?"

The Supreme Grandmasters' speaker replied, "It was sailing to Le Havre in France, and the Princess was heading home to Persia."

Another man spoke, "We must have men watch all the main ports, both here and in France."

The speaker for the Supreme Grandmaster continued. "We posted them immediately, but we have lost contact at this moment."

Several of the speakers began to speak amongst themselves.

"Then we have lost them. What a waste."

"They must be gifted seers to evade our traps, three times on the journey and once on the boat. No wonder our brother was so excited with the child's potential."

"Also, the ability to "bewitch animals at such a young age is intriguing." For a time, the meeting went quiet, the members all contemplating the loss of potentially exciting new members.

Then one of the elders addressed the meeting. "Do we know if the bird carrying our brother's spirit was close to the girls when it died"

The Supreme Grandmaster replied, "We do not have this information. What is your point, brother?"

"Have we considered the possibility that our brother did not fail? After all, he was a gifted seer."

The Grandmaster raised his voice in anger. "How did he not fail? He is dead, his memories gone, and the girls have escaped. Of course, he failed."

The elder continued, his voice calm and patient. "Maybe that was all part of his plan."

Silence descended once again on the meeting.

"Explain yourself, brother."

"If he foresaw that he could contaminate them by sacrificing himself near the girls. Then in years to come, if either child had a leaning toward the dark, it would manifest itself. He probably foresaw this happening, and it is more feasible than a child outwitting one of us."

"Very interesting. As you say, it would explain how a child could outwit a Grandmaster."

The elder continued, "For a Grandmaster to give his life on the off chance that one of the girls could be turned, he must have foreseen at least one of them becoming a mighty member of the 'Primevil,' possibly even a future Queen."

The Supreme Grandmaster agreed. "In that case, Grandmasters, I think we must agree there is a greater possibility he did not fail - and that our brother's memories have not been lost after all.

We will send messengers to all the ports to keep a lookout, but I fear if these girls have the foresight, we think they have, we are wasting our time. Only time will tell if our brother's sacrifice has worked, so all we can do now is wait.

On the other hand, we do know who helped arrange the deception. It was Lord Monkton, and I am informed that he is Prime and that he has been a thorn in our side for many years, as was his brother, whom we killed when he crossed us. However, his youngest son is becoming interesting as well, he formed a close bond with the younger of the twin girls, and now he too can communicate with the forest creatures."

The Supreme Grandmasters' speaker fell silent as another speaker raised their head. "An impressive skill, to be sure, but is it beneficial to us? The birds again began to chatter between themselves.

When they fell silent, a fresh speaker raised its head. "Supreme Grandmaster, we feel this is a minor skill and of no benefit to us."

The speaker's head fell forward, and the Supreme Grandmaster concluded the meeting. "In that case, we will take our revenge on Lord Monkton. He has a substantial estate and many vulnerable tenants. Once again, I feel it is time to show him it is not wise to go against us. I propose we instigate a fresh wave of raiding parties against his tenants. We will make them pay for this outrage. Our members have been getting hungry of late, and I say we let them feast for a while. All those in favor."

The birds went crazy. The supreme Grandmaster did not wait for the speakers to raise their heads.

"Motion passed."

The Supreme Grandmaster closed the meeting, and one by one, the birds flew away.

14. EARLSWOOD MANOR 1996 AD

She knew this day would be the most momentous day of her life. Alice Llewellyn had the gift of foresight. It was hereditary and had passed down the female line for thousands of years. An ancestor had foretold in the early sixteen hundreds that one day she would be reunited with her lover once again. At last, after many lifetimes, she would once again be reunited with her soul mate, the only man in all her lives she ever truly loved.

It was a union connected by an ancient calling, a 'Prime' feeling that crossed the ages and locked them together. The most powerful emotion of all... love, a love that echoed through the generations, never to be denied or forgotten.

Unknown to him, she had been calling him for years, lifetime after lifetime, century after century, as he had done for her.

Saul is coming, and I can feel him getting closer. So, Jed was wrong after all. Paul Masters is Saul, and he has been reborn and is coming back to me. She could sense he was getting closer by the second, and the wait would soon be over.

Alice's mind was filled with doubt and anxiety. *Would he remember me? Can he sense me as I can feel him? Jed said he was blind to his 'Prime' heritage. A stray, as we call them now. What if he cannot remember who he is? Should I tell him? Is it just a matter of reawakening his memory? Jed said he did it with his mother, and she, too, was a stray. Only time will tell. Can I guide him to the light? He has been brought up living in a city and was exposed to its temptations.* She shuddered involuntarily and shook her head, clearing her thoughts.

Alice had woken early. This was the day she had been waiting for all her life, this life, and a dozen others. Alice was always up early as manageress of this hotel, but it was well before dawn today. Alice could not sleep. She had showered and spent time putting on makeup and took her time combing her long black hair that fell to her waist, she knew Saul loved her hair long. She put on her best working clothes and kept herself occupied.

Paul Masters sat at the wheel of the Bentley convertible. He had parked the car on the hill overlooking the Earlswood estate, and it gave him a panoramic view of the manor house and its grounds. Far off to the right, he could see the lake and the woods. In the distance, the town of Glastonbury and the remains of the Abbey, and high on the Tor the Saint Michaels chapel that overlooked the surrounding area.

He sat there deep in thought as he took in the surrounding views. He remembered his father and grandfather talking about the estate when he was young, and it was one of his few remaining memories of his father. He was familiar with this place, and he couldn't determine why.

Have I dreamt about it?

He shook his head wordlessly. He could not remember seeing a photograph of the old family estate either. He chewed his lip thoughtfully and wondered why it looked so familiar. It had been his family's ancestral home in the early twentieth century. Then again, maybe, it was one of his mother's so-called inherited memories.

Maybe I can get some answers, who knows?

Like a salmon returning to the river of its birth to spawn, it was a calling, a message embedded in his DNA. He could feel something drawing him here and had no idea what it was, but he knew he needed to be here. A business opportunity arose, which he took, and now he was here at last.

His grandfather had told Paul many tales of his youth. It was centered around the estate and growing up in the manor house, playing in the woods, and swimming in the lake. His great-grandfather had sold the manor in the nineteen twenties and had moved the family to America. Later it was converted into a hotel. Now the property was once again up for sale.

A motorway to the south bypassed the property and had taken their customers and most of the profits. It was a downward spiral from then on. His family in America had heard that it was on the market - and Paul, who was still in his mid-twenties, was here to represent the family, a family whose fortune was built on the design and construction of golf resorts. As the sport took off in America, so did their finances.

Paul's task was to compile a report on the viability of transforming this estate from a run-down hotel to a premier golf resort. As he sat there, his thoughts turned to the conversations between his father and grandfather when he was young. The family was sitting around the dinner table, the topic, discussing the possibility of turning this estate into a golf course.

Once again, Paul took in the views, the fields, the woods, and the lake and nodded his head approvingly. *Well, there is certainly enough land, and the lake could be a helpful feature. So far, it all looks promising. I think it is time to look at the manor house itself.*

He started the Bentley and glided down the tree-lined road. It was late morning when he arrived at the estate. There was a green wedge of grass down the center of the driveway, and he made a mental note. *There is no room for two-way traffic on this lane, and we may need to widen this unless we can make it a one-way system.*

Alice was about to select a pen from a jar of pens when her head filled with the noise of a car driving over gravel. Although the car was a mile away, she could sense it with every fiber of her body and knew he had entered the estate.

He's here. He is finally here.

The jar of pens fell to the floor and shattered into a thousand pieces. Alice tried to keep calm but found it difficult, she was accustomed to controlling her emotions and meditated regularly. It only took moments before she was again under control, and outwardly, she was calm, personified.

He is here. My love is here.

He would come to the rear of the house. She was sure of it. Quickly she made her way to the upstairs window, which overlooked the rear of the property. His car pulled into the courtyard in front of the back entrance. Her legs felt like jelly, just like when she saw him first.

He's here!

Paul parked the Bentley in what he assumed was the front of the manor house, where he sat for a while, taking time to look at the house and grounds, and was once again lost in thought. *I can't remember seeing a photo of the house either, but everything looks familiar. Déjà vu, I think they call it. Ok, what was it, my grandfather said. First impressions are crucial.*

Paul took out his Dictaphone and spoke into it. "Well, it's old, probably older than America. The land. There is plenty of land, enough for even a large golf course. It would be a nice feature to encompass the lake. I'll check it out later to see if it's workable."

He switched off the Dictaphone and continued with his thoughts. *The lake could be a feature. Yes, first impressions are good. The house, however, maybe a different kettle of fish. Yes, it has character, and it looks grand, imposing even. Could we drag it screaming into the twenty-first century? That's the question. Here we go. It's time to have a look inside.*

Alice watched from the upstairs window, and her heart was pounding. She watched as he got out of the car, paused, and looked at the house. His eyes drifted, taking in the view of the surrounding countryside. He stood there for several minutes. From above, she could see his head turn towards the lake, and then towards the woods, the church, the Abby which now lay in ruins, and in the distance the bustling town of Glastonbury, and beyond that the Tor with St Michael's tower on top

Is he remembering? The town was a tiny village the last time he was here, the wood was a forest. Has it changed, Saul?

Paul turned to the rear door. She heard the old heavy doorbell ring. *It is the same bell? Can you remember the tone?* Her excitement was palpable. *He is here.*

She could hear someone moving down the corridor.

That would be Jed, coming to open the door. He would be wondering why someone had come around the back. It will take Jed a few moments, then he too will remember why.

She felt her heart racing, and Alice took a deep breath, let it out slowly, and used her training to bring it once again under control. *At last, he is here, after nearly four hundred years, he is here – but will he remember me?*

As he pulled the old bell rope for a second time, Paul heard bells ringing inside the manor house. Again, a feeling of familiarity overcame him.

"All right, all right. Keep your hair on." The muffled voice came from deep inside the building. The large oak door opened, revealing a man in his late forties, he was about six feet tall, well built, with thin receding hair. He spoke with a strong Welsh accent. "Yes, can I help you?"

"I'm Paul Masters."

For a moment, the man looked confused. "Well?" the man said abruptly.

Paul, who was a little taken aback by the response, countered, "I have a room booked."

Jed managed a faint interrogative "Ah ...?" Then added. "So, you are a guest are you Sir? You have come to the wrong entrance. Guests usually go to the front of the property."

Paul's brow furrowed in confusion. "Oh, sorry. Isn't this the front?"

The man laughed. "No, Sir. It was four hundred years ago, but not now. Not to worry, let me put a light on and you can come through this way." If Paul could have seen his face, he would have seen his smile. Jed shook his head. *He has changed since I last saw him. So, Alice has called him at last. O God I hope the world does not come to regret it.*

Jed shuffled over in the dark to switch the lights on. Before Paul could step inside, a heavy gust of wind struck Paul and took his breath away. Seeing the heavy oak door about to slam him in the face, he leaped into the darkened room as the door slammed shut. Suddenly the room was in total darkness. A second later, it could have done him serious harm.

Alice, who was watching from above, smiled inwardly. She expected something like that and spoke verbally for her own benefit. "What a rude Witch you are. You really should learn to let bygones be bygones."

Jed raised his voice in the darkness. "Are you alright, Sir? Please stay there until I put the light on. Don't move."

"What caused that?" Paul said indignantly.

Jed shrugged his shoulders. "It's just the wind, Sir. Wuthering, as they say around here, blows right through the house it does. The front door must be open, and it could be a storm coming.

Paul pursed his lips and his brow creased. "You could have fooled me. I didn't feel a breath of wind before."

Jed made light of it. "Must be the wind, Sir. Doors don't shut by themselves, do they? If you follow me, we will go through to the main desk, and I'll book you in."

Paul followed the man through the house and along narrow dark wood-lined corridors. Paul again had the feeling of déjà vu and felt the hair lifting on the back of his neck. After turning the last corner, Paul found himself in a well-lit foyer as Jed opened the register on the desk.

Alice made her way down the stairs and watched him from a distance as Jed booked him in. *He looks so young, but his eyes are the same, and he still has a straight back. His hair is a lighter color. No beard though. He has a forceful jaw, and his mouth is wide with plenty of teeth, typical American. Oh, and his lips are thicker. He pulls his mouth to one side when he smiles, just like he used to. He looks so different, but at last, after all this time, He's here.*

First impressions are always important. Paul Masters could hear the words again as if they were said yesterday. It was advice his grandfather had given him when he first joined the family business ten years ago at the age of sixteen. His eyes drifted around the lobby. Classic old English, dated yet, familiar, classy but tired. The receptionist's Welsh accent broke his reverie.

"Right, Sir, my name is Jed, and I'm the assistant manager. So, you say you have made a reservation? May I have your name, please?"

Paul's voice had the edge of irritation in it. "As I have already said, Paul Masters."

Jed ignored the sarcastic remark. "So, you did, Sir. Paul Masters, yes, here we are. Jed could not hide the surprise on his face. "According to the email, you asked for the master bedroom?"

"Yes, that's correct. Is there a problem?"

"Well, not really a problem as such - it is just that we haven't let that room out for a very long time. Is there a particular reason you want that room?"

Paul smiled sheepishly, and Jed realized it was a copy of his mother's. "My family used to own this property, and it was my grandfather's room. He said if I was ever to stay here, it must be in that room. He said it was the most beautiful room he had ever seen, south-facing, large windows with views down the lake."

Jed was troubled, but his face belied his worry. "I see, Sir. It's just it has not been used or rented for a long time. It will take some time to get that room aired and ready for you, and we have many more rooms with beautiful views."

"I want that room. It is most important – and I don't mind waiting. It's not a problem for me as long as it will be ready for tonight."

Jed had not anticipated this and knew he must do all he could to prevent it from happening.

"I see, Sir. I must point out that it's got a bit of a reputation, and not many of the locals request that room. It's also the most expensive room we have."

Paul waved his arms dismissively, "Not a problem."

"Do you not want to know how much, Sir?"

Paul shook his head. "No, Jed. The company will pay."

Jed took a deep breath. "Right you are, Sir. How long will you be staying?"

Paul thought for a moment and chewed his lip, another of his mother's mannerisms. "I "m not quite sure, but book me in for one week first, and we will see how we go."

"Very good, Sir. Are you here on business or pleasure?"

"A bit of both. I have some business to take care of locally, but I would like to trace back some of my ancestors. As I said before, my family used to live in this property."

"You could do with talking with Alice, the manageress. Her family has lived in the neighborhood for centuries."

"Thank you, Jed. You must point her out to me sometime."

Jed smiled openly. "Just look for the most beautiful woman you have ever seen, and it will be her."

Paul returned his smile and pursed his lips before commenting sarcastically. "Wow, and she works here?"

Jed nodded his head in agreement and ignored the sarcasm. "Yes, Sir. She works here. Now Mr. Masters, if you can give us a few hours, we will get the room ready. We have a restaurant with a bar, and it's open for guests."

"Thank you. Would you get someone to take my cases up to the room when it's ready and have them put the car away?"

"Certainly, Sir, I'll ask Alice to do it for you."

Jed pressed the bell on the desk, and Alice looked up. He caught her eye and called her over to him. Alice's heart began to flutter with excitement.

Let him see me first, see if he remembers.

She walked past Paul without looking at him, and up to the desk. Jed said nervously, "He's here."

"Obviously," Alice said, her eyebrow lifting cynically. She let her eyes discreetly slip towards his face to get a closer look and held her breath. *I could love that face.*

"Could you park his car please, Alice? I can't leave the desk, and there is no one else on duty that can drive?" Jed had raised his voice so everyone could hear and then lowered it to a whisper. He expects us to do it, and what's more, Alice, he is demanding the master bedroom."

The color drained from Alice's face. "What! can't you stop him?"

Jed did not hide the exasperation in his voice. "How? I have tried everything I can think of.

Alice closed her eyes in despair, and when she answered, her voice was little more than a whisper. "Get Susan to go and scare him with ghost stories or something and see if that will do the trick." Alice lapsed into thought. *Thinking about it, of course, he would want that room. It was his. How stupid of me.*

Jed interrupted her thoughts. "Oh, by the way, Alice, the head office has said that we are to treat him like royalty."

Alice frowned. "Did they say why?"

Jed shook his head. "No, Alice. Do you think you could find out?"

Picking up the keys, she turned and, once again, walked past him without paying him the slightest interest. She could feel his eyes watching her. *Please remember me, Saul. Take a good look.*

Paul had to agree with Jed that she was beautiful, and his heart missed a beat at the similarity of the woman in his dreams. He was momentarily lost in thought. *I know her from somewhere - or someone just like her. Or, is she the woman I have been dreaming about all these years? Her hair is the right color, I wonder what color her eyes are.*

The formalities sorted, Paul went into the bar, which was almost empty. He looked around again, trying to gauge his first impressions, and made a mental note. *They don't seem to be very busy, no wonder they are going bankrupt.* After ringing the bell on the bar, a familiar voice called out. "Be with you in a minute, Sir."

Moments later, Jed, the receptionist, came through to the bar. "Right, Sir. What can I get you?"

Paul smiled ruefully. "Do you do everything around here, Jed?".

Jed snorted. "It certainly feels like it some days, Mr. Masters, and today is one of them."

"Can I try one of your real ales, Jed?"

"Certainly, Sir. This is a local Brew, a favorite of mine. See what you think of it."

Paul spotted a seat by the window, sat himself down, and took time to take in the decor and feel of the place. And again, he was lost in thought. *It will take a lot to bring this into the twenty-first century, but the whole place has a very homely, familiar feel. We will need to modernize, but we must keep the character to make it work.*

One of the guests, a lady in her mid-thirties, came over to Paul. She had long, curly red hair. She was attractive and had ample breasts which she did not try to hide. Her smile was warm and inviting.

"I hear you have booked the old master bedroom?"

"Yes," Paul got to his feet politely and returned the smile.

"That's very brave of you."

"Brave, what on earth do you mean by that...?" He held the word, and she introduced herself.

"Susan, Susan De Winter. Don't tell me you weren't warned about the goings-on in that room?"

Paul shrugged his shoulders. "Jed said that it had a bit of a reputation. But I didn't ask what it was?"

"You should not sleep in that room without knowing all the facts. Why don't you buy me a drink, and I'll tell you about it?"

Paul thought the lady was attractive even though she was a few years older than him, although certainly not his type. However, he had nothing better to do and felt it would be nice to have some company to help pass the time.

"Certainly. What would you like, Susan?"

She sat down before replying. "Scotch, scotch with water."

Having rung the bell on the bar, Jed again came through from reception. "Could I have another of your real ales, a different one this time, one you can recommend, and a scotch with water for the lady?" Jed looked across to see who it was who was sitting with him. *Good girl, Susan.*

"The lady is not bothering you, is she, Sir?"

"No, she seems fine, just friendly."

Jed looked in the direction of the lady. "You should be careful, Sir. She can get a bit too friendly if you keep buying her drinks if you get my drift."

Paul laughed. "I'll bear that in mind, Jed, thanks for the warning."

Paul carried the drinks back to the table. The lady was checking her face in her compact mirror, and Paul noticed her emerald green eyes.

"Here we are, one scotch with water. Are you a guest here, Susan?"

She shook her head. "No, I live locally, and I have a table booked. The food is quite good here, and I don't cook."

"Sorry, I haven't introduced myself. My name is Paul, by the way. May I say your eyes are so strikingly green, are they contacts?

Susan studied the young man, trying to determine if it was a compliment or a pass. She licked her lips, savoring the scotch and hedging her bets, and smiled.

"They are real, Paul, everything you see is real."

Paul felt his face turning red and let his eyes fall away from hers, they rested on her bosom.

"Those too."

Paul turned his eyes away, "Sorry, Susan, it was meant as a compliment. "Your eyes are so striking set against your red hair."

Again, she licked her lips before replying, enjoying his discomfort. "They say your eyes are a window on your soul, Paul. You can tell a lot about people from their eyes. Don't you think?" He once again held eye contact, and her smile turned into a full-blooded laugh. "If it was a compliment, Paul, I will take it as such, anyway, I was only messing with you."

Paul cleared his throat. "So, Susan, why am I brave to want the master bedroom? I've heard that it's quite special and extremely beautiful, fit for a Queen, that's according to my grandfather."

Susan took a sip of her drink and eyed the young American, and her face became serious. "I personally haven't dared go in that room. They usually keep it locked these days, but there have been rumors of strange goings-on for years. Just think, why would you never try to let the best room in the hotel?"

"What do you mean by that? Do things go bump in the night, that sort of thing," he said jokingly.

"More like guests being "bewitched by the room itself, never wanting to venture out. People would book in, and you would see them a couple of times, then they would just stay put in the room, never venturing out. They would have breakfast, dinner, and supper all in the room."

"That Doesn't make sense. You think I am brave because that room is beautiful?"

"It bewitches you. They say you lose yourself if you stay in there." Susan's face was still serious. "Then, there are the disappearances?"

"Disappearances?"

Susan took a second sip of her drink. "Yes, weird they are."

Paul tried to hide his irritation. "Explain "weird.""

Susan looked from side to side as if she were about to impart some well-kept secret. "Well, about twenty years ago, a guest booked in, usual pattern, the first couple of days mixed with all the guests, friendly-like. Then he started to stay in his room more and more, he had his food, and everything in his room then didn't go out at all. Then one day, he was gone."

Paul shrugged his shoulders. "You mean he just booked out? That Doesn't seem weird."

"No, he disappeared, vanished, and left all his clothes."

"Maybe he just thought it was cheaper to leave his clothes there than pay the bill."

"That's what the police thought at the time. The room was locked from the inside, and the key was still in the lock, and the only other exit was a sixty-foot drop to the ground." She took another sip of her drink.

"Twenty years ago, you say." Paul fell silent for a moment and was lost in thought. *That's how long it's been since my father disappeared.* "Do you remember the date this happened?"

She shook her head. "Not exactly, but Jed should be able to help." Paul appeared to be troubled by this, and Susan wondered whether she had already succeeded in scaring him off.

"Yes, of course, Susan. That's interesting. I will ask him later."

Susan thought she was on a roll and continued. "Rumor has it that it happened before, in the late eighteen-hundreds, and twice in the twentieth century, the same thing, left all their belongings, door locked, gone."

Paul did not try to hide the irritation in his voice any longer. "So, now and again, someone leaves their gear then goes without paying."

She ignored the sarcastic remark and continued, "Then there are the deaths?"

Paul shook his head in disbelief. "Oh, do tell."

Eagerly Susan continued, "There have been two to my knowledge. The last one, I think, was in the early eighties. As I said, Jed will tell you the dates. Then there was one in the sixties."

"Susan, that's about one every twenty years?"

Her face was still stern. "You can mock. I am sure it has been twenty years since the last one. I've warned you, but it's your choice."

A waiter approached the table. "Miss De Winter, your table is ready now." She finished her drink and got to her feet.

"Let's see how brave you are in that room after a week. Rather you than me." With that, she followed the waiter.

Paul finished his drink and approached Jed at the bar. "Do you have any other ale I could try, Jed?"

"Yes, several, Sir. Are you getting a taste for them?"

"My grandfather said to try them all, he said it was the thing he missed most about the UK."

Jed smiled at the American. "He liked our ale, did he? When did he leave for America?"

"He left as a young boy when my great-grandfather sold this place. But he was stationed here during the Second World War. That's when he got a taste for your ale. Susan said that someone went missing from that room twenty years ago, the door locked on the inside, and left all his belongings. Do you have a name?"

Jed continued to pour the ale. "Can't recall the name, but I remember being told he was a Yank like you. I was on holiday that week."

"Is there any chance you could find out the name and date?

Jed shook his head. "You can see how busy I am, and I'm short-staffed at the moment. I would have to go through all the old registers. I'll do it as soon as possible, but it will probably be tomorrow at the earliest.

"No rush, but I would be very grateful."

Jed continued to dry the glasses, his eyes trying to measure the young man. "Has Susan been trying to wind you up with ghost stories and all that?"

"Yes, she was very trying."

"I see, Sir. It didn't work then?"

"No, of course not, Jed. Should it?"

Jed shook his head and kept his face serious. "Me, I wouldn't want to sleep in there for all the tea in China. It did get a bit of a reputation. So much so that people came from miles around to stay in that room. You know the type, spiritualists, paranormal experts that sort. People were looking for answers, hoping to find the answers to life's questions, that sort of thing. It was very good for business, though!"

"Did they, Jed?"

"Did they what?"

"Find anything?"

"Find any ghosts? Not that I'm aware of. They were all seeking answers to the most basic question humanity has?"

Paul's face looked puzzled.

"What question would that be?"

"Why are we here? What is the purpose of life? It's the question most people ask at some point in their lives unless they know the answer. Jed studied every nuance on Paul's face, measuring his reaction to that statement, but saw nothing. "Is that why you wanted the room, Sir?"

"No, no. As I said before, I have been told it's quite a special room, my grandfather's old room."

"I can arrange for a different room if Susan has put the wind up you?"

"Thank you, Jed, but I'm sure I'll be fine."

Some other guests came into the bar, and Jed moved off to serve them. Paul took his latest glass of ale over to the table by the window and once again took in the views. In the distance, he could see the ruined Abbey, and above it, St Michael's tower on top of Glastonbury Tor. Absentmindedly Paul drew his finger around the rim of the glass, making it sing. His thoughts drifted back to his childhood once again, to a time twenty years ago and a conversation his mother had with him. *Your father seems to have abandoned us. It's been six months now, not a word, not a phone call, nothing.*

His father had gone to Europe on business. This usually meant looking for sites for various new golf courses. His mind began working out the different permutations.

He could have booked in here! Dad and grandpa often discussed the suitability of turning this place into a golf club. The time seems right. If it was him, it would explain why he never contacted us.

15. THE MASTER BEDROOM 1996 AD

After a couple of hours, Jed informed Paul the room was ready. Paul followed him along the wood-paneled corridor and up the centuries-old oak staircase and came to the master bedroom. "Here we go, Sir, the master bedroom for Mr. Masters." Jed chuckled at what he perceived was a joke and opened the large oak door whose hinge creaked and moaned, showing their displeasure at being disturbed and stood to one side.

After entering the room, which was in the shape of a pentagon, he saw the whole of one wall was taken up by adjoining tall windows. The early evening sun was streaming in highlighting the dust motes that danced in the air - happy that they had been disturbed from their long slumber.

There was a king-sized four-poster bed covered with cream-colored silk drapes at the center of the room. On the wall opposite was a large painting of a beautiful woman. It stood five feet tall, and it was the only painting in the room. All the other walls were covered with mirrors from floor to ceiling, and with the mirrors reflecting the sunlight, the whole room was bathed in light. Taking it all in, Paul understood why his grandfather said it was one of the most beautiful rooms he could remember.

"Jed, the room is as lovely as gramps said. I see now why he told me to book it."

Paul walked out the open window that led to a balcony and took in the view of the lake and in the distance the tor on a carpet of mist. Looking down, he could see a sheer drop to the ground of at least sixty feet, as Susan had said.

Walking back into the room, Paul turned his attention to the lady in the painting. "What a beautiful woman, Jed."

Jed joined him, admiring the painting. "Yes, she was a beauty, all right."

"Strange, but her face seems familiar. Who was she?"

"One of the Monkton girls I can't remember which one, but it Doesn't matter as they were identical twins."

A gust of wind suddenly filled the room, and the curtains billowed until the door slammed shut. Unperturbed, Jed commented, "Storm's coming, so we had better leave the window shut, Sir."

Paul ignored the wind, his eyes still focused on the painting, stirring memories that echoed through the ages, a familiarity just out of reach. He quipped, "Maybe you upset the lady in the painting. Maybe she wants to be remembered. Maybe she's one of your ghosts."

Jed tried once again to get him to change his mind.

"You could be right. Maybe Susan has put the wind up you after all."

Paul laughed. "I'm joking, Jed. Just a joke - Wuthering wind, no doubt."

Jed sighed and shook his head as he realized he had failed to dissuade Paul from sleeping in the room. "Of course, Sir, whatever you say. Will that be all, Sir?" Jed lingered long enough for Paul to give him a tip, and he called back as he left the room, "breakfast is between seven and nine. Sleep tight."

Paul studied the painting, and once again the feeling of déjà vu overcame him. "Lady Monkton, you look so familiar. Are you the woman that has haunted me in my dreams all these years? He found himself staring at the picture, studying every detail, her hair, her smile, how she held herself, and the color of her eyes. She was captivating.

Walking around the room, he noticed the reflection of the painting was always in view. As he stood there, he realized someone had arranged the mirrors so that you would always see the reflection of the painting wherever you were in the room! "Whoever had designed this room must have been in love with you, my lady."

There was a sash cord to the right of the picture, and Paul pulled it, and the curtains closed, hiding the painting. Sleep did not come easily. His thoughts centered on the familiarity of the house, the surrounding land, and the lady in the picture. There also was the constant feeling of déjà vu that troubled him. That, and Susan's comments were playing on his mind.

He removed his clothing and collapsed on the bed. He was exhausted, his head fuzzy with jet lag. His leg muscles quivered and twitched in spasms screaming for rest. He lay there listening to the sounds coming from the building itself. The house, like all houses, creaked and talked to itself at night. He had to admit Susan's ghost stories had put him on edge. He rolled over, punched his pillow, and called out, "all old houses creak and moan," hoping it would comfort him.

When sleep finally came, he plunged headfirst into a seething cauldron of dreams, and they reflected the echoes in his mind. He was riding a horse at a gallop through the woods. In front of him was another rider, a woman. For some reason, he was chasing her. She was wearing a white garment that billowed behind her in the wind. He could feel the wind on his face, in his hair. Blood coursed through his veins, and he could feel his heart pounding with excitement. The woman looked behind her and laughed her face full of life, her eyes vibrant green. They were always green in his dreams. She let out a scream as she realized she was about to get caught.

The horses continued to weave through the trees, their lower branches grazing his head. He could smell the sweat of the horses filling his nostrils. Shortly, she would be within reach. He pulled alongside her, matching her stride for stride. He looked across at her, and yes, her eyes were green, green like emeralds, blazing with life and excitement. He stretched out his arm to grab her harness and realized she didn't have one and was guiding the horse with her knees. Suddenly she veered to the left, and he overshot, and she was gone.

He turned the horse and walked back in the direction she had taken, there was no sound. He took a deep breath tasting the air. There it was, the smell of perfume mixed with the sweat of her horse. She was near, very near. He continued to strain his ears, and there it was, she was giggling, unable to contain her excitement.

He dismounted and tiptoed through the bushes. Suddenly she rushed past him on foot. He grabbed her gown, and as she wriggled to get free it ripped like paper. She was completely naked underneath. Their eyes met. Yes, they were like sparkling green emeralds. Again, she darted away, laughing, leaving the remnants of her garment in his hands. He ran after her until he could hear water, running water. He could smell the damp air as it danced past the stones in a hurry to get to the lake below. Now he knew where she was going, and he slowed to a walking pace.

The sound of running water now filled his ears. He could smell the damp moss, and the grass, it was their special place. He let his horse walk free and tip-toed through the undergrowth. The moon lit the grassy knoll, its light dancing seductively through bare-branched trees.

"What kept ya?" The voice was female, and the accent was pure West Country. She was lying naked on her stomach with her head resting on her hands and her feet high above her knees. "Well, my Lord, has cat got tongue?"

He knelt and took in her beauty, and he gasped. Her eyes were the eyes that had haunted him throughout his life. She cupped his head in her hands and pulled him down upon her, her body writhing, in need, of longing. As is the way of dreams, the scene changed, and she was now on top of him, and her breasts, like ripe melons, hung down before his eyes, their nipples brushing his lips. His body was filled with urgency and, finally, release.

The cold between his legs returned him to the land of the living and he let out an agonized groan of desolation and disappointment as he realized it was once again, just a dream.

*

After a shower, he went down to breakfast, his mind full of questions. Why the same woman? It's always the same woman. Could it be, after all these years, I have finally found the woman of my dreams - but four hundred years too late?

There was a mixture of guests, and he noticed the majority were elderly. He scanned the room and spotted Alice, who, unbeknown to him, had deliberately positioned herself on the last table with an empty seat. He studied her from a distance. *Yes, she is beautiful, Jed, you were right and so out of place here.* Nervously, he moved closer and went over to her.

"Is anyone sitting here?"

Alice at once noticed the American accent. *Well, he has lost his West Country twang.* Alice lifted her eyes from the newspaper and looked at the chair. Resting the newspaper sarcastically on the table, she leaned forward, examining it, then sat back down without speaking, and turned her attention to the paper.

"I take it that's a no, do you mind if I join you?"

She presented him a copy of the Mia smile and removed the newspaper that she had deliberately left to prevent anyone from sitting there.

"By all means."

Alice folded the newspaper in half and continued reading, and ignored Paul Masters completely

"Lovely morning," Paul said over the top of her newspaper, and his heart missed a beat when he saw the color of her eyes.

Alice drew her eyes from the paper and took in every aspect of his face. *His eyes are the same: same lips, but thicker. Oh God, I should not look at his lips. His hair is lighter. I would love to just run my fingers through his hair. Just sit on your hands Alice Llewellyn - you're behaving like a schoolgirl. It's just as curly though. I think He's taller. He obviously hasn't remembered me yet. But he came to the back door! He must remember the house as it was. That's a start. Oh God, just look at him. He is so handsome. Please, Saul, do you not remember me? What's that? He is saying something.* It brought Alice out of her reverie.

"Pardon?"

"I said, it's a lovely morning. Jed says your family has lived here for generations."

Alice pulled herself back to reality. "Ah, You're Mr. Masters, I take it. "Yes, my family has lived in the area for hundreds of years. Jed told me you wished to trace your family tree. If you need any help, just ask. How was your first night's sleep, Sir?"

Paul waved his hand dismissively. "Slept like a log, and please drop the Sir. My name is Paul."

He reached across and held out his hand, and Alice took it. As they shook hands, their eyes locked together. Alice felt a tingling sensation run up her arm. Had he felt it too? As Paul held her hand, unknown images flashed through his mind, echoing someone lost in time. *Those eyes are the same. I am sure of it. She could be the woman in my dreams.* He continued to hold the handshake longer than expected, but Alice did not mind. She was touching him once again.

Paul, for a while, fell silent, the echoes becoming clearer. He was having flashbacks. Scenes flashed through his mind, multiple scenes. Children playing in a stream, covered in mud. White-robed people were dancing within a circle of standing stones. He was lying on his back, a woman sitting astride him on a large flat rock, and, like him she was naked. Was she the woman he dreamt about last night whose dress ripped like tissue paper? He shook his head, clearing his thoughts.

"What a strange sensation I am having. You seem so familiar, yet I am sure we have not met." Alice ignored his question, released his handshake, and fired one of her own.

"Are you here in England for business or pleasure, Mr. Masters?" She noted he was evasive with his reply, simply saying that he was in property and wanted to trace his roots. Alice gave him some tips on tracing his family. She suggested he start at the church and that he should talk to the vicar, Steven Weston. He asked where she had parked his car, more small talk. But Alice had found out what she needed to know. The big surprise to Alice was that he wasn't troubled by Ursula in the night. Any memories he may have had had not surfaced, she was sure of it. Finally, Alice made her excuse to leave and made her way back to Jed at the reception desk.

"Well, Jed, he doesn't remember much yet. He was evasive about his business, and all he would say was that he was, in "property."

"Do you think it is definitely him? You're not letting your heart rule your head?"

Alice's face lit. "It's him. We connected when we touched."

Jed could not hide the relief on his face. "I am so glad you have waited so long." After a long pause, he measured her reaction again, and his face belied his concern. "Alice, be careful, don't be blinded by love, if you think he is leaning towards the dark, you must warn us."

She snapped. "Why! so you can kill him?"

Jed closed his eyes in anguish. "let's hope it doesn't come to that, but he could destro…"

Alice cut him short, and she snapped. "Yes, I know he could destroy us all." After an awkward silence, she dropped her voice to a whisper. "If it comes to it, I'll do it, I'll do the killing."

Jed's face brightened trying to ease the situation and he quipped. "Do you think Paul intends to move back here?"

"We will see. It's early days yet, and he may just be responding to my enchantment, my calling. He said he was going to the church to trace his family tree and wanted to know where his car was parked."

Jed was looking at the register hiding the fact they were talking about him. "He keeps looking at you. Alice. He's doing it right now."

"Good, keep looking, Saul." *Just remember me. Holy Mother, please help.*

Jed coughed and looked down at the register once again. "He's coming over."

Alice turned to face him. "Can I help you, Mr. Masters?"

"May I have my car keys, and please call me Paul. Which is the best way to the church?"

Alice again gave him one of her well-practiced smiles and pointed in the direction he should go. "Through the gate, you came in at the rear of the house, up to the T junction, and turn right. Or if you would like a pleasant walk, you can go along the left-hand side of the lake then just head for the spire on the church. It's about four miles."

"Thanks, but I'll take the car."

Alice smiled openly, again it was her Mia smile. "In that case, I will see you tomorrow. It's my half-day today. Bye, for now, Mr. Masters." As Alice left the room, she was sure his eyes followed her.

Paul Masters could not get her out of his mind. *She is just the most stunningly beautiful woman I have ever seen, and yet she seems so familiar it's untrue. I'm sure it's her*

After collecting the Bentley, Paul pressed a button on the dashboard and lowered the electric roof. He started the car and drove down the gravel drive toward the gates. The sun was shining and the countryside glided by. He took a deep breath and filled his lungs with clean West Country air, taking in the different scents, the damp grass, and the trees. Scents that were alien to a city boy. He let his breath out slowly, he was finally here, and it was time to relax. He could hear the birds singing. After growing up in city after city, life felt good for Paul Masters.

On exiting the estate gate, which was wide enough for one vehicle only, the car came to an abrupt halt. The engine had died entirely! He checked the fuel gauge and found it had plenty of fuel. The electrics seemed to be working. He pressed the start button again and again. Nothing, the car simply would not start. I don't believe this! It's a Bentley for goodness" sake. He tried thumping the steering wheel several times and gave up. He left the car where it was and made his way back to the manor on foot.

Back at the reception, he walked over to Jed at the desk. "Houston, we have a problem."

Jed looked up and smiled. "Mr. Masters, back so soon. What is the problem?"

"The car. It's broken down, and I'm afraid that's not all. It has stopped in the middle of the main gate, and I can't start it or move it."

Jed shook his head in disbelief. "The Bentley? We will need to get it shifted quickly. Is it your car, Sir?

"No, Jed, it's a hire car."

"If you can give me the details of the hiring company, I'll get it sorted."

"Thanks, Jed." He pulled out his wallet and gave Jed the number. Paul let out a sigh. "Damn, I don't fancy walking all that way to the church, though. I really wanted to go there today."

"You're not into walking then, Mr. Masters?"

He shook his head again dismissively. "Not today. Got too much to do. Could you book me a taxi?"

Jed picked up the phone, and then a thought hit him and the slightest of smiles creased his lips. "I'll tell you what, Sir, it's Alice's half-day today. I'll ask her if she can take you down in the horse and trap if you like."

"Do you think she would do that?"

"It won't hurt to ask. Alice normally takes one of the horses out for exercise on her afternoon off, I can give her a ring if you like."

Jed picked up the phone and rang her number. "Alice, it's Jed here. We have a bit of a problem. Mr. Masters's car has broken down. You said you would take one of the horses out this afternoon. Why not take the horse and trap and show him the estate and then run him down to the church at the same time? Then maybe give him a heads up with his family tree." Putting the phone down, Jed turned to Paul. "She said, give her thirty minutes."

Paul smiled. His day was going to turn out ok after all. "That's very kind of her, Jed?"

Jed gave him a broad smile. "We aim to please, Mr. Masters. Would you like a beer while You're waiting?"

Paul nodded his approval. "Yes, good idea, now I'm not driving. A small one, if you please, Jed."

He positioned himself in what was becoming his favored spot by the window. Paul waited, taking in the views. His mind drifted back, imagining what it was like in years gone by. *It does seem familiar, the whole place, the house, the lake, even the woods, like a dream that you can't quite remember.*

After a while, a female voice called out from behind him and disturbed his reverie. "Mr. Masters."

Paul turned to see Alice dressed casually in tight denim jeans and a white blouse. Her hair was loose and fell to her waist. She was wearing white trainers, and in her hand, she was holding a horse crop. Paul stared, open-mouthed. *God, she's beautiful. Jed was right.*

"Ready to go, Sir?"

After a pause, he collected himself. "Yes, thank you, this is very kind of you."

"Well, Mr. Masters, we aim to please as they say." She whipped her thigh lightly with the horse crop, turned, and walked to the door.

He followed her to the horse and trap and studied every curve of her body, the white top which was almost transparent, and the jeans that looked like they had been sprayed on, and again, he was taken by her cat-like grace. "If you don't mind me saying Alice, you dress down well."

"Well, thank you, Mr. Masters." She then paused before adding, "I think… Climb aboard."

"Please call me Paul."

"Mr. Masters, we are not allowed to call guests by their first name."

"You can make an exception for me, surely."

Again, she smiled. "Very well. Yes, out here, but it will have to be surnames only in the manor."

"That's fine by me."

"So, Paul, here we go." With a gentle brush of the horsewhip, the horse moved away. "We will go down alongside the lake. Tell me, Paul, what sort of business are you in?"

"My family buys and sells property."

"Are you looking at something in the area?"

He shook his head dismissively. "I'd rather not say because it usually affects the price if people know You're interested in a property. If a deal gets done, I'll tell you then. Let's not talk about work. Tell me about you, Alice."

Alice looked across at him, her face full of surprise. "Mr. Masters, why on earth would you want to know about me?"

"Just humor me."

"Let's see," she said thoughtfully. "There's nothing much to tell. I was born about a mile away. I went to the local primary school. Then I went to the local high school. Then I went to the local college, and I've only ever worked at the Manor. I started as a waitress, and I now run the place, end of. It has not been an exciting life."

A voice unbidden echoed to the forefront of her mind, one of the thousands which are part of the collective conscience of Alice Llewellyn. *Don't be a stupid child. Why would he ask if he is not already interested? You must revive his memories quickly while there is still time. Take him to the tower.*

"University?"

"No, I've never even left the county."

"You have never even left the county?" Paul could not hide the astonishment in his voice. "Have you never wanted to travel?"

She shook her head. "I belong here." She paused for a while as if deep in thought, then continued. "I feel comfortable here. Have you not felt you belong somewhere, somewhere special?"

Paul shook his head dismissively. "No, we didn't stay in the same town or city for more than two years. I do like this place, though. I can understand why you like it so much; I could belong here."

They sat in silence as Paul took in the scenery. Alice, for a time, was lost in thought. *Yes, you belong here, Paul, and you will realize it soon. Just please remember us.*

Looking across the lake, he could see a lady on the far side wearing a long white dress or nightgown.

"Alice, the lady in white on the far side of the lake, who is she?"

Without looking, Alice seemed dismissive. "No one you need to worry about."

"It's only, she seemed very near the edge?"

So, Paul, she is making herself visible to you, is she? I need to distract him from her. "Paul, why don't you tell me about America?"

Paul's face lit, and Alice could see his pride and love for his country written across his face. "America? Well, America is big and bold as brass. It's a country where dreams are made, and everyone is busy making them happen, in the cities, especially!"

Alice pursed her lips, and a frown formed on her forehead. "I don't think I would like it. I've seen your cities on the television, everyone running around like ants. People are too busy making a living to stop and see the world around them."

"Alice, it's not all like that, and it's a slower way of life in the country - and we have some spectacular countryside."

She nodded her head in agreement. "Yes, I will give you that, but I don't think I would feel safe there. No, I don't think America is for me."

"Why do you say that Alice"

Alice snorted. "Everyone has guns. You're all gun mad. You shoot anything that moves animals, and even people, and most of the time just for fun. You argue with someone, he pulls out a gun, and bang, you're dead. Your kids even take them to school." His forehead creased in surprise, and she realized she had touched a nerve.

"You think it's as bad as that?"

She shrugged her shoulders. "It might be the back of beyond here, we haven't got mains gas, but we do have television, and it's not even headlined news anymore."

Paul shook his head in disbelief. "It's not that bad, Alice. I think you would love it."

Again, the voice within Alice's head prompted her. *The tower. It might wake him up – take him up there.* In the distance, Saint Michael's Tower sat perched like a sentinel on top of the great hill surveying the landscape for miles around. Paul's eyes were drawn to it.

"What's that building on top of the hill?"

Alice answered without looking up. "Saint Michael's Tower."

Paul continued to stare. The tower dominates the landscape for miles around. The Tor itself is 518 feet high, and the building is situated at the very top. Its image is burned in the memory of everyone who has lived in the area

Alice prompted. "You get amazing views from up there. I usually go to the top once a week or when I want to think about something that's troubling me. You can see for miles and miles, it's very comforting."

Paul was tempted, and silently he thought it would be a good idea to get an overall view of the Earlswood estate. It would certainly help in his feasibility study for a golf course.

"I think I will climb to the top one day this week. Do you get a good view of this estate from up there?"

The voices again prompted Alice. *Today, Alice.*

"I was going to go today. If you want, we could leave the horse and trap at the bottom of the Tor, and I can show you the quick way up."

Paul looked surprised. "Would you?"

Again, her smile emphasized her beauty. "Of course, we still have all afternoon to go to the church. It will give you an excellent overview of the landscape and be helpful if you plan to buy property around here."

They quickly felt at ease with each other's company and soon found themselves at the edge of the town. Alice parked the trap in a field at the base of the Tor and, without tethering it to a bush or shrub, jumped down cat-like and landed lightly on her feet. "The horse won't go far," she said as if reading Paul's thoughts."

By the time Paul climbed down off the trap, she was already striding up the hill.

"You need to keep up, it's really good exercise."

Paul watched from behind as she strode off in front of him. She had a lithe feral grace unusual for one so tall and skipped lightly from rock to rock with athleticism and confidence. Finally. he caught up, panting.

"You do this every week?" He said between breaths

"Yes, and when I want to think - it's quite magical up there."

The path got steeper and narrower, Paul fell behind and had a great view of her rear, the tightly fitted denim jeans showing every curve of her buttocks and the painted whirl of muscle and sinew in her legs. They were on all fours now as the hill got steeper still. The gravel rolled down the hill towards him. It was intentional, Alice never left anything to chance. *Keep looking, Paul. My bum looks just as good as it did when I was Sarah.*

"How do you like the view?" she taunted.

For a second, Paul thought Alice could read his mind. "What?"

Alice pursed her lips, hiding her smile. "The view from up here - it's amazing, don't you think?"

Paul was still staring at her rear. "It certainly is - the countryside is not bad either."

Alice laughed and continued to stride up the hill. *Yes, keep looking, Paul Masters.*

Paul started gasping for breath. "It's getting pretty steep - is this the way everyone comes?"

"No, Paul, this way saves about fifteen minutes, it's not much further."

Paul noted that she was not even out of breath. Finally, they reached the summit.

The view from the tower on the top of the Tor is magnificent. Paul stood at the entrance to the roofless tower and looked out over the Somerset countryside, and an unbelievable feeling of déjà vu overcame him.

Alice watched him as he gazed into the distance and studied his features. He was different from Saul. Saul had dark curly hair and a full beard, Saul was also more robust and muscular. Paul's hair was blonde, not curly, but still wavy. She mused. *The blonde mass of hair softens his face a little. He has a sharp nose, a forceful jaw, and a wide thick-lipped mouth.* She smiled to herself. *He still pulls his mouth to one side when he smiles, He's different but still handsome, and I am in love with him already.*

"A penny for your thoughts."

He answered her, but his eyes were fixed in distance or time. Alice was unsure which.

"It all seems so familiar, yet I know I have never even seen a photo of this place. I have an uncanny feeling of déjà vu. Grandpa used to come up here, and he has described it to me. I often pictured it when I was young, but it does seem so unbelievably familiar. Even so..." He fell silent for a while, and Alice watched, she could see the confusion written across his face.

Alice prompted. "Even so?"

"The hill I remember was in the middle of a lake, not surrounded by green fields and farmland."

Alice managed a faint interrogative "Ah...?" *How silly of me last time we were up here was wintertime, sixteen twenty - I think – and yes, it was an island then.*

"How old was your grandfather Paul?"

Paul pulled his eyes away from the view and studied her. She patted the ground encouraging him to sit against the tower. He sat down next to her and rested his head against the wall. Alice's heart lifted. *Yes, touch the tower, listen to the stones.*

"What a strange thing to ask?"

"Humor me."

"He was born in nineteen hundred and one. Why?"

She glanced sideways at him and noticed his eyes were strikingly blue, enhanced by the sky, and her heart missed a beat. She mused once again. *Yes, I could love those eyes.* "I just thought your grandfather had seen it in the winter, it used to flood the levels below, but he is not old enough. They were all drained by the beginning of the twentieth century."

Paul shook his head. "Ah, no, it must be somewhere else, I'm sure it is a memory - not a description." Alice studied his face as again he took in the views and thought it might be a good time to prompt him.

"Have you ever heard of inherited memory, Paul?"

Their eyes met once more, and for a while, neither spoke, Alice watched as his brow creased in thought.

"Well, yes, my mother and grandfather both believe in it. Do you think that's what this is?"

Alice pulled her eyes away from his to aid her concentration. "Could be, you are from a local family. This tower has been here for hundreds of years, and before that, there was a Roman fort, and before that, the Celts had a whole community built around it only accessible by boat."

Paul watched as Alice also stared into the distance, seemingly lost in thought. When he did not interrupt, she continued. "Have you ever heard of the fabled Isle of Avalon?" He looked at Alice and simply nodded.

"Well, you are sitting at its highest point. We were safe here before the Romans came and slaughtered my people."

This time Paul did interrupt. "Your people?"

Again, their eyes locked together, and Alice measured him, unsure how much to divulge once more.

"Our people Paul. Avalonia's, Celts, Druids, or Pagans as they called us. You were from a local family - they were your ancestors too." Their eyes held fast, and he didn't argue, so she continued. "Celts were in Britain before the Romans and before the Anglo-Saxons ever set foot in Britain. This area was very inhospitable, always flooding. The Celts who had settled in the area further north of Somerset, in what is now the country of Wales, had a name for this area which they could see across the Bristol Channel. Their name was Gwlad yr Haf, which is Celtic for the "land of summer," because they could see the vast area of green land where they could go once the winter floods had receded. You could have inherited that memory from one of your ancestors, but yes, this hill was an island every winter."

Paul did not laugh or dismiss the idea and again turned his eyes to the surrounding fields. When he did not comment further, she continued, her eyes still fixed on the past.

"Paul, this is the place of our ancestors." She emphasized the noun, and he turned and studied her face. "The cradle of our blood and bones, a holy place, a refuge from those that wished us harm. Safe within the bosom of the creator, for thousands of years we were safe here, then...."

Alice got to her feet abruptly. "Enough. Time to go, things to do and all that, let's get you to the church."

They made their way back down the Tor taking the shallower tourist route and found the horse waiting patiently for them.

16. MIDSUMMER DAY 1996 AD

Alice parked the trap by an old Yew tree just outside the churchyard with a wooden bench under it. "There's a nice patch of grass here that will keep the horse contented." She said, then casually walked off and let the horse walk free once again." Alice led him to the churchyard and pointed toward several Family tombs. "If you start with gravestones, the oldest and most important graves are usually nearest the church."

"Tell me, the lady in the painting, is she buried here?"

Alice turned sharply. "Painting?"

"In my room?"

Alice's brow furrowed. "Ursula." *Why would he want to know about Ursula? - Oh God, has she been calling him too?*

"So, that's her name. Jed said he didn't know who it was." Paul noticed the puzzled look on her face.

Alice pursed her lips. "I know her name was Ursula. She is not buried here, but her twin sister is buried under that large yew tree, where we parked the horse and trap."

Paul followed her gaze to where the horse was grazing. "She's not buried in the main part of the churchyard then. Why is that?"

Alice again paused for thought. *There are things he needs to know, but not yet. He wouldn't understand.*

"I am not sure, but I think the locals thought she would be happier there. They were probably right. That magnificent tree is much better than any headstone."

Alice turned and studied Paul's face before asking the next question. "Why the interest in the painting?"

He rocked his head from side to side and bit his lip, contemplating his following comment. *How do I answer that without sounding crazy?* "She seems very familiar. I can't think why, but I am sure she reminds me of someone. Maybe I dreamt about her, who knows."

A feeling of dread gripped Alice's heart and silently she wondered if Jed's worst fears were coming to fruition.

Alice's attention was drawn to the yew tree, and she noticed the tree covered in fresh green buds. Alice smiled inwardly. *Sarah knows. She can sense him too, deep under the tree's roots. She knows he is back. Yes, Sarah Saul's back - your lover, is back.*

"Look, Paul, the tree thinks springtime has come again, all fresh new growth. See the leaves, new fresh green leaf buds in midsummer!"

He smiled at her enthusiasm for nature and the world around her. "You seem to be in tune with nature, Alice."

She tilted her head and studied his face once more. "Are you not Saul? Do you not see the seasons, the cycles, the patterns, the births, and the deaths? Everyone and everything have a time and place. Sometimes the time and place are out of sync, but in the end, it all falls back into place as it should. You probably don't notice those things living in a city, but you would if you stayed here long enough. *Just like it's falling back into place for you.*

"That's very profound, Alice, but my name is Paul, by the way."

"Why?" Alice replied with a puzzled expression on her face. "What name did I use?"

"Saul."

Again, Alice presented him with a smile, and the green of her eyes, reflected by the sun and trees, took his breath away. "Sorry, Paul, a slip of the tongue. I knew a Saul once, and you remind me of him. Why the interest in your family tree?"

"It's like you were just saying. I'm trying to find where I belong. I feel something is missing in my life, and I need to find what it is. I can understand why my ancestors lived around here though. It's a different world from what I am used to, it's so calm and peaceful."

She studied Paul's face once more and realized she already felt a deep physical attraction to him. There followed an awkward silence, bringing Alice out of her reverie.

"Right Paul let's get started. What names are you looking for?"

"Well, Masters, obviously for one, then there's the Giffords, the Monktons on my mother's side, and the Llewellyn"

Alice looked shocked. "Llewellyn, now there's a surprise."

"Why?"

"My surname is Llewellyn, Alice Llewellyn."

The smile stretched across Paul's face. "Really, then we could be related."

"It's possible. People say we're all related if you go back far enough."

"Wouldn't that be something?"

Alice chuckled to herself, thinking. *Of course, we're related. You're my lover, husband, best friend, father of my children, and ancestor. Get your head around that one, Paul Masters.* Pulling herself back to reality once again, she continued.

"How far have you gone back with your family tree?"

"Early nineteen-hundreds. I have only just started."

"You've not gone back very far then?"

"As I said, I've only just started looking. Have you traced yours back?"

Alice's eyes creased with amusement. *I can't tell him I can trace my lineage back to the "Primaeval soup at the beginning of time. He really would think I'm crazy.* "I know mine back to when they built the manor."

"You are joking, all the way back to fifteen ninety-nine."

She pursed her lips and shook her head. "No, I'm not joking."

"How on earth did you go back so far?"

"It's not difficult, especially when your ancestors stayed more or less in the same place." Again, her thoughts drifted. *Remembering every one of their lives helped.*

"I take it they all felt they belonged here, like you."

"Very much so. Right, let's get you started. If I remember correctly, there are crypts close to the church with the names Masters and Llewellyn. You will find gravestones for the Monktons and Gifford's down there by the fence. I'll talk to the vicar and tell him to expect you, and then I'm going to the florist to get some flowers."

Alice walked over to the vicarage, a rambling old Victorian house, and admired the perfectly mown lawn and roses in full bloom which covered the red brick walls.

She knocked on the door, and Steven Wilson, the vicar, opened it and greeted her with a smile. "Alice, how nice to see you." He planted a kiss on her cheek as she walked in. "I'll put the kettle on. Tea?"

"Yes, please. Steven, Saul's here looking at the gravestones in the churchyard, he has started tracing his family tree."

The vicar knew she had been waiting a long time for this day. "So, he's finally answered your calling and has come back to us. Does he remember you?"

"Not yet, but the signs are good. He came up to the old front door at the rear of the Manor, probably remembering it was the front in his time. He says everything looks familiar to him, but only time will tell. The only fly in the ointment is he insisted on staying in the master bedroom. Again, probably remembering it was once his."

Steven looked surprised. "How's the old Witch taking that?" He noticed the worried look in her eyes. "Strange thing is, she didn't bother him last night, although he did say he didn't sleep well."

Steve poured them both a cup of tea and proffered. "Maybe she's mellowing in her old age?"

Alice pursed her lips before answering. "I doubt it, Steven."

He eyed Alice warily. "You need to keep a close eye on her. I talked to Jed, and he is very worried, well, we all are. It could be curtains for us if she gets her claws into him and turns him to the dark.

"Don't I know it? The Witch tried to slam the door in his face when he arrived. Oh, and I think she stopped him from leaving the estate today."

He looked up as he poured the tea. "How did she do that?"

"His car broke down between the gate posts on the rear entrance, the one on the estate boundary. It is a Bentley, so I think it's unlikely to be the car."

Steven put in. "It sounds like she's up to her old tricks! She's probably toying with him?"

"You could be right, and she is making herself visible for him... on the lake."

"Well, at least you know he is 'Prime' if he can see her."

"Oh, and he's probably coming across to see you. He wants help with births, deaths, marriages, etc."

The vicar again smiled. "I'm free all afternoon, so it's no problem, but Alice, you need to keep him away from that room, we just can't risk it."

When she did not reply, he raised his voice, and his anger shook her. "For God's sake Alice, he imprisoned her there nearly four hundred years ago. Do you really think she will leave him be? She will possess him, kill him, or turn him to the dark."

Alice turned her eyes away from his, she knew he was right and sighed heavily. "Steven, I don't know what to do, we have even tried frightening him with ghost stories."

He eyed her with compassion. A statement like that from Alice was unheard of. He placed his hand on hers to comfort her, and he put on his vicar's voice, filled with compassion and understanding. "Alice, you love him, don't you?"

She pulled her hand away angrily; she was not used to showing any sign of weakness to anyone and snapped. "You know I do-I always have."

"Then use your womanly wiles. You're a beautiful woman, entice him to your place before it is too late for him and us."

Again, she sighed heavily. "You don't think it is too soon, he might think I am easy."

Steven shook his head in dismay. "Alice, this is the nineties, people do this sort of thing these days, so stop living in the past."

For a while, the room fell into an awkward silence.

Alice took a sip of tea and added. "He thinks his name's Paul, by the way."

Alice drank the rest of the tea, kissed Steven, and went to the florist. She collected a dozen red roses, returned to the churchyard, and placed one on each of her ancestors" graves.

Paul saw her from a distance and walked over to her.

"That's a nice touch, Alice. Some of the graves you put flowers on go way back?"

She looked up at him from her task and shielded the sun from her face with her hand. "Yes, gone but not forgotten." The sun shone on her face and reflected the vivid translucent green of her eyes, and again his heart missed a beat. "How are you doing, Paul, any luck?"

"As you say, there are loads of graves with the names I'm looking for, and I've written them down. You have put a rose on a couple I want to check out, so you never know we could be related."

"That's interesting. You should go to see the Vicar now - he is expecting you. I'm going to do some shopping in town, and I'll see you in about an hour. If you finish early you could rest beneath the yew tree, and I will meet up with you there. You have had a busy day, haven't you? You must be tired. If you feel tired, you must rest there against the tree." Paul was not aware of the melodic tone of her voice, but the enchantment was cast.

An hour or so later, Alice returned to find Paul asleep, and her heart lifted as she saw him laying with his back resting on the trunk of Sarah's yew tree. He appeared to be at peace with the world. She observed him for more than an hour and resisted the urge to run her fingers through his hair as her mind drifted back to their wedding night. They had galloped away on the 'Arabians' deep into the forest to be alone and made love for the first time. Sated they had fallen asleep. She woke first and roused him by running her fingers through his hair.

Her hand hovered above his head, and she pulled it away sharply. She could see he was dreaming; his eyes, hands, and feet were twitching. She smiled. *He's running. I wonder who to, or from what? He is as close to Sarah as he has been for almost four hundred years.* She looked up at the new growth on the tree. *I see You're happy, Sarah.*

A voice unbidden deep in Alice's mind replied. *Thank you, Alice. At last, we are together once more. Why did you have to enchant him to sleep here by me?*

He is blind to his 'Prime' heritage, a stray as we call them these days. Help him to remember for the sake of us both. Oh, Sarah, He's waking up.

Paul opened his eyes to find Alice sitting there and watching him.

"Alice, how long have you been there?"

"I have just got back. Sorry if I woke you, I said you looked tired." Her smile was genuine and reflected her love. Again, she felt the involuntary impulse to run her fingers through his hair and pulled back.

"I have had just the most amazing dream."

Alice lay down on the grass and rested her head on her hands as she did on her wedding night four hundred years before - and looked into his eyes. "I'm all ears, I love dreams. Do tell?"

"I don't know where to start. I was in a forest, and it was nearly dark. There were dozens of young people dressed in white, dancing, drinking, girls chasing boys, boys chasing girls. There were people in the water swimming. I think it was the lake down by the Manor House. And there was a circle of old-fashioned torches on the ground, the ones on a stick with flames coming out. Then there was some sort of ceremony. There was lots of chanting and music in the background."

Thank you, Sarah. I think he is beginning to remember. Alice's face belied her knowledge. "They were all dressed in white, like druid robes, you mean?" *Come on, Paul, remember.*

Paul's eyes looked distant as he recalled the dream. "Yes, they were all wearing that type of outfit, and they wore hoods. They were dancing around some trees. They had a lamp or some sort of light in one hand. I have had similar dreams for years," His voice dropped to an awkward whisper. He gave a dismissive laugh and shook his head. "Listen to me, telling you all my secrets."

So, you have been remembering. Oh Saul, you poor thing. Wake up. Alice prompted him. "Maybe you remember past lives like we were talking about, or maybe You're picking up vibes from the old yew tree. It is well on its way to being four hundred years old. Like I said on the top of the Tor, it could be inherited memory, or maybe you're listening to Sarah's story before she moved on. Perhaps it was her you dreamed about and not Ursula, after all, they were identical twins. Alice gave him a warm smile to make him think she was joking.

She silently spoke to the voice in her head. *It's happening, I think he is beginning to remember. Well done, Sarah.*

As Paul and Alice climbed back into the trap for their journey back, he quipped. "You are in tune with nature and the world around you, you even know how old the trees are."

She laughed openly. "That one's easy, the yew tree was planted when Sarah died. But enough of this. It's time to head back, and its way past dinner time."

They headed back, making small talk at ease with each other's company. The sun was shining and the birds were singing. The long grass in the meadow had turned to seed, their seed heads dancing a melody with the wind. It was one of those rare summer days in England when the sun was strong and the wind light, with not a cloud in the sky.

Passing the lake, Alice took time to point out the swifts and swallows skimming the water and drinking on the wing, trying to open his mind to the natural world that was so alien to most city people. Paul noticed the lady in white on the far side of the lake. "She's still there."

"Who?"

"The lady in white, standing on the far side of the lake."

Alice chewed her lip, and Paul noticed a frown crease on her forehead. She tried to make light of it. "Sorry Paul, I can't see who it is from here. Maybe it's one of your dancers from the woods that's lost her way - the ones in your dream."

"Very funny, Alice. I knew I shouldn't have told you." Again, Alice's thoughts drifted. *Keep looking, Witch. You're not getting your claws into him this time.*

She whipped the horse gently, and they trotted back to the Manor. As she was removing the harness, Alice turned to Paul. "Would you like a ride? For a while, Paul fell silent. Alice, sensing the possible double meaning, added. Horses, I mean?"

"Oh, I see. Do Americans ride horses? What do you think?"

"Would you like to go Thursday evening then, cowboy? It's forecast to be another lovely evening, and I have nothing planned?"

"I'd love to," Paul said almost too eagerly, then wondered if he could still remember how.

Paul returned to the manor reception and went over to Jed. "Have I missed dinner?"

Looking up from his register, he presented Paul with his usual easy smile. "No, Mr. Masters. They are still serving if you'd like to go through." Paul turned to leave but Jed stopped him. "By the way, Sir, they came for your car and have taken it away."

"Did they say what was wrong with it?"

Jed shook his head. "They said it started the first touch of the starter. But they took it in to get it checked over."

"That's strange. Did they say What's happening about a replacement?"

"No, Sir. They said you were to contact the office."

"Thank you, Jed."

Jed noticed his confused look and shook his head. "We are here to please, Mr. Masters."

"Jed, do you think you could find out the name of that missing person for me today."

"I'll do my best, Mr. Masters but I have got a lot on. I'm afraid it might have to be tomorrow or the following day. Jed was distracted as he spoke and looked at someone behind Paul.

As Paul followed his line of sight, he couldn't believe what he was seeing. Standing in the doorway was a party of twenty Druids, all wearing white robes. *White robes, like in my dreams.* Then he repeated the thought verbally, barely audible, and full of wonder. "White robes, like in my dreams."

"Pardon," Jed said, interrupting his thoughts.

Paul replied without taking his eyes off the party of Druids. "Are they real Druids, Jed?"

With a diffident shrug of his shoulders, Jed replied. "Suppose so dressed like that. They are probably "Prime Druids," there are a couple of weddings shortly, so they are probably here for them. We get a lot of Druids this time of year - Glastonbury is a magnet for them. Saint Michael's Tower on the top of the Tor is a sacred place for them, a Holy Place."

Paul continued to stare as he had seen nothing like it in America. Two white-haired elderly men whose hair and beards looked like they hadn't seen a barber for years were resting on gnarled poles. Surrounding them was a party of eighteen mixed-age people, some wearing robes, and some dressed normally.

"Why, this time of year, Jed?"

Jed cast his eyes upwards in amused exasperation. "Do you not know what day it is?" When Paul shook his head slowly, he continued. "Midsummer's eve. Their Holy day."

"Oh."

Again, he turned to watch them. "Is that where they are going to get married on top of that, Hill?"

Jed corrected him. "Tor. There, or the standing stones at Avebury. There is also a massive gathering at Stone Henge, but that's just Druids, not 'Prime.' Anyway, Stone Henge is too far away and much too busy for a wedding tonight. So, you see, Alice and I will be very busy in the early hours of the morning. I will see what I can do about the missing guest, but today will be a struggle."

"Thanks, Jed. That's all I can ask."

Paul was about to leave, but Jed stopped him. "How did you get on tracing your family tree with Alice down at the church yesterday?"

"Yes, good. I have got lots of names, and I just need to start linking them all up. There is a chance I could be related to Alice. One of the lines I'm following on my mother's side is the Llewellyn's."

Jed let out a surprised laugh. "Well, you know what they say. If you go back far enough, we're all related."

Paul nodded in agreement. "That's exactly what Alice said."

"Great minds, yeah. Is your room to your liking Mr. Masters?" Jed studied the young man's face, weighing up his reaction.

"Great Jed, I don't know what all the fuss was about."

Jed nodded thoughtfully and did not hide the concern on his face. *So, Ursula still hadn't troubled him. Why?*

*

After another night of restless dreams, Paul approached Jed at the desk.

"Good morning, Mr. Masters. Did you sleep well?"

"Yes, fine, Jed."

"Still no ghosts then?" Paul laughed but didn't comment.

"Will you be working today, Mr. Masters?"

"I don't think so. I haven't sorted out a car yet, but I'm in no hurry, so I think I'll take it easy for a couple of days. Alice has suggested we go horse riding Thursday at two-thirty."

Jed drew his eyes away from the register. "You ride back home in the states, Mr. Masters?"

"I Haven't ridden since I was fifteen at summer school, and I must admit I am a bit apprehensive. Jed, could I ask you something about Alice?"

"Ask away."

"I take it she's single, she doesn't wear a ring?"

The hint of a smile creased Jed's lips. "Yes, Alice is single."

"Does she have a boyfriend? I mean, she's a beautiful woman?"

Jed shook his head. "Not that I know of. I told you she was a beauty - you fancy your chances, do you, Sir?"

"I've only known her a couple of days. But it's like I've known her for years. She's easy to talk to and very down-to-earth. I can't stop thinking about her."

"I think down-to-earth describes Alice to a tee. I can't remember seeing any boyfriends, though. I think she's waiting for the right person. She lost both her parents last year, knocked her for six it did. If I remember correctly, there wasn't a boyfriend with her at the funeral."

Paul held eye contact with Jed. "She's not gay, is she?"

Jed laughed. "Alice! I don't think so."

Paul let out a sigh of relief. "Good."

Jed smiled at his reaction. "What's your plan for this morning, Mr. Masters?"

"I think I'll take a walk around the grounds and get the feel of the place."

Jed looked surprised. "I thought you said you didn't like walking."

Paul turned and left and answered as he went out the door. "I don't mind walking, but I had too much to do yesterday. I'll see you later, Jed."

17. GLASTONBURY HENGE 1996 AD

Paul Masters walked out of the front door of the manor house and made his way around the estate. His purpose was to plan each hole, green, and bunker for the upcoming golf course. He went clockwise around the lake. On this side of the lake, the reeds and bulrushes were twenty to thirty feet deep. You couldn't get near the water's edge. The trees came right down to the water about a mile further on. Here the bulrushes disappeared, revealing a shingle beach. Again, Paul found himself deep in thought.

It is a natural swimming hole with a shingle beach and no bullrushes, so it must be deep water. Could we develop that?

He walked along the beach, turned, and looked back to study the woods. *Even the wood seems familiar, this is so strange. Why should I think the trees are familiar?*

The wood itself got thicker as he continued around the lake's edge. Here he came across dense areas of brambles and thorn bushes and had to turn away from the lake's edge and turn deep into the wood. When he followed the path, another feeling of déjà vu overcame him.

I'm sure this path will double back on itself shortly. Am I going crazy, or is all this inherited memory? If it is, I am so glad I came to Earlswood, I should have done it years ago.

He found the path did indeed double back, and he felt the hair lift on the nape of his neck.

He continued to weave his way through the wood. Unknown to him, they were the secret labyrinth of paths that only the Druids knew. Eventually, he came across a clearing in the trees and stopped abruptly. It was about one hundred feet in diameter, and there was lush green grass underfoot.

He looked around the clearing and couldn't believe what he was seeing. There was a circle of trees around the perimeter, and all of them were upside down. The trunks of the trees were at least a foot across and twenty feet high. The roots had been left in place and functioned as branches. Paul's eyes turned to the large oblong stone slab, four feet by ten feet, rising from the ground to waist height. It was not central but near the middle of the circle.

What on earth is going on here? It looks like an Altar, or could it be a film set? It must have been here for a long time. Why would anyone want to turn trees upside down? What's even weirder is that I feel I know this place. Could this be what I have seen in one of my dreams? I must ask Alice about this later. If anyone would know, she would.

Moving on, he completed a full circle of the lake. He planned out different holes for the golf course in his mind and returned to the old barn that he thought they could convert into a clubhouse.

Back at the Manor, he ate by himself. One of Paul's favorite pastimes was people-watching, and he studied the various guests in their different attire. There were plenty of Druids, others that resembled Witches, and others that just seemed weird.

Everyone appeared friendly - if not a little high. The corner of his mouth twitched as his face reflected his thoughts. *It's just like Halloween back home.*

The staff appeared very busy, and he made a mental note wearing his business hat. *An unexpectedly busy period for the manor, how could we build this into our business plan for this place?*

He continued to look for Alice, but she and Jed were nowhere to be seen. After several beers, he made his way back to his room, had a shower, and collapsed on the bed. Propping himself up on a pillow, his eyes were drawn to the picture, and he studied it for a while. *From back here, it looks even more like Alice, except the lady in the painting has got hard eyes, but that could be down to the artist.*

Looking at all the different mirrors surrounding the bed, he could see the lady in the painting in every one of them simultaneously. It was like the room was full of women. *It's very clever. Whoever designed this room has positioned the mirrors on purpose to create this effect. Whomever it was must have been really in love with this lady. The result is fantastic.*

She seems to be standing in the middle of the room like a hologram.

Jet lag and the stress of the journey finally began to catch up with him. Feeling very tired, he found it uncomfortable with these women looking at him and decided to draw the curtain covering the picture. He quickly dropped off to sleep, which this time was much deeper.

He once again dreamed about the woman in the picture, or was it, Alice? They were deep in the woods again, and she was wearing white. They had ridden to this spot, which was special for them. He couldn't think why, but he just knew it was. It was down by a lake or a stream.

Once again, they were running. She was in front and was very fast. There was laughter, the lady squealing with excitement knowing she was about to be caught. He reached out to catch her and grabbed the tunic, and she turned and twisted around. The garment ripped, revealing her naked breasts. They both froze, looking deep into each other's eyes. This was their moment, their first time. He went to kiss her, but she ducked out of the way and ran off deep into the wood squealing with delight.

He followed her to the hollow at a walking pace. It was their special place. When he parted the bushes, he found her lying on the ground. He smiled when he realized she was virtually naked. She pulled him down to her as he knelt, raked her hand through his hair, and kissed him expectantly.

Her tunic, to his surprise, was not the white cotton of the Druids but silk, so fine it was transparent. He cupped his hand over the remnants of the silk gown. Her breast was young and firm. She squealed with delight and called out to him. "We have waited so long. I thought this day would never come."

She began lifting his robe off him, eager to feel him next to her. Paul took control and lifted it over his head. She fumbled with the garment around his waist, frantically undoing the laces. "Laces?" Paul looked down, and his mind was full of confusion. He was wearing a short skirt embroidered with strings of seashells and wooden beads. *A skirt? How come I am wearing a skirt?* Her hands were now holding his manhood, stroking it, caressing it. Paul looked down at her and saw she was looking up at him, and the green of Alice's eyes took his breath away.

Paul gasped and sat bolt upright in bed, covered in sweat. It was a continuation of his last dream. *It was Alice! I am sure it was Alice. God, no. I've woken up at the best bit again. This is the same dream that has tormented me all my life, always the same woman, long dark hair, green eyes, full of life, and the robes, always white robes. It was either Alice or that woman in the painting, how did I know what she looked like?*

He looked outside and could see it was now dark. Still feeling unbelievably drained, he decided to call it a day. Again, sleep quickly overtook him, but the dream was different this time.

He was feeling anxious because someone was splashing around in the water. There was a crowd of people screaming and cheering. Someone he knew was in trouble. He couldn't think who, but it was someone special.

He needed to get to this person, to help. The crowd was so dense he couldn't see who it was. Then suddenly, the crowd went quiet, but he still couldn't see. Then once again, the crowd began to roar with excitement. His whole being screamed to him that he needed to help, but he didn't know why.

Again, Paul woke and lay there lost in thought. *Well, I wish I had gone back to my first dream. What was that one all about? I can't remember having so many dreams. Maybe it is this house, perhaps this room. As they say, it's had some strange things happen here. Can you listen to yourself, Paul Masters? Are you letting Susan De Winter's ghost stories scare you?*

Paul once again went back to sleep, and this time he slept solidly, not waking until he heard people walking around outside.

After quickly showering, he went down for breakfast. Again, Alice had positioned herself where he would sit. She was eating her breakfast but at the same time writing on a clipboard. He made a beeline straight for her. "Morning Alice. May I join you?"

She beamed her welcoming smile at him. "Of course, Mr. Masters, please join me."

"Alice, do you have to call me Mr. Masters, Paul, please?"

She lowered her voice. "Mr. Masters, you know the rules. In here, You're a guest, outside, You're a..."

"Friend?" He prompted.

Alice smiled and nodded her head. "Yes, friend will do. So, how did you sleep last night, Mr. Masters? I didn't see you at the evening meal."

"I must have slept for ten hours solid. It must be jet lag, although it Doesn't usually take me this long to get over it."

Alice's eyes gazed into the distance, trying to picture flying. "I have never flown in a plane or had jet lag, so I wouldn't know."

Paul stirred his coffee and felt comfortable enough in her company to return to the subject of dreams once more. "I had a dream again last night; I don't know why I dream so much here."

Paul went quiet for a while, then he announced. "I had a dream about you, or I think it was you."

Alice smiled, and her face lit. She reached out and put her hand on his, her green eyes twinkling mischievously, she studied his face intensely. "Really. Tell me did I have any clothes on?"

Paul was taken aback for a second. "What?"

"You heard, Mr. Masters." She opened her eyes wide and raised both eyebrows, teasing him. "What, I do believe You're blushing."

He drew his eyes away from hers, unsure if she was laughing with him or at him. He answered dryly, "I'm not telling, after all the stick you gave me about my first dream under the yew tree."

Her eyes were still open wide, enjoying his discomfort, and she suppressed her smile. "Wow, so I didn't have any clothes on."

"I didn't say that."

She laughed openly. "Still blushing,"

For a moment, a feeling of intense déjà vu overcame him, and he gasped at her beauty and the familiarity of her smile. Was it a memory? Was it the woman in his dreams? He turned away from her laughing eyes and stared into his coffee thoughtfully. "No, I'm not."

I had a second dream as well, a bad dream. It was about someone in the water down by the lake. A crowd had gathered to watch, and I couldn't see what was happening and for some reason, it made me extremely anxious. I don't quite know why, but I was trying to get there to help someone, and I couldn't get near enough to see. I thought it was someone I knew and that they were possibly drowning, but it didn't make any sense, if they were why were the people laughing? It upset me. So, Alice, have you any thoughts on that one?"

Alice managed a faint interrogative "Ah ...?" Her mood quickly changed from being jolly to one deep in thought.

A thought she kept to herself. *So, Saul was watching.* After thirty awkward seconds, when neither spoke, Alice broke the silence. "Are you still up for a ride tomorrow afternoon?"

"About that, Alice, it's been over ten years since I've ridden a horse. I had lessons at summer camp, that's all."

"But you have ridden?"

"Yes."

"Then I'll get Molly saddled up. She's as gentle as you can get, and we can take it steady. There is someone I would like you to meet. Anyway. Riding a horse is rather like riding a bike, you never forget how. Shall we say two-thirty at the stables?"

"Two-thirty is fine by me, but why not go today? It's a lovely evening?" Alice finished the rest of her tea and set the cup down. "Sorry, Mr. Masters, I have to oversee a 'Prime' wedding later and have things to prepare." Alice left the table and disappeared down the corridor that led to her office.

Returning to his room, Paul walked over to the curtain. He pulled the cord covering the painting of Ursula and took in every aspect of this woman. In his mind, her beauty was breathtaking. His eyes were drawn to her long black hair and deep green eyes that seemed to burn deep into his soul. Her lips curled at the edges with the hint of a smile, lips that drew you to them, imploring you, demanding you to caress and kiss. The neck was swan-like, her bosom full. In the back of his mind, there was still that uncanny feeling that he knew her.

She just looks so familiar. Is she the one in my dreams? I can't tell. It could be Alice, though, she and Alice have green eyes. These eyes, however, seem much harder. The lips are the same and they both have the same swan-like neck. She is so much like Alice. He shook his head, trying to clear his thoughts. Maybe I have been dreaming about Alice all these years.

Finally, he drew himself away from the picture, opened the balcony window, and stepped out. He breathed in deeply, savoring the summer scents. *It is lovely here. Why did my grandfather leave?*

Paul put on his business hat, began studying the grounds, and planned the golf course layout. *We could put the first hole over by the car park to the left. We then go to the left of the estate, behind the lake, and continue down to the church. Then we go up to the town and back to this side of the lake. We could put the eighteenth tee down by the old barn, and it could be converted into the clubhouse, fitted out with a bar, changing rooms, and showers. It could be kept separate from the hotel. There's enough land, and the lake would work well. It could work. We could turn this into a first-class golf venue.*

He walked back into the room and left the door wide open to cool the room down from the summer day's heat. Again, his eyes were drawn to the woman. "You're haunting me, do you know that." He said it out loud for his benefit and blinked his eyes as she appeared to be standing in front of him. "What an amazing effect these mirrors give, they're almost as good as a hologram." Eventually, his eyes became heavy, and sleep overcame him.

The sleep was deep and the dreams stronger, and darker. It was pitch dark, and Paul couldn't see a hand in front of his face. Then slowly, his eyes were drawn to the light from the window. *I'm still in my room.* Suddenly he felt her lips on his, he opened his mouth to speak, and her tongue was already deep inside his mouth, searching, dancing with his. *Alice? It must be Alice.* He tried to touch her face and found he could not move his arms. He pulled against the restraints to no avail.

"Alice?" His voice reflected his uncertainty. Then he heard laughter, and she whispered. "Shush."

"Alice, I know it's you?"

"Don't talk, just enjoy." The accent was much stronger. It was still Westcountry, but different. he was unsure. *Who else could it be?* She trailed kisses and soft bites along his face, and his cheek, and then bit the nape of his neck, sucking hard. He closed his eyes, enjoying the myriad of sensations. Her tongue danced down his Adam's apple, down to his nipple, which she took in her teeth and bit gently.

"How did you get in? Did you have a spare key?"

"Shush, I said."

Paul closed his eyes and surrendered to her skillful tongue. Moving lower, her kisses tantalized his belly button. He tried to twist away and found his legs were fastened too. "Why the straps, Alice?"

"Why, so you can't escape, silly."

His pulse quickened, and his breathing became shallow in anticipation. Fingers with long nails raked through his hair. You love me, don't you? You have dreamt about me all your life. I have waited so long for this. We are at last together, you love me, don't you – say it. He felt her caress his manhood, lifting it close to... He could feel the heat of her breath.

"Say it!" she screamed.

"Oh yes, Alice," he whispered, and as her name left his lips, it was a prayer. "I think I've always loved you."

When there was no further involvement, he again called out, God, please don't tease." Finally, his pulse slowed to normal as he realized it was once again a dream, and the feeling of loneliness and disappointment overcame him intensely.

*

Paul lay in bed for a while waiting for his blood to cool and his pulse to slow. *God, that was different – bondage? I don't think I have ever dreamt about bondage before, but I have dreamed of Alice Llewellyn. Now I am sure of it, it must be her. Oh God, I really can't get her out of my head.*

Noise from below his window drew him from his bed. People were talking in whispers. He walked out the open balcony window, enjoying the cool summer breeze on his skin, and breathed in deeply. Looking out into the darkness, he could see a trail of lights like fireflies all in a line. People were walking around the far side of the lake.

A loud noise down below drew his attention back to the courtyard. Someone had knocked over a bucket. He strained his eyes to see who. One of the 'Prime' Druids from the wedding party had fallen over. In his hand was a lamp, not a torch but a hand-held oil lamp. Getting to his feet, he ran off in the direction of the lake.

Paul watched him as the light took the same path as the others. *Where is he going this time of night? Yes, of course, Alice said that they celebrated until the early hours of the morning. I bet he is going to that place I found in the wood.* Paul looked at his watch, it was ten-thirty. *I have got to see this for real, it might explain why I have had dreams about Druids all my life.*

Paul Masters followed the same route he had taken several hours before. There was a full moon, and the path seemed easier to follow in the dark. He continued, keeping the water to his right until the way ahead was blocked by brambles. He then turned inland, following the path he subconsciously remembered from years gone by. He switched off his torch when he heard music ahead and crept closer.

The music stirred something deep within his soul. He was now on his knees, edging ever closer.

He found the circle lit by fire torches staked in the ground around the perimeter of the upturned trees. The large Altar Stone appeared to be covered with a red blanket and was offset from the center. A woman sitting cross-legged was on a large cushion in the middle of the circle. Paul blinked, rubbed his eyes, and took a closer look. The woman's skin was colored red from head to foot, and if not for a transparent veil around her shoulders, she appeared to be completely naked.

People were dancing circularly, weaving in and out of the upturned trees. Some were playing the flute or a pipe as they danced, others simply carried the oil lamp in one hand and held the hem of their tunic in the other. The effect of the lamps was mesmeric as they twisted and turned. *I know this dance, this is the same dance I always dream about - exactly the same, and I must say - seeing it for real is beautiful. This is it. I am about to get some answers. This is the place I have been drawn to all my life.*

Paul watched. His eyes were transfixed. He saw the beauty, the joy, the familiarity, and the purity. People were laughing and undoubtedly enjoying themselves. The women wore loose flowery dresses and danced barefoot with bells on their ankles and wrists.

Suddenly a white barn owl flew down and landed on the Altar. The dancing and music stopped. Everyone watched as the bird made its way to the woman sitting on the cushion. Nothing was said. Eventually, the woman bowed to the creature, and it flew away.

The woman took the shawl and covered her head, hiding her face. She clapped her hands, and the dancing once again started in earnest. The woman sitting on the cushion turned her head slowly and looked directly at Paul, who immediately ducked low out of sight.

The celebrations continued for about an hour until the woman in red got to her feet. Suddenly the music stopped, and the circle emptied of people and formed a circle around the perimeter. They still held the oil lamps in their hands and began to hum with the backing of the pipes and flute. Two people, hand in hand, made their way to the Altar. They wore very little, and their bodies were covered in runes, scrolls, and symbols of some sort.

Paul smiled to himself as he remembered drawing them on Jenny Walker's butt ten years before at college. He could not contain his excitement. The answers he had been looking for all his life were here, playing out before him. His eyes were once again drawn to the couple walking to the Altar. He noticed the man was wearing a skirt like the one in his dreams and the woman a body-length transparent veil. They bowed their heads before the woman in red, and the music stopped.

Paul could not hear what was said, but eventually, the woman in red laid a branch on the shoulders of each of them and touched their foreheads. The couple turned, and the man raised himself upon the Altar and lay back. Various thoughts swam through his mind. *What on earth is he doing - is it some sort of sacrifice?* As he watched, the woman covered simply by the veil climbed up and knelt above him, straddling him. He shook his head in wonder and could not believe his eyes.

The woman turned to the lady in red and waited for some sort of signal. Another man and a woman made their way to the Altar and stood at the couple's side. The music started once again; however, it was just the hum from the onlookers. The woman in red nodded, and the woman on the Altar sat herself down upon her partner. The couple observing them turned to the lady in red and bowed. *Are they having sex?* He thought.

The crowd began cheering and clapping. The woman got to her feet almost at once, and the man joined her, and they once again stood before the woman in red.

He took in the priestess's beauty. Her dark hair flowed freely to her waist, her bosoms firm and proud, her body slim, athletic, and from head to toe was colored bright red. Again, he was lost in thought. *If they were having sex, I think she was easily pleased. God the Priestess, or whatever she is, is a beauty. What on earth is going on?*

The lady in red then tied their hands together with a rope or something, Paul could not see with what, and the couple went once again to the outer circle to join the others who congratulated them.

The woman in red turned once again and looked directly toward Paul through the veil. He ducked down low out of sight. The pure white barn owl still peered down upon him from above, so he sank lower into the undergrowth to be sure he couldn't be seen - and continued to watch.

The people below again began to dance, and the echoes in his mind were reawakened. *I remember this, but how? When? It's got to be ancestral memories – it's got to be.*

As the evening wore on, the couples began to lay on the ground and watched those with youthful exuberance as it became a dance of the last man - or woman standing. When they finally stopped, everyone cheered. The circle then fell to silence, and the woman in red again sat upright, serenely watching over them.

The scene was lit solely by the flickering light from the firesticks, and without prompting, all the couples began to pair off and lie on the ground, and the conversation began to fade. Paul couldn't see what was happening, but the sounds were that of people making love. The scene did not shock him, and he could feel the love, the peace, the tranquility.

He also began to feel awkward. Like a voyeur, an intruder peeping through a keyhole. As he looked up, the owl was still there. The woman in red also stared unblinkingly in his direction. It was time to go.

Paul walked back, unsure of what he had seen. However, he was comforted that he was getting closer to the answer to his reoccurring dreams.

Paul slept in the following day and missed breakfast because it had been nearly daybreak before he got back to his room. The first thing Paul did was close the curtains that covered the picture, as he wanted privacy, especially from green-eyed women.

He slept like a rock all morning and did not go down until they were serving dinner. After dinner, Paul walked over to the stables, where Alice was already saddling up the horses. Jed was watching from the upstairs window as they began to talk. He smiled wickedly, slotted two cartridges in his shotgun, and made his way directly to the woods.

Alice greeted Paul with a smile. "Mr. Masters, you're early."

He returned her smile. "It's Paul now, remember? We are outside the hotel,"

Alice drew his attention to the horse she was saddling. "Paul, this is Molly. Molly, meet Paul. Another lovely day, don't you think?"

Paul instinctively rubbed the side of the horse's ear, comforting her. "Nice horse, Alice. Not that I am an expert. How are you? I didn't see you last night?"

Alice eyed him warily before answering. She was pleased to see his affection for the horse and noted the creature sensed nothing unpleasant in Paul's nature. "I'm fine, thank you, busy night last night." She changed the subject. "Jasper, you've met."

"The horse from the other day?"

"You've got it. I will follow up if you would take Molly's reins and lead her out. They walked outside, and Paul managed to get on his horse without looking like a fool.

Alice mounted hers, and they made their way through the estate. Paul found himself at ease with the horse in no time at all.

"You look like you have been riding for years, Paul. You're a natural."

He smiled nervously. "I think Molly knows what to do, and she's making it easy."

They talked for ages, feeling comfortable together just walking their horses. Secretly, she hoped riding through the estate on a horse would stir some long-lost memory. It seemed like only yesterday they had galloped through the woods on Morag's 'Arabians.' They loved to race, it was in their blood, and Alice hoped it was still in his with all her heart, just waiting to be awakened.

Alice tilted her head listening. "There's someone that wants to meet you." She said and let out a loud whistle. One of the largest dogs he had ever seen came running across the field.

"Paul, meet Ghost."

"Wow, that's one big dog. It's like a wolf."

Alice smiled at his description. "She may have some wolf in her somewhere, you never know."

"I take it she's yours."

"Yes, and here's someone else." Turning around, Paul spotted a horse running towards them. "This is Poppy. As you can see, she is in foal."

Alice waved her finger at her in a mock admonishment. "You shouldn't be running like that in your condition, You're a naughty girl."

"Good grief. She looks massive." He shook his head in disbelief. Alice at once comforted her, tickling her behind the ear. "She's due any day now, Paul."

Paul fussed both the horse and the dog, who was vying for his attention for a while and then fell silent. After a pause, he asked. "Do they just run around wild on the estate?"

"They do, but they don't wander far from my cottage. The cottage is just through those trees. They heard us coming."

Paul's brow creased. He turned and looked at Alice and couldn't hide the surprise on his face. "You live here on the estate?"

"I live here in my cottage. It's been in my family for hundreds of years, even before the manor house was built."

"So, it's not part of the estate, and here's me thinking all the property here was part of the estate."

"No, Paul, it's not part of the estate." Alice eyed him warily. "It seems you know a lot about the estate. Is that why you're here? The property you're looking at. Is it the hotel?"

Paul shook his head. "Alice, I'm not at liberty to say."

Alice looked shocked. "It is the hotel then!"

Paul didn't answer, and there was an awkward silence for a while. "Alice, it's more than my job's worth to say what properties we are looking at," Alice noted that he was now avoiding eye contact with her. She took a deep breath and sighed. *So, it is the hotel, and he does not want to lie to me.* She pressed him further.

"Properties? So, we're talking more than one." A double shot rang out from nearby and startled Molly, who at once started to gallop into the distance.

18. MORAG'S COTTAGE 1996 AD

Alice urged her horse into a gallop chasing Paul, whose horse now sprinted away in the direction of Alice's cottage. Paul was startled and fell forward, holding the horse by the neck.

Alice cried out from behind him. "Lean back. Pull the reins towards your waist." Paul's horse was already in full flight. It had passed the jarring canter stage. The ride now smoothed out as the horse galloped to full speed. Alice pulled up alongside him and called out loudly. "Pull the reins towards your waist, hard!"

"It's ok." Paul cried out at the top of his voice. "I'm all right. I remember what to do."

Alice galloped alongside him and looked across at him. She smiled when she saw he was laughing.

Paul felt the wind in his face, and after his initial panic, he found himself alive again with an adrenalin rush the likes of which he hadn't felt for years. He let out a scream. "Yahoo!"

Alice shouted to overcome the noise of the hooves. Take your weight on your feet and lift your bum off the horse and let her have her head." They galloped alongside one another for more than a mile.

For Alice, looking across at him, time went in slow motion. *It's been nearly four hundred years since we did this. God, he looks magnificent.*

Alice called out, "She's making her way home, where she feels safe. Just let her go where she wants and enjoy the ride."

Ghost now joined in running alongside them both, and Alice's joy was complete. The horses galloped into the woods, weaving in and out of the trees. Alice deliberately galloped past him as she had done in their earlier life, turned her head backward, looked at Paul, and laughed.

Paul shook his head in disbelief. Once again, he had the feeling of déjà vu. The horses began to slow to a canter, and then to a walking pace. Paul saw the cottage through the trees and, after taking the weight off his legs, lowered himself back into the saddle. When they came to a stop, Alice spoke first.

"You, ok?"

Paul let out a gasp. "Phew, it was a bit scary, especially when she started to gallop, but it was great when she was at full speed."

Ghost started to bark, and Alice remarked. "Ghost said she enjoyed it too." Paul ruffled Ghost's neck and began to stroke her. He then turned his attention to the property. "I take it this is your house."

Alice corrected his terminology. "Cottage. Yes, welcome to my home. I didn't intend for us to come here today, but as we are here, would you like a cup of tea?"

Paul pursed his lips. "How about coffee? I haven't got into tea yet."

"Of course, I forgot you are an American. No coffee, sorry, a beer, would you prefer a beer?"

Paul's face lit. "Beer would be great."

Alice demounted nimbly and let the horse walk free. "Sit yourself down on the porch, and I'll grab a couple of bottles."

Alice disappeared into the cottage. Moments later, she returned with two small beer bottles but no glasses. Handing one to Paul, they chinked bottles. "Cheers."

Looking around him, Paul, once again, had that feeling of déjà vu. "Alice, it's lovely here, it's strange but it all seems so familiar."

She followed his gaze as he took in the surrounding area. "I think so."

"Is it just you?"

"Apart from my animals, yes. My parents died a year ago in a car crash, and I've been on my own ever since."

"How awful." He studied her face intensely. "Jed did tell me, what a dreadful thing to have to deal with. Do you like living on your own?"

"I'm comfortable with it for the time being." She changed the subject as it was still too painful to talk about. "You managed the horse well - I said you were a natural."

He laughed nervously. "Scared the life out of me at first, truth be told, but wasn't it great when she got up to speed."

She agreed. "There's nothing quite like it when you let them have their head."

Paul scanned the scenery, taking in all the views. "Was that a gunshot back there that frightened the horse?"

"There isn't supposed to be anyone shooting today, especially near my property, and yes, it sounded like a shotgun. Someone was probably shooting pheasants." Alice smiled inwardly; she knew who had fired the shot.

Paul, unsure of what Alice had just said, repeated the word. "Peasants?"

Alice laughed and shook her head. "No, Paul, we aren't allowed to shoot peasants in England. I said pheasants, game birds. They were introduced from China hundreds of years ago. They're not native birds, but we breed them here, thousands of them. It's big business and contributes thirty percent of the income to the estate." Her eyes turned to Paul measuring his reaction. "How silly of me if you are looking to buy the place, you probably know that."

Again, an awkward silence descended on them until Paul changed the subject.

"I thought you didn't like guns?" He watched as her brow creased and she chewed her lip, and he realized he had spotted a tell-tale, her reaction to an awkward question. She turned her eyes to the ground.

"I don't like killing anything for fun. Why big businesses pay tens of thousands of pounds a day to send employees out into the countryside to blast little birds to death is beyond me."

This time it was Paul's turn to study her reaction. "Yet here you are running the place."

Her face became serious. He had touched a nerve. "Yes, but I'm not comfortable with it. If I didn't do it, someone else would. In this modern business world, everything must make a profit." She sighed heavily. "They built a motorway ten miles south of here. It was years ago, before my time. It took all our passing trade, so we had to diversify. We introduced shooting and fishing to complement fox hunting. She shook her head. "I don't agree with that either, but there we are, what will be will be. Tell me, how will you make a profit when you buy this place?"

Before he could respond, she put up her hand to quieten him and called out. "Ghost, where's Poppy?" Ghost got to her feet, lifted her nose into the air, searching for her scent, turned, and ran back the way they had just come.

"Something's wrong," Alice said and started to run in the same direction.

"What on earth makes you think there's something wrong," When there was no reply, Paul chased after her. Ghost had stopped running about eight hundred yards from the cottage. When Alice reached the horse, she found her lying on her side under the trees.

Kneeling beside her, Alice began to comfort the distressed animal. "Poppy, Poppy, what is it - I told you not to run, you silly girl." Alice was kneeling beside the horse and looked up at Paul. "I'm sorry, Paul. I'll have to stay with Poppy. Something's wrong. She's trying to give birth, but something's not right."

Paul could see Alice was concerned. "I haven't got my cell, Alice. Have you got one? I could ring for a vet?"

She shook her head dismissively. "No point, there's no signal here."

He turned to go. "I'll ride back to the hotel and use the phone there."

Alice placed her hand on his to stop him. "Paul, I know what to do. Don't worry."

He looked shocked. "You're sure you can manage this."

"We'll be fine, but you go back if you wish. I don't need help from any vet."

"You're certain. You're sure?"

She continued to stroke the head of the horse, and Paul could see she was in distress as the tears ran down her cheeks. "You can go if you want, I'm afraid this will not be pleasant."

"No way."

"Paul, this could take ages."

Paul was adamant. "What can I do? I'm staying to boil water, rip blankets, or something?" This brought a smile to her face, and she wiped the tears away with the back of her hand.

"In that case, go into the cottage to the bathroom. It's through the front door, and the second on the left. You will see a large jar of petroleum jelly. Could you get that? Then go into the stable, and on the joist hanging from the roof, you will see several ropes. Could you bring those?"

Paul hurried off to do her bidding. In the meantime, Alice meditated, silently searching for the memories of her ancestors. She found dozens that had come across the same problem. Alice listened to several as she cradled the horse's head. Like Sarah and all the ancestors that came before her, she had the same telepathic skills. She at once sensed what was wrong. As her ancestors had said, the foal was breached.

A breached birth was dangerous for both the horse and foal, but the knowledge stored in the countless memories of her ancestors could be accessed quickly. This had happened hundreds of times in her past lives, not just to horses but to cattle, wolves, and dogs. Some survived, and some Didn't. Of those who didn't, the knowledge gained was not wasted. It was stored deep in the memories to be accessed by her or any of her brothers and sisters to make sure that they didn't make that mistake again.

Paul came running out of the cottage, quite out of breath.

"Here's the rope and Vaseline you asked for. How is she?"

"The foal is breached, so this is bad. I might lose both f them."

Paul was shocked. "Then I must get the vet."

"We haven't time, Paul. Thank you for staying, but again we don't need a vet. I'm afraid this will get very messy on our first date. Are you sure You're up for it?"

"Of course, I'm sure. Are you sure you can do this?" He bent over, resting his hands on his knees, to catch his breath. "So, this is a date, is it?"

Alice was concentrating on Poppy, but she could sense his smile. "I've seen this done before, but we've run out of time. I'll lose her before any vet can get here.*

Alice took off her long-sleeved blouse, leaving her wearing just a bra. She applied the Vaseline up her right arm to her shoulder. The horse was still lying on its side in distress and was frothing around the mouth. She could smell the fear emanating from the creature.

"Paul, hold her tail and lift it. I need to examine her internally." With that, she inserted her right hand into the horse. "Something's very wrong. Oh no!"

Paul cried. "What is it?"

"No head."

Paul answered in an astonished voice, "What! It hasn't got a head?"

A smile creased her mouth, and she replied patiently, "No, Paul, the head is not where it should be." Alice inserted her arm fully into the horse. "The foal is facing the wrong way. It's trying to come out rear end first. She will die if it does. The only way around this is for me to tie a rope around the rear hooves, and together, we pull the foal out backward, legs first. Pass me that rope quickly."

Paul passed Alice the rope and watched as she skillfully tied a slip knot in the end and created a loop. "What we must do now is pass the loop over both rear hooves. I'll do that, and then you must pull the rope. Can you do that?"

Paul did not hide the irritation in his voice. "Of course, I can."

"Right, lift her tail again." Alice inserted the rope inside the horse, and her arm disappeared up to the shoulder. The horse was now in even more distress, and Paul felt the need to console her by stroking her head.

"I've got it on one leg, but I can't find the other." After a couple of minutes of pulling and pushing, she managed to find the second leg. "Got it. Now, If I just get the loop over the second leg like that. Yes, I've done it. Paul, pull the rope, but gently." Alice held the rope so the knot slipped tight over both hooves. "Pull the rope harder. That's it, the slip knot has worked." Alice then pulled the legs forward while Paul pulled the rope. "Ok, we're in position. Get ready to pull hard."

What I need you to do, Poppy is stand up. Come on, girl, stand up, and you'll be all right, but you must stand. Come on, girl, you can do it.

"Alice, what are you waiting for?"

"She needs to stand up, Paul. It will be much better if she can."

Alice then repeated the instruction verbally for Paul's benefit. "Come on, Poppy, stand up." Poppy obeyed and promptly got to her feet. "Ok, Poppy, big push. Paul, would you pull hard on the rope? Yes, that's it. Now stop." Alice again inserted her hand, checking everything was in place. "Ok, Poppy, this time push hard. You can do it."

"Paul, pull hard, now." Two hooves appeared first, then the rear legs. Alice now held the rope with Paul. "One big pull, now." She said and switched to talking to the horse telepathically. *Push Poppy, push.*

Moments later, the foal slid out feet first, followed by the placenta. Poppy turned around and at once started licking the foal.

Alice removed the rope, cleared the membrane from its face so it could breathe, and then stood back.

The foal began to move. It tried to stand, its feet splayed, but it was unsteady. Then with its rear feet locked in a wide position, the front legs pushed up and locked into place - and it began to shiver.

Poppy continued to clean the foal, and the couple stood without speaking for several minutes, sharing the moment with the horse, and both were engrossed in the beauty of life.

Paul shook his head in disbelief. "You did it, you saved them both. That was amazing!"

Alice turned to face him, and her face reflected her relief. "We did it, Paul. I couldn't have done it by myself. Thank you for staying."

Paul turned to Alice and kissed her lightly on the cheek. She flushed at the unexpected familiarity. Her eyes met his, and this time it was her heart that fluttered.

For God's sake, kiss him back.

Alice recognized Sarah's voice as it echoed from the deep recesses of her mind, and as he went to turn away, she pulled his face closer and kissed him on the lips. When she released him, their eyes locked together each measuring the other.

Paul smiled and cleared his throat. "I wouldn't have missed that for the world. Poppy looks ok now."

"She would have died. It was touch and go. The foal was trying to come out backside first, and the legs would have folded back, and the foal would have been too big to go through the birth canal." Her eyes were drawn to his hair which was now covered in Vaseline and horse. "Err, sorry, Paul, I seem to have greased your hair."

He wrapped his arms around her and pulled her closer. "Don't worry it was worth it."

They stood in silence and watched Poppy clean the foal for a while. Feeling steadier on its feet, it took its first step, then another, and another. Immediately, it started looking for the mare's teats and, after finding one, began to suckle. They looked at each other, smiled, and Alice casually took Paul's hand.

Paul asked thoughtfully, "How did it know how to stand and where to find the teats?"

Good question. Time to awaken some lost memories of your own. "We call it "Prime inherited memory." We all have it to some degree." *Except you, that is.* "It's a message built into our DNA and imprinted over millions of years. The foal knows it is in danger the second it's born. It must be ready to run to escape predators. It's life or death, the survival of the fittest. Those that didn't remember to stand and be ready to run, didn't survive in the wild. It also knows it must suckle as quickly as possible to get energy and get its mother's scent on her. Without the milk passing through the foal, the mare could reject it, not realizing it was hers. In their world, the sense of smell is more important than sight. They need both, but they rely more on the sense of smell."

Paul's eyes were fixed on the foal, engrossed at the moment. "How come we don't have inherited memory?"

She smiled patiently. "We do, Paul. When a baby is born, it too wants to suckle, no one shows it how. That's inherited memory. We all have it, but to a much lesser degree than animals."

He turned to her once again. "Alice, where did you learn to do that with the breached birth.".

She gazed into the distance with unseeing eyes, momentarily lost in thought. "I watched a friend do it years ago." She took a deep breath and shook her head: *dam, my first lie.*

"Could I ask you something else?"

"Ask away."

"How did you know Polly was in trouble? We were half a mile away, so you couldn't possibly have heard her."

Her mind went into overdrive.

How can I explain that without telling him I can communicate mentally with other creatures? I can't tell him Polly called me. "Polly and Ghost are inseparable, and they are always together. When I realized she hadn't caught up with us after we got back from our ride, I put two and two together." *That was easy. I'm getting good at lying.*

He turned his attention to Ghost and ruffled her fur. "You've got Ghost well-trained, and she seemed to understand you completely when you asked where Poppy was."

"Yes, she's a good girl, aren't you, Ghost? Goodness, will you look at the state of me, of us?" A thought came to her. *As Steven said, I think it is time to get him out of those clothes and maybe awaken some more memories. After all, he did not pull away when we kissed.* Again, Sarah's thoughts came unbidden to the surface. **For mother's sake, Alice, he wants you, can't you tell? Strike while the irons are hot.**

"They will be ok now, Paul, let's leave them to it."

Alice verbally instructed Ghost. "Ghost, you stay, stay with Poppy. You watch over her." The dog rested on the ground, with her head on her paws, watching over the horse.

Alice turned to Paul. "I think we need to get cleaned up. Let's go back to the cottage; I think we deserve another beer." She looked up at the sky. "It's getting dark. I didn't realize."

As they walked away, Paul noticed Ghost did not try to follow.

"Alice, will Ghost stay with Polly because you told her to?"

"As I said, they are very close. She would have probably stayed anyway." As they walked back to the cottage, she felt a thrill when he held her hand.

"Alice, I really enjoyed this afternoon. I think I will probably remember it all my life."

"Me too, Paul. Alice said thoughtfully. "It has been quite special. Strange, I feel comfortable around you, considering we are from different worlds."

He squeezed her hand. "I don't think I've met anyone like you, Alice Llewellyn."

Alice again presented him with the smile Mia perfected four hundred years in the past. *I'm sure you haven't, not for nearly four hundred years.* "Really, Paul. I'll take that as a compliment." She then prompted. "Do you not feel like we have known each other for years?"

He couldn't hide the smile on his face. "That's exactly how I feel, and it's like renewing an old friendship."

Alice smiled to herself. *It's a lot older than you think, Paul.* They arrived back at the cottage, and Alice put the lights on. She looked Paul up and down and then looked in the mirror herself before adding. "Goodness, You're as dirty as me. I'll put your clothes in the washer-dryer. I need to get cleaned up, Paul. I'll just run the shower. Get a couple of beers out of the fridge. You can jump in when I've finished if you wish."

To Alice's dismay, the shower was freezing cold. She cleaned off the worst of the blood and Vaseline but couldn't stand the cold. Wrapping a towel around her, she called over to Paul. "You might want to take a rain check on the shower. There is no hot water, the boiler has been on the blink for ages, and I think it's finally given up the ghost."

He called back to her. "We should go back to the manor and have a shower there. I'm sweaty and covered in blood." His heart again missed a beat when she walked into the room with a short white towel wrapped around her. "Alice, you've still got blood in your hair."

"Have I?" She said and turned to look at herself in the mirror. "I couldn't stand the cold any longer. The water is colder than the lake." *There's an idea, he always loved to swim in the lake.* Alice paused for a while, then turned to Paul. "There's a thought. Do you fancy a swim? It would clean us off."

Paul could not hide the surprise in his voice. "Go swimming in the lake, but it's dark?"

"At least it would clean us off." She again gave Paul one of her most captivating smiles and raised her eyebrows invitingly. *Go on, Paul, you know you want to.*

Paul took the hint. "Do you know Alice, I walked around the lake Tuesday, I thought then it looked tempting."

Alice taunted him once more. "I will if you will!"

"I'd love to, but what about swimming costumes."

She shook her head, teasing him. "I usually go naked, but I will wear my bikini as we have only just met." She put her tongue in her cheek and added, "I have a spare pair of bottoms if you would like to try them, but they would not hide much." She looked down at the bulge in his trousers and shook her head. "Sorry, Paul, it looks like none of mine would fit you."

He returned her smile. "I'm wearing boxer shorts, so let's go for it."

"Paul, I'll get changed. Let me have your clothes. I can stick them in the washer-dryer. They should be cleaned and dried by the time we get back."

Alice returned wearing a white bikini swimsuit and a couple of towels and took his hand. "Alice, I can't believe we're doing this, going for a midnight swim."

Her eyes danced with his, and she raised her lashes. "It's all in the name of hygiene." Her smile was open and full of life, and again, Paul's heart missed a beat.

"Of course, Alice, lead the way."

On this side of the lake, the shallow water around the edge was covered in water lilies, so Alice held on to Paul's hand and led him down to the water's edge.

"Paul, if we go past the weeping willow tree and around the bend, there is a boat landing stage. I normally swim off that. It's nice and private, so no one can see us from the Manor."

Paul tiptoed through the long grass, enjoying the sensation. "You swim here often, Alice?"

"In the summer, yes, but only when it's hot. Ghost loves to swim with me."

Right on cue, Ghost joined them on the landing stage. Alice bent down and fussed the dog. She then gave the creature one of her sternest looks. "I thought I told you to stay with Polly?"

Alice then communicated with Ghost mentally. *Is she all right? Are you sure? Ok, if You're sure that she's all right.*

She then switched back to verbal commands for Paul's benefit. "Ok, Ghost, but only a quick swim, then you go back to Polly."

Taking the lead, Alice, followed by Ghost, ran along the jetty and leaped feet first into the water. Still, in mid-air, Alice cried, "The last one in is a sissy."

Not to be outdone, Paul ran and dived in at speed. Upon surfacing, he cried out. "No, no, no!"

Alice swam over to him. "Paul, what's up?"

"Alice, my boxer shorts have gone, and they have come off completely. Can you see them?"

Alice laughed. "You should have jumped in like wolf and me. Don't worry, Paul, I don't usually wear a swimsuit here, and I only did tonight because you were here. No one comes down this side of the lake, especially this time of night."

"You're here."

Alice cocked her head to one side, teasing him. "Well, Mr. Masters, are you shy of little ole me?"

Paul pursed his lip and shook his head disapprovingly. "Well, Miss Llewellyn, you have me at a disadvantage."

Again, Alice taunted him. "So how do we rectify it, Mr. Masters?"

"In all fairness, I think you should take yours off as well,"

Alice presented him with a face reflecting mock horror. "What! In your dreams, lover boy. If You're trying to live out your fantasy dream, you will have to catch me first."

Alice turned and swam out into the middle of the lake, and was quickly followed by Paul.

Alice being a competent swimmer, took Paul by surprise. It was about three hundred yards before he caught up. Alice started to scream as she realized he was almost upon her. Finally, Paul stretched his arm forward, grabbed her bikini bottom, and stopped swimming. Before Alice could stop, she found them around her ankles. As she turned to face him, he laughed, holding the bottoms above his head, and began to taunt her by spinning them around on his finger.

"Now we're even," he laughed and let them spin off into the distance. "Whoops-sorry."

To her dismay, Alice cried out. "No! They're brand new." She watched as they fell below the surface and let out a deep sigh. She swam back towards Paul and stopped about a yard in front of him. Both looked at each other, hoping they knew what the other was thinking.

"Mr. Masters, that's not funny. I'll be adding that to your account."

He laughed openly. "Alice, the look on your face says it is worth it."

The moon was high in the sky, and it was a clear night. There they stayed, treading water, looking into each other's eyes, unsure what was about to happen.

Down below, Alice could feel the spirits of the lake around them as she trod water. The Princess was there, Morag also. Alice's mind moved to the realm of the spirit world. *I feel you, Mia, and you Morag, and, yes, he is back amongst us as you prophesied, but he hasn't recovered his memories yet. Like Sarah, I, too, love this man, and I want him more than life itself. But I want him to love me for me. Then, if he Doesn't recover his memories, both Sarah and I will still have him. Princess Mia, it is Paul I'm swimming with, not Saul, but Saul's memory is getting stronger. He is recovering them more and more, day by day. I will ask Sarah to be patient and please be happy for us all.*

Paul and Alice continued to tread water, looking at each other just out of reach. Sarah once again prompted. *For mother's sake, Alice, you will never lose your virginity at this rate.*

Alice made the first move. She swam closer and put her arms around his neck. He held her close and unfastened her bikini top at the same time. Alice raised her eyebrows in shock and horror once again. "Mr. Masters, what is going on behind my back?" *So, you are interested. But are the instincts yours or Saul's?*

Alice released him and backed away, letting the top sink to the bottom of the lake.

"The top is useless without the bottom." She stated and lapsed into thought. *Do I care? If it is Paul, then both he and Saul are mine. If it is just Paul, I am sure I can help him recall his lost memories. Flesh-to-flesh would be a good start.*

Paul now moved closer, embracing her once more. "I feel I'm falling in love with you, Miss Llewellyn."

Feeling his skin touching hers for the first time in four hundred years, Alice quipped, "You've always been in love with me, Paul-you just didn't realize it."

She pulled him closer. "Flesh to flesh, Paul Masters. Who would have thought that this morning?" Still holding her arms around his neck, she lifted her legs and wrapped them around him. Paul was now treading water for them both. They kissed and held it even though they were sinking to the bottom of the lake. Finally, their feet touched the mud, which brought them to their senses, and they surfaced and gasped for air.

Ghost started to bark as she saw them return to the surface. Alice turned her attention to her. "Ghost, go back to Poppy. You've had your swim. Go, check on Poppy." The animal turned and swam to the shore. "Three's a crowd, Paul."

"It's amazing. That dog knows every word you say."

She turned and watched the dog swim to the shore. "Yes, she's a good girl Paul, let's swim for a while." Alice smiled to herself, thinking. *She knows every thought too, Paul.*

Paul's attention was drawn to lights emanating from the bottom of the lake. "Alice, look at the phosphorescence in the water. It's sparkling all around us. I've swum at night before, but I have never seen it like that."

Alice smiled inwardly. *I'll tell him one day, but he is not ready yet. I think he would drop his cork leg if he knew he was swimming with the lake spirits.*

They swam for about fifteen minutes, idly talking about nothing like lovers do. Nearing the far bank, Paul recognized the spot he saw earlier in the day, the one he thought would make a good swimming hole. "I know this place, Alice. We can get out here."

"How on earth do you know that?" Then a thought occurred. *Is he beginning to remember?*

"I walked past here this morning, and I thought then that it would make a good swimming hole. There's something I want to show you."

Alice resisted. "It's dark, and even I'll get lost in there."

"It's a full moon, Alice. Come on; it's not far." Paul held out his hand and led her out of the water.

"Where are you taking me, Paul?" *I wasn't expecting this.*

"It's a surprise, you'll see. They both felt self-conscious as they stepped out of the water together, naked. Alice looked down at Paul's manhood and commented to ease the situation.

"He looks cold."

Paul let out a groan. "Alice, you really know how to destroy the moment." He took her hand and pulled her. "Come with me." Paul led Alice by the hand, taking her into the wood.

"Paul, are you sure you know where You're going?"

"It's not far, wait and see."

As he guided her through the trees, another thought hit her. *This is the way to the circle. He can't be taking me to the Henge, how could he possibly know about it or the labyrinth of paths to get there? Surely, he is beginning to remember.* Twisting and turning through the bushes that only the Druids knew, they entered the circle.

"Here we are, Alice."

Alice stared at him in disbelief. "Paul, why have you brought me here? And how on earth did you know about it? No outsiders know it's here?"

He smiled openly. "I found it yesterday when walking around the lake, and it's just like I saw in my dreams - and look at this lovely soft green grass to lie on."

"Paul, you can't find this place by accident. Do you know where you have brought me?"

"I was hoping you could tell me. Do you know?"

"Of course, I know. I've lived here all my life. It is a holy place, a place of worship, and you should not be here."

She grabbed his hand and tried to pull him away, but he stood firm.

"Is that the Altar?" Paul pointed to the large oblong stone offset to one side of the circle.

"Yes, Paul, that is the Altar."

"I thought they were always in the middle - they always are in my dreams. Why is it offset?"

Alice shook her head in disbelief. "So, suddenly you are a Henge expert. What a strange thing to ask?"

"It just feels wrong there."

"You're right, Paul, it should be in the center, but someone moved it hundreds of years ago. There is a tale about it, and I will tell you one day. It will surprise you but I haven't got time now. We must go." She again tried to pull him away, but again he stood firm.

"Alice, who come here?"

She pursed her lips. *He is not ready for this.* "People, country folk, normal people who still believe in the old ways."

"Druids?"

She sighed heavily. "Nowadays, it is mainly Druid or 'Prime,' but Druid is a broadly used term. Many people come here for comfort, worship, and peace of mind. Some come to escape from everyday life's rigors and get closer to their creator. Others just come to be alone, even if it's just to connect with nature again. People marry here. They hand-fast, they step over brooms. They share their harvest. They give thanks to their creator. "Paul, I will tell you about it some other time, but we should go. It is wrong for you to be here.

"Wait a minute, Alice. Hand-fasting, stepping over brooms?"

Alice wrapped her arms around herself, trying to keep warm. "Paul, I will tell you about this place some other time. There are many things to tell you, but you are not ready yet."

Paul stood firm. "Alice, you don't understand. I've been here many times in my dreams or somewhere like this. The dreams I have had since I came here, I think they were all about Druids, white robes, and all that. Alice, please don't mock me, but there is always a woman in my dreams, the same one every time, and Alice, it is a woman who looks exactly like you or the one in the painting in the Master bedroom."

Paul studied every nuance of her face. *Oh God, she will think I am mad. I shouldn't have said that.* Alice's smile returned instead of the expected sarcasm, replacing her frown like sunshine after rain. Even in the moonlight, he could see the glint in her green eyes.

She reached up, put her arms around his neck, and kissed him gently. "Paul, you have remembered at last. I have been dreaming of you all my life too." *This life and a dozen others, but you still are not ready for that.*

"Remembered what, Alice?" She held him around the neck, studying his eyes for any signs of recognition, but all she saw was confusion, so she decided to change tack.

"Right, stepping over brooms and hand-fasting. Have you never heard of either of them before?

Paul shook his head, so Alice continued.

"A hand-fast can be a marriage or an engagement ceremony, depending on your beliefs, country, and time period. It is when they tie the couple's hands together with the ground ivy vine to cement their union as we do, or a rope or strip of fabric in more modern times. You'll find the ivy on the floor of the wood." She waved her arm vaguely, showing where it could be found. It's where you get the saying tying the knot in modern marriages. In times gone by, it was done when two families wanted their children to be married at a future date, like an engagement.

"Ok, I get that. So, what on earth is stepping over brooms?"

"What do they teach kids in America these days?" She said jokingly. "Stepping over brooms is a marriage ceremony. They simply lay the brooms on the ground and step over them together, and, hey presto, they are married. It represents sweeping out their old life and getting ready for their new one together."

Paul's eyes drifted around the circle, and Alice could see their wonder. "All that sort of thing goes on here?"

"Yes, Paul."

"I thought this was a sleepy little town, with nothing happening. This is amazing."

Alice laughed. "One thing is for certain, Paul, Glastonbury is not your average sleepy country town." Paul looked up at the roots towering above him. "The trees are all upside down in the ground, with their roots in the air. Why is that?"

She shook her head. "That's a silly question, Paul. If you put the trees in a circle the right way up with their roots in the ground, they would simply grow, and how would you tell where the forest ends and the sacred circle begins."

"You're mocking me, Alice."

"No Paul, I will explain quickly, and then we must go. Tens of thousands of years ago, the people who arrived at these ceremonial places were hunter-gatherers. Bye, the way - that's how long this one's been here. They were ignorant, primitive people. To see trees coming out of the ground upside down seemed magical to them.

It was agreed by the tribe elders that the tribes would meet once, or maybe twice a year. The only time reference they had were the longest and shortest days. So, now the groups of hunter-gatherers wandering around the forests of Britain had a time and a place to meet up. Without the inverted trees, It would be like looking for a needle in a haystack."

Paul gazed up in the night sky, and the cloud-striped moon shone eerily through the roots, which spread out like malformed fingers grasping for the clouds.

Paul turned to Alice, his eyes searching. "Do you come here, Alice?"

Alice paused for thought. *Ok, the million-dollar question, do I tell him and frighten him away? Make him run from the crazy woman who lives in the wood with animals. Or do I lie?* Alice let out a heavy sigh. *Oh dear, I'll have to tell him. Our lives together could depend on how he reacts to the answer, and his response could change our lives forever. Holy Mother, let him understand.*

"Yes, I come here. I am the guardian, the guardian of the henge."

19. THE HAND-FAST 1996 AD

Paul looked stunned. "You are the guardian?" His eyes took in every nuance on her face, measuring her reaction. "So, what does that entail?"

Alice rocked her head from side to side nonchalantly. "Mainly guiding ceremonies." *Go on, Paul run from the madwoman.* Paul, however, did not run. Alice studied his face and could see he was confused and had many questions.

"Who do you worship, Alice?"

She gave him her broadest smile. "The Earth Mother, the creator. Who do you worship, Paul?"

"Well, God, of course."

Alice nodded and continued, "The one God, the Creator?"

"Yes."

She smiled again and shrugged her shoulders. "In that case, we both believe in the true God, as do most main religions." The confusion on Paul's face deepened. When he did not respond, she continued. "The name may be different, and in our case the sex being a woman figure, but you must always remember it is humanity that creates the divisions in how to worship God."

Paul fell silent, taking in Alice's comments. "So, you say we all pray to the same God?"

"God has been given many names by humankind since man became aware, but the message is the same. You must look past the name, and the sex, and see the message, it is the same for most true religions"

His eyes burned deep into hers. "So, what do you think the message is?"

"The same as all true religions, which is to treat all humankind and the creatures of the world with love, kindness, compassion, tolerance, forgiveness and to have the self-discipline to control your anger when others fall short of your expectations, And to be content with what God has given you, and when you have become fully conscious, guide others to achieve the same."

Paul shook his head in disbelief. "Wow, Alice, that is a profound statement. Do you believe that will ever happen?"

"Paul, that's what we 'Prime' do. We always have since the beginning, before the Romans, before the Druids, before the Celts. We guide humanity toward the light, and by doing so, hope humankind will remember the answer to the first question, "why are we here?"

Paul shook his head deep in thought. "Let us hope so."

Alice had given up trying to pull him away from the circle.

"What sorts of ceremonies are performed here?"

"Harvest, you would call it thanksgiving. There are weddings, funerals, remembrance days, birthdays."

"You read about orgies and sacrifices and that sort of thing going on in these places." Alice fell silent, obviously deep in thought. *How much do I divulge now? How much is he ready for?*

Alice didn't try to hide the sarcasm in her voice. "Well, I haven't sacrificed anyone for ages, and as for the so-called orgies, I must have missed those!"

"What about last nigh...?"

"That is enough, Paul, you are being silly, and I'm getting cold, and you should not be here."

"Sorry Alice, I've upset you?" Paul moved closer, took her in his arms, and kissed her gently.

Alice noticed the intensity had gone out of his eyes and felt her heart flutter when she realized he was not going to run. All she saw now in them was love.

"Aren't you worried I will sacrifice you on the Altar, Mr. Masters?"

"You're mocking me again."

"Of course, I am, but seriously Paul, I'm a simple country girl with simple beliefs. This Henge is a holy place for us, and if this shocks you and you think I'm weird, run away now. If we're going to make love now in the circle, which is sacred in my mind, we will be spiritually bound together forever whether you like it or not. This place is for weddings, and it's not to be taken lightly. If you just want to make love, we can go back to a warm bed.

Paul picked her up in his arms, sweeping her off her feet. He looked deep into her eyes. "Alice Llewellyn, I want you more than anything in the world, and I've run to you, so I'm not going anywhere. We belong together."

"Paul, be serious. We have only been together a few days."

His voice was as warm and rich as melting butter. "I can't explain it, Alice. It's like I have known you for years, and I feel I have been looking for you my whole life."

Paul carried her into the center of the grassed area, and they lay together, but when Alice wriggled to get comfortable, she felt a stabbing pain in her back.

"Paul, this is too painful. There are twigs and stones under me, and it's hurting." They got to their feet. "Paul, if you want us to be tied together, we should be doing this properly on the Altar, so get up."

"What, like the guy last night?"

"Whoa...It was you. Alice took two steps backward, measuring him, and could not hide the surprise on her face. "So, you were watching from the trees, I knew someone was there, but I thought it was a shy relative. When Paul let his eyes fall, avoiding her gaze, an awkward silence descended upon them. "Paul, that was a 'Prime' wedding. It was an intimate and sacred ceremony and very personal, and that was very naughty of you. Do you know what we do to naughty boys?"

He tried and failed to hide his smile. "Er, no."

She lifted her right eyebrow cynically and kept her face stern and judgmental. "You must be punished." Again, she stretched out the silence and narrowed her eyes, maximizing its effect.

"Right, on the Altar now."

Paul hesitated and was unsure if she was angry or not. It wasn't until he saw her lips twitch suppressing a smile that he remembered to breathe.

"You heard my sacrificial lamb, on the Altar now - and lay on your back. And if you saw what happened yesterday, you know what to do - I won't be long." Alice pushed him towards the Altar, and he lifted himself with ease. He then lay back and waited.

Alice planted a kiss gently on his lips. "Paul, you should run now if you're going to. It's your last chance."

"W - why, what are you going to do?"

"Paul, if you love me like you say you do, you must trust me, so lay back."

"In that case, I'm staying, Alice. I have been drawn here all my life, to this spot, to you. I have been in love with you even before I met you, and I have never been more certain of anything in my whole life."

Alice kissed him lovingly on the lips. And held his lower lip between her teeth and pulled gently. In that case, I need to go and prepare myself for you, so make yourself ready and close your eyes. Whatever you do, don't move."

He heard Alice move off into the woods and called out. "Where are you going?"

Her voice echoed from the darkness. "Won't be long, oh, and keep your eyes shut."

After five minutes, she returned. "Are your eyes still shut, my sacrificial lamb? Not even a tiny bit open."

"Shut tight," he said as a smile crept across his mouth.

"Now, Paul, I want you to keep very still. Do not open your eyes. It is still a test, and if you really love me, you will keep them shut." Alice kissed him on the lips and moved down to his nipples, which she bit just a little too hard.

Paul responded. "Ouch!"

"Shush, quiet wimp," she said between kisses.

Her kisses moved lower to his stomach, teasing him. Paul lay there in agony, ecstasy, and anticipation but he wasn't sure which. Alice climbed onto the Altar and straddled him, and after she had aroused him, bent her knees, and lowered herself onto him. "Eyes still shut, Paul?"

"Yes, of course." Alice began to tie an ivy vine around his left wrist and attached it to her right.

"W - what are you doing?" Paul asked anxiously.

"It's a test to see if you trust me enough to keep your eyes shut, I'm just tying your wrists, my sacrificial lamb."

As the bondage dream was still fresh in his mind, Paul began to panic and started to lift his head. "You're tying me down?"

Alice pushed his head back down. "Stay there. You have been very naughty, so don't you dare move." Alice used her sternest voice and then added. "I am only tying our hands together - don't worry."

Paul felt her lips on his once again, and he began to calm down. Lifting herself to her knees, she took hold of his manhood and guided him into her. She lowered herself gently into place and gave a little squeal as she sat lower until he was fully inside her. She then sat upright, motionless.

"You can open your eyes now, Paul."

Paul saw that Alice had painted blue lines and scrolls all over her face, and blue circles around her breasts and arms. There were runes and symbols on different parts of her body, and he could see that she had tied their hands together.

"You look… Wow, you look pretty erotic." As he spoke, she began to rock backward and forwards as if in a trance. Paul asked, "Why have you tied our hands together? Is this what is called hand-fasting?"

"Yes, we are now tied." She replied and then bent her head and began to tease his nipples again.

"Are we married?"

In my eyes, yes. I said we would be if we made love in the circle. Just lie back and enjoy the moment. She then tried to put something in his mouth. Here Paul, eat this, it will calm you down."

"What is it? I don't do drugs?"

"Don't be silly, where would I have got drugs from? We swam across the lake naked, didn't we? You said you trust me, I've already had one, so just eat it. It will make our union more intense. We are going to be here most of the night. Trust me, you'll need all your strength for later." It tasted and had the texture of dried meat, so he swallowed it.

Alice began to lift herself up and down at a faster pace as Paul's senses began to dull from the effect of the mushroom. His mind started to turn in on itself, and nothing else existed outside his body. But was it his body?

Paul looked around the Henge, and people were watching them, long-lost friends, friends he hadn't seen for a very long time, and his heart lifted. He couldn't remember their names, but he felt glad they were here. A feeling of peace and tranquility overcame him as he heard Pagan music echoing in the recesses of his mind. It was a joyful celebration.

His mind drifted, and he watched from the circle's edge. He could see Alice sitting astride another man, and Paul was filled with anger. He studied them further and realized it was his brother and Alice's sister, and he too began applauding them as they honored the Earth Mother.

His mind drifted once again, and he was back on the Altar, and all he could feel was the rise and fall of Alice.

She, however, could feel the spirits in the circle. They were all there, Morag, Lord Monkton, Sarah's mother Mia, all her ancestors, and their descendants, Sam, Jake, Eleanor, and Luna May, all bearing witness.

Alice's breathing began to rise, and Paul lifted his hands to her breast, cupped them, and twisted her nipples that were standing firm. This encouraged Alice to speed up, and she began to move her whole body up and down harder and harder.

Paul sat upright and slowed her by wrapping his arms around her. "Slowly, Alice, make it last," he whispered in her ears as he kissed her neck lovingly. Paul took control and began to rock gently as he waited for Alice's heart and breathing to slow. "That's better, nice and slow."

"I can't believe we are back together, she whispered,"

"Sorry, what did you say?"

"I can't believe we have found one another, I have been waiting such a long time."

Paul continued to rock back and forth. "Me too, I have been drawn to you my whole life."

"What, only this one?"

Paul laughed, assuming she was joking.

"Saul, I have waited so long for this, and I can't wait any longer." Alice pushed him backward and once again took control. She urgently began forcing her pelvis down hard again and again until her body was wrapped in spasms, and she couldn't move. Paul, in turn, exploded inside her, and Alice collapsed in a heap on top of him, motionless.

They lay entwined, sated. Time stood still. Eventually, Paul drifted into a deep trance and spoke a single word phrased like a question.

"Sarah?"

Alice listened. Had she heard correctly? Did he say, 'Sarah?' "Paul, what did you say?" The reply came, but it was not Paul's voice.

"It's Saul, you called me."

"I did?"

"You must be Alice, one of our descendants?"

Excitement flooded through her; Saul was speaking to her for the first time in almost four hundred years.

I am, and Sarah's memories are here within me. She has been waiting for you for so long, Saul. Paul is of your line also. As you now realize, he is carrying some of your memories, not all of them, but he is recovering them quickly now that he has returned home. Saul, I must rest now. You can revive the memories of Sarah within me until sunrise, but I must warn you. It is only Sarah's memories, as she is still buried outside the churchyard under the yew tree."

"No wonder I could never find her," he said, and Alice could hear the sense of despair in his voice.

Both Paul and Alice drifted into the background as the memories of their ancestors took control.

*

Paul returned to the land of the living at the crack of dawn. Unbeknown to him, their bodies had been used by their ancestors passionately throughout the night. The dawn chorus was in full swing, the birdsong so loud, their song was an almost discordant force. Alice was still straddling him, and her head had fallen forward resting on his chest. Lifting his arms, he stretched his muscles, which were cold and numb, then placed his hands on her buttocks and gently caressed them. Alice now joined him back in the land of the living, literally.

"Hmm, my sacrificial lamb is waking up." Alice kissed him on the Lips and wondered who would wake up, Paul or Saul?

"I am so cold and tired, and I think I passed out."

Alice relaxed. *Definitely Paul.* "What can you remember before you passed out?"

"We made mad passionate love, my Druid Princess, again and again, it was weird, like I was standing back watching someone else, and if I might just point out, I lasted a lot longer than that guy last night."

"What!... That was a wedding, and you only have to penetrate once at a wedding."

"Oh, really, I didn't know, you should have stopped me. Hang on a minute, you were on top, you were in control – and you said this was a wedding."

"Hmm, yes, so I, err.... sorry. Anyway, I am not a Druid Princess, not in the full sense."

"What are you then, Alice?"

We have been called many things by humanity across the ages. What is he ready for – The guardians – The watchers. She smiled to herself, *even Angels.* She studied his eyes, unsure how to answer. *I have even been called a white Witch, now that really would scare him off.*

'Prime.'

"Just 'Prime,' nothing else. I had never heard that name until you and Jed mentioned it."

Alice planted another kiss on his lips. "Never mind. I'll explain it all one day. The truth is, I'm just a normal country girl who still believes in the old ways."

Paul's head was full of questions. "Why the blue paint, the circles, the lines, and where did you get blue paint from out here?

"First, it is not paint, it's woad. We keep it nearby for ceremonial purposes. Humankind has used it since the beginning of time to decorate their bodies, and you should have done the same in the true sense of the fastening. The decorations, again, are for ceremonial purposes, and this one was a hand-fasting ceremony."

"So, we're married?"

"We have tied the knot, Paul, but don't worry. It's not recognized by law, so you can run if you wish. I said that to see if you were serious about me."

"Who said anything about running? I have been looking for you all my life, but it's time to make a move, I'm starving and freezing."

Alice looked around them. The darkness of night was giving way to the grays of the morning. "It's getting light; we should head back.

Alice climbed off Paul. As he got up, Paul realized he was covered in blood. "One of us is bleeding. I'm covered in blood, but I'm not hurt. Is it you?"

Alice shook her head in disbelief. "Of course, it's me, Paul."

"Are you hurt?"

"For goodness sake, I was a virgin. Where do you think the blood came from?"

It was Paul's turn to stare in disbelief. "You were a virgin? but you must be twenty-four or five?"

She pursed her lips and placed her hands on her hips. "I take it you were not?"

Paul dropped his head in mock embarrassment. "No, sorry."

Alice's face creased with a smile. "Don't feel ashamed. Being an American, I didn't expect you to be. As I said, I'm an old-fashioned girl, and I was just waiting for the right man."

"What about the ceremonies? You were there last night."

Alice narrowed her eyes and pursed her lips, giving him her most indignant stare.

"Yes, what are you saying? Just because I attended did not mean I made love to anyone. Anyway, you did not see me with anyone, did you?"

For a while, Paul looked perplexed.

"I could not see anyone's faces from where I was. Where were you?"

Alice laughed and stroked the side of his face lovingly. "Why Paul, I was the one on the cushion."

Paul looked shocked. "The Priestess?"

"The Earth Mother, Paul."

Paul wrapped his arms around her and gave her another kiss. "Wow, well, I must say you look great in red." He rocked his head from side to side, obviously deep in thought. "Why you?"

"What do you mean – why you?

"Well, I thought it would be an Arch-Druid conducting the ceremony?"

"Well, it would be if it was a Druid wedding. But like I said last night the 'Prime' are different. We go way back before the word Druid ever existed, and we are on a slightly different path, still Druid, but much older, hence the Earth Mother.

Alice returned the kiss. "Anyway, time to go. The swim will clean us off."

They walked back to the water hand in hand. The early morning mist swirled around, and the scene was as timeless as Adam and Eve, two lovers together once again as in centuries past, but only one of them could remember.

Alice found Poppy in the stable, accompanied by Ghost and the new foal, as they arrived back at the cottage. Paul and Alice walked over to the mare, who seemed proud of the filly. They stroked the two horses, and then Alice turned her attention to Ghost. "You're a good girl too."

Alice took Paul's hand. "Paul, I'm ready for bed. Will you join me?"

"I'd love to, but won't they wonder where you are at the manor."

Alice shook her head. "I'm the boss, remember. I'll give them a ring and tell them I'm not up to it today."

A frown creased Paul's brow. "I thought you couldn't get a signal on your phone."

Alice pursed her lips and lowered her head, hiding her eyes. "I lied. Sorry."

Paul shook his head in disbelief. "But the vet, the horse could have died?"

"The horse was safer with me than any vet, Paul. I didn't want to argue with you, and time was running short, so I needed to take matters into my own hands. I do apologize for misleading you."

Paul ran his hand through his hair in exasperation. "You were that confident you could save her?"

"Yes, more than anyone else on the planet, especially with you there to help."

Paul again shook his head, unable to understand her reasoning. "But you said I should go back to the manor."

"Yes, but you Didn't."

"But I could have done."

"No, not in a million years would you have left me then."

He tilted his head, studying her. "How would you know that?"

"I know you, Paul Masters, better than you think." She lifted her lips to his and kissed him lightly on the mouth. "You will soon realize how well I know you and your dreams. She repeated her mantra in her mind. *Please, Earth Mother, after all this time, let him remember me. I could not bear it to be this close, and him still blind to us.*

A multitude of voices burst into her mind, all recommending the same thing. *Induce him.*

Alice answered them telepathically. *It's too dangerous, it could kill him. I'm not going to risk losing him yet - not until there is no other choice.*

"Ok, Paul, did you, even for a second, contemplate leaving me to do it on my own?"

He continued to shake his head. "Not for a second."

Alice gave Paul a gentle kiss. "We did ok, though, and now I am ready for bed. Are you coming?" She held out her hand to encourage him and presented him with the Princess Mia smile perfected centuries before.

Paul kissed her on the nape of her neck, looked lovingly into her eyes, and gasped at the beauty and depth of his woman. He could feel his soul drowning in them. He took a deep breath and sighed. "Ok, but I'm on top this time."

End of Book 1

CONTINUED IN BOOK 2
'PRIME': THE WITCH-QUEEN

"If you have enjoyed this book or even just liked it a little, I would ask you to please leave a review wherever you bought it, even if you got a free promotional copy. I would consider it a personal favor as I'm on a quest to get 100 reviews of this book, and I can only do it with your help. Reviews are the lifeblood of books, especially for debut authors who rely on review rankings to promote their books.

TO LEAVE A REVIEW IN THE COUNTY YOU PURCHASED THE BOOK, SEARCH USING THE ISBN CODE

Book 1. Prime: An Echo in the Stones.

Paperback ISBN. 9781838530624

eBook ISBN. 9781789260205

Footnote

So, after centuries of searching, two of our protagonists, have been drawn together once again. This, however, is only the beginning of their story, and it leaves us with many unanswered questions.

Will Paul recover his ancestral memories naturally and realize who he once was - and what his relationship with Alice was in his earlier existence?

Will he survive if Alice must induce them?

Will Paul return to America? or be drawn towards the secret rituals encompassing the henge and the 'Prime' Druids? Or the dark satanic rituals of the Primevil?

In nineteen-ninety-six, we find Ursula's spirit trapped in the Master bedroom and Sarah's spirit entangled in the roots of the yew tree in none consecrated ground. How did they come to this fate, and why?

Will the 'Primevil' Grandmasters seek revenge on Lord Monkton and his sons in 1605 AD?

Will Lord Monkton's relationship with Morag continue now he knows Princess Mia is nothing more than a spirit?

Can Morag keep up the deception of being Robert Llewellyn and Princess Mia and manage to raise the children safe from the clutches of the 'Primevil'?

Will the 'Primevil' overthrow humankind and lead them to misery and desolation?

Will Paul Masters be attracted to the dark as the vicar forewarned?

The saga of the Prime and the Echo in the Stones is far from over.

To order the second paperback in the series, search, 'Prime: The Witch Queen,' by James Watson.
Or by searching the ISBN code.

Book 2. Prime: The Witch Queen.

Paperback ISBN. 9781789726558

eBook ISBN. 9781800686076

If you would like to read excerpts from the next book or leave comments on the story so far, please go to

www.jameswatsonauthor.com

I hope you have enjoyed this book as it was my debut novel. It was written, printed, and published by me. I started the original book almost forty years ago. However, the arrival of the first of my three children diverted my path, and my priorities changed. It wasn't until I retired that I had the time and energy to complete it.

Unknown authors only get noticed through reviews and rankings in the book sales charts, and to do that we need the books to be rated. So as a personal favor to me, if you have enjoyed the books, would you please review and rate them from wherever you purchased them?

Yours in anticipation.

James Watson.

Web page jameswatsonauthor.com

Follow on Facebook

https://www.facebook.com/James-Watson-Author-108784507263356/?

Please review via the following worldwide links.
I hope you have enjoyed this book as it was my debut novel. It was written, printed, and published by me. I started the original book almost forty years ago. However, the arrival of the first of my three children diverted my path, and my priorities changed.

It wasn't until I retired that I had the time and energy to complete it.

Unknown authors only get noticed through reviews and rankings in the book sales charts, and to do that, we need the books to be rated.

So as a personal favor to me, if you have enjoyed the books, would you please review and rate them in the country you purchased them?

Yours in anticipation. James Watson.

Join my mailing list for further updates and preorders. Web page jameswatsonauthor.com

https://www.facebook.com/James-Watson-Author-108784507263356/?

To order or review, use these worldwide links.

Australia

Book 1 Prime: An Echo in the Stones
Amazon.com.au https://www.amazon.com.au/Prime-Echo-Stones-James-Watson-ebook/dp/B07BNVQXPV/ref=sr_1_1?crid=1TNOI18KV5RGY

Book 2 Prime: The Witch Queen
https://www.amazon.com.au/Prime-Witch-Queen-Stones-Book-ebook/dp/B086RWZWYT/ref=sr_1_1?crid=2I6SR9X5ZYE66&keywords=Prime%3A+The+witch+queen&qid=1690031374&sprefix=prime+the+witch+queen%2Caps%2C240&sr=8-1

Book 3 Prime: The Gathering of Souls
https://www.amazon.com.au/Prime-Gathering-Souls-Echoe-Stones-ebook/dp/B08VJDT9P4/ref=sr_1_1?crid=32KQM1NO0MLZC&keywords=Prime%3A+The+gathering+of+souls&qid=1690031778&sprefix=prime+the+gathering+of+souls%2Caps%2C220&sr=8-1

Book 4 Prime: The End of Days
https://www.amazon.com.au/Prime-End-Days-Echoe-Stones-ebook/dp/B0B37CTHMD/ref=sr_1_1?crid=2ASEL3K9JSNOA&keywords=Prime%3A+The+end+of+days&qid=1690032276&sprefix=prime+the+end+of+days%2Caps%2C235&sr=8-1

Canada
Book 1 Prime: An Echo in the Stones
https://www.amazon.ca/Prime-Echo-Stones-James-Watson-ebook/dp/B07BNVQXPV

Book 2 Prime The Witch Queen
https://www.amazon.ca/Prime-Witch-Queen-Stones-Book-ebook/dp/B086RWZWYT/ref=sr_1_1?crid=1YVII2LCQRKX0&k

eywords=prime%3A+the+witch+queen&qid=1690032881&s=digital-text&sprefix=prime+the+witch+queen%2Cdigital-text%2C206&sr=1-1

Book 3 Prime: The Gathering of Souls
https://www.amazon.ca/Prime-Gathering-Souls-Echoe-Stones-ebook/dp/B08VJDT9P4/ref=sr_1_1?crid=HHXTMISMIUNG&keywords=prime%3A+the+gathering+of+souls&qid=1690033011&s=digital-text&sprefix=prime+the+gathering+of+souls%2Cdigital-text%2C138&sr=1-1

Book 4 Prime: The End of Days
https://www.amazon.ca/Prime-End-Days-Echoe-Stones-ebook/dp/B0B37CTHMD/ref=sr_1_1?crid=348FA1UQBB78&keywords=prime%3A+the+end+of+days&qid=1690033122&s=digital-text&sprefix=prime+the+end+of+days%2Cdigital-text%2C139&sr=1-1

America

Book 1 Prime: An Echo in the Stones
https://www.amazon.com/Prime-Echo-Stones-James-Watson/dp/1838530622

Book 2 Prime: The Witch Queen
https://www.amazon.com/Prime-Witch-Queen-Stones-Book-ebook/dp/B086RWZWYT

Book 3 Prime: The Gathering of Souls
https://www.amazon.com/Prime-Gathering-Souls-Echoe-Stones-ebook/dp/B08VJDT9P4

Book 4 Prime: The End of Days

https://www.amazon.com/Prime-End-Days-Echoe-Stones-ebook/dp/B0B37CTHMD

United Kingdom

Book 1 Prime: An Echo in the Stones
https://www.amazon.co.uk/Prime-Echo-Stones-James-Watson/dp/1838530622

Book 2 Prime: The Witch Queen
https://www.amazon.co.uk/s?k=Prime%3A+the+witch+queen&i=stripbooks&crid=28X4IQUYA5Q2P&sprefix=prime+the+witch+queen%2Cstripbooks%2C102&ref=nb_sb_noss

Book 3 Prime: The Gathering of Souls
https://www.amazon.co.uk/Prime-Gathering-Souls-Echoe-Stones-ebook/dp/B08VJDT9P4/ref=sr_1_1?crid=2VH4RQE8V2U05&keywords=Prime%3A+the+gathering+of+souls&qid=1690034673&s=books&sprefix=prime+the+gathering+of+souls%2Cstripbooks%2C70&sr=1-1

Book 4 Prime: The End of Days
https://www.amazon.co.uk/Prime-End-Days-Echoe-Stones-ebook/dp/B0B37CTHMD/ref=sr_1_1?crid=2Y8HBGPK0WTBZ&keywords=Prime%3A+the+end+of+days&qid=1690034866&s=books&sprefix=prime+the+end+of+days%2Cstripbooks%2C72&sr=1-1

About James Watson

James Watson is now retired and lives on the south coast of Devon in the UK, overlooking the sea with his wife, three children, four grandchildren, and a labradoodle.

Living in the West Country, James has spent a lifetime studying Pagan, Celtic, and historical folk law. He was always drawn to the Neolithic landscape of the moors and the rich diversity of Standing Stones at Stonehenge and Avebury which inspired him to write these novels.

Printed in Great Britain
by Amazon